Cat Zero

+33:00:37

+00:00

ZY045

Jennifer L. Rohn

CAT ZERO

Jennifer L. Rohn

Bitingduck Press
Altadena, CA

Published by Bitingduck Press
ISBN 978-1-938463-66-2
© 2018 Jennifer L. Rohn
All rights reserved
For information contact
Bitingduck Press, LLC
Altadena, CA
notifications@bitingduckpress.com
http://www.bitingduckpress.com
Cover art by xxx

Publisher's Cataloging-in-Publication
Rohn, Jennifer [1967-   ]

Cat Zero/by Jennifer Rohn–1st ed.—Altadena, CA:
Bitingduck Press, 2017
p. cm.

[1. Marshall, Artemis (Fictitious character)—fiction
2. Laboratories, Scientific—fiction 3. Virus diseases—Transmission—fiction 4. Detective and mystery
stories] I. Title
ISBN 9781938463662

LCCN 2017938932

For Richard, always

PRAISE FOR CAT ZERO

"*Cat Zero* is that rare beast, a racy novel with a sound scientific background. Postdocs will love it. Ph.D.s will gasp. And the general reader will enjoy a smart romantic thriller in which an intelligent, independent and, yes, beautiful, researcher confronts her demons while fighting to succeed in a male-dominated world. Will she find love along the way? Read it to find out—I did, and loved it!"—Simon Mawer, author of Man Booker Prize-shortlisted *The Glass Room*, and *Trapeze*, *The Fall* and *Mendel's Dwarf*

"Absolutely gripping. A fast-paced story that opens the lid on the secret world of the laboratory and shows us what scientists are really like—as human and fallible as the rest of us."—Pippa Goldschmidt, author of *The Falling Sky* and *The Need for Better Regulation of Outer Space*

"A potent mix of science, thrills and romance... Fans of Michael Crichton will love it."—Mark Edwards, author of number-one bestsellers *The Magpies* and *Because She Loves Me*

"A mysterious outbreak of cat plague sends an intrepid virologist on a hunt to find the source of contagion in this gripping page-turner. Nobody writes about scientists quite like Jennifer Rohn, who captures not just the technical details of research, but also the complex humanity of the endeavor."—Jennifer Ouellette, *Cocktail Physics*

"Cat Zero weaves together the complicated, sometimes archaic, social hierarchies of researchers with the thrill of a new scientific discovery. But you don't have to know anything about science to follow along with the mysteries in this book: Why are cats falling ill in Kent? What's going on with Artie's strange colleagues down the hall? And will she hook up with her postdoc—or should she stay away? At the end of the book, we have some answers. But like real scientific discovery, the end is just the start of a whole new set of possibilities."—Eva Amsen, Easternblot.net

"This book purrs. It does that thing that cats do, playing with their toy, gently poking at it, softly lobbing it in the air, then, eventually, lunging. I'd recommend it for those who like the interplay of scientific lives, permeated with motives and mystery."—Grant Jacobs, *Code For Life*

"Very human scientists go about their lives and work, seamlessly blending into a fascinating tapestry as they try to solve the scientific mystery of a disease plaguing a cat population, which spills over into the human population. I loved getting to know the main character, Artie, a female scientist who deals with all of the plusses and pitfalls of being a woman, a scientist and a woman-in-science. Her personality shines through in Jennifer Rohn's work."—Joanne Manaster, *Read Science*

"Within the stylish package of a pacy thriller, Jennifer Rohn gives us a glimpse of what it's really like to work in a scientific laboratory: the academic rivalries and jealousies, the gender politics, the frustrations of painstaking experimental work and the excitement of new ideas and breakthroughs. For once in a science-based novel, everything here is plausible – which makes it all the more alarming, and all the more compelling." — Philip Ball, award-winning author of *Critical Mass*

"[T]he final chapters are absolute emotional roller coasters. I could not put the book down. I had to know how it ended. But I am not telling. You will have to find out for yourself. I give it five purrs and two paws up."—Susan Johnston, *Goodreads*

ESSEX

N
W   E
S

← to LONDON
(27 miles)

The River Thames

• CLIFFE

• GRAVESEND

ESTUARY
KENT

The

• ROCHESTER
RAINHAM •

Kent Downs

SOUTHEND-ON-SEA

NORTH SEA

ISLE of GRAIN

River Medway

SHEERNESS

MINSTER

ISLE of SHEPPEY

Sheppey Crossing

the Swale

Whitstable Bay

the Marshes

SITTINGBOURNE

SEASALTER

FAVERSHAM

PROLOGUE

THE OLD WOMAN OPENED THE door and leaned out into darkness.
Wind rippled through the unmown grass, shafted coolness through the heat of the room behind her. The treetops surged, splintering moonlight and shade into a heaving stormy sea that obscured the back yard's familiar features.

Disoriented and dizzy, she steadied herself with a trembling hand, forgetting why she had opened the door.

Something distressing, something imperative. Breathing in the dewy-green earth smells, she forced herself to focus.

The cat. That was it. *Her* cat. Her cat Mackenzie, who had failed to come home for his supper earlier that evening. She could not recall something like that ever happening before. He had, in fact, been acting off for a few days, skittish and irritable, and looking like he'd lost weight. He'd even bitten her—nothing serious, but he hadn't done that since he'd been a kitten. She should probably take him to the vet in the morning.

The woman called Mackenzie's name with a quavering voice. Caught her breath, waited and tried again. In a few minutes, a dark shape emerged from behind an inky-black patch of shrub. The moonlight caught its eyes, emerald fire, panicked. He lunged towards her in a blur and she reached down for her beloved companion—completely unprepared for the swiping paw, the fiery slash across her left hand.

She cried out, snatching her hand to her mouth and tasting salty rust. The animal seemed to deflate before her eyes, bowing his head as he slunk into the house. Still in shock, she watched him stagger right past his food bowl and disappear into the living room.

The vertigo hit again. She lowered herself down to the floor, flinching at the symphony of complaining joints and muscles and wondering if she'd ever be able to get back up again.

Minutes passed, perhaps hours. She could only stare as her blood oozed from the scratch onto the ancient grey linoleum, one scarlet drop at a time.

CHAPTER 1
The Perils of Abbreviation, Gender-Neutral Variety

Artie Marshall was considering the article in her hand, trying to decide whether to file it under "Cat Viruses, General" or "Feline Endemics, Global" when a knock at the door postponed the decision. To someone compelled to excessive subdivision, filing was always painful.

"Hi," Artie said, looking up at the man—or boy, more accurately—who hesitated, one foot in the corridor and one in the disaster area that was one day destined to become her office. "Can I help you?"

The student, a blond twenty-something with a perpetually throttled look, was attired in pressed trousers and a white shirt: a dead giveaway in this place. He frowned at the sheaf of papers in his hand, frowned at the room number, and frowned at Artie before alighting on something obviously more encouraging over her left shoulder.

"Dr. Marshall?" His eyes bulged with asphyxiated relief.

Artie heard the screech of Mark's chair and reminded herself for the fourth time that day to bring in a can of WD-40.

"Not me," Mark said, sounding amused. "Her. And it's Professor Marshall."

Artie offered the student a smile and an outstretched hand, and he nearly recoiled.

"You must be Ryan," she said, trying to decide whether she would file him under "Rabbit, Scared" or "Loser, Clueless."

"But I was expecting..."

"A man?" Artie said. "Common mistake. 'Artie' is short for Artemis." When he didn't respond, she added, "My parents had a thing for Greek mythology."

"I'm sorry?"

Mark coughed over his laughter before explaining, "Artemis, as in the virgin hunter goddess."

"Daughter of Leto, born after she and Zeus got it on behind Hera's back," Artie said.

"Didn't Zeus give birth to her himself, sprung fully formed from his forehead?" Mark asked.

"You're thinking of Athena."

"Ah, so I am."

"There might have been a mistake," the student said, looking optimistically at his papers again.

"PhD studentship?" Artie said. "The Department of Molecular Virology? Feline leukemia?"

At his miserable nod, she said, "Take a seat, Ryan, I'm perfectly harmless."

"Extra chairs haven't arrived yet," Mark said, as the student looked around in confusion. "Pull up one of those crates."

After about five minutes of interview it was clear that he was never going to work out. Artie struggled to extend the conversation to half an hour as a formality before allowing him to slither away.

She sighed and met Mark's eye. Mark shrugged.

"Are they removing part of the frontal lobe as a university graduation requirement these days?" she asked.

"I doubt we've been seeing the top students."

"What's scaring them off?" She studied the face of her first ever post-doctoral fellow—a post-doc she had been very lucky to secure, she was starting to realize.

"Maybe we should tone down the whole mythology angle."

"I'm serious, Mark. My youth? The lab's outmoded research topic? Heatherfields as a whole?"

The Institute had been founded by Rupert Heatherfields, a prominent entomologist, when he'd gathered together the first utopian cluster of interdisciplinary scientists in 1883. The organization, more like a think-tank than a private research facility, was still going strong in the original building. Its aura of sleepy, old-world charm was enhanced by its location, hidden away in the leafy north-London suburb of Mill Hill, worlds away from the hard-core labs jostling within internationally renowned campuses in the center. As such, it was not much rated among modern biologists, with their medical bent and their twenty-first century pragmatic cynicism.

Mark leaned back in his chair and gave her his habitual grin, the one that started as a twitch at the corner of his mouth before gradually taking over the surrounding territory. It still disconcerted Artie that he was older, and she was supposed to be the boss.

"All three," he said. "And if they're not deterred by that, seeing the state of this office pretty much caps it."

Artie's high spirits experienced a rare dip. "You had no idea what you were getting into, did you? Ever have second thoughts?"

"Not a chance," he said. "I came here because I wanted to work with the top feline leukemia specialist. You're it, Art."

"I almost wish I'd persuaded you not to come. For your sake, I mean."

But her tone wasn't convincing, and he obliterated the argument with a sweep of his hand. "If you can flourish in a passé field, so can I. I reckon there's room enough for two rebels in the system."

For the hundredth time, Artie silently blessed the day that Mark's email had arrived. Mark Reynolds, who had sprung fully funded from a modest but hard-working avian virus lab in Bristol, already had eight years of post-doctoral experience when he got restless and developed an interest in an even more obscure topic.

"Why the shift?" she'd asked him at the interview back in April, which had taken place over too many pints down at the Victoria Arms.

"Honestly? I'm tired of chickens."

"No, really. Give me some legitimate reasons... and make them good, or I might not hire you."

They had both known she wasn't serious. After only an hour in his presence, Artie was convinced that he was the one to get her lab off the ground. His CV demonstrated an impressive breadth as well as depth, and despite his light-hearted tone, she could sense the intense intellect underneath. Although Artie berated herself for being so unscientific, she drew confidence from his tall, sturdy build and tree-felling arms, with that bearish dark-brown hair curling around his head and over most of his exposed surfaces. In fact, she had the peculiar conviction he was somehow the older brother she'd never had.

"Right." He held up a finger. "Your papers are insightful and take a stab at serious evolutionary questions. Not like everyone else's, pretending their arcane little treatise is going to cure human disease. You seem to want to understand the deeper implications of the biology for its own sake."

"Hmmm... you obviously haven't read the shameless pandering in my latest grant application to Cancer Research UK."

"Second," he said, ignoring her embarrassment. "I know this place is a backwater, but I'm well into the eccentric intellectual vibe."

Artie make a noncommittal noise. Eccentric was certainly one way to describe Heatherfields, which ran rampant with interdisciplinary oddballs who had never produced important medical cures, lucrative patents or Nobel prize-winning research.

"And third," he said. "Can I be frank? You've been appointed here at a very young age—that must mean something. You're obviously someone worth learning things from."

"If Phil hadn't retired, I assume you would've gone to Edinburgh instead?"

He just smiled. "He may be brilliant, and he may have transmitted only a fraction of his knowledge to you, but I prefer your style. Fourth... I'm interested in AIDS, and it was becoming increasingly clear that studying it in birds was a waste of my time."

She shifted in her seat. "Mark, I hate to break it to you, but feline leukemia virus went out of fashion as an AIDS model decades ago. And even the feline immunodeficiency virus model's not ideal—you should really be looking at monkeys."

"Not interested," he said. "I don't want to study animals in cages. I want to study a natural virus in its natural host population. Cats are the way forward, Artemis."

"You're preaching to the converted," she said. "And call me Artie. Better yet, 'boss' will do nicely."

Artie's reminiscences were dislodged by a knock on the door. She looked up to see Fiona, the third and final member of her new research team, poking a head into the office.

"Any luck with that student?" Fiona said, making a face. "He wandered into the lab by mistake and tripped over those cables Mark was messing with. The way he swore at me... well, it sounded like he's not too keen on women."

"He'd fit right in at Heatherfields, then," Mark muttered.

"I don't think he'll be troubling us further, Fiona."

"Thank God for that." She seemed considerably cheered.

"As gormless as that boy was, he was also our last applicant," Artie said, picking up the troublesome article again as Fiona disappeared.

"Don't worry." Mark, as usual, projected an aura of equanimity. "There's always next year. Besides, students are hard work. Let's get the show running first before we worry about expanding your empire."

◡

A FEW DAYS LATER, THE office was sorted out to mutual satisfaction—except, of course, for Artie's filing.

"The only thing we're missing is a window," Artie said, looking at the reprint on the top of her pile. She was wavering between "Mutations, Non-coding" and "Genetic Variants, Minor."

Mark glanced up from his laptop. "I got cornered by some nerd up in Behavioral Psych at lunch. He was telling me about his preliminary specs for a solar periscope, designed specifically for people who work in basements."

"Oh, Mark..." Artie was extremely gullible, and Mark clearly delighted in testing the limits of her credibility.

"I'm serious," he said. The scary thing, knowing Heatherfields, was that he very well could be. "It's a simple metal and mirrored affair, requiring only a modest series of holes drilled through the ceiling, and apparently it can go a long way towards alleviating something called Subterranean Displacement Blues."

"Isn't that a Bob Dylan song?"

"Laugh all you like, but I think you might be presenting with some of the major symptoms, Art."

"Don't you have some important stretch of the internet to surf?"

"Let's see... Manic energy," he pronounced, not noticing her sudden discomfort. "Workaholic tendencies. Reluctance to leave said basement. Excessive caffeine consumption..."

There was a knock on the door.

"Did someone mention caffeine?" A woman was standing in the doorway, dripping with rain and hugging a polystyrene box to her chest. "I'll trade you a couple of dozen blood and saliva samples for a decent cup of tea."

"Mary!" Artie jumped to her feet. "Give me your coat—you're drenched! And how did you get past Cerberus on the door?"

"I threw him a big juicy steak," she said, placing the box on Artie's desk. She peeled off the sodden outer layer to reveal a prim grey skirt suit. "Nice office, you two."

"We're still arguing over the feng shui," Mark said, "so we compromised on the plastic palm tree."

"It's hideous," Mary said, tilting her head critically.

"Mark, be a love and stash those samples in the freezer, would you?" Artie hung up the coat and switched the kettle on.

"Yes, ma'am." Mark swept up the box in his large hands. "Anything for me in here, Auntie Mary?"

"No immunodeficiency cases this time, I'm afraid," she replied. "But I did manage to score you a spectacularly disgusting thymic tumor."

"Really? Hey, cool!" He hurried out the door, already prying away at the tape.

"I've said it before and I'll say it again," Mary said. "He's lovely, Art—so polite and well trained."

"And he keeps his fur groomed and his litter box tidy as well."

"How's his lab-side manner?"

"Fabulous," Artie said, perching on her desk. "You should see his research proposal. It should fit in nicely with my main project—maybe a bit too ambitious, though."

"Reminds me of someone I know."

"His work will require lots of samples, Mary."

"Hmmm... also familiar."

Artie grinned. "Feel free to tell him to back off if he gets too demanding. After all, you weren't put on this earth solely to supply us with cat spit."

"Mark, demanding? He could charm the bone marrow out of a rabid moose."

"Getting many of those in your surgery, Mary?" Mark slipped back in and threw himself into his chair.

"No hoofed quadrupeds, but plenty of overweight poodles and depressed budgies."

"How can you tell if a budgie's depressed?" Mark asked.

"It sits on the sofa eating chocolates and watching re-runs of *Friends*."

"Right, you two." Artie rapped her knuckles on the desk. "Down to business."

Mary tucked her straight black hair behind her ears before pulling out the familiar red leather notebook. Making herself more comfortable, she launched into an amusing description of all the feline illnesses she'd seen in her small vet practice in Gillingham over the past few weeks. Then she rattled off second-hand anecdotal accounts from her colleagues from around the Medway area, and finished with her usual digest of some relevant local cases in the vet journals. Artie scribbled rapid notes, and she and Mark took turns peppering Mary with questions.

Artie had known Mary since University. Later, the two women evolved easily from friendship to scientific collaboration when Artie developed an interest in feline leukemia virus, an affliction that still popped up now and again in Mary's practice. Artie had come up with a controversial new theory about the way the virus mutated and spread in cats, but to test it, she would have to study the genetic signatures of many viruses over a number of years to chart their spread. Such an approach would be difficult and had never before been attempted in cats, so she was in the process of thinking up new strategies to grapple with the logistics. But more crucially, she would need samples from a large number of sick cats, and Mary's connections with vets all over Kent county had been invaluable.

"That's basically it," Mary said. "Unless you're interested in hairballs. Listen, I've got to run—a seminar at the Royal Vet, and the Northern Line is a shambles today. Have fun with the samples."

"And, Mary..." Mark looked at her imploringly with his chocolate Labrador eyes.

"I'll keep my eyes peeled for cat AIDS," she promised.

ARTIE HAD LEARNED EVERYTHING WORTH knowing about feline leukemia virus from Philip Cox, one of those old-timer veterinarian scientists who used to figure so prominently in the virology scene, but who were rapidly becoming extinct in the genomic age. In fact, Cox had worked fifteen years longer than the University of

Edinburgh had wanted him to, but he had been undeterred by cajoling, pension-en-hancing bribes and finally outright blackmail, using his celebrity status to maintain a dynamic research lab right into his late seventies. All of this had been fortunate for Artie, who turned out to be the last post-doc he ever hired. Cox, too, had tried to dissuade Artie, just as Artie had felt duty-bound to be open with Mark, whose reasons for wanting to work with her had sounded all too familiar.

"Feline leukemia virus is dead, Dr. Marshall," Philip Cox had told her. He might have inspired awe at that first interview seven years previously, having only recently stepped down as President of the Royal Society, but Artie was not easily spooked. "There are still a few good labs in the States, but they've gone over to simian and human AIDS viruses almost completely. It won't do your career any favors to special-ize in it now." He glanced at her CV. "Even more of a pity after such an auspicious beginning."

"It's what I want to do," Artie said. "I've got new ideas, and they involve under-standing natural disease patterns. Mouse viruses"—the topic of her PhD disserta-tion—"are too artificial, too lab-bound. Whereas feline leukemia is infecting cats all over the world."

"I am aware of that, Dr. Marshall." But the great man finally smiled. "Very well, but don't say I didn't warn you in four years' time. And I might be too dead to write you an effective reference letter."

∽

HAPPILY, PHILIP COX WAS STILL alive, and Artie often suspected that it was precisely this letter that had secured her prestigious appointment at Heatherfields the previous February. There were other scientists her age at the institute, but very few of them had tenured senior positions (the job title was "Professor," even though its recipients were not required to sully their thought processes with undergraduate education).

Or maybe it was because she was as much of an anachronism as the institute itself. Throughout her career, she'd been good-naturedly teased for her propensity to hunch over forgotten anatomy treatises in the underground archives of medical schools, or to attend seminars on particle physics or chaos theory just to look at the scientific method from a fresh angle. She sent emails to molecular paleontologists about the cause of death in mummified Egyptian cats, to behavioral zoologists observing lions in the Sahara, to classical Greek scholars for the latest translational take on some an-cient feline plague. She was, in short, exactly the sort of person that Heatherfields was looking for, and had to increasingly struggle to find. Some aspects of the Institute's culture had not evolved much since its Victorian origins, so it was probably this as much as Philip Cox's blessing that had caused its Inner Sanctum to disregard her distinct lack of a Y chromosome.

Her special qualities, however, had not been enough to prevent the Institute's elders from bestowing the bare minimum of space and resources—ones more ap-propriate to a negligible visiting Fellow than to a full-fledged professor. When she'd interviewed, they'd whisked her around the above-ground portion of the building: ornate, high-ceilinged rooms combining the antique splendor of the original décor with all the state-of-the-art accoutrements of the thoroughly modern. Some of the labs even had stained glass windows, splashing geometric wedges of color all over the workspaces.

But when she'd arrived in February, Artie had been shocked to find that her designated laboratory space was not in the fourth floor Department of Molecular Virology proper, but one cramped and windowless room orphaned down in the basement, lodged between Virtual Immunology on one side and Theoretical Epidemiology on the other. A basement that had none of the magnificence of the main building, having been only minimally refurbished some time during the grim Sixties—and which had obviously deteriorated since. The carpets were shabby, the paint was peeling and there was a perpetual dampness that imparted a permanent fungal odor.

And it wasn't just a matter of aesthetics. Molecular virology was a communal endeavor, requiring not only casual consultation with other specialists in the field but, more importantly, several rooms of shared equipment. The upshot was that any researcher Artie hired would have to spend a lot of time trekking up and down six flights of stairs to complete most experiments, or waiting for the mythically slow lift—an Edwardian-era affair known to seize up with alarming regularity.

"It's good exercise," Mark had said at the interview, when she admitted to yet another disadvantage of accepting the job. "And the conversations in the basement's coffee room have got to be worth it for sheer entertainment value. Theoretical Epidemiology is marginally self-explanatory, but what exactly *is* Virtual Immunology? Do they just *pretend* to come to work every day?"

"It's a new field," Artie had replied cheerfully. "They're building a computer simulation of the human immune system. They've managed to get the T-cell program sorted, but right now they're struggling to make the virtual antibodies behave. We've talked about collaborating on virus antigen recognition."

"I'm sorry I asked." But Mark's shake of head had been admiring.

And sure enough, after only a few weeks she couldn't imagine being anywhere else. Possessing a keen interest in almost everything, Artie soon became a popular colleague, as nothing is more endearing to a virtual immunologist or a theoretical epidemiologist than a willing audience who hasn't heard their theories before. Sir Rupert himself, if he'd been able to see past the damning impediment of her sex, would probably have watched her social development with benevolent accord. And Artie's sociable nature wasn't only scientifically useful; it had inspired a neighbor, just in the past week, to offer a small room that she and Mark could use for an office.

"Belonged to a former PhD student," Ben Crombie, one of the immunologists, told her as he flicked on the light to reveal towers of stacked, dusty boxes. "After eight years and no thesis, went bonkers, turned up half naked and gibbering in Lancaster Gate underground station. Used as storage ever since—right next to your lab, seems a shame to go to waste. I'll have a word with Salverson, but I can't imagine he'll mind."

Artie was relieved that her new team seemed to be settling in well despite all the inconveniences. Mark was a careful, competent scientist, and his way with machinery proved invaluable for setting up the laboratory. He had not used his slight age advantage against Artie, instead showing a remarkable willingness to accept instruction and advice. She found his air of serenity soothing. Fiona was young, breezy and hard-working, filling up the lab with laughter and the latest music, and the three of them got on well. Sometimes Artie could not believe that she really was running her own lab at last, but so far, all the evidence was pointing in that direction.

∾

"MY DEAR ARTEMIS!" A DEEP voice accosted her after lunch, when Artie was leaving the dining hall. "I've been looking for you everywhere."

"Susan," Artie said, spirits flagging. If she hadn't dawdled over her dessert, making one of her many lists, she would've missed this encounter entirely.

Susan Tavistock, Professor of Ecology, was a formidable presence: six feet tall, her broad-shouldered, blown-dry and tailored power-dressing style imparting more than a passing resemblance to a Thatcher-era politician.

"We missed you at the women's group gathering last night," she said, eyes managing to appear bright and cool at the same time. "The students were particularly disappointed."

Aside from Susan, Artie was the only other female professor in the entire nine-floor building.

"I had a lot on my plate," Artie said. "Maybe next month." She didn't have the heart to break it to her that, in her experience, the 'us-versus-them' mentality more than helped. The trick to infiltrating in science, she'd found, was to fit in, not to stick out. To placate, not provoke. To just play their game instead of incessantly crying foul.

Susan pressed her lips together, inspecting Artie's clothing: black jeans and a pink T-shirt bearing the logo of a London breast cancer charity. Artie was aware that the shirt was a lot tighter than it used to be, thanks to a recent laundry mishap.

"It must be so difficult down there," Susan said. "Just one male post-doc and no role models... I don't know how you manage without the support."

"If you're talking about Mark," Artie said, "then I couldn't ask for a more understanding colleague. And the lab heads in the basement are fantastic. Nice guys all."

Susan regrouped. "There're only two of us—you owe it to the younger ones to provide the inspiration and example they need to thrive."

Artie fidgeted under Susan's heavy stare.

"Listen... I just don't believe in all that stuff," she finally confessed. "The best way I can set an example is to just get on with my work and be successful, rather than moping about complaining about how oppressed I am."

Susan paused. "You know, the pressure and activities of the women's group played a major role in getting you shortlisted for your position."

"Really?" Artie said. "And here I was thinking I'd got in on my own merit."

Artie tried to walk away, but Susan grabbed her arm and spoke to her in a low voice.

"I'd think very carefully before you abandon your own kind," she said. "You might think they're on your side, but it's all an illusion. When they get tired of looking at you, you might find them a bit less helpful."

When Artie got back to the office, Mark looked up and said, "What?"

"Susan Tavistock," she said. "According to her, I've betrayed the sisterhood."

Mark just looked amused. "She's on the losing side, Art."

"You don't think it would be politically imprudent to piss her off?"

He leaned back in his chair. "You've only been here four months, but you're already far more respected than Tavistock will ever be."

"How would you know?"

Mark shrugged. "Men talk. I listen. As long as I don't actively defend you, they assume I don't mind overhearing the gossip."

Artie took in the implications. "They assume you're on their side, you mean."

Another shrug. "Possibly. I figured it was more useful for you that way."

"What have they been saying about me?"

"This and that," he said. "But I think you're on the right track, whereas Tavistock's just digging herself in deeper. I wouldn't worry about alienating her if it gives you a buzz."

Artie returned to her filing, trying not to picture herself as a topic in a male-only Heatherfields beer session. She had no doubt that her professional exploits were only one of the items under discussion.

ARTIE TENDED TO USE THE solitary Heatherfields evenings to catch up on her relentless email correspondence. As she sat at her desk that night, she was aware as always of the emptiness of the building. It was a paradox to her how silence could be so heavy, a gravity that she could feel more than hear, pressing against her eardrums and the hairs on her arms like an impending weather system. She was a spinning top that did not relish the consequences of wobbling to rest, and the weighty sensation made her want to fight back with brisk monologue—mental light and color against the gathering darkness.

She activated a random playlist, filling the office with music before turning to her Inbox.

The first letter was from a Russian expert on feral cat behavior whom Artie had contacted the previous week. She liked to imagine each email exchange as a spoken conversation, dreaming up suitable voices for the colleagues she had never met.

"Thank you for your interest in our research," the note began—Artie assigned her a seductive purr, like a morally ambiguous Bond girl. "Indeed it is true that after a scratching fight, we have observed wounded cats being licked by non-wounded individuals, which undoubtedly could facilitate the spread of any blood-borne pathogens, but as far as supporting your theory of a saliva-to-blood selected variant..."

After firing off a suitable response, Artie opened the next email, from an aging Australian large-animal virologist:

"Yes, I've heard that urban myth about that highly infectious canine lentivirus," he said—Artie assigned him a lilting, crocodile-wrestling accent—"but who hasn't? And no one's ever published anything convincing, so I still stand by my theory that they simply don't exist. Must be something protective in the dog genome..."

"Artie, you're way out in left field on this one," Dr. Bud Fisher drawled. Because she sparred with him all the time at conferences, she knew exactly how his Texas twang sounded. Fisher was one of the few nominal feline leukemia scientists remaining in the world—though even he now devoted more than half of his lab to monkey viruses.

"I mean, epidemics over endemic prevalence! And even if you're right, honey, how on earth you gonna see it? Be like looking for a pin in a needle-stack." She could almost hear the coy pause. "Honestly, maybe you're going a bit nuts over there, all alone with an abandoned paradigm. Why don't you come on over to primate lentiviruses like everyone else? The water's fine!"

And so on, bursts of ebullience from all over the world, and for as long as it carried on she would be cradled in a secure hammock of scientific curiosity and companionship.

Until the final message, which had nothing to do with her research. She experienced a twinge of nervous embarrassment as her eyes raced across the screen.

"Yes, vee have been looking extensively at hereditary factors in this particular disorder." The note was from Dr. Frederik Vissel, an Austrian whose voice would surely bear a passing resemblance to Sigmund Freud's. "I have attached, with compliments, zee file of our most recent paper in press at the *European Journal of Psychiatry*. And might vee also call your attention to a recent review article by one of our colleagues..."

Artie queued up the documents to print and gathered her things together. She could hear exactly what Mark would say if he knew about her exchange with Vissel.

"Why don't you go up to Behavioral Psych and have a chat if you're interested in mental illness? They're desperate for conversation up there. And I know you think in tangents, but what could this possibly have to do with feline leukemia? Is this some sort of AIDS dementia link?"

Which was precisely why Mark was never going to find out.

Putting on her jacket and hoisting her backpack and laptop over one shoulder, she locked up and padded down the corridor. Song lyrics still swirled around her head, insulating her from the building's hush as she headed for the stairwell door.

That was when she noticed that the usual late-night light in room B302 of Theoretical Epidemiology was extinguished.

"Great," Artie said out loud, peering into the dark office. For the first time since her appointment at the Institute, she was going to have to deal with the alarm system.

"This is all a formality," Ben Crombie had told her on her first day, when he'd shown her how to work the basement's frighteningly complex security panel. "You'll probably never need to set it—Rennie in B302 works till midnight every night of the week except Sundays, and regular as hay fever."

And Ben had been right—until this evening. Because the alarm would be triggered by corridor motion as well as unauthorized entrance, the last to leave had to ensure that everyone else in both departments really was gone, lest someone emerge unwittingly from their office later and set all of Heatherfields ablaze with light and sound.

Artie worked late most evenings, but her last tube train departed just before midnight, so she had always been silently grateful to this Rennie, whoever she happened to be. There were a few people floating around Theoretical Epi who were rumored to be reclusive or even downright strange. She was aware of a handful of nameless faces spotted occasionally in the corridors, so she supposed this mysterious Rennie was one of them. Room B302 led to at least one inner room, but its door wasn't angled to offer a line of sight into its secrets.

When Artie, always eager to make a new acquaintance, had pumped Ben for information about Rennie, she had found the garrulous man unusually reticent.

"Anti-social," Ben said shortly. "Gets furious if you interrupt. Best steer clear—the rest of us do."

Artie made sure the sticky note with Ben's scribbled instructions and the four-digit code for the alarm was still pressed into her diary, then tromped the entire length of the basement's L-shaped corridor, feeling foolish as she called out, "Hello? Anyone still here?" Not a sausage, either virtual or theoretical. Ben said they'd tried an informal clocking-out system in the past, but a few of the more scatty among the staff seemed incapable of remembering to tick off their names. Artie thought she would probably count herself as one of those.

She headed back towards the stairwell, then paused at the communal lavatory. No noises issued forth, but in theory someone could be inside. She was just raising her hand to press the swinging door back when its surface fell away a millimeter beneath her palm.

It all happened in less than a second. She jumped, a primitive noise squeezing from her throat as she was confronted with a man towering above her: early sixties, face lined and cragged like a weathered butte and yet entirely expressionless, granite-colored eyes almost catatonic under severe white brows. If he was similarly startled, she was unable to detect it.

They stared at one another, snagged in a bubble of thundering silence, for an indeterminate length of time—a second? ten? twenty?—as Artie's heart rioted in a wake of adrenaline. Just as she was struggling to throw off her shock, say something, perhaps opt for an apologetic laugh, the man slipped past her without a word. Artie slumped against the wall and watched the apparition take a dozen slow strides, open the door to B302 and disappear into darkness.

The laugh came out of her after the fact, even though she felt shaky. She ought to know better than anyone about the ambiguity of nicknames. Rennie wasn't a woman after all, any more than she was a man. There had been something familiar about him, something that was making her very uncomfortable. *Furious*, Ben's voice whispered in her mind, hinting at revulsion, even fear. Nevertheless, she seemed unable to stop herself as her feet began walking towards B302, as she put her hand around the metal handle and turned it. When her eyes adjusted, she noticed a light issuing from the open door of the inner room, bluish and faint but there all the same. It had probably been on all along.

She stepped into the outer office, a sparse arrangement of bookcase and filing cabinet, bare-surfaced desk and chair. She had never seen anyone working there. She reached over and slid open the desk drawer—it was empty. Glancing more closely at the bookshelf, she saw that the neat rows of cardboard binders were unlabeled and did not contain any pages. Now she wondered if the office were just a protective blind, a buffer zone of normality against the real activities in the rooms beyond.

"Hello?" Her upbeat, no-nonsense self. "Can I speak with you for a moment?"

Silence from within, but Artie could sense a motion, not so much a sound as a temporary dimming: something passing in front of the unknown light source.

"We've got to discuss this alarm thing," she said. "I very nearly locked you in."

Still no response. There was a creak of weight settling into a chair, then nothing.

This was ridiculous. She crossed the room and looked through the open door. The man sat with his back to her in the dark at a vast computer screen. She made out about a dozen other monitors, spread evenly along the walls, each of them occupied by graphs or columns of numbers—the collective origin of that faint glow. In the central area was a small table and two chairs, but the room was otherwise bare. Artie made out another door in the back, offering access to an unknown number of additional rooms, additional mysteries.

She then became aware of a soft rhythmic patter over the hum of the computers: one of the man's hands lay on his knee, twitching with a small, repetitive movement. His other hand rested slack on the mouse, and on his screen, a three-dimensional tangle of curves that resembled a lily rotated slowly around a Y-axis, each thread a slightly different color.

"Rennie?" she insisted, hearing the annoyance in her voice—a voice that was not used to being ignored.

With no warning, the man spun his chair in one forceful motion to face her, making her step back involuntarily.

"My name isn't Rennie," he said, voice as deep and melodious as a rumbling train. "It's Henry. What can I do for you, child?"

His eyes had lost their unfocused glaze and were now animated with intense curiosity. But even though the apparition had transformed into something less strange, the weird familiarity she'd initially sensed was still there, lurking just underneath the set of his face, the twitching of hand on trouser-leg. His wild ivory hair was lit up in pastels from the monitor—aquamarine, rose, lime and amber—as the exotic shape spun lazily behind him.

She should remind him to leave his light on and make her escape. Ben had warned her, Ben who was not at all excitable or given to melodrama. And she was in danger of missing the last train. Instead, she said, "What's that on your screen? What are you modeling?"

He paused, long enough for Artie to inhale and exhale half a dozen times. There was something about his inspection that made her feel, uncomfortably, that she looked familiar to him as well.

"A hypothetical epidemic," he finally said, in that exquisite voice.

Artie felt herself relax, feet restored to solidity, her normal inquisitive nature trumping the oddity of this entire exchange.

"It's beautiful," she said, which sounded so unprofessional she could kick herself. A pause.

"Yes," he replied, as if its beauty were the entire point. Maybe, for him, it was.

"An epidemic of what?"

"Avian influenza," he said. "Pandemic-strain avian influenza, if Patient Zero had infected six other business passengers en route to Heathrow. Monday morning. Two of the infected individuals are on their way to an international symposium at Earl's Court with over twelve hundred registered participants from thirty-five different countries."

Theoretical Epidemiology, she thought, with a thrill of insight. The science of what-if, of worst-case-scenario. What if your most terrible nightmare came true? An Ebola outbreak at Paddington Station. A mutant of HIV that could be spread by sneezing or insect bites. A smart bomb full of smallpox, detonated over downtown Tel Aviv.

"What happens?" she asked breathlessly.

He turned slightly, face at three-quarters, and clicked with the mouse. One of the threads, a vivid lavender, unstrung itself and shot towards the abscissa. Another click, and a new shape rotated in space, more bloated and amorphous.

"This," he replied. He leaned closer, then called up a spreadsheet of numbers and began entering new ones with one hand—the mouse-hand, the hand that wasn't flopping on his knee in an endless tic.

"I don't understand," Artie said. "Can you explain what—"

"No," he said, voice as cool and implacable as iron. But there was still no fury here, only a bottomless inky pool of calmness.

"But—"

"I want you to leave now." He stopped entering numbers and took hold of the mouse again, eyes still fixed on the screen. "Good night, Professor Marshall."

His voice held an indefinable quality that was both dazzling and impossible to fight, and Artie the fearless, Artie the irrepressible, turned and fled.

∾

SHE SAT IN THE EMPTY train carriage, shooting underground towards Hampstead. Normally she filled the silence of her evening journey home with a stack of unread articles on her lap, but tonight, she couldn't concentrate. Instead, she played and re-played the strange encounter with Rennie-slash-Henry.

She could still see the simulation of the avian flu epidemic rotating in space on Henry's computer screen, superimposed over the scratched plastic surface of the opposite window, over her own slumped reflection: dark blonde hair in a rational bob, heart-shaped face too soft for the resolve, the ambition, the sheer will underneath, and a body too feminine to be taken seriously in a man's world, even when she tried to hide it under sensible clothing. But if male colleagues wrote her off on first glance, this attitude seldom persisted after she opened her mouth. She could win over almost anyone when she flexed the true depth of her determination and enthusiasm, even as her intellect tended to temper their initial animal desires. She thanked the gods of genetics that, unlike Mary, she had not been cursed with a lilting soprano interface that men seemed born programmed to underestimate. Artie's own voice was a cool, flowing alto, not given to hysterical swoops or breaking readily in emotional situations.

Or at least, not in conflicts of a professional nature.

What on earth was going on in room B302? Why hadn't Ben just leveled with her about its strange inhabitant, and why had he fobbed her off with the wrong name? It was embarrassing. Why had he labeled *furious* a gentle man who was merely peculiar? She felt a flutter of uneasiness, remembering how Henry had known exactly who she was, but pushed it aside, focusing instead on the beautiful graphic representation and the lush colors that had bathed his intent face. She knew nothing about the man, but she recognized genius when she saw it, and was already in the thrall of attraction that genius tended to exert on her.

What could this sort of knowledge do for her particular passion? Could it help her to understand the spread of particular cat viruses, moving across the sea of underlying infection like surfers skimming ahead of the waves? What *shape* would such an outbreak have, and what sorts of factors might distort it? She thought about the Inner Sanctum at Heatherfields, an anonymous grouping of older men who guided the Institute's interests, and how they were rumored to be cryptically intuitive. Could her relegation to the basement near Theoretical Epi have been a calculated maneuver, a nudge in the right direction? Was she supposed to have met Henry all along?

Unfortunately, the answers to these and other questions were at least nine hours, and a lonely night, away.

Or maybe not so lonely. Artie knew as soon as she saw the light behind her front window curtains that there was going to be trouble. Heart pounding, she fumbled with the keys, wishing for the dozenth time that she had changed the locks. But she had the vague idea that it might be illegal to lock her husband out of a jointly owned house before anything was settled, and she didn't want to give Calvin's solicitor yet another mark against her.

She shut the door and slipped her burdens to the floor, sensing the air with practiced vigilance. He was near, his cologne the merest suggestion in the air, calling up a swift medley of joy, fear and finally revulsion, as if the last two years had been compressed into a second.

She stepped into the lounge. Cal sat relaxed on the sofa, facing the switched-off television. His hair was darkened to the hue of damp straw and slightly curled from the heat and humidity of the night. He looked up and gave her that smile, the one that had knocked the breath out of her when they'd been introduced in a bar in Grassmarket in Edinburgh, friends of friends of friends. There was no telltale glass or bottle now, but she knew immediately that he'd been drinking.

"Artemis," he pronounced, fairly distinctly, so there'd been enough alcohol to make him affectionate but not enough to make him cruel. Artemis, the name he used when he wanted to seduce.

"I thought we had an agreement, Cal." Artie was suddenly exhausted, desperate to get him out of the house. Even solitude was less dangerous than Cal in charming mode.

"But I know how much you hate being alone." There was no concern there, only that mocking knowledge, whose calculated use against her had heralded the beginning of their end, at least for her. Maybe he had drunk more than she thought.

He stood up and started the long approach across the empty acres of the room, moving with the inexorable fluidity of a pursuer in a nightmare. She shrank against the wall, but still he came until he was putting out a hand, running it along her shoulder and down her arm. Despite herself, she felt her body react, not to flinch but to crave. And it wasn't only to his touch, but his smell, his warmth, the hundred little physical promises shedding from his skin. The prospect of companionship. And the shameful memory of last week, when she had been too weak and lonely to resist.

Instead, she said: "I want you to leave now."

Henry's words, she remembered. And something of Henry's placid, impenetrable strength mixed in with her own habitual resolve. To her amazement, Calvin dropped his hands.

"If that's how you really feel," he said, "then maybe you'll be a bit more helpful with the divorce process."

Charm, warmth, coercion discarded as useless skins, his cool scales glistening beneath, and then the carefully timed closure of the door, a pointed full stop. Cal was the master of the parting shot, but Artie knew that this evening, the victory belonged to her.

Nevertheless, there was no law about fastening the door-chain behind her.

CHAPTER 2
Keeper and Kept, The Fine Line Between

IN THE MORNING ARTIE WENT straight to room B302, but the door was locked. The lights were on, though. As she rattled at the useless handle, then spent a fruitless minute knocking, several passing employees threw her startled looks before glancing away in embarrassment. Then she walked past her own office and tapped on Ben's door.

"He's not in yet," Raisa, one of his post-docs, said. "I'll tell him you popped by."

Disappointed, Artie retraced her steps, more slowly this time, and went into her lab. Fiona was working in the tissue culture cabinet, singing along to music, already well progressed with the daily chore of keeping all the feline cell cultures maintained.

"Everything okay, Fi?"

"Yup," the young woman replied, manipulating towers of plastic dishes with thoughtless efficiency. "I've finished PCRing up those latest samples from Mary as well."

"Fantastic," Artie said. "Mark will be thrilled."

She went back to her office. Her own post-doc wasn't in yet, but that wasn't surprising. She made a cup of tea and switched on her computer. Navigating into the Heatherfields homepage, she performed a personnel search using the keyword "Henry."

There were only two hits in the Theoretical Epidemiology department. The first, Jason Henry, was known to her, an amiable PhD student who was always trying to find a fourth for a game of lunchtime bridge. The other name was not familiar: Henry S. Manfield. She clicked on the link. Room number: B302. Telephone extension: none. Email address: none.

Artie blinked. How odd.

Rank: Professor. Affiliated staff: Simon Renquist, another unfamiliar name. To have only one post-doc was also very unusual. Artie already had two people on her team; Ben had six, and someone as old as Henry ought to have a dozen at least. But maybe theoretical fields were more solitary by nature than the experimental sciences—just one's brain and a computer.

Simon Renquist. *Rennie*, she thought. This must be the furious one she'd been warned about. But where had he been last night, and why hadn't Ben mentioned Henry at all?

Artie started scouring the scientific literature online and pulled down an unexpectedly large amount of material about Henry S. Manfield. The man seemed very prominent in the field, cited repeatedly by other epidemiologists. There was a hefty publication record, both articles and books, almost all of them in the authorial guise of "Renquist and Manfield." Their publishing partnership extended back 24 years—so this Rennie had probably been around for slightly longer than that, meaning he was not likely to be a mere post-doc. Indeed, when she went back to the Heatherfields page and clicked on his name, the rank came up as Associate Professor. He did have a telephone and email address, she noted.

Artie downloaded a few of Henry's recent articles, trying to get a sense of his work through the thick patina of jargon and mathematics. From the way other scientists referred to him in their papers, it was clear that he was a maverick, inspiring scorn as much as awe and admiration. His theories about the spread of infection were bold, audacious, trend-resisting. In short, he seemed precisely the person who could help her with her own unfashionable theory.

The thought that he might not wish to do so did not even occur to her, despite the way he had dismissed her the night before. In Artie's world, everyone could be cajoled eventually.

She picked up the phone and dialed Rennie's number, but after about ten rings there was a click and the call got shunted to Reception. No voicemail either, she thought, putting the receiver back in its cradle. What was wrong with these people?

"Morning, Art." Mark stepped into the office, pausing to give her a closer look. "What's up? You've got that feverish glint in your eye."

"What do you know about Henry Manfield in room B302?"

"Brilliant rebel-hermit," he said without hesitation. "Wildly infamous amongst other Epi types, but too odd to mix with mere mortals."

Artie's eyes widened. She hadn't expected an informed response.

"He's got an attendant called Rennie to keep him out of trouble," Mark went on. "I've never met either of them, though. All very Victorian, stashing a batty old uncle in the wardrobe, don't you think? Apparently they've even got a private lavatory."

A lavatory Henry did not keep to, after hours, when his "keeper" was absent.

"How," she said slowly, "do you know all of that?"

"Ben told me."

"Ben told you? At one of those all-male pub sessions, I expect."

There was a small silence.

"That's not fair," he said. "We were just having a random lunch, as I recall. In fact, I think I asked you along, but you were too busy."

When she looked away, ashamed at her outburst, he said, "You know, I thought you'd realize by now that I'd be the last person to give you the traditional Heatherfields treatment."

"I know," she said, passing a hand over her eyes. After Calvin's intrusion, she'd slept poorly. "And I'm sorry, Mark. It's just that I specifically asked Ben for the same information, and he was evasive."

Mark hung up his jacket and sat down at his desk.

"I get the idea that Ben's proud of where he works, and considers Henry a blight on it," he said, serenity restored. "And Ben's obviously dead set on impressing you. But he didn't mind someone as lowly as me knowing, so I'd be flattered, not offended."

"Hmmm." The thought of Ben trying to impress her was not a welcome one.

"And why the sudden interest, anyway?"

Artie was about to describe her midnight encounter, but then for no good reason, changed her mind. "He's done simulations with bird flu," she said vaguely, "and I think he could help us with feline leukemia. Let me show you one of his papers." Overflowing with enthusiasm, her fingers were already calling up some of the relevant articles on her laptop.

But Mark said, "He doesn't collaborate with anyone except Rennie, according to Ben. In fact, he doesn't *speak* to anyone else. Hasn't opened his mouth for decades, apparently."

"But—"

"He's not... *normal*, Art." He sounded almost apologetic at having to cool her ardor.

Artie looked up slowly from her screen and met his eye. "What flavor of *not normal*?"

"Autism or Asperger's, something like that. I don't know the details. But Rennie's meant to be fiercely protective, so I wouldn't get your hopes up."

Just like that, the previous night's encounter came back to her in a new light. At the time, she had interpreted the man's behavior as merely strange, the sort of strangeness one could find at the fringes of normal behavior, especially late at night after a long day of mental exertion. His reaction at the lavatory entrance was just surprise, and his failure to answer her queries, mere absent-mindedness. But now it made sense why Henry had seemed familiar; her cousin was afflicted with high-functioning Asperger's syndrome, and she belatedly recognized the signs.

And yet the description didn't seem quite right: it couldn't explain completely the overall weirdness that had emanated from Henry. She felt a prickling of discomfort on her skin as the reality superimposed itself over her memory—there must be more to the story than that. And as far as talking, after the initial refusal, he'd had no problem at all speaking to her. Surely Ben had been exaggerating, just another false rumor cemented into certainty in the retelling.

"You stopped by, Artie?"

She looked up to see Ben himself in the doorway, as if her musings had summoned him. For the first time she recognized the eagerness that Mark's quietly observant eyes had long since noted. She hoped the immunologist's shyness would postpone an uncomfortable scene for as long as possible. And in the meantime, she was not above using whatever assets her gender gave her, to offset the majority of times when they proved a distinct disadvantage.

"I want to talk to Simon Renquist," she said with a big smile.

He looked appalled. "Why?"

"Can you get me an appointment? The normal channels—door knocking, telephoning—don't seem to be working. I'd send him an email, but that seems ludicrous, seeing as how he's sitting about twenty meters away."

She could feel Mark's amusement as he stared innocently at his screen, and could just imagine him trying to guess which force would win—Ben's revulsion about the situation in B302 or his attraction to Artie.

Ben sighed, running a hand through his floppy hair. "I can try, but doubt he'll be up for it. Not exactly the collegial type."

"This is ridiculous!" Artie said. "They work down the corridor, and this is meant to be an interdisciplinary institute. Who invited them, if they weren't willing to uphold Sir Rupert's banner?"

Mark coughed.

"It's a special case," Ben pleaded, face gone pink under his ginger thatch. "You see..."

"Don't bother—Mark's already been decent enough to explain." She let her displeasure radiate like the steam off an iced drink on a sultry terrace table.

Ben swallowed. "Listen, Artie, I'll do what I can."

"Thanks, Ben—you're wonderful."

"And you're shameless," Mark said, bursting into laughter after Ben left.

"Shameless, but effective." Artie shrugged. "And it's all in the name of science. Besides, it's your fault for pointing out his soft white underbelly in the first place."

"I feel like I've let the side down."

"How long has he carried the torch?"

"No idea," Mark said. "But he only started acting obvious when you stopped wearing your wedding ring."

Artie glanced down involuntarily at her hand, at the faded white stripe that persisted from last year's tan.

There was an awkward pause, and then he said, "Sorry. I think I just crossed the line."

She looked up at him. "I always thought only women noticed things like that."

"Well, Ben's got an incentive. And I..." He gave her a rueful smile. "I've always had an eye for detail."

"Never mind," she said. "It's not a deep dark secret or anything. I recently chucked him out for bad behavior."

"Oh," he said. "I'm sorry, Art."

"It's no big deal." Her voice sounded brittle and bright to her own ears.

He looked at her thoughtfully for a few moments before going back to his computer screen. Artie queued a few papers by Renquist and Manfield to print, cursing herself for having allowed this little scene to occur. And it wasn't Mark's fault at all, but hers, for sullying the professional sphere with real life, with the maneuverings of sex and all its consequences. Gender-disadvantaged in a chauvinist's paradise or not, she felt embarrassed for how she had manipulated Ben.

IN THE END IT TURNED out not to matter, because Ben didn't have any luck with Rennie.

"I'm sorry," Ben said, slipping into a seat across from her in the otherwise empty coffee room that afternoon. "Managed to speak to him, but says he's too busy right now, reiterated his usual policy of non-collaboration."

"Too busy," Artie said disdainfully.

"Might be telling the truth there," Ben said, rubbing a finger over his freckled, crooked nose. "It's a full-time job dealing with Henry, and Henry works pretty much all the time. I don't envy Rennie's position. Or blame him for being surly, to be honest."

For a second, Ben paused, and Artie felt a prickle on her skin, a sense that Ben was deeply uncomfortable but trying hard not to show it.

"How did this whole thing come about?" she asked.

"Rennie was Henry's PhD student, ages ago," Ben said, reluctantly. "His only one... all a bit mysterious how Henry chose him. I mean, why he decided to talk to him, trust him with his work. Up until Rennie, Henry was a one-man show. The Inner Sanctum had recruited him for their usual inscrutable reasons, set him up down here with an healthcare attendant and left him to it."

"How did he disseminate his ideas if he couldn't speak?"

Ben stirred some sugar into his coffee. "When you think about it, it's amazing how fully you can participate in academic science without being physically present. Henry's a powerful writer, submitted prolifically to journals, both articles and correspondence. Of course, until Rennie came along, there was no one to go to the international conferences and really advertise the research, so in those days, he was on the fringes. I'm sure someone like you appreciates how important the social aspects of science can be."

He flushed a bit, and Artie felt her heart go soft for him. She didn't find him at all attractive, but he was kind, and she was determined to be on her best behavior.

"I know exactly what you mean," she said. "Papers get ignored with no face on the podium to hype them up... and sometimes it's difficult to sense the trends unless you're working the conference bars, hearing all the gossip."

She thought abruptly of Henry's hypothetical avian flu situation, two infected individuals spreading deadly virus particles like careless rumors.

"Bet you're good, in the bars."

She laughed. "I *do* have a way with networking," she admitted, taking a sip from her mug. "So Rennie stayed on then, after he got his PhD?"

Ben nodded. "And never left, became the official face of Renquist and Manfield. Doing all sorts of mysterious things in there now, strictly via email and phone—hear they've even got contacts with the Ministry of Defence."

"Hmmm. But this Rennie—is he just the mouthpiece, or is he an intellectually equal partner?"

"No idea, Artie. He stopped going to conferences years ago, once Henry was established. And he never had an independent career, so how could he be judged? I suspect, though, that it's mostly Henry."

"Poor Rennie," Artie thought to herself, and aloud, said, "I really appreciate your efforts, though, Ben."

"Sorry I couldn't be of more help." He paused. "Listen, Artie, I don't suppose—"

"Ben," she said quickly. "How did you contact Rennie? Secret knock? Smoke signals?"

It took him a few seconds to answer. "I'm the fire officer for the basement, so I've got his telephone extension number."

"The one that gets answered, you mean. Could you..."

"No, Artie, I'm sorry," he said, truly remorseful, and Artie wouldn't let herself press further as he got up and left her to stare at the silty remains at the bottom of her mug.

༄

WHEN ARTIE GOT BACK TO the office, she decided, ludicrous or not, that she was going to send Rennie an email. She kept it brief, saying nothing about her late-night encounter with his mentor, merely mentioning that she'd read some of his papers and thought that they might have an area of mutual interest. She deliberately did not mention Henry's name, reasoning that it would be politic to treat Rennie as an equal partner unless she found out otherwise. She described her controversial theory about the spread of mutant viruses in a few sentences, then typed: *I know you're busy, but just give me thirty minutes of your time and I'm sure you won't regret it.*

Classic Artemis Marshall, she thought as she scanned it over. She would have made an amazing used car salesman.

She clicked on the button and sent the message across the corridor and down three doors into B302. She imagined the answering beep of Rennie's computer as the two men hunched over their keyboards in the twilight, spinning gossamer graphics into space and dreaming about death and contagion. Two and a half decades... it was enough to make anyone bitter. So she was willing to forgive a little honest resistance.

At least for a while.

༄

ON FRIDAY NIGHT, ARTIE WAS wandering through the dim rooms of an exhibition at the Tate Modern. She'd long since lost Mary within the shadowy crowds—viewing art was a solitary endeavor for both of them, and she knew they'd catch up later in the café for the full post-mortem. Meanwhile, a brothelful of orange-skinned odalisques glowed at her from the walls, with their knife-slash noses and their unearthly expressions, expressions that seemed to fluctuate depending on the angle of inspection: now bored, now coy, now wicked, now dreamy. Never modest, though, Artie realized. The models knew that she was watching and this did not perturb them; this, in turn, made her feel uncomfortably like a voyeur.

Modigliani was not an artist Artie had thought she liked. She'd had a vague impression, gleaned from posters and postcards, of trashy, ill-formed girls, touching themselves with ambiguous intentions like a teenage male fantasy. Mary had expressed a strong preference, though, and her friend was so sweet-tempered and obliging that Artie was always happy to allow herself to be overruled on the rare occasions when they differed.

But Artie found out that she'd been wrong. True, she despised on principle this timeless obsession that artists had with female nudity—it was not only predictable, but subtly offensive. Calvin had been fond of theorizing that this aversion was a subconscious, redirected loathing of her own voluptuousness, and by extrapolation, of her feminine side. But these particular paintings were beautiful, regardless of the subtext.

She hadn't been much into art until Calvin had bought her the subscription to the Tate and indoctrinated her into his own passions. She never bothered to read the labels or the historical notes, to pore over the catalogs, to dissect the influences and symbolism as Calvin had; instead, she just soaked in the colors and allowed the manic energy of her thoughts to come to rest: *used* the art, for her own purposes. Afterwards, she often found that something that had been troubling her at work—a strange experimental result, say, or a block she was experiencing in writing an article—would shake itself loose. More subconscious activity at work there, Calvin had explained, as usual trying to demystify something that Artie found amazing.

"You're a scientist," he would say when she'd ask him to stop. "Deconstructing mysterious things is what you're supposed to *do.*"

But then, Calvin had never been very good at separating work from pleasure, especially when it came to his wife.

Displeased that thoughts of Calvin had disrupted her enjoyment, Artie left the exhibition. Mary was already sipping a glass of wine, lost in thought, when Artie caught up with her in the back of the bustling museum café. She scanned the room as she sat down with a cup of tea.

"Looking for someone?" Mary said.

"Calvin normally lectures on Friday evenings, but I always feel paranoid here. It's *his* territory, if you know what I mean."

Mary studied Artie solemnly. "Have you seen much of him recently?"

Artie busied herself with milk and sugar, spoon and teabag. "He's taken to dropping by the house unannounced."

"Oh, Art. What does he want?"

"Sex, ostensibly."

"My God! You don't let him have it, do you?"

Artie just took a sip of tea from the glass cup, burning her mouth in the process, and Mary shook her head.

"How long has this been going on?" Mary asked, her eyes large and wary. She had never liked Calvin.

"Maybe five visits since he packed his bags… but I've only given in twice."

"*Why,* Artie?"

"Why's he visiting or why have I given in?"

"Both, you idiot."

"He's trying to punish me for my sins," Artie said, after a pause. "He knows I'm lonely, and this is the only way he's got left to bully me."

"*Your* sins," she nearly spat, in an uncharacteristic bout of bile. "And why don't you flip him onto the floor and break a couple of his ribs?"

"I don't want to make Cal's solicitor's day," she said.

"Okay, I'll let you off the hook about the disfiguring and dismemberment, but you don't have to *sleep* with the toad."

"He's always been able to intimidate me. That's the whole point. That's why I've got to get out."

"It's practically rape, Art." Mary tossed back the last of her wine. Despite her bluster, Artie realized that Mary was close to tears. Crying when angry: yet another female characteristic that Artie had neatly avoided in the genetic lottery. Disadvantageous or not, it gave Artie a twinge now.

"If I were you," Mary added, when Artie didn't reply, "I'd pick up some young brainless thing at a pub and take him home if you're that lonely. It would be a hundred times less dangerous."

∽

ARTIE'S TOLERANCE FOR RENNIE'S DIFFICULT situation was put to the test over the weekend and well into the next week, when her inbox remained stubbornly empty of his reply. Twice a day, once in the morning and once after lunch, she rang his extension, but no one ever picked up. By the following Friday afternoon, she was genuinely irritated.

"He's a coward," she grumbled to Mark. "Doesn't he..."

"Know who you are?" Mark said, amused. "You sound just like a celeb getting pulled over for speeding. Tell it to the judge, lady."

"He could at least have the decency to answer."

"Do you answer all your mail the same week?" he asked reasonably, and seemed to interpret her fuming silence correctly.

That evening, after Mark left, she pulled out her diary to remind herself of upcoming commitments. When the pages flopped over to the sticky note with Ben's instructions for the alarm system, she began to smile.

She made sure all the lights were on, turned on the music to maximum volume and worked diligently on her email for several hours. At ten, when she would normally leave the office, she remained in her seat, tapping her audacious opinions into the void. Time bled away and city-bound trains departed without her as she parried with zoo keepers, retrovirologists and small animal veterinarians around the world.

At some point after midnight, there was a knock on the door.

She looked up at the pale face staring at her through the oblong rectangle of glass. Not the pale of fear or of genetic stock, but the paleness of someone who never goes out into the sun.

Heart pounding, she silenced the song on her computer and motioned the man into the sudden stillness. Looking very reluctant, even more reluctant than the gormless PhD candidate, he turned the handle and committed one foot to her office. Tall, malnourished, late forties. Dark brown hair cut for utilitarian purposes more than style, and a spectacularly ill-thought-out combination of clothing. If she saw him in a crowd, she would never give him a second glance, except perhaps for his eye color— the dark cloudy blue of an alpine lake, fathomless and enigmatic.

"You're the last," he said, almost inaudibly, but with a dismissive undertone, as if she were a student, or one of the housekeeping staff. "Do you know how to set the alarm?"

"Are you Rennie?" she asked, unable to filter out her eagerness.

Anger flashed across his face, quickly squelched. *Furious.* In a second, Artie knew exactly what Ben meant.

"My name," he said tightly, "is Simon." Then his expression acquired new comprehension and the subterranean anger intensified. "*You* must that new woman professor." He made the word *woman* sound like a curse. "It's you who keeps ringing, isn't it?"

"Who did you think I was before?" she said. "A *secretary*?"

His chin tightened, which Artie interpreted as a yes.

"I take it that Ben didn't pass on my message," he said.

"Oh, he did."

"Then why do you keep ringing?"

"If you ever answered your phone, I wouldn't have to."

"I don't have time for female tricks," he said, contempt flowing from his movements as he turned to go, and Artie was on her feet before she knew it.

"Wait!" It was all going wrong. "I didn't mean to insult you—I genuinely thought Rennie was the name you went by. And I only want to talk with you because I admire your work."

He paused, still half in and out of the doorway. "Rennie's what they call me to wind me up."

"They?"

His gesture took in the entire basement.

"I'm sorry, Simon, about the ambush. But I didn't see how else to get your attention."

He came back into the room, crossed his arms and leaned against the wall. The fury seemed to have faded for the moment. "I was going to answer your message eventually, Dr. Marshall, honestly. It's just that I'm about a month behind Henry's correspondence as it is…"

There was a different quality in his voice now: weariness, almost desperation.

"What did you think of my theory?"

He looked at her dispassionately—the color of his eyes was uncanny, and made her feel strange. Eventually he said, "There wasn't enough information for me to judge how applicable our models might be—but even if they were, I simply have no time to commit to any new projects."

His gaze drifted awkwardly towards the floor, and Artie wavered over a response. The man was clearly impervious to charm, with his disdain of "female tricks" and the closed door of his body language. The usual coin of flattery had also flopped, so a sheer intellectual approach was called for.

"I've got to go," he said before she could speak, still not looking at her. "You're okay with the alarm?"

"Come have a drink with me," she challenged. "Let me tell you more about my theory."

"I'm sorry." He shook his head, not looking the slightest bit regretful. In fact, he looked as if she'd just suggested something offensive.

"But—"

"Good night, Dr. Marshall," he said, exactly as Henry had.

It hadn't gone even remotely as planned, Artie thought after he'd vanished. He was supposed to have accepted her offer, and ideally, given her a hand with the damned alarm and a ride home afterward to boot. Smiling at her own folly, and nowhere near defeated, she picked up the phone and rang for a cab.

BEFORE ARTIE SET OFF TO Kings Cross station on Saturday morning to catch a train to Edinburgh for a weekend with friends, she composed a short email to Simon Renquist from her study at home. She attached the electronic file of one her recent review articles about her theory, purposefully selecting the most erudite of the lot, the most removed from medical implications and focusing on the sheer abstract merits of the work. Like Mark had said at the interview—the deeper implications of the pure biology. Artie had a flair for selling her work; this particular paper, though a bit off-the-wall, happened to be her favorite. It could certainly grab attention—if such a feat were possible with a man like Simon. She didn't write anything in the body of the message, just a subject: *humor me, it's only five pages.*

"YOU'RE LOOKING EXCEPTIONALLY WELL, MY dear," Philip Cox observed before sinking his fork into the cake: multiple sedimentary layers of different shades of chocolate, adorned with yet more chocolate frosting and shavings, with a healthy dollop of cream on the side.

Nothing had changed, Artie thought with amusement. Philip had only to set one foot into the café before the staff were whisking the house special to his usual table, with affectionate quips about their "favorite Prof and his sweet tooth" and a wink at Artie, who was also well known.

"I still don't know how you keep so trim," Artie said, settling into her low-fat carrot torte. "You should've had a cardiac arrest ages ago."

In addition to the daily cake, she knew that Philip ordered the Full Scottish for breakfast every morning at the establishment next door.

"Good genes, Artemis," he intoned, like he always did. "And how are you finding Heatherfields? Coping with the famous attitude?"

"Men are wired quite simply, Phil," she said. "It hardly seems sporting, but I'm being gentle with them."

He grinned, enhancing the skull-like appearance of his head. "I had a feeling it wouldn't be a problem for you. How's the research?"

This was the opening she'd been waiting for, and she launched into an enthusiastic description of the lab, Mark, and the expanded collaboration with Mary. When she mentioned Henry Manfield, Philip frowned.

"Manfield... a tough old nut, I hear. Although if anyone could crack him, it *would* be you."

"Have you met him?" she asked eagerly.

He shook his head. "But many years ago, I received a visit from his student... dark-haired, pleasant fellow, very likable."

"Simon Renquist?" she said dubiously.

He nodded, dealing with a prim mouthful of cake before carrying on. "That's the one. He needed some specialized information about HIV entry, wanted to speak with me personally. He thought there was epidemiological evidence that HIV used more than one receptor—years ahead of everyone else on that point."

Artie smashed some crumbs against the plate with her fork. "Likable in what way?"

Philip dabbed a smudge of chocolate from his lips with his napkin. "Well, you'd have to be enthusiastic to come all the way up here for a few simple questions. Brimming with energy and enthusiasm, that one. And evangelical fervor—referred to Manfield in almost a deferential whisper." He chortled softly at the whimsies of youth. "Otherwise quite sensible, and a quirky sense of humor."

"He's still there, you know," she said. *Albeit in an unrecognizable form.*

Philip raised feathery eyebrows. "How unfortunate. Lingering is seldom healthy. You know my philosophy, of course, the same for post-docs as students: In and out, like a surgical strike."

∾

SIMON RENQUIST SAT IN HIS kitchen, writing up a record of the day's events in his journal. So little happened to him that he'd been ritually filling up this same notebook for years without reaching the halfway point. Nevertheless, he couldn't bring himself to stop, as if these brief paragraphs were the only evidence that he was actually alive.

H. calm. Clear night yesterday, Venus prominent. Looking forward to summer solstice and the earlier nightfall in coming weeks.

A.M. had the gall to email me after what happened on Friday, with attached article. Would not normally bother, but look forward to seeing first-hand evidence that her appointment to professorship over my application was down to sexual politics as opposed to independent thought. Then at least there's a logical explanation

Simon stopped short of finishing the sentence with the obvious:—*not that it would make me any less angry.* Instead, he nearly punctured the page with a full stop before closing the notebook. He placed a hand on the laptop that sat, sealed like a disapproving mouth, on the kitchen table, and hesitated. The truth was that he didn't really want to read Marshall's article, even if it meant scoring points against her. True, if her intellectual credentials did turn out to be false, which was in his estimation a statistically fair probability, it would give him a satisfactory opportunity to email his opinions to that effect—which ought to stop her from bothering him in future.

Simon shook his head in the dim light of the bare light bulb. He was acting childish, he knew. He should let the now unchangeable fact of this woman's existence roll over him like everything else. If it hadn't been her, someone else would have secured the professorship—there was no use denying the truth. And knowing his luck, Marshall would turn out to be highly qualified and perfectly decent. But the pugnacious persona he adopted in his journal was always on the rampage—and bore little resemblance to the powerless man who wielded the pen. What would really happen, regardless of the paper's content, was that he would write Marshall a polite, brief rejection, severing all future contact, and that would be that.

So why even bother wasting his time? Sunday evenings were sacred: Henry went home early one evening a week, for his own inscrutable reasons, and Simon had five or six blissful waking hours of freedom and solitude. He dreamed about those hours all the rest of the week, how it would feel to sit in his small, shabby kitchen and read for pleasure—books on astronomy and history, mostly, anything that would transport him away. How it would feel to take his weekly, two hour-long run along the golf course, pounding his frustrations into mindless pulp beneath his trainers—so much more satisfying than the scant half hour he allocated for exercise the other six nights of the week. How it would feel to escape the drone of the computer fans, the stress of the backlog of work and correspondence, and, above all, the never-ending storm front of Henry Manfield's moods.

It was only five pages, after all. Simon opened the laptop with a sigh.

ON MONDAY MORNING, ARTIE WASN'T really surprised to see that Rennie hadn't replied to her email.

"Any luck bagging your man?" Mark asked her in the laboratory that afternoon, where Artie was sitting at the workbench, pipetting over a rack of plastic tubes. She'd told him the story that morning, and every time she checked her email he teased her for an update.

"Were you cruising for men up in Scotland?" Fiona said, rather a connoisseur of that particular topic.

Did the entire basement know about her separation?

"No, she's after someone in this corridor," Mark said. "B302."

"Mark, for heaven's sake! Not in front of the children."

Fiona put down her pipettor. "Not old Rennie, I hope? I've heard he's violent."

"Violent?" Mark paused in the act of whooshing out the door. "As in bad temper?"

"No, as in Grievous Bodily Harm," Fiona said. "As in restraining order."

"Where did you hear that?" Artie asked. She met Mark's eye, and could tell he was thinking along similar lines.

Fiona shrugged, hands moving over the PCR machine with rote grace. "We technicians hear things. Things you lot are too busy to pick up."

"Why do I get the impression," Artie said, "that when you say *busy*, you actually mean *clueless*?"

"Tell us more," Mark said casually. "Think of us as a charity case."

She shook her head. "No can do. Privileged information... but highly reliable."

"Second hand? Third hand?" Mark said.

She pressed her lips together, gloved hands shifting back and forth, back and forth from tube rack to the gleaming metal bed of the machine. "No, from the one who needed the court order. That's all I'm saying, okay?"

Later, Artie was finishing her solitary lunch in the main dining hall, the burble of hundreds of scientists echoing in the high-ceilinged room. The space was bathed in sunlight streaming through the leaded-glass windows, reflecting off the polished walls and the scuffed, antique tables. She was just scraping up the last of her vegetables when Mark appeared, a resolute expression on his face.

"I don't like it, Art," he said, sitting down across from her with a cup of coffee. "You're not planning any more midnight rendezvous, are you?"

"I might be," she said.

He just looked at her, so she said, "A, there's no other way to talk to him, B, I'm not afraid, and C, he's absolutely no match for me."

"How tall is he?"

"Maybe six-one?"

"Come on, Artie, he's got half a foot on you, not to mention..."

"The all-important Y chromosome."

He sighed impatiently. "The testosterone advantage, I was going to say."

"If I were a man, we wouldn't be having this conversation."

"For Christ's sake, I'm about as egalitarian as a bloke can get, but biology is biology, and it's stupid to deny the obvious differences!"

"The differences are obvious, all right," she said. "He looks like he's been sitting at a computer for twenty years, and I've got a black belt in karate."

He put down his coffee slowly.

"Really?"

"Really—I could have you on the floor in five seconds, mate." She took a demure sip of Coke. "I can arrange a demonstration if you like."

Despite himself, Mark started to laugh. "Just when I think you couldn't possibly produce another facet, you surprise me, Artemis Marshall. What next? Closet baroness with an estate in Derbyshire? Booker Prize-winning novelist under a pseudonym?"

"I do a mean Victoria Sponge. When's your birthday?"

"Okay, I'll concede that you can protect yourself in an ordinary situation." He lowered his voice. "But if he really is violent... I happen to like your provocative nature, but I can also see how it might be infuriating to someone of another temperament. You know what they say about anger, how it can translate to inhuman strength. And he might have a weapon."

"Yeah, like a stapler or something."

"Artie." He made her look at him by sheer force of will. "Making assumptions is a dangerous business, and you know absolutely nothing about this man. I'm really enjoying my post-doctoral stint here—I don't want to find myself without a boss."

She couldn't look away from his frank gaze, couldn't bring herself to say something flippant.

"What do you want, Mark?" she finally said.

"Just let me be there the next time you lure him into the office. I won't say a word, I promise."

She shook her head. "One person is already too many for someone like him. I'll be fine, honestly."

Mark stood, face completely neutral. "Fine, but don't say I didn't warn you."

❧

LAST FRIDAY'S STRATAGEM WOULDN'T WORK twice. That evening, around eleven, she shut down her office and retired into the tissue culture annex of the lab, leaving the lights out. After checking that the computer's glow wasn't visible from the main corridor door, she worked at her laptop in a chair in the corner, neck sore from the awkward angle and wondering what imbecile had named them "laptops." At the time when she would normally leave the building, she snapped shut the computer, left it on the chair, picked up her backpack and went to stand quietly in the shadows by the main lab door. If she positioned herself just right, one corner of the lit entrance to B302 was visible.

She felt foolish, elated, and yes, despite her earlier bluster, scared. What had got into her? Hiding in the dark like a teenage prankster from a bitter, oppressed, apparently misogynistic man—from a random element with a reputed criminal record. She knew that Mark was right to be concerned, and knew she would probably have taken the same advice if it had come from a woman. Which made her undeniably stupid, to hold principle over personal safety.

Time moved sluggishly, but the solitude didn't prey on her, because she knew she wasn't truly alone. On the other side of that lit door, two men sat working, two men who held the key to releasing her beloved brainchild into the sunlight.

Weary, she rested her head against the door, allowing her thoughts to slide, and then the click of a door alerted her, the memory of a black shape's passage dislodging from her blinking lashes. How long ago? A second? A minute?

Now she heard a strident beeping noise undulating down the corridor. She must've dozed off. Blood rushing, she opened the door and dashed down the dim corridor towards the man standing with his back to her at the security panel, lights flashing like a mini apocalypse around his head.

"Wait!" she cried.

He swiveled around, lights strobing off his skin with heated urgency.

"I don't *believe* this," he said. "Where in hell did *you* come from?"

They stared each other down, Artie wasn't sure for how long, until the alarm changed to double time, going up an octave in pitch.

"Abort it, you idiot! Enter the escape code!" She had no idea what it was.

He hesitated, looking at the panel and then back at her.

"It's past the point of no return," he said.

"Well, go through then! Hurry up!"

"I don't have my pass with me—do you?" When she shook her head, he said, "I don't have time to deal with that dolt on Reception—come on, quick."

"But Simon, how are we going to get out afterwards?"

"Just come *on*."

Confused, she followed him to B302, surprised at how rapidly he moved. She'd had him down as a lethargic, laconic nobody, but there was energy in his movements, and ungainly strength. As his wiry fingers manipulated the door handle, she could imagine them wringing the life out of something.

He shoved her through the door. When they were both safely inside, she opened her mouth to protest at the rough treatment, but he put a finger to his lips, striding over to the inner entrance to Henry's lair and closing it. Artie leaned against the closed outer door, trembling and light-headed from the cacophony of the alarm, and two things happened simultaneously: the spiraling klaxon went silent, and Simon slowly approached, glaring down at her with calculated menace.

"I really should call Security and get you thrown out," he said. The tone was soft— not the softness of a gentle spirit, but the softness of a strung-out, on-the-edge parent who has finally managed to get the baby asleep.

"I haven't done anything wrong." She kept her voice down too, but she could feel the quiet preparation flowing into her arms, her shoulders, her hands: dozens of *kata* priming themselves to be adapted for a real-life encounter. Her body knew exactly what to do if he came after her with his right, his left, or with both, if he kicked, how to disarm him if he attempted to pull out a concealed weapon. These were things that she didn't have to plan; they would just happen.

"Don't insult my intelligence, Dr. Marshall." His face was expressionless, but she sensed that the fury was somewhere close to the surface. "This wasn't a coincidence; this was premeditated harassment."

"I only wanted a quick corridor chat." She felt, suddenly, like a very small child, and flushed with shame.

He stood there, acknowledging that shame, approving of it, and then said, "You ended up with a bit more than you bargained for, didn't you?"

There was a second or two of silence, and then both of them started laughing at the same time, hands over their mouths to blot out the noise. It was a sick kind of laughter, the sort people indulge in when hearing of natural disasters and then immediately regret. Simon laughed like someone who had forgotten how, staggering backwards and falling into the chair, doubling over, then raising his head to look at her with tears streaming down his face, and Artie just stood there against the wall with shaking shoulders, struggling to control herself.

After about a minute, their moment of joint hysteria trickled out, and Artie felt completely out of her depth, the fear returning as he wiped his face matter-of-factly with his sleeve and continued to look her over, humor gone as quickly as it had arrived. He was out of his depth too, she realized. And she had no idea what he was going to do next.

"We'll have to call Security anyway," she said, "to get out."

He was sitting between Artie and the telephone, and she didn't have her mobile on her—it was, she belatedly realized, inside the backpack she'd forgotten to grab when the alarm roused her. She measured distances, calculated the span of his arms.

"That won't be necessary," he said. "We've got a private exit here, through the back."

"Oh." She looked at him for a moment. "Can I have those thirty minutes now, or are you just going to chuck me out?"

"Women like you always get their way in the end, don't they?" A look of distaste crossed his malleable face.

"You don't know a thing about me."

"Well, I know you're manipulative, after your two recent performances," he said. "And I assume you've been using your looks all your life."

"And I assume you've been discounting women who look like me all of yours, without even bothering to find out what's underneath!"

Unexpectedly, he gave her a sardonic smile. "You're right, I have. And I've yet to be proved wrong—although I certainly concede a statistical margin of error."

She opened her mouth to retort, but then he added, "Actually, I'm not being fair. After this weekend, I'd be reluctant to discount you outright, despite your immature behavior this evening."

"Don't tell me you actually read my paper?" Her indignation melted into astonishment.

He nodded. "But I won't be able to collaborate with you, as I made it clear before."

"Was it because you aren't interested?"

"No, I was intrigued." This concession, she could see, galled. "Your thesis is sound, and testable, and provided you'd generated enough raw data, we might have been able to model your phenomenon using our techniques."

As he spoke, she got the distinct impression that he was no mere mouthpiece. Could there be more of Renquist in the team Renquist and Manfield than Ben had led her to believe?

"In fact," he said, "we could probably extrapolate from feline viruses to infectious epidemics in general—at least those agents prone to mutation. It could be a very valuable exercise for the larger scientific community."

She felt a little thrill in her chest. "Then why—"

"I'm sorry." He shook his head. "As much as I'd like to help, there just isn't time."

"Because Henry's interests come first." Disappointment made her disdainful, which she immediately regretted.

But he just said, "Exactly. Now I really have to escort him home now, before he gets restless. Do you need me to call a taxi, Dr. Marshall?"

"*Professor* Marshall," said a deep rumble from the open inner door, the door that neither of them had heard open in the intensity of their conversation. "Where are your manners, Simon?"

Simon's mouth slowly opened as he stared up at Henry, standing a few feet away with his eyes locked on Artie and an article in his hand. It was, she realized, a printout of the paper she'd sent Simon.

"Professor Artemis Louise Marshall," the rumble continued, "Pembroke College, Oxford, top first in Biochemistry; PhD in Microbiology awarded from Harvard University, under the mentorship of Jasper Richards; dissertation title, *Evolution of murine leukemia virus variants under unique conditions of spread*, during which she published five first-author papers, two of them in *Nature*..."

Both Artie and Simon remained paralyzed as Henry Manfield recited the rest of her career highlights from memory. Artie, who seldom blushed, was blushing for the second time in five minutes, so hard that even the roots of her hair felt molten. Simon, meanwhile, was staring at Henry with a combination of consternation, bewilderment and panic, reduced from confident, angry adult to chastised child in less than a moment. Somewhere underneath her own confusion, she felt pity for his weakness and his situation, pity and an unavoidable corollary of scorn. How could anyone let himself be subjugated so severely?

When Henry stopped speaking, he looked at Simon expectantly.

"Professor Marshall," the younger man finally said, rising to his feet with a tremor in his voice, and only thinly disguised rage. "Allow me to present Professor Manfield."

"We've already met," Henry said shortly. He was playing with Simon, she realized with horror. "Come round tomorrow night at eleven, child, and we can discuss your proposal."

With that magisterial proclamation, he went back into his room and shut the door behind him.

The stillness in the room expanded thunderously until Artie wanted to scream just to make it stop. Simon just stood there, rubbing the stubble on his face. Eventually, without looking at her, he said, "And when you two met before... did he actually speak?"

She nodded, but then realized he couldn't see that, so cleared her throat and said yes.

"Straightaway?"

"Well, no. But I was... pretty persistent."

"I bet you were." His voice was cold.

"I didn't know he was ill then, Simon! I didn't know I wasn't supposed to come in—I'm new here. But I had to set the alarm, and the door was unlocked..." She described what had happened. "Where were you, anyway?"

"On the roof," he said.

"On the *roof*?"

"Do you realize," he said, "that this is the first time that he's talked to a single person besides me? Not counting the time he shouted incoherently at Ben and practically tried to kill him?"

Artie opened her mouth, shocked, and then just shook her head.

"And were you ever going to tell me about it?" he said. "It's important to keep track of his behavioral symptoms. It might bear on his medication."

She found herself twisting her hands painfully. "I would have. I just... it was so weird. I felt like I'd broken a rule."

"I see. Even when you're being straight, you really aren't, are you?" His eyes glittered at her, icy lakes. "This whole thing, wanting to talk to me, has been about infiltrating Henry, hasn't it?"

"No..." She stumbled, confused. "Well, yes, in that I wanted to talk to both of you. You're a team, aren't you? I was just trying to get in however I could."

"Well, you're obviously in now," he said. "If you hadn't deceived me, I might have learned to trust you, been happy to work with you. But you did, so I want it to be clear that I'll only be doing it because Henry will force me to."

"Don't be like that, please." She ran a shaking hand down her face. "And why do you let him treat you like that, anyway?"

"It's not something I care to discuss with you."

As Artie sat in the back of the cab, the sodium streetlights blurring by, she didn't feel any of the emotions she might have expected after scoring a collaboration with Renquist and Manfield. She just felt a sense of foreboding. The peripheral anxieties that were never far from the center of her resting mind seemed to flutter against the window glass, demanding entrance. She turned away from them and focused hard on the driver's head, dark and anonymous and reassuringly real.

CHAPTER 3
Divisions, Those Apparent Only On Closer Contact

THE NEXT MORNING ARTIE'S EQUILIBRIUM was fully restored. As soon as she opened her eyes, happiness moved in to replace the previous night's disquiet. Those feelings, she decided, must have been the result of simple tiredness and the after-effects of almost tripping the Heatherfields alarm system. The air coming through her open bedroom window was cool and sweet; breathing deeply, she parted the curtains and filled her nose with the dewy mown-grass essence of mid-June. She could hear bees buzzing in the flowering jasmine climbing up brickwork below the window, the practical cheeriness of an electric mower from a neighbor's yard. The sky was a cloudless blue, smudged lavender on the horizon: another perfect day.

My project is going to take off, she told herself. My theory is going to conquer the world.

She wrapped the worn black belt around her white *gi* and tied its ritual knot. Padding into the lounge, she performed her daily series of *kata*. The calming effects of the movements, their familiarity, the murmuring of Japanese numbers, *ichi, ni, san,* the sensation of hard wood against the bare soles of her feet and thrill of the power of her own body—all of these things reinforced her good mood. Artie Marshall would never let another human being oppress her, no matter how intelligent. Artie Marshall could not be defeated.

She took a shower, rinsing the curves that so beguiled or infuriated the world, depending on the eye of the beholder. Standing in front of the open wardrobe in her underwear, she chose a light cotton dress and sandals, even though it would accentuate her femininity. For some reason, she didn't care today. A slow breakfast over the newspaper, and freshly ground coffee instead of instant; something about the summer morning made her dawdle, even though she normally rushed through the episodes of her life when she had to be alone. Today, solitude was acceptable—even pleasurable.

The result of all this was that she was a full two hours late to work. When she stepped into the office, Mark looked up from the scientific journal he was reading.

"I want to say *what kind of time do you call this*," he said, "but I'd sound ridiculous."

"Even more than usual." Artie gave him a smile, her fondness for the world expanding to encompass him as well.

"I was worried about you," he admitted. "I thought you'd had another encounter last night, and that it hadn't gone as well."

She took off her cardigan and saw Mark noticing her dress. She wouldn't normally, and wondered what was infecting her this morning. Hormones, undoubtedly.

"I did, actually," she said.

Mark raised an eyebrow. "So where did you dump his body?"

"I was in a merciful mood," she said. "I agreed to a collaboration instead."

His eyes widened. "You're joking, Art. No wonder you're dripping with smugness."

She gave him a brief sketch of the encounter with Simon. After a moment of hesitation, she confessed about Henry speaking to her, after first cautioning Mark not to mention it to anyone else in the institute. For some reason, she didn't think it was right to reveal that it had not been their first verbal exchange. Something about that dreamlike chat in B302 and the rotating pastel lily on his screen seemed to demand secrecy.

"The first person in twenty-five years," he said, shaking his head in awe. "You're not so much a scientist as a force of nature. So when do we have our first meeting?"

"Actually..."

"I'm not invited, am I?' He looked away.

"Listen, Mark." She perched on the edge of his desk. "Henry's illness... it's not as if we can just traipse into B302 and have a normal group meeting. Simon's skittish about the whole thing as it is. I need to go slowly with them."

"Soften them up, you mean," he said. "Is that why you're wearing that little number?"

She met his eye defiantly, lips pressed together, then retreated to her own desk and turned her back on him. Underneath her irritation, however, she realized that the last thing she should have worn was something so revealing, given Simon's barbaric attitude. And then she thought that bringing Mark along would probably be the best thing she could do to make him take her seriously. But this idea nettled her even more. Besides, she instinctively knew that Henry wouldn't speak if Mark were around, and that anyone knowing about him speaking to *her* would somehow be betraying Simon's trust. She had made that mistake once, and was desperate to win him over, no matter how long it took.

"Artemis," Mark said. She looked over, and was relieved to see his contrition. "I was well out of line. Forgive me?"

"As long as you forgive me for excluding you at this stage. I'll try to bring you on board as soon as I can."

"I appreciate it," he said. "I'm dying of curiosity. And... you're convinced it's safe?"

She made reassuring noises, but when she thought about it afterwards, she wasn't entirely sure that it was.

❧

ARTIE'S DAY PASSED IN THE same relaxed mood. She spent the rest of the morning in the basement's small conference room with Fiona and Mark, discussing recent research results. Unlike many male scientists Artie knew, Mark did not talk for the sake of hearing his own voice. Back when he'd first arrived, aside from a few requests for clarification he'd remained largely quiet at these weekly meetings. Not, she had sensed at the time, because he was naturally reticent or detached. In fact, his easygoing outlook on life and quick-thinking banter had already gained him numerous lunch and pub invitations from the other post-docs. Instead, she got the feeling he was just keeping his ears open as he scribbled on his notepad, intent on absorbing all the new details.

Sure enough, he'd gradually gained his footing, becoming more like an equal in helping to shape the team's direction. This was done so tactfully that Artie never felt a threat to her overall authority. In parallel, she was growing to understand the way he thought, to catch on more quickly to his intuitive leaps. Scientific chatter was like a game with its own rules: the interplay of ideas, the mad speculation tempered with cool rationality, the moment an idea crystallized or a conceptual log-jam broke down—or a perfect theory shattered into a million pieces under close scrutiny. Members of one of the Theoretical Epidemiology labs, whose weekly meeting was booked directly afterwards, were always having to pound on the conference room door to extract them at the appointed time. Often, they were still in heated discussion as they filed out, and the conversation carried on into the office.

For lunch, Ben invited her team to dine with his group at a nearby terrace restaurant, and they lingered far longer than they ought to have, drinking iced tea, looking out over the green valley below and exchanging Heatherfields gossip. As always, the most popular topic was the perennial speculation about who the Inner Sanctum actually were.

"My mate up in Population Genetics reckons that Salverson is actually deep in the whole thing," Mark said, "and that his Institute directorship is just a clever blind."

"Ludicrous," Ben said. "On what grounds?"

"An overheard telephone conversation," Mark said, "But from his description, I don't think the evidence is all that conclusive."

"Besides," Raisa said, "Salverson's too sensible to be in a secret society. They probably have all sorts of handshakes and have to wear scarlet robes or something—I can't see him going for all that shit."

As the others nodded, one of the newer students leaned forward. "Does anyone understand why Heatherfields is run like this, anyway? You'd think in this day and age they'd be forced to be transparent."

"Forced by whom?" Artie said. "It's a private foundation. They don't need to kiss anyone's arse, if the endowment is anywhere near as bottomless as rumor has it."

"Just think how much trouble they'd be in for the sexist recruitment policy," Raisa mused, "if they had to answer to anyone."

"Not sure it would make much difference," Ben said, with an apologetic look at Artie. "Plenty of conventional research institutes get away with pretty much the same thing. Just a lot less overt about it."

And on the chatter spun. Artie enjoyed the feeling of sun on her skin, the radiant glow she could feel developing on her face, bare arms and legs; she enjoyed watching Mark flirt outrageously with Raisa and Ben's other female post-doc. Once when he caught her watching, he winked, and she gave him a covert thumbs up.

For the rest of the day, she and Mark were happily involved with a departmental meeting on the fourth floor, listening to a series of post-doctoral research talks from their colleagues in Molecular Virology. As much as Artie admired the weird and tangential projects in the basement, it was a relief to immerse herself in her true passion.

Mark had given the final presentation and, though she knew she was biased, his seemed by far the best talk in weeks, and she brimmed with secret pride throughout.

Artie had always been voluble and irrepressible at meetings like this, keen to ask questions and to offer advice. The first time she'd attended, the others had obviously been startled by her performance. But as the weeks had gone by, they'd become accustomed to her enthusiasm. A few of the female PhD students, clearly not receiving much attention from their own supervisors, had started making regular pilgrimages to the basement to speak with her personally. Unlike Tavistock's activities in the women's networking group, Artie took this form of role-model mentoring very seriously because it was positive and practical, and she herself had enjoyed similar support at the start of her career. But it wasn't just the younger women—nearly all of the post-docs, male and female, had solicited her opinion on some scientific issue by now.

The only blight on the meeting had been the exchange that occurred afterwards with Peter Hastings, the department Chair.

"Very impressive, Reynolds," he said to Mark as people were bustling out of the conference room around them. His hard eyes flicked in Artie's direction before refocusing on him. "You know, if you'd like, we could arrange some extra bench space for you up here so you wouldn't have to keep coming up and down the stairs. I know how *limited* Artemis' facilities are."

"It's kind of you to offer," Mark said, "but I can assure you it's entirely unnecessary."

"If I didn't know better," Artie said, as she and Mark were trooping down the stairs, "I'd say Hastings was trying to poach you."

"Oh, he is," Mark said.

Artie stopped flat, hand gripping the worn brass rail, and turned to face him.

"What do you mean?"

"He's already asked me privately if I'd care to transfer my fellowship to his lab."

"The slime! What did you say?"

"I said no, of course."

Artie took a few more steps, then came to a stop again, her heart beating a bit faster.

"Not that I blame him," she said, before forcing the next bit out. "If you'd rather move, I'd entirely understand. I know how difficult it is to negotiate the experiments with the current set-up."

"Forget it, Art," he said. Then he looked at her more carefully. "You're not trying to get rid of me, are you?"

"Of course not! I'm just thinking of your best interests."

He looked her over a moment, so long that Artie became aware of the dust particles floating past his face, caught by the light from a series of copper-colored glass windows in the stairwell.

"It's in my best interests," he said, "to work for someone who's about ten times more intelligent, and about a hundred times more original, than a worm like Hastings."

"I bet you say that to all the girls." Despite her laugh, she felt almost weak with relief.

"Besides," he said. "It's grim up there. No music, no good conversation. Like pipetting in a crypt. And their attitude is more Visigoth than Victorian—they're giving Fi a hard time."

"Are they now?" Artie felt herself tense up: maybe she'd have to have more than a few words with Hastings, some day soon.

"I'd watch him if I were you," he said. "He's worse than your standard issue chauvinist—he loathes women. And I sort of get the impression that he considers you a threat."

But when Artie pressed Mark for more details, he told her it was only a feeling and started back down the stairs.

Artie, though, wondered what else Mark might have picked up from conversation with other men when she wasn't around.

THE REST OF THE BASEMENT was deserted when her eleven o'clock appointment with Henry Manfield finally arrived. Artie was relieved to feel no fear, only an almost unquenchable anticipation. She grabbed her notebook and strolled over to B302, where the lights were on, and knocked briskly.

After a few moments, she knocked again, louder and longer, but still nobody appeared. She didn't want to startle Henry. Trying the handle, she found the door unlocked, but she allowed it to close again, thinking quickly. It was just like the first night; an unlocked door and no Simon. But this time, she wasn't going to go behind his back.

I was on the roof, he'd told her.

Artie had no idea how to get to the roof of Heatherfields, or what amenities it might offer to someone like Simon, but she was the last person to be put off by the unknown. The main building didn't arm its independent alarm system until the porter went off duty at 1:00, so she'd be okay. She took the lift up to the eighth floor, which was as far as it went, and entered the main stairwell, but this route didn't go up any further either. Then she wandered around the dark corridors until she finally located an auxiliary stairwell in one corner of the building.

There was a book propping the heavy metal door open, and a flow of cool air sinking from it. Leaning down, she saw that it was a paperback copy of Kaplan and Sadock's *Pocket Handbook of Clinical Psychiatry.* It was, in fact, an older edition of the same book that never left her bedside table, and this gave her a twinge of unease. She slipped through the door, careful not to dislodge the book, and went up the dozen or so stairs until she'd reached the second door, also kept ajar. It was harder to make out the title in the dark, but she managed it eventually: *One Hundred Years of Solitude.*

She shivered, standing there in the shadows. The open door served up a slice of sky, dotted with pale stars, and the flat concrete expanse of the roof, interrupted by ventilation shafts and antennae, glowed a faint grey. She pushed the door wider and stepped outside.

Simon was there, to her right near the railings, on his knees and busy with something she couldn't see. She took a few steps to one side: a thick, black tube on a metal tripod. A telescope.

She didn't think he was aware of her, and stood there, wondering how to alert him without causing alarm. But then he spoke first, without turning around.

"I'm glad you worked it out, Dr. Marshall."

"Can you please stop calling me that?" She hugged her notebook to her chest as the summer night's coolness pressed into her sunburnt skin.

"What should I call you? *Professor*?" His voice was mocking.

"Artemis," she said, unable to imagine a breezy nickname ever emerging from his lips.

"Artemis, then... when Henry's not around. As you may have noticed, he has a thing about titles."

She went closer and sat down on a protruding rectangle of concrete, watching him fiddle with the instrument's angle. "Was this some sort of test, to figure out where you'd gone? Did I pass?"

"You passed." He put his eye to the ocular, made another adjustment.

"Will he be angry that we're late?"

For the first time, Simon looked over at her, eyes cool and impatient. "He doesn't have any concept of time. We could waltz in three hours from now and he'd never dream I'd disobeyed. Sometimes I do things like that deliberately, just to give myself some semblance of..."

He clamped off the sentence before it could betray him, returning to the ocular. To Artie, the man before her consisted of two clear layers: a childlike maelstrom of anger and despair and god knows what other human emotions, and a hard outer shell that was cracking against the strain of containing it. As she watched his long fingers move on the apparatus, she recognized that the ritual was calming him down. Willing herself to be patient, she studied his profile. The starlight suited his pallor much better than the harsh fluorescence of the basement, or sunlight. He, more than anyone else in the basement, seemed evolved for underground existence.

"So that's why I'm here?" she finally asked. "So we can be late?"

"No," he said. "After what you said last night about letting Henry walk all over me, I wanted to see if I could exert control other another living creature. And here you are: I *made* you come. So maybe I'm not entirely ineffectual."

"You didn't have to do this to know you've got power over me. You've already made me act like an idiot to get closer to what you know."

"But it's not *me*, is it? It's *him*."

He hates Henry, she realized. Almost as much as he loves him.

"I've already explained," she said. "Someone on the outside can't see the distinction. But I refuse to believe you're not heavily complicit, after so many years."

"Why do you want our help?" he asked bitterly. "Prestige? Fame? A vaccine for AIDS? Even more notoriety than you already have, with your full professorship and your *Nature* papers?"

"No," she said. "I just want to know. I want to understand what's *happening*. I want to know how it *works*."

She expected him to sneer at this, but instead he just nodded. "And your idea, your theory; I assume it was just one of Philip Cox's cast-offs?"

She smothered the surge of irritation, all the more difficult because he wasn't the first man to imply as much. "Phil spent most of his time on the links at St. Andrews, perfecting his putt and dreaming about virus receptors—he wasn't terribly interested in mutation. I came up with the idea from some stuff I was doing in Boston, wrote it up for the fellowship. Phil didn't even want to read it over before I submitted it."

"And your dissertation work?"

"Well, Jasper got me going, but I swerved away pretty quickly. I was into different things." She wondered where all this was leading.

"And how does it feel, to have an independent idea, to realize it? To have everyone know that no one else but you was responsible?" He had stopped fiddling, hands on his threadbare knees, and was watching her again. She noticed then that the look on his face had morphed from contempt to curiosity, as if his hard shell had dissolved without his even noticing.

"It feels wonderful," she said slowly. "It's what I live for."

He nodded, unsurprised. "And how do you rationalize those feelings? Doesn't appreciating, even needing the recognition negate the moral high ground of just wanting to *know how it works*?"

"No," she said immediately. "I'm keen to know the answers, and I'm keen to be the acknowledged author of the ideas. I can't see how one negates the other."

He nodded once more, and she understood that she'd somehow passed again.

"We're up here for five reasons," he said. "We've covered two of them already. Do you have time for the next three, before we go downstairs? I realize that other people actually have lives, schedules."

"I've got all the time you need," she said. "But before you continue, can I ask a question of my own?"

He thought about it. "If you must."

"I've heard you went down for assault," she said, all in a rush. "Is it true? Is it safe to be alone with you without bringing my post-doc along as a bodyguard?"

One of the first rules of self-defense was to keep the element of surprise for as long as possible, and she was happy to play the weak female as part of a larger plan of ultimate domination.

He absorbed her words, perfectly unruffled. "The short answer is, I was falsely accused of GBH, and the charges were eventually dropped. It's a matter of public record, if you'd care to check."

"No, that's okay, I'm satisfied." And oddly enough, she was. "Your turn."

He rearranged himself so that he was sitting back against the railing, not exactly facing her, but not exactly not.

"After yesterday, I wanted to hate you," he said. She could hear the evidence underneath his even voice. "With your independence, your autonomy, your whole career ahead of you. The fact that people actually *like* you, are happy to do things for you. Do you know how much it cost Ben to contact me?"

She swallowed, shook her head.

"I suppose you'd have no way of knowing," he said. "I wanted to hate you because you automatically fit in. Because you're already a full professor, and I'll never be.

Because you thought you could just snap your fingers and I'd tumble over myself to make your perfect life even better."

She really ought to protest, but in a way, he was absolutely right. And anyway, he spoke like someone who was accustomed to working things out in his mind, someone who seldom had to deal with the inconvenience of a response. His blocks of words, carefully organized into discrete sections and produced without much of a pause between, didn't invite them.

"And Henry speaking to you," he said. "In a way that was the worst. That hurt the most."

"I understand," she said. "And I'm really sorry."

"But that's just it," he said. "None of it is your fault—which made me want to hate you even more."

He reached up absently and gripped the iron railings, arms outstretched: a scarecrow, all bluster and no resolve.

"I've been up here for a few hours," he said, a bit quieter now. "When Henry zones out, he's gone for a while, and I can escape. I come to the roof when I'm so angry I... can't bear it any more." There was no doubt about it: the structure of his sentences was breaking down now: he was in unrehearsed territory. "When, if I stayed, I probably *would* get violent, for a particularly cruel remark or vicious slight. None of which are his fault either, you see—it's the illness, right?"

She wanted to yell at him, to shake his scrawny shoulders, to rattle his lethargic brains against the side of his skull. Why did he take it? Why hadn't he walked away, five, ten, fifteen years ago? Get the hell out, get another position somewhere else? Instead, knowing she wouldn't be able to hide the contempt underlying her honest sympathy, she said nothing.

His thumbs on the railings tested the metal, up and down. "Seeing the stars puts it all into perspective. I may think I've got a wretched life, that I'm insignificant, but then compared to the vastness of the universe, we're all insignificant. Even *you*." He eyed her a moment, as if expecting her to protest. "It's the one way I can truly belong to the human race—my utter inconsequentiality in the grand scheme of things."

He looked at the sky for a moment, and Artie considered those pale points of lights, knowing how uncomfortable their uncompromising scrutiny would feel if Simon weren't with her. The poor man.

Simon bowed his head. "So I was sitting up here, dreading eleven o'clock, and that's when it suddenly occurred to me: how would it be to have someone to talk to? About the work, even about Henry? To have an ally of sorts—even if it *was* a woman?"

Barbaric fuckwit, she thought, keeping her face neutral.

"I've got over forty collaborations," he continued, "but it's entirely virtual. And Henry doesn't discuss—he just mandates. I don't think science is supposed to be like that."

"Definitely not." She forced her voice to be kind, encouraging.

"So I decided..." He looked up at her. "It's too soon to know yet whether I even like you, or ever will. But I'm not going to hate you. If we're going to work together, we'll need some sort of truce in place."

"That's what I want too," she said. "I want to regain your trust—I've bungled the whole thing completely."

He sniffed, as close to humor as she'd yet seen from him. "If you'd done it any other way, nothing would have happened. And as much as you've irritated me this past week, I have to admit that it's more excitement than I've had in years."

She felt a weight lift off her and slip up into the stars: it was in the bag, and the rest was mere formality. "I think we're on point four, if I'm not mistaken?"

He nodded. "About Henry—there are a few guidelines. You ought to have been told this when you arrived. Do you have any experience being around mentally ill people?"

She hesitated. "Yes, I do. Quite a bit."

He gave her a peculiar look, but didn't enquire further. "Henry's not textbook Asperger's; he's considered to be a very unusual case. He has lucid phases and cata-tonic phases: on or off, nothing in between. It's best to let him make the first move in communication. Avoid eye contact, even if he initiates it—don't worry, he won't think it's rude."

"I think I've broken that rule already," she said.

"How did he react?"

"He didn't, I don't think."

Simon shrugged. "Okay. And this is really important: *never* touch him—and keep in mind that his radius of personal space is much wider than average. Don't contra-dict him more than once on any point, no matter how trivially."

"I see what you mean about having unsatisfactory scientific conversations," she said, rather shocked. "How can you talk science without dissent?"

"Those are the major things. On everything else, you will follow my lead and defer to me. Is that clear?"

"Perfectly."

"And, Artemis..." He spoke her name like someone not used to being on a first name basis with anyone. "From what little I've seen of your personality, you seem to be fairly... excitable."

"Hmm."

"I think it's best to stay as sedate as possible when you're around him."

"I'll do my best."

Simon dropped his hands from the railing, reached over to caress the telescope as if it were the head of a beloved son.

"Number five, I presume?" she said.

"An unusual planetary conjunction," he said. "Mars, Jupiter, and Saturn. Not ideal viewing conditions in London, of course, even this far north, but being next to the golf course keeps the light pollution down, and the moon has set. Some of the larger satellites are visible. Would you like to see?"

Artie was burning with impatience at the thought of Henry, spinning his colorful computer lines in the dark, but all she said was, "I'd love to."

∾

WHEN SIMON LED HER INTO the inner chamber of B302 at last, Henry was hulking over his terminal, busy with a spreadsheet. He did not acknowledge their entrance.

Artie was terrifically disappointed. Had she passed every last one of the disciple's tests, only to fail with the master? Simon, catching her eye, seemed to sense her anxiety and transmitted a look: *Be patient, Dr. Marshall.*

"Have a seat," he said in a normal voice, taking a chair at the central table and indicating another chair opposite. He opened up a notebook lying there, and Artie did likewise with her own, hyperaware of the looming, oblivious presence of Henry Manfield a few meters away.

"Your paper was quite abstract," he said, uncapping his pen. "I'd like to hear more concrete details about the virus and your current research."

She opened up her mouth, then paused, flicking a quick glance at Henry's back, but Simon nodded his head. His right hand, resting on the blank page of his notebook, wriggled *go ahead* fingers at her.

"Well," she said, her voice sounding artificial to her own ears. "Feline leukemia virus—FeLV—is related to HIV, but it doesn't exist in epidemic form. It's an ancient disease, so it's already everywhere at a constant, low level."

"What's the prevalence?"

"It depends on what you're counting—pet cats, stray cats, cats that live in multi-cat households. Indoor versus outdoor cats. But generally, it's as low as one to three per cent of healthy cats, and much higher if you're testing sick ones."

"Tell me a bit about the viral replication strategy," Simon said. "This will strongly influence the choice of mathematical model."

"As viruses go, it's almost ridiculously simple," she said, making a quick sketch in her notebook.

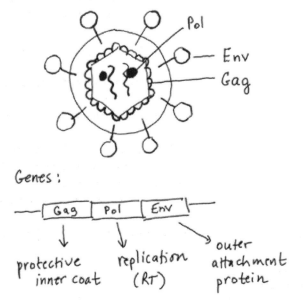

"FeLV has just three genes," she said, pointing to each in turn. "First is Gag, which makes the protein shell that protects the genetic material. Gag is also what standard FeLV veterinary tests pick up."

Simon jotted something down on his pad and gestured at her to continue.

"Pol, short for polymerase, makes a couple of proteins involved in replication," she said, "including reverse transcriptase or RT, the enzyme that copies the genome—which it does rather messily, with lots of mistakes. Is that an issue?"

"We have mathematical ways of dealing with error-prone replication," Simon said.

"Good. And last we have Env, the envelope protein covering the outside of the virus particle. This allows it to dock onto the host cell it's attacking."

"OK. So after the virus enters the cell, how does replication occur?"

Artie explained how the RT enzyme ran off many genome copies, and how another virus protein inserted them randomly into the cat genome. "Once the so-called 'provirus' is inserted, it essentially becomes a permanent part of the cat's genetic makeup. It can fool the cell into making everything needed to assemble thousands of new virus particles. These particles then bud off the cell and initiate more rounds of infection."

She described how, due to the frequent mutations, the virus existed not so much as a single strain but as a swarm of slightly differing individuals, altering and evolving as they passed like a microscopic storm from animal to animal. Artie's theory supposed that certain combinations of variants spread over the top of the underlying infection in a manner more reminiscent of an epidemic.

"I'm interested in the error-prone nature of virus replication," Simon said. "Are these mutants just dead-ends? It seems like a very wasteful strategy."

"That's the fun bit," Artie said. "The mutants, no matter how defective—even if they're so defective that they can't replicate themselves, or make all the proteins—can survive just fine by hitching a ride with all the normal viruses around them. When the particles are being assembled, the dud ones can get packaged up along with the normal, replication-competent viruses that came in during the same swarm."

"Well, that will clearly affect the mathematics. Another issue that could muddy the waters is vaccination—is there any?"

"Yes, but it's not one hundred per cent effective, and many cats don't get vaccinated. Feline leukemia is still nearly the top cause of feline deaths."

"So do you obtain the DNA sequences of the full-length virus genomes from each of your samples?" he asked.

"Recently, yes. But at the beginning I didn't have the resources. We were using a quick and cheap shortcut, inspecting something called the SNP signature... 'Snips' for short. It's a sort of crude fingerprint of virus mutations that we can work up by chopping up the DNA and analyzing the patterns. Different mutations give you different Snip signatures."

"Did you bank the original samples so you could go back and get the full sequences retrospectively?"

"Yes," Artie said. "In fact, Fiona has started on this as a side project already, although we'd need to prioritize it now."

"I'm sure you've already realized this," he said, "but you're going to need a lot of virus signatures to make any sort of meaningful statistical analysis. And you haven't been here very long."

"Actually, I've been gathering data for years from the same geographic since the 2010, ever since I started in Phil's lab. Of course I've sped up quite a bit since setting up here, with the extra help, but there's still a lot of older material we can use."

"Where do you get your data?"

"We've got a cohort of cats in Kent, pet cats seen in a particular surgery," she said. "And access to about thirty other vet practices. The prevalence may be low, but we don't have a problem finding them."

"Wouldn't feral cats be more appropriate?"

"Maybe, maybe not," she said. "They're two entirely different populations—and they intermingle in neighborhoods. I'm interested in both, but it's difficult to sample strays, to follow them up."

"Still, your phenomenon will be more artificial with pets, won't it?"

His eyes on her were keen, incisive. Artie wondered whether he was deriving an illicit thrill from contradicting her more than once on a particular point within earshot of Henry.

"It all depends on what you want to know," she said. "You could argue that domestic cats are a better model for human disease—not that I'm particularly interested in all that. Anyway, it would be very misleading to assume that feral cats in populated areas of Great Britain are truly natural."

He conceded the point in the end, and they carried on. Soon Artie had relaxed into the enjoyment she always took from scientific discourse, and found herself able to forget about Henry altogether. Simon's attitude now was almost unrecognizable; it was as if he'd unloaded all his anger against her on the roof, and underneath that was his normal self: courteous in a strangely formal way, measured and respectful. Himself, perhaps, before the past twenty-odd years had warped him beyond recognition. Or maybe this was his scientific persona, an artificial construct kept carefully partitioned from the angry mess that was the rest of his life.

Either way, he was a careful listener—probably not too surprising, Artie thought, given his usual submissive role. But he wasn't passive with her at all. The more details she revealed, the more he challenged her. She tried not to be distracted by what he was scribbling on his pad—not a transcription of her details in words, but unintelligible things: formulas, mathematics, even a rough line graph or two. His hand moved quickly in that weird, tilted gait that left-handed people employ, and as the page filled up with markings, as he turned one and started on the next, she received the impression that he had fallen into a peculiar mental state, where absorbing her words and analyzing them were as natural as breathing. A world where concepts became numbers, and numbers became concepts.

Finally she fell silent, and he made a few more notes, stared into space, then said, "La Fontayne. I think we ought to try the La Fontayne algorithm as a starting point. It all fits."

He looked at her, eyes refocused.

"Okay," Artie said. "Can you explain it? I'm no mathematician, but I want to understand, at least the basics."

"I can give it to you in simple terms." Simon leaned forward, pushing his pad towards her across the table and picking up his pen with obvious enthusiasm.

"The La Fontayne is out of the question."

Both Simon and Artie started in their seats at Henry's rumble.

"It's all wrong," the older man said, rotating his chair to face them. "Doesn't fit the dynamics properly. We'll go with Meyerhof-Hernsley model instead."

Artie saw Simon's entire frame tense up, then the deliberate letting go of the muscles. "Actually, Professor, with the mutation rate she's described, and the infectivity index... to say nothing about the prevalence of vaccination... surely Meyerhof-Hernsley would grossly underestimate the rate of spread."

"Nonsense, lad." This was delivered in a father-knows-best sort of tone that made Artie clench her teeth. Still, she was eager to witness Henry defending his difference in opinion. After soaking up all those elegant words he'd deposited in the pages of the most prestigious journals, she was finally going to experience his genius in its full glory.

But there was only silence. Henry, she realized with confusion, was not going to elaborate further.

She waited for Simon to stand up for his own viewpoint, but he only tossed his pen onto the table and lifted one shoulder in eloquent surrender. Then she remembered the rule: he'd already used up his sole contradiction allowance. Meanwhile, his low-level anger was back. It must be there all the time, she thought. *Endemic.*

But Artie hadn't used up *her* allowance. What were the rules when there was one point, but two people? The rules hadn't been invented—Henry had never dealt with multiple contenders.

"With all due respect, Professor," she said. Simon's eyes widened and he made an almost imperceptible shake of his head, but she couldn't seem to stop. "Maybe it would be best to run both models in parallel? Of course using the Meyerhof-Hernsley is a brilliant idea, and obviously preferable..." She had no idea what she was talking about, but Henry was a man after all, and Artie knew about men rather well. "Nevertheless, perhaps it would be informative to compare the two methods."

When nobody said anything, she paused, coloring her earlier silky tone with a bit of boredom. "You could consider the La Fontayne as a sort of negative control."

She smiled, not looking directly into Henry's eyes but at someplace vague beyond, and for an indeterminate period there was only the hum of the computers, ventilating the heat of a dozen ongoing simulations. With her peripheral senses, Artie could feel Simon's tension on one side, and somewhere above her gaze, she received the impression that possibly, just possibly, the esteemed professor's eyes were inspecting the curve of her bare legs crossed one over the other. She became aware of her own body, then, the heaviness of her breasts, the crescent of sweat on one thigh where skin touched skin, the sluggish pump of blood making her hanging foot twitch almost imperceptibly.

"An excellent suggestion, Professor Marshall," Henry finally intoned. "We shall run the two models in parallel. Simon will see to it."

And with that, he turned to face his screen once more, as absent as if he'd been swallowed up by the floor.

Artie stared at Simon across the table, watched as he struggled to suppress his emotions. He stood up, motioned her to follow him out of the room and into the blind office. She cast one last look at Henry, at the fierce angles of his profile as he dreamed into his monitor, and then forward at the swift, curt movements of the younger man's arms and back as he crossed the room, opened the door to the corridor.

It's finished, Artie thought with a growing weight of despair. He was going to terminate the collaboration and chuck her unceremoniously out of B302, never to return. Artie had promised to follow his lead, but when he threw down his pen, she'd ignored his signal and pressed on. Henry hadn't seemed affronted, but what did she know about his moods, his behavioral patterns? In a rush, she recalled what Simon had said before, about Henry attacking Ben. Why hadn't that properly registered at the time?

Simon stepped into the corridor and kept walking. He was heading for her office, she realized. Artie followed him as he opened the door and held it open to allow her inside. As she brushed past, she could sense him flinch away to prevent physical contact.

But when Artie turned to face his wrath, he was leaning against the closed door, staring at her not in anger, but in awe.

"How did you do that?" he demanded.

"It's called charm." She sat down at her desk, suddenly weary. "One of those feminine, manipulative qualities that you aren't too keen on, remember?"

"I take it all back, Artemis." His mouth twisted through a series of shapes—bewilderment, disbelief and finally a sort of morose glee, transforming him into someone almost, but not quite normal. She didn't think he could ever look normal. "And you really trusted my opinion enough to risk his displeasure, enough to split my energies into two separate analyses?"

"I didn't even think of that," she said, dismayed. "You're clearly overstretched... can you..."

"Spare a bit of time for something I honestly want to do, as opposed to something I've been told *to* do?" His smile took another bitter turn. "What do you think?"

"Do you two differ very often?"

Simon sat down too, rubbed his shaggy dark hair. He looked as if he hadn't slept or eaten properly in the past decade. "We never used to—there was always this amazing synergy. What you said before about science without dissent—well, we never seemed to need it. It was almost like we were parts of the same brain."

For no good reason, Artie felt a chill ripple the hairs on her bare arms.

"What's changed? And when?"

"I guess it's been fairly gradual." He looked surprised, as if it was something he'd never thought to ask himself. "But we had our first major disagreement last year over a simulation we did for the Ministry of Defence about smallpox terrorism."

"Who won?"

"Who do you think?" His restless fingers worried at the broken seam of his shirt cuff, bits of threads coming unraveled. "And I hope an attack like that never really happens, because I still think he got it wrong."

Her stomach drifted uneasily inside her. "The MoD *acted* on his advice?" What she really meant was, *theoretical epidemiology isn't just an intellectual game?*

"Of course." His shrug was bony, casual. "We're one of the Government's consultants. Business has picked up over the past few years."

Another shiver, and Artie took her cardigan off the back of her chair and slipped it on.

"What's wrong?" he asked.

"I'm just thinking about how insignificant feline leukemia is in the bigger picture—and how you've obviously got more important things to do."

"Nonsense." His tone was sharp. "Theory is useless without a constant influx of new facts. I already told you how I thought your model might be applicable to more general scenarios. The exercise will be valuable for us—Henry would never have been interested otherwise, charm or no charm."

"Okay." She remembered the original point. "But why do you think you're no longer agreeing?"

"I haven't the slightest idea."

"Maybe you're developing your own style? Rebelling a bit?" *Growing up*, she didn't dare say.

He considered this, and Artie watched as the split in the cuff seam enlarged, revealing a tongue of pale skin underneath. "I don't feel I've changed. I think he has. He talked to you—a complete stranger! He's more impatient, lucid for shorter periods..."

"And he's showing poor judgement."

"Arguable, in a theoretical field with no correct answers." His entire posture had stiffened. Despite everything, he couldn't seem to help defending his mentor. How many times in the past had people accused Henry of being unreliable because of his Asperger's?

"Maybe he's... slipping a bit?"

"No." He glared at her. "No, there's nothing wrong with him. And you didn't really answer my question before. Why did you insist on La Fontayne when Henry wanted something else?"

"To be honest, I would have preferred going with your method alone. But that would've been pushing it too hard."

"How could you know? You were bluffing—you haven't a clue what either of those algorithms does."

How indeed? But all she could think of was how Simon had questioned Henry, and how Henry refused to discuss all the possibilities. He might be a genius, but she knew which was the better scientist.

"I don't really know, for sure," she said. "Feminine intuition?"

He looked appalled. "Why do I have the feeling I'm going to have to get used to those sorts of answers?"

"Think of me as an analog interface," she said. "I'd better introduce you to Mark. You'll appreciate his cold, rational masculinity."

"I'm not so sure..."

"For heaven's sake," Artie said. "Just pop by the office tomorrow when Henry's lapsed into screensaver mode and have a cup of tea. Or aren't you allowed out into the corridors until after dark?"

There was a flicker in his eyes—anger and wistfulness in equal measure.

"I could just stop by. Couldn't I?" He lifted his arm, extended it, spread his fingers wide towards her. "I feel..." His fingers vacillated in empty air.

"Liberated?"

"Yes, that too... but what I meant was, I feel like I've scored a point against Henry, for the first time ever. Even though you were the one who made it happen."

"It's teamwork, Simon," Artie said. "That's what science is all about."

SOON AFTERWARD, SIMON ESCORTED HENRY home, grateful that his mentor remained in an uncommunicative mode. How many times had the two men paced the short walk from Heatherfields to Henry's flat like speechless automata? Thousands? Tens of thousands? Although it was after midnight, the air was still hot, the breeze lifting lank strands of hair from his damp forehead, rustling the bushes in front of the terrace row on their right. The feel of the air evoked childhood memories: late nights in the old neighborhood, running wild with other children, hiding and scheming; the sensation of wet grass, of painful gravel, of smooth still-warm pavement on the toughened soles of bare feet.

Simon had not run wild since.

Bats swooped and dived over the golf course on the other side of the street. A close, sultry overcast had spread over the sky, but behind this, Simon knew that the planets still shone down like benevolent angels, hanging in a conspicuous cluster that almost no one in the city of nearly eight million knew about, or if they did, would care.

Had Artemis Marshall cared, as she peered obligingly into the ocular of his telescope? He didn't trust the woman, with her smiles, her bare limbs and the way she had managed to subvert Henry so quickly. Of course he was pleased that she'd changed Henry's mind about the La Fontayne, but that didn't mean he approved of her methods. After all, she would probably do the same with him one day, and he was not optimistic about his chances against someone so skilled in arts he had so little understanding of or experience with.

He'd known about her even before she first emailed him, of course. Artemis Marshall had been hard to avoid—first the flurry of her upcoming arrival, another professorship in a long line being awarded to someone besides him, and then the actual event in February. He'd heard her before he'd seen her, a boisterous laugh from the coffee room he made a point never to enter, and an answering chorus of appreciative, mostly male chuckles.

The previous Friday, when she'd lured him into his office, he'd been unsurprised to finally meet the person who belonged to the laugh. It all fit. She was beautiful and confident and about as unscientific as a person could look, with her gleaming hair and bottle-green eyes. In fact, he'd thought at the time that she rather resembled a sleek, smug version of the cats she studied, secure in the knowledge that there would be fresh cream awaiting her every morning of her life. She didn't belong in a lab; she should be pushing a trolley in an airplane or reading out the evening news—an opinion that had more to do with statistical probability than outright chauvinism. It was hardly Simon's fault that women who looked like Artemis tended, on average, to fill roles requiring such an appearance. The proof was in the numbers, and Simon, a keen statistician, was not afraid to make assumptions based on the bell curve. She had been the perfect case study, a set of facts fitting into the algorithm so precisely that the curves of the graph—simulated versus actual—had overlapped.

But actually getting to know her had confused his initial analysis. The intellectual content of her article shocked him, and if he'd suspected that Philip Cox was responsible for the words, talking with her about her work had killed that theory outright, making him regret that he'd been open about his own prejudices and made to look a fool. Not that she'd rubbed his face in it. In fact, in their subsequent conversations she hadn't seemed smug or shallow at all, just polite, even sympathetic. And this failure to conform to her appearance, to his initial expectations, was a distinct threat. As intriguing as it was to experience a change in his normal routine, a routine so steeped in the inflexible paralysis of Henry's illness that it fettered him like concrete, he couldn't help feeling that something dangerous had slipped into his stagnant little world.

When he led Henry to his door, he saw the glow of a cigarette and smelled the sweet flow of tobacco in the heavy air. Samantha, the night home help, sitting on the step and radiating impatience.

"You're late," she snapped, not even bothering to make eye contact.

"Sorry," he muttered, as Henry drifted past them and through the open door.

"Anything I should know about?" The bored, dutiful voice this time, and he felt a whisper of her ashes against one of his forearms, where he'd rolled up his sleeves against the heat.

"That woman he spoke to before..."

"Yeah?"

"He's done it again this evening. I don't think it's a fluke."

"Okay." She took one last drag on the cigarette before smashing it into the flagstones. "I'll speak to Dr. Caruthers."

They exchanged a few more words, Samantha's gaze never once intersecting his—had it ever? As he walked towards his own nearby flat, almost melting with the relief of being alone at last, he remembered that, as unpredictable and manipulative as she might be, Artemis Marshall had at least looked at him as if he existed.

ARTIE RETURNED HOME TO A red winking eye of disapproval: Calvin on the answering machine, probably because she'd ignored the two voicemails he'd left earlier that day on her mobile, as well as the accusatory email.

"Artie dearest, I hear you've missed another appointment with my solicitor. Why insist on handling it yourself and then not show up? Anyone would think you didn't want the bloody divorce. Please call me tomorrow—this is getting old."

Artie erased the message, but she couldn't erase his words from her head.

Discomfort encroached from the shadows around the entrance hall, so she flicked on the lights, went into the lounge and turned on the television, chatter and laugh track as a second line of defense. It was hot and airless, so she opened up the windows and got herself a glass of ice water. Wandering back into the lounge, where the night air hardly made a dent in the temperature, she sat back on the sofa and began to interrogate herself.

Why hadn't she gone to the solicitor's, exactly? She'd carefully arranged her schedule that afternoon to fit in the appointment, including an hour on either end for the Underground journey. After the terrace lunch, she'd done a bit of lab work, and when it was time, she'd gone to her desk, picked up her handbag, and—what? She just hadn't felt like it. She'd put her bag back down and retreated to the lab.

Her mind tried to slide away from the analysis, but she forced it back. She was sure she wanted the divorce; there was no question on this point. Calvin's abuse had gradually increased from casual ribbing to outright cruelty, all of it fueled by an obsession with alcohol that was only nominally under control. And she was under no delusion that he would ever change—he had been like that all along under his slick disguise. So what was the problem?

The answer was obvious, no matter how uncomfortable: as long as she was married, in theory, then she wasn't truly alone. She could use her status as a prop against the darkness, even if Calvin was no longer physically present in her life. But this was a madwoman's logic: not following through with the divorce was wholly irrational, and she was determined to ring Calvin in the morning.

CHAPTER 4
Outbreaks, Subtle Differences Between

DETERMINATION, THOUGH, IS A SHIFTY devil, even for someone as strong-willed as Artemis Marshall. As she stood in the entrance hall on her way out the next day, listening to the tinny ring of Calvin's mobile phone in her ear, her finger pressed the hang-up button before she'd consciously made a decision to do so. Furious with herself, she tried to work up the momentum to call him again. But before she could do so, the phone began to ring in her hand: Calvin, of course. She switched off the phone altogether and buried it in her handbag.

When she got to work and checked her email, there was a brief message from Simon. He wrote that he would be too busy after all to stop by and meet Mark, but that he would appreciate her coming round at nine the following evening to give him some preliminary data for the simulations.

Coward, she thought, zapping his words away with an irritated click of the mouse. Everything about the day so far was suboptimal.

Later that afternoon, an unexpected visit from Mary cheered her up.

"Your security is getting really lax," she said from the office doorway. "He didn't even look up from his tabloid when I signed in, let alone ask me who I was or what I wanted."

"I am *so* glad to see you," Artie said. "I've been trying to decide where to file this damned article for the past five minutes."

"What's it about?"

"Feline immunity."

"What are my choices?" Mary, well used to this line of enquiry, sat down and put the unusually large polystyrene box onto the floor with a sigh of relief.

"'T cells, helper subset' or 'MHC recognition, class II.'" Artie frowned. "Or possibly, at a stretch, 'Granzyme B, signals upstream of.'"

Mary rubbed one of her biceps reflectively. "Why don't you just have a file called 'feline immunity' and lump them all together?"

"Too broad—how will I ever be able to find what I want?"

"She's so old-fashioned," Mark said, coming in. "Heatherfields has online subscriptions to almost every relevant journal. Nobody actually *stores* papers anymore."

"I can't think unless I can doodle in the margins," Artie said defensively.

"With her feather quill and ink pot," Mary said. "Listen, do you two have ten minutes?"

"Have as much time as you need—it's a long trip." Artie glanced at Mark, and he nodded.

"I have a dinner engagement in Chelsea," Mary explained. "But this is so hot, I probably would've made a special trip."

"Sounds promising," Mark said. "Please tell me it's to do with immunodeficiency. And that that box is full of juicy samples."

"Right on both counts." Mary took a seat and pulled out her red book. It was only then that Artie realized how excited her friend actually was, and she began to register a delicious flutter of scientific anticipation.

"What about the samples?" Mark cast an anxious glance at the box.

"I didn't want to take any chances with these—they're on dry ice, so no hurry."

"Dry ice?" Artie echoed. "What's the occasion?"

"There's something going on in the Isle of Sheppey, in the village of Minster," Mary said. "Three dead cats, the first one from a household in the center of the village, and then two more from a multi-cat cottage down the road a week later."

"And AIDS, you said?' Mark's eyes were fired up.

"It looks like it." Mary hesitated. "Freddie, my vet colleague from Sheerness, dealt with the cases, and he was kind enough to take some extra samples for us. He did full necropsies, to be honest—the man's got endless enthusiasm when it comes to poking around the innards of a dead cat. I repeated the standard feline leukemia ELISA test on the samples in my surgery, and it was negative."

"Feline immunodeficiency virus, then." Mark slumped back, deflated.

Mary's lips twitched. "Do I detect a note of prejudice?"

"Mark only has eyes for FeLV," Artie explained. "FIV is too trendy."

"Well, he's working for the right person," Mary said. "But I don't think it's FIV either. The standard FIV ELISAs were also negative, though we're still waiting for results to come back on the more reliable test—it can take up to a week. But Freddie's been road-testing a new FIV detection kit developed by a mate of his in America that's supposed to be a lot more sensitive, and that came up negative for him."

"Is the test reliable?" Artie asked.

"Freddie thinks so." Mary looked at them both uncertainly.

"What is it?" Artie prompted.

"It was clearly some sort of immunodeficiency," she said. "They all had a similar suite of opportunistic infections, and that typical wasted appearance. But it didn't look quite right to me for either FeLV or FIV—both owners reported an unusually rapid degeneration. Days, as opposed to weeks. And they had some pretty unusual bowel symptoms."

"Two households," Artie said slowly. "I take it they were outdoor cats."

Mary nodded. "Unfortunately. Freddie's promised to be on the lookout for more cases in the neighbourhood. Meanwhile," she tipped a chin at the box, "I've brought you samples from all three cats—bloods, bone marrow, spleen and kidney. Freddie's banked the rest in his freezer if you're interested in any other tissues." She paused. "He was hoping to be a co-author if you ever write this up."

"Of course!" Artie said. "And you too, it goes without saying."

"This is fantastic," Mark said. "If it's not FeLV or FIV, we'll know in a day or so, depending on Fiona's social calendar. What if it's a new cat immunodeficiency virus? We can name it!"

"Boys and their priorities," Mary said with a smile.

"Freddie's mate's kit," Artie said. "How's it different from the standard FIV ELISA test?"

"It's pretty different," Mary said. "Instead of looking for antibodies against the virus, it's designed to detect the Gag protein on the virus itself. It's meant to be a lot more sensitive."

"The most likely explanation," Artie said, "is that what killed these cats is a virulent new strain of FIV that has acquired a mutation in the Gag protein and is therefore invisible to the detection kit. Even though the virus capsid is usually pretty stable, there is certainly a precedent for at least some variability there."

"Either way, I reckoned it was right up your street," Mary said, standing up. "I hate to shift your paradigm and run, but I don't want to keep my date waiting."

"Tall, dark and handsome?" Mark asked.

"Short, stooped and balding," she replied. "My father, if you must know."

As soon as she left, Mark practically pounced on the box.

"What do you think, Art?" he asked, pulling off the lid and ducking away from the resulting plume of white steam. "Could it be one of your mythical mini-epidemics at last? Would make it a hell of a lot easier to track with such a conspicuous phenotype."

"I don't want to get my hopes up prematurely."

"You, not getting your hopes up? Come on."

"Okay," Artie conceded. "I do admit I have a sneaking suspicion we might be in business. Just imagine, Mark... a virulent new strain of cat AIDS, spinning out of the general population! *Nature* will be knocking down our door." She executed a happy little twirl on her way to the kettle, already imaging the reaction at the next International Retrovirus Symposium.

"That's more like it. What'll it be, boss?"

This was just a courtesy—Mark was perfectly capable of making the decision. Nevertheless, she appreciated it.

"Ask Fi to do a quick PCR of the three viral genes separately with both FeLV and FIV primer sets," she said, "since we're not sure what we're dealing with. Then we can decide how to deal with the sequencing."

"Right."

"Oh, and Mark—try multiple primers on the Gag gene, in case we're looking at a major new mutation. If you and Fi are overstretched, I can give you a hand."

"As if we'd trust you with something as important as this. Don't you have a grant to write or something?"

❧

WHEN ARTIE FOUND HERSELF UNABLE to concentrate, she went up to the second floor library. Libraries had always played a central role in her scientific life, and one of the first things she'd done on arriving at the institute was to seek out the perfect hiding place. And she'd found it straightaway: a carrel of carved mahogany tucked into a seldom-visited corner. There, in this niche with its illusion of solitude, she could read and think and let her mind relax from her usual mania, secure in the knowledge that other patrons bustled about just out of visual range.

The Heatherfields library was not, on the whole, a popular place. There were epochs in the geological past when meteors had struck the earth and wiped out entire phyla of exotic species. Artie had a feeling that the late twentieth century had undergone its own cataclysmic impact when scientific journals began to be available online. The result was a tendency to laziness, and a general avoidance of all things printed. The PhD students Artie had interacted with at Heatherfields showed an alarming propensity to only read papers published in the last five years—unless they could somehow avoid reading altogether. It was only a matter of time before the early journal articles were forgotten completely. And then there were the ancient medical and natural history books, which she doubted anybody was ever going to bother to scan and upload. Random trawler that she was, she could lose herself for hours in their musty pages and elegant language. And things would pop up, from the most tangential sources, things that she had not even known she wanted to know in the first place.

When she stepped through the arched doorway of the library, the late afternoon light seemed to ooze like honey. The larger stained glass windows were colored ruby and amber, bending reality still further. As usual, the cavernous space—carved up with multiple layers of mezzanines connected by catwalks and spiral staircases—was moderately populated. But most of the scientists were greying; she didn't see anyone young enough to be a student, and the few post-docs in evidence were skulking by the shelf that displayed recent glossy editions of the more popular journals.

She passed through the reading section and the stacks, male heads turning toward her in a wave as she went by. This reaction was as familiar to her as the flow of air over skin, and elicited a similar level of conscious recognition—that is, none whatsoever. She made her way to her hiding place and sat down. A diamond-shaped window of bubble-shot glass stained iris and emerald abutted the carrel. Through it, light fell onto her hands, purple and green, slightly more intense against the untanned strip where her ring had been. She realized then that her hands were aging, and experienced an old memory: her own childish hand, pale and smooth and perfect, resting on her mother's larger version, long and tanned and elegant, criss-crossed with tiny wrinkles. At the time it had seemed that she would never own hands like those, yet now hers were the same. The only difference now was that she no longer coveted that experienced skin with its allure of adulthood. Turning into her mother felt like an inevitable process that she was powerless to prevent.

No, she wouldn't think of that. She had come to think about a far more promising topic. It seemed as if Mary's news, so hard on the heels of the Renquist–Manfield collaboration, was too serendipitous to be true. Before this, Artie had had only the infrastructure in place—all of the thousands of baseline cat virus samples she and Mary had collected over the years, and the means in the laboratory to identify their sequences in a streamlined fashion. Of course this had represented a lot of hard groundwork, work that Artie was proud of achieving. But she had nevertheless lacked two essential components, components that had now fallen into her lap from the sky, one after the other: a potential new virus strain whose progress she could chart from the very beginning, and a cutting-edge mathematical technique to study it properly. She had kept her reactions with Mark suitably muted, as befit a professor at a prestigious institute. But with an intuitive and entirely unscientific tingle, Artie was sure her project was on the brink of greatness.

FIONA PICKED UP THE LAST blood sample, which had been treated at collection with anticoagulants by the enthusiastic vet, Freddie. Her hand sure and steady on the syringe, she layered the blood over the golden liquid cushion at the bottom of the plastic tube. Her movements were fluid despite the awkward angle imposed by the glass shield of the biosafety flow hood, and Artie loved watching her work: she had the focus of a child coloring with crayons, trying to stay within the lines. Despite her many years of experience, Fiona had somehow never picked up the usual bad habit of sloppiness. Like the best technicians, she understood intuitively when taking shortcuts was permissible and when to adhere strictly to the cookbook.

Mark and Artie had been standing by the microscope chatting about the Minster outbreak, but had both lapsed into silence as Fiona began to work with the blood, hypnotized by the vibrant coloring in the tubes.

"Get lost, you two," Fiona said. "You're making me nervous. And turn up the music on your way out."

Mark and Artie retired meekly to the office and were laughing over one of Mark's quips when he cleared his throat and looked pointedly over her shoulder. She looked around too, the smile fading from her lips.

Calvin stood framed in the open doorway, so completely out of context that she was rendered mute. He was dressed in a suit and tie, which meant he'd come straight from a lecture, and he held a single red rose, an offering that baffled her more than his sudden presence in the basement. She was almost transfixed by the flower: its perfection, its shape, its deep color. A dozen different impossible feelings welled up and got pushed around her body by her racing heart.

"Artemis," Calvin finally said. Despite the use of her full name, she knew immediately that he was sober: the most frightening state of all. She remembered with a flush of queasy shame what had happened the last time he had managed to get his hands on her.

"How did you get in here?" She struggled to master her confusion, aware of Mark tensing up behind her.

"I told the man on the door it was our wedding anniversary and I wanted to surprise you." He snapped the rose in two, producing a sick sound like a bone breaking, and tossed it accurately in the bin. A few petals fluttered to the floor, like spots of blood around his polished shoes. "Clever ruse, wasn't it? And ironic, too, since you couldn't even stick out the full year."

"What do you want?" Her voice came out steady, but she knew he would see through her. Seeing through her had always been his special talent.

"What do you think?" He loosened his tie and looked Mark over briefly before returning his gaze to her. "A cozy set-up you've got here, Artie dearest. Is *he* part of the remuneration package?"

There was a space of silence, and then she said, "Get out."

Calvin clucked sympathetically. "Don't tell me your condition has deteriorated so much that you can't even *work* without—"

"You heard her," Mark said.

"Oh-ho, he speaks as well!" Calvin said. "That can be such a disadvantage, don't you find?"

Mark stood up to his full height and put one hand on the telephone. "Security gets rather bored in this place," he said conversationally. "I gather the frustration mounts."

"Don't bother," Calvin said, suddenly tired of the game. He reached into the inner pocket of his suit, pulled out an envelope and tossed it onto Artie's desk. It landed with a heavy thud. "The mountain comes to Muhammad. It's self explanatory, even for a ineffectual bitch like you."

Mark picked up the phone, the stretch of his mouth halfway between a smile and a snarl.

"I'm finished here." Calvin turned from Mark to Artie, inspecting her for a moment with a look in his eye that made her heart crumple. "Please deal with it promptly so I can get on with my life."

After he disappeared, Artie dropped her face into her shaking hands, hearing the click of the telephone returning to its cradle. She would not cry, *she would not cry*— there was nothing she despised more than a woman who lost control in public. She wished fervently she were somewhere else, that Mark had been safely sequestered in the lab, that she'd called Calvin in the morning and prevented this entire scene in the first place. She could feel the skin of her face burning her palms, followed by the hot moisture of tears, and willed Mark to walk out too, and leave her to pull herself together in peace, even as she knew that leaving was the last thing that someone like Mark would do.

She felt the inevitable hand on her shoulder and nearly recoiled.

"Could you give me a few minutes alone, please?" She was trying to blot him out through the closed heels of her palms.

"I don't mind sticking around."

"I mean it, Mark—get lost."

"Only if you're truly all right." He paused. "Are you?"

She nodded, then shook her head, all with her face still covered as she began to cry in earnest. She heard the door shut, the flick of the cheap plastic Venetian shades which protected its rectangle of glass, the click of the lock, the familiar screech of Mark's chair being pulled close as the hand returned to her shoulder, making no demands. The tears had been building up for weeks, and now they were escaping against her will, flowing forth with no regard for decorum or scientific rationality. But Artie would not be defeated; making a fierce effort, she eventually smothered them back and raised her head.

"You might feel better if you let yourself finish crying," he suggested.

"Fuck that. I don't cry, okay?"

Mark shook his head and looked around, at a loss. Artemis Marshall was not the sort who would need a box of tissues in her office. Finally, he pulled a folded white cloth from his pocket.

"It's clean," he said, and she took it, trying to remember the last time she'd seen anyone under forty with a proper handkerchief.

"I'm sorry you had to see that," she said, mopping her face. A tremble still infected her voice, and she vowed to squelch that too.

"Why? It's not your fault he's a shithead." Beneath the civilized brown of his eyes was an intensity that she thought might be the masculine desire to pound Calvin into the floor. As much as she disapproved of primitive gender roles, she couldn't deny it felt gratifying.

"It's my fault I married him." She blew her nose. More tears trickled down, and she wiped at those too, confounded at the continued mutiny.

"I trust he wasn't a shithead at the time."

"I'm sure he was, but I was just too stupid to see it," she said. "And it's my fault he had to chase me down here—I've been absolutely useless. I'm sorry you had to see that."

"You don't have to be ashamed that this happened in front of me, Art. I'm glad I was here."

She shook her head, and he looked at her more carefully.

"Are you pissed off at me for defending you?"

She had to laugh, then. "I should be, but truth be told, you were magnificent. He's a coward at heart—you played it perfectly."

"I know his type rather well," he said. "Listen, I think you could use a drink."

"But it's only six. Fiona—"

"Will be ecstatic if we get out of her hair," he said firmly. "Come on."

NEAR THE END OF THE afternoon, Simon found himself out of printer paper. He was always careful to replenish office stocks in the late evenings so that he wouldn't have to mingle with the rest of the basement denizens, but the previous night's activities had disrupted his routine. And today especially, he did not want to walk past Artemis' office after making such a big point about not having time to meet her team. But Henry would be needing paper in a few minutes, and Henry did not tolerate delays.

He went into the blind office and was just putting his hand on the handle when he saw the door to Artemis' office open. A muscled, hairy arm appeared, propping back the door, and then Artemis slipped out, followed closely by the arm's owner: a large, powerful-looking man in a T-shirt and faded jeans. Her post-doc, more than likely. No wonder she'd been considering his services as a bodyguard.

Simon stepped to one side of the rectangle of glass, making himself invisible from the corridor. They were both burdened with laptops and backpacks, and when Artemis turned away from locking the door, he got a good look at her face.

Simon did not mix with people, so the finer subtleties of body language tended to elude his comprehension. Nevertheless, he had become very attuned to extreme moods after twenty-six years of trying to predict and fend off Henry's tempers, and he could see that Artemis was upset. Mark, he noticed, was hovering over her like a protective brother. Then he murmured something that made her smile wanly, and the pair walked past towards the basement exit.

Simon leaned against the door, momentarily disoriented. He had only just got used to Artemis' transition from manipulative airhead to intelligent protégé to kindly ally to wily, fearless warrior, all in the space of a week. The prospect of her going full circle and being a fragile female after all did not appeal to him, even though it would vindicate his initial hypothesis.

But no. This time, he was going to wait and see what else unfolded before he settled on a final assessment of disdain or disappointment. She was an unstable algorithm; slippery, resisting facile categorization, like an epidemic with too many variables to predict the outcome.

When he was sure they were gone, Simon opened the door, stepped into the corridor and began walking, eyes fixed on the worn mauve carpet. People slipped by on his left and right, but he did not register more than their shoes.

∿

IN THE END, MARK PROCLAIMED the weather too fine to sit in a stuffy pub or bake on a terrace, so they picked up a bottle of wine and some snacks from the supermarket and took the tube to Hampstead, stopping by Artie's house to drop off their things. Mark idly read the spines of the bookshelf in the lounge while she changed clothes, threw some cutlery and cups into the bag and grabbed an old blanket, and then they walked to the nearby Heath.

"Where to?" Mark asked, hefting the grocery bag as they stood, knee-high grass whispering over their legs in the hot breeze.

"Parliament Hill," she said decisively, starting to stride in that direction. Calvin had always insisted on the willow-shaded lakeside bank at the bottom of Kenwood bowl, so Artie instinctively chose one of the furthest extremes.

It really was a lovely evening. The park was seething with life: picnickers, dog-walkers, strolling lovers, pram-pushing *au pairs*, sunbathers, shrieking children. The wind tousled the oak leaves, powered kites, pushed Frisbees wildly off their intended trajectories. With Mark's companionship and a universe full of pleasure-seekers in broad daylight, she felt her earlier despair fade.

This was the first time they'd done anything together besides pints at the Arms, and she was aware of a sense of uncertainty about the whole jaunt, just as quickly dismissed as ridiculous. Mark's entertaining chatter on the way here had already cheered her up. He had not broached the topic of the incident with Calvin, instead relating anecdotes about his old Bristol colleagues until she finally gave in to laughter.

It was even windier on the top of the hill, the blanket rearing like a live thing when they attempted to smooth it over the lumpy grass.

"To new beginnings," Mark said, touching his plastic beaker of Cabernet to hers before starting to wrestle a slab of cheddar from its packaging.

"Meaning what?"

"Whatever you like. Our basement empire. Collaborating with the batty epidemiologists. Mary's cat plague. Your divorce."

She took a large sip, felt the wine warm her throat and radiate downward.

"I'm not trying to pry," he said after a moment, head down and still focused on his work. "But if it would make you feel better, you could tell me about him."

Artie watched the knife flash as the pale oblong of cheese transformed into thin, perfectly symmetric slices, soft and yielding in the heat of the sun and glistening with beads of whey. The sight made her nauseous, and she took another gulp of wine. A Roma tomato received similar treatment from the knife, so carefully that not a single blob of pulp escaped, and then he sculpted off planks of baguette and assembled a couple of sandwiches. In his fingers, and she saw the same competence that he exerted over the lab equipment: a deep muscular understanding of how things worked. In another era, he would have been a carpenter, or a clockmaker.

"If this is you trying not to pry," she finally said, lightly, "I'd hate to see you being pushy."

His eyes glanced up, a flicker of brown, before returning to the bread. "It's not a crime against feminism to drop the superwoman act for one second, Art."

"I think I've done a pretty good job of that back at the office already."

"Ah, so you have."

Mark gave her a smile and started in on a sandwich, letting his gaze roam over the rooftops of Highgate with crumbs dribbling down his chin. Leaving her own untouched, Artie nearly emptied the cup of wine and then lay on her back to stare at the sky. The clouds were long ragged threads against blue, tinted rosy-gold and combed in the same direction: *mares' tails*, her mother had called them, harbingers of storms—though there was nothing but sun in the current forecast, an impossible summer high that persisted beyond all expectation. Which just went to show how unreliable such maternal observations had ever been.

No, she wouldn't think about her mother. She would inspect the sliver of moon, wonder at how it was the exact hue as the clouds—if it weren't such a distinctive shape, she'd never know it was there at all. She would focus on the prickles of grass through the weave of the blanket, the perspiration forming on her bare skin just as quickly dried by the breeze, the guitar playing nearby, gusty vocals over top, a spattering of laughter snatched away in the mobile air. Far above, a jet excreted a precise plume of whiteness, and she compared it to older, longer trails that had long since lost their integrity, smeared and disintegrated.

"The divorce," she said at last, "was my idea. He didn't want it at first, but I insisted. I had to wait two months before I was legally allowed to apply for divorce under Scottish law—a full year of marriage. Those two months felt like forever, but now that they're finally over, I'm afraid to follow through."

"Why?" His voice was quiet, but there was tension there as he settled onto his back, joining her in contemplating the sky. "You're not afraid of anything, Art. He isn't... hurting you, is he?"

"No. Like I said, he's a coward."

"Good." He whooshed out his breath. "I didn't think you were the type. But you never can tell."

A wedge of geese flew over, slaves to the magnetic lines that criss-crossed, invisible, over the globe.

"My little sister," he said, a while after the geese had disappeared. "She's a lot like you—unstoppable, doesn't take any shit. Turned out she'd been letting her husband batter her for years—none of us had any idea. He was a master of discretion."

"Oh, Mark." She turned her head, but his profile was set and his eyes were fixed on the sky. "I'm sorry."

"And there was something about your ex, today... the way he mutilated that rose. The way you reacted."

"Nothing like that," she said briskly—though privately, she thought that some might classify Calvin's behavior as a kind of battering.

"Anyway, that's why I've been pestering you," he said. He turned his head towards her, met her eye. "It's not normally my style, but after what happened with Rebecca..."

"I understand, Mark. And...thanks." She paused, feeling a number of forces working within her: the wine. The moment. The pressure of untold words, aching at the back of her throat. "Actually, I'd sort of like to go on, if you still want to hear."

"Of course." He rolled his head back to study the clouds, and so did she. In only the half a minute or so that she'd taken her eyes off them, they had already shifted to new patterns, their color deepening to orange and pink.

"Are you having second thoughts because you still love him?" he asked.

"No. He killed that some time ago."

"So...?"

"There's no way to say it without sounding like an idiot, Mark."

An impatient sigh. "You should know by now that's the last thing I'd ever call you."

"I'm afraid of being alone."

There was a long pause.

"You mean, of being single?" A hint of incredulity had slipped into his tone.

"God, no, of course not," she said. "No, I mean literally. I can't stand solitude. It frightens me, sometimes to the point of complete immobility." She felt herself tensing up, made an active effort to resist. "Being married kept it away for a while. And the divorce will bring it all crashing back." She took a breath. "In fact, it's already started."

"I'm so sorry," he said, after a few surprised moments. "I never would have guessed."

As he reached for more wine, Artie became aware of the swifts, swooping and diving so far above that they were tiny pinpricks, insignificant life forms in the vastness of space, so far that their high-pitched *scree-scree-scree*-ing, that perennial soundtrack of summer, could no longer be heard. In a flash she remembered how lonely the stars had looked on the roof, and those planets swimming at the end of Simon's telescope. A shiver passed through her, and she took a breath, concentrated on Mark's bulk next to her—she didn't have to take her eyes off the swifts to sense his warmth and his breathing. She had been using people as similar props all her life, with none of them the wiser: strangers on the bus, neighbors clattering dishes or walking across parquet in adjacent flats, actors on television, email correspondents and voices on the radio. And Calvin had been the ultimate prop.

Not at first, of course. At first they'd been in love, and she'd been safe for all the right reasons.

Mark topped up both of their cups, then said, "So it's a sort of phobia?"

"That's a good a way to describe it as any."

"Any idea why you have it?"

"No." She felt vaguely guilty not telling Mark the complete story, but how could she explain? Look how Calvin had reacted, and he was meant to be a *professional*.

"Have you ever sought help?" he said.

No ridicule, no disbelief or pity, just his usual calmness. She felt her muscles start to unclench.

"I'm afraid of therapists, too," she admitted.

"Is that why your shelves are loaded with psychiatry textbooks and journals? Are you trying to treat yourself?"

So close, and yet so far from the truth.

"Cal hasn't had a chance to clear out all his stuff yet," she said. "He's a shrink."

"Oh, dear. I see where this is going."

"It's not what you think, Mark," she said. *Not even remotely.*

"Hmmm." He raised his head enough to drink some wine, then noticed that her cup was empty again, refilled it. "But you're no longer living together, right?"

She nodded, taking another drink. She was starting to feel light-headed from the alcohol.

"So what difference would it make to finalize things?"

"None whatsoever." She sighed. "That's the whole point, Mark. I'm acting like an irrational, pathetic wreck. My marital status, it's become almost like..."

"A placebo?"

His voice was gentle, and then suddenly the tears were back, and Artie, who seldom cried, was crying again for the second time in as many hours. Mark put his arm around her, pulling her in, and she pressed her face against his chest, let the tears soak into his T-shirt. After a few minutes when the shirt was soaked through, a few paper napkins appeared discreetly in front of her face, and she blew her nose and carried on sobbing, determined to have it out once and for all. If she was going to act like a helpless female, she might as well do it properly.

It was a great relief to allow herself to let go, to disappear into Mark's solid human warmth, to pretend that she was the sister he cared about so much. She had never had a functional family, had never been looked after like other children—it had always been she who had to be the caretaker. It had made her strong and independent, and she was proud of her strength, but it also meant that she'd grown up seeing vulnerability and weakness as the worst sort of sin.

But she didn't have to be ashamed: it had finally become clear that Mark wouldn't think she was a bad person, and nobody from Heatherfields would know about what was happening on top of this hill in the growing twilight. A hill that, with her eyes shut and the grassy wind in her ears, transported her back in time to that night on the summit of Arthur's Seat. And this made her cry even harder, for the loss of Calvin, for the way his love had twisted into hate as seamlessly as a Möbius strip.

She could still see Calvin's face, blotting out the starlight, feel the movement of his finger tracing the arc of her throat. And the lassitude of exhausted muscles—how long had it taken, that walk from the Grassmarket across town and then up to the very top of the hill?

"I don't even know you," Calvin had said, in wonder, "but I know I'll love you forever. How can this be possible?"

And later, much later. The sneer, the condescending cast, when she'd burst into his office on Rose Street and told him with high excitement about her appointment to Heatherfields. It was only then she realized that her husband, despite all his overt encouragement, was actually not too keen for her to achieve the same academic rank, especially not at such a markedly younger (and by inference, undeserving) age.

What was it he'd said, exactly? *Affirmative action must be getting a bit out of hand these days.* And after she'd exploded with anger, he'd said: "You're acting a bit crazy, Artie dearest." The disapproving hands, folded one atop the other on his desk. "Any more of that and we'll have to ring up my esteemed colleagues and have you locked up."

Enough. She wouldn't think about Cal any more. When she eventually stopped crying, Mark didn't take his arm away and she felt no urge to move either. They didn't speak; they just breathed, listening to the wind and thinking their own thoughts. When the sun slipped under the horizon, the temperature plunged almost instantly and she moved in closer. He took his arm away then, but only long enough to fold her end of the blanket over her before restoring his grip, keeping the thick fabric in place around her.

She wasn't consciously aware of when consolation eased into the first stirrings of desire. She became aware of the weight of his arm, the mass and bulk and measure of him, the sound of his breathing. As she did so, that familiar heaviness settled within her body's center of gravity, accompanied by a feather-tickled sweep of nervous impulses over skin.

She had always had a healthy sexual appetite and was comfortable enough with her body's needs not to be perturbed or confused by them. After all, it was a logical response: Mark was a potent male, with his powerful muscles, his feral body hair and the salty suggestion of his scent, and she had not had regular sex for several months, or satisfying sex for even longer.

If it were anyone else but Mark, she almost certainly would have pushed things further. But she didn't dare risk what was shaping up to be a perfect team. She'd heard cautionary tales from female colleagues who'd dallied with their male post-docs and then lost them when it all went wrong. Or worse, retained them as employees with the roles reversed, the balance of power shifted against them, helplessly subjugated by the thrall of their feelings. In the face of these prospects, mere lust, for someone as strong-willed as Artemis Marshall, was a mosquito whine in the ear, easily brushed aside.

As if aware of her thoughts, Mark twisted around so that he was on his back, all without letting go of her. She knew he was being his usual polite self and removing his erection to a less problematic locale, and acknowledged the happiness of being wanted, even if nothing would ever come of it. At the same time, she pitied men as a class, who had no choice but to wear their desires on their sleeves. How much more convenient to be a woman, with everything running deep and secret and, if she chose, no one the wiser.

"Some day it won't hurt any more," Mark said, after clearing his throat. It was the first time either had spoken in nearly half an hour. "And meanwhile, you might find yourself feeling less lonely if you made a clean break and started getting over him."

"I know that," she said. "When I'm happy, the problem's always been manageable. And, Mark."

"Yes?"

"I *am* happy, you know, about everything else in my life. I'm so thrilled with our lab, and with you, to be honest. I'm lucky to have you."

He gave her a squeeze. "Post-docs are common as bacteria in the current job climate."

"Nice try, Reynolds, but you can't gloss over the truth. You're a true find. That's one thing I've never understood: what are you still doing on the post-doctoral baggage belt? With your CV, you could've started your own lab three years ago."

"Not interested," he said. "I'm not a leader, not a schemer—I don't have an ounce of ambition in my body. I just love science: *doing* it, not organizing it. Working with my hands at the bench, not writing grant after bloody grant."

"Why don't you become a technician, then, at least get some job security?"

"I tried it, actually," he said. "Nobody would hire me, I was so over-qualified. They just assumed it was temporary insanity, that I'd eventually move on."

"Why didn't you tell me before?"

"I had to make myself indispensable first."

"Be serious, Mark."

There was a silence. "I didn't know you well enough—I didn't want to scare you off with my aberrant behavior."

She laughed. "What's the world come to, if not wanting the universe at your feet has become aberrant?" She paused. "Maybe we can come to some arrangement."

"That's sort of what I was hoping. You, your project, Heatherfields: it's exactly the type of situation I could settle down into."

"I couldn't bear to pay you a paltry tech's salary, though. Let's use up your fellowship, wait until we've published a few papers and I've gained some influence with the Sanctum..."

He laughed, too. "Only Artemis Marshall could believe that she could actually *influence* the Sanctum. Why not gravity, or the tides?"

"Not a problem, Mark—just you wait. How does the title Associate Professor grab you?"

"Like a barnacle," he said, which was such an absurd image that they both started chuckling again. When their amusement trickled out, Artie said, "Can I ask you something personal, seeing as how I've..."

"Go ahead, Artie. I'm an open book." He had plucked a thick piece of grass and was chewing at it like a proper yokel.

"You don't have a girlfriend, do you?"

"Nope."

"Can I ask why? I mean, someone as charming as you. Ben's post-docs are swooning all over you. It doesn't make sense—you should've been married ages ago."

"I'm not the marrying kind, actually." His smile was faint in the dusk. "Although I'm an avid fan of women—especially beautiful ones. You must've noticed the evidence a few minutes ago."

This threw her, but she wasn't about to be out-cooled by Mark.

"So you're a professional cad?"

"Of course not!" He tilted his head to give her a reproving glance before looking back up, the piece of grass bobbing complacently. "One-night stands aren't my style. I just don't have it in me to be in love."

"You don't *love* people?'

"No, that's not what I said. I mean, I just don't fall *in* love. I feel respect, affection, admiration, loyalty... love, I suppose, in the manner of our friend Plato. And lust. But nothing more."

"Are you sure it's not just semantics?"

"Positive."

"Have *you* been to a therapist?"

He shrugged. "Several. Apparently it's to do with my upbringing. But in all other respects I'm happy, as mentally healthy as a horse. I try not to let it bother me."

"So you don't stay with one woman for long?"

"Yes, but not by choice," he said. "I would quite like something long-term, maybe have a child or two, but they can never handle my limitations, eventually give up and move on. It's sad, really, but I do understand."

"Jesus, Mark." She looked up at the first stars—the faintest suggestion of starness, really, in the deep blue. "You must be dragging a string of broken hearts a mile long."

"I can't take responsibility for that," he said, a bit sharply. "I'm always up front from the beginning—utterly explicit. But women, they always assume they can change the unchangeable."

Why not gravity, or the tides?

"I'm sorry, Mark. It must be hard on someone like you, inadvertently hurting all these people you... you like."

"Yes," he said. "Almost as hard as them leaving me afterwards."

They lapsed into silence. What a pair they were, Artie thought. Unable to love; afraid of being alone. Was one really any weirder than the other? How fragile the human mind; how rare that condition that the textbooks liked to refer to as "normal."

$\sim$

AFTER MARK WALKED HER HOME and took his leave, Artie put on some loud music and removed Calvin's envelope from her backpack. She spread its contents onto the dining room table and uncapped a pen, ready to deal with the divorce papers once and for all. But after she took out the last sheet of legalese, her fingertips encountered something stiff and irregularly shaped at the bottom of the envelope.

Premonition was a lightness in her gut. Trembling, she fished out a short strip of photos, the sort produced in a series of four in booths at train stations. A pair of images of herself and Calvin stared up at her. The expressions were bewildered: two new victims caught in the relentless headlights of love. Of course she remembered exactly where and when they'd been taken. After watching the sunrise from Arthur's

Seat that first night, they'd stumbled back to town and stopped at Waverley station before finding some breakfast—the most delicious fry-up Artie had ever eaten.

What was it Calvin had said when he pulled her, giggling, into the booth? Something like, "We might think we'll always remember how wonderful we feel right now, but that's just a delusion. Let's make some *evidence*."

The first two photos were only slightly differing straight shots, Cal behind her, head on her shoulder, both of them grinning like idiots. She could picture the last two well, even though they were now missing, severed with a rough scissors cut. Laughter forgotten and intoxicated by proximity, they'd succumbed to a fervent kiss, witnessed only by the heavy flashes. A stammering commuter eventually had to tap on the booth, wondering if they would be finished any time soon—which had set the laughter off all over again.

Shivering, Artie burned the photos in the kitchen sink, watching with fascination as the flames devoured her face and its happiness melted into black. She'd received the love, and Calvin had kept the lust. Had he burned the remaining shots too, or was he going to save them for his own inscrutable reasons? She didn't know which prospect was more disturbing.

CHAPTER 5
Identities: Mistaken, Forgotten, and Otherwise Obscure

SIMON ACTUALLY HAD THREE TELEPHONE extensions in his private office in the rabbit warren that sprawled behind B302. The first was the useless one whose number was published in the Heatherfields directory. The second was the emergency extension, known only to the porters and Ben Crombie. And the third, the one that was ringing now, was the one used by the Ministry of Defence.

Simon picked up the receiver and listened for a good few minutes. Timothy Brees, his normal contact at the newly established Suspicious Diseases Unit of the Defence Science and Technology Laboratory, had learned years ago not to bother with pleasantries, either before or after disseminating the requisite information. Simon could tell that Brees despised him. The feeling was mutual, the way Brees treated him like a secretary: "Would you be so kind as to inform Professor Manfield that a recent unusual outbreak of disease has been reported in Faversham, which we have reason to believe..."

It was exactly what Simon did not need—another bioterrorist scare. They always came to nothing, but nobody seemed to realize that Simon had *important* things to do. More things, in fact, than could possibly be done in the allotted time. After hanging up, he turned to his computer and activated the small device that would give him the continuously fluctuating eight-digit code he used to access his MoD guest account.

The details of the case that Brees had sketched out came up on the screen, and Simon's anger faded away in his habitual curiosity at a new problem.

༼ つ

DOWN THE CORRIDOR, ARTIE AND Fiona sat at one of the workbenches in the lab, looking at the results of Fiona's attempt to detect virus signatures in the blood samples from the three cats that had died so mysteriously in Minster.

Fiona flipped a few pages back in her lab notebook and shuffled through the various digital images with agonizing slowness, giving Artie tantalizing glimpses of various bright bands of DNA in the process.

"You could at least wait for me to finish labeling all the lanes," Fiona grumbled—she was not a morning person like Artie. "I've got a raging hangover."

"C'mon, Fi, I'm dying here. Did anything come up positive?"

"Mark will kill us for not waiting for him."

"Mark should get up a bit earlier if he wants to catch all the hot news. He's getting lazy in his old age."

"Sorry I'm late," Mark said, striding into the lab. "I had to park my wheelchair."

When Artie caught Mark's eye, his smile intensified ever so slightly. She had woken up embarrassed by the intimacy of what had occurred on Parliament Hill, but any fears she might have entertained were vaporized in that one simple exchange. Instead of awkwardness, there was a subtle new bond, unspoken but undeniable.

Mark pulled up a stool and Fiona showed them the first image.

"Well, one thing's clear," she said, running a finger along a neat column in the notebook. "All three cats are negative for FIV."

"But were the controls OK?" Mark asked. "I hadn't tested those new primers yet."

Fiona nodded. "I've included our normal FIV Petaluma strain plasmid as a control—all positive, all products the expected size."

Artie studied the image with a slow nod before pushing the notebook towards Mark.

"I'm pretty sure those cats had feline leukemia virus," Fiona said. "But not all the primer pairs worked."

"Show us, Fi," Artie said.

Fiona retrieved her notebook, turned a page and tapped on a second image, which showed a pair of glowing bands on a black background. "Here, see? We've got a positive signal with the FeLV Pol primers. Clear as mud."

"Beautiful," Artie agreed. "How come your PCRs always look so much better than mine?" When Mark opened his mouth to retort, she said, "Shut it, Reynolds. I wasn't talking to you."

"But the Envelope primers are negative, all three cats," Fiona said. "Controls are fine on the FeLV-A/Glasgow strain, so we know it's working."

"And the Gag gene?" Mark said.

"One primer set negative, the other positive," Fiona said. "The primers spanning p27 are negative, but the broader set came up. The size is too large, though... about 400 basepairs bigger than it ought to be. Identical in all three cats, though."

She pointed out the relevant bands, which were running higher than the control plasmid, freighted with their extra burden of DNA sequence.

"An insertion?" Mark speculated.

Artie nodded. "Possibly. I'm not surprised we're seeing some mutations in the Envelope gene, but it's rare to get such drastic changes in Gag."

"At least it explains Mary's negative ELISA result," Mark said.

"We're going to have to do some sequencing to get a better idea what's going on," Artie said. "Can you start that today?"

Fiona nodded. "Already planned on it."

"Did you book time with the sequencing department yet?' Mark asked.

When Fiona shook her head, Marked leapt up and went over to the phone.

"The Hastings lab has been on sequencing overdrive," Fiona said. "There's a massive queue—but luckily I'm mates with the guy in charge, so I can probably convince him to slip our samples in ahead."

"That reminds me," Artie said. "Mark says the Hastings crew have been hassling you up there."

She made a face. "Mark is such a snitch."

"Is it true?"

"Yeah." She sighed. "But it's nothing I can't handle—or haven't seen before."

"Are you sure?" Artie studied her technician: the strong profile, the impervious blue eyes, the way it sometimes seemed as if she were far older than her years.

"Of course. Just stupid insults—the sort that if you react, you look like you don't have a sense of humor."

"I know exactly what you mean," Artie said, thinking of Calvin, and just as quickly shoving him out of her mind. "Do you want me to have a word with Hastings?"

"No!" She lowered her voice. "Jesus, Artie, you have absolutely no idea, do you? Just leave it, okay? They'll get bored eventually."

❧

MARK CAME INTO THE OFFICE a few minutes later to find Artie staring dreamily at nothing.

"You took that rather calmly," he said.

"I was trying to act professional in front of the troops," Artie said. "Three dead cats, Mark! Definitely FeLV, and all with the same major mutations—we could be onto something wild and wonderful!"

"That's more like it," he said. "I was starting to wonder if you were okay."

"I'm fine," she said. Taking a breath, she stepped over that unspoken gap for the first time. "In fact, I made a start on the paperwork last night—thanks to your encouragement."

There was her embarrassment again, but Mark just nodded.

"Any time, Art." He paused. "I mean that literally, you know." He went over to his desk, scribbled something on a sticky note and passed it to her. "It doesn't matter how late."

She looked up from string of numbers, but he was already slouched in his chair, calling up his email. Artie put the sticky note into her wallet and got to work too.

❧

Thursday, 19 June

A. is coming this evening to initiate our joint project. I'm under a lot of pressure with Brees, but he'll just have to wait. A bit worried—H. has been acting unusually. Last night, right in the middle of lecturing me (quite unnecessarily) about the Raijvoort Theorem, he took off his shoes for no good reason that I could see, and all without breaking off speaking or acknowledging what he was doing. Five minutes later, he put them back on, still lecturing. Today, I've noticed that he's started to repeat things that I say to him. At first I thought he was taunting me, but now I'm not so sure.

Simon put down his pen at the soft knock at the outer door of B302, closed the notebook and set it by his designated terminal in the main space. He stood up, noting that Henry was still oblivious, communing with his avian flu simulation with a flurry of fingers over the keys. He hadn't spoken for hours, for which Simon was grateful. Having the random element of a third party in their midst made him more than a little nervous.

Artemis stood poised behind the glass oblong in that way she had, somehow both tensed and relaxed. It seemed familiar. Like a cat, he realized as he held open the door for her. All that was missing was the swishing tail.

"Not too busy for our date, I hope?" Her smile was friendly, but he heard the dig underneath, and the anger flickered inside his stomach.

"Come on in." He kept his voice level.

When he led her through the main room, he saw Artemis eye Henry's silent bulk warily. He took her right through and into his little office, knowing that Henry would not approve but hoping that she'd be in and out before he was even aware of her presence.

She unloaded a pile of notebooks and an external hard drive on his desk, looking around curiously as she sat down. Then she fixed that feline gaze on him.

"Why didn't you come by, Simon? Mark was disappointed."

"I told you—I..." He trailed off, somehow unable to keep up the pretense. "You don't realize how difficult it is for me here."

The words sounded trite and whiny, and he expected her to bat them aside like a cat toy, tell him how friendly everyone in the basement was, or accuse him of being irrational.

"Actually, I have a pretty fair idea," she said.

He didn't know how to handle her sympathy, so he inspected the surface of his desk instead.

"But the thing is, Simon... people are adaptable. If you started acting more sociable, they'd come around. Especially with me on your side."

There was no modesty in the final statement. Her place and influence at the center of things was a scientific fact, not subject to doubt or debate.

"Not everything can be changed simply because you want it," he eventually said.

A strange look passed over her face. Then she shook her head, dispelling it. "That doesn't mean you shouldn't try."

"I don't get along with people," he said. "I never have done."

"That's not what Phil Cox told me."

When he looked up sharply, her mouth only hinted at a smile.

"I had coffee with him last weekend," she explained.

"He remembers me?"

"Phil's memory is cast-iron," she said. "But I'll admit that at first, I wasn't sure we were talking about the same man."

"In a way, you weren't," he said.

Simon had almost forgotten about that trip to Edinburgh. It had been during his first year as Henry's PhD student—a time which belonged firmly to the *before* phase of his life, a life that was now so decidedly *after* that he might as well have died and been reincarnated as a lower species—a slug, say, or a bottom-feeding fish. Something blind, grey and helpless. Before he'd got trapped, before he'd lost Laura, before everything had changed forever.

"Would it really hurt to try?" she said.

"It's too late," he said. "Besides, after what happened with Ben..."

"What did happen?" She tilted her head at him, then widened her eyes. "Ben getting attacked... and your assault charge. Were they related?"

"Oh." He paused. "You haven't checked up on my story? I didn't think you'd take my word for it."

"I thought I could trust you."

Feminine intuition, he supposed. A thoroughly rattling, illogical prospect.

"You wouldn't have been told the truth anyway," he said, "so maybe it's just as well."

She shook her head at him, not understanding.

"It was a long time ago," he said. Then he sighed, gave in. "Maybe ten years. Ben had just arrived. You know what he's like—eager and puppyish and desperate to be friends with everyone."

She nodded, amused. "Puppyish: that's perfect."

"Well, he'd been briefed about Henry, but he hadn't quite internalized what it meant, I guess. He wanted to meet him—and one night, while I was in one of the back rooms and out of earshot, he came in."

"This is sounding familiar," Artemis said with a grimace.

"When Henry didn't respond to Ben's greetings, Ben apparently touched Henry on the shoulder. Henry made the most amazing sound—an unearthly scream I've never heard before or since." He stopped to swallow. "I'm not sure exactly what happened next. I came running, there was a crash and then the fuses blew—it was pitch black. I could hear a scuffle, Ben whimpering, this loud crack..."

"Jesus, Simon." She looked shaken.

Good, he thought. Maybe now she'd realized how close to disaster she'd actually come.

"By the time I found the torch, there was a wrecked monitor, glass everywhere. Ben was on the floor with a broken nose—bleeding, unconscious. Henry had disappeared."

"What did you do?"

"Well, I revived Ben. He was too frightened to be angry—that only happened later. He refused my help and took a cab to the hospital. I finally found Henry wandering around in the car park. It took me ages to calm him down. I think he was more terrified than Ben."

There was a short silence, and then Artemis said, "How did the police get involved?"

"The next day was a Saturday. I found out from one of Ben's team where he lived, went round there to see if he was okay, to apologize. Ben wouldn't even open the door. When I got back to my flat, they were waiting for me."

"But you didn't do anything!"

"I didn't understand either, at the time," Simon said. "And you have no idea how furious I was."

She started to say something, then apparently thought better of it.

"I only found out the whole story later," he said. "Ben had been confused by the blow to the head; when he woke up and found me crouched over him, he somehow thought that *I* had hit him, not Henry. Henry wouldn't speak for himself, of course, so there weren't any reliable witnesses."

"God," she said, eyes wide.

He realized what a relief it was to tell someone else about this humiliating incident—the most humiliating of his entire life.

"I was standing there in my front garden," he said. "The neighbors were all staring at me, the cops were doing that thing they always do on television, telling me I was under arrest for assault, that I didn't have to say anything, but that if I did... And the anger just vanished: I went completely clear-headed."

Artemis seemed somehow both tensed and fluid there in the chair opposite him, hair glinting and bare arms paled by the fluorescence.

"That's when I knew," Simon said. "I worked out what had happened, and decided I would go along with Ben's story. I could plead self-defense—it was late, the light's always dim in there. Anyone could have mistaken Ben for an intruder. I thought they'd let me off lightly."

"Surely that wasn't necessary! Henry couldn't be held responsible, could he, with his illness? After all, Ben had been warned." She made a face. "Unlike me."

"Yes, but what would happen then, Artemis? He wouldn't be charged, but it would be the end of his appointment at Heatherfields. It would be too dangerous— the Inner Sanctum would never let him stay." He wished she would stop staring at him. "He has no living relatives, so he would've ended up in an institution, doped up on anti-psychotics or sedatives for the rest of his life."

"So you went down to protect him?"

"In the end I didn't have to," he said. "I was released on bail, and Salverson came round to see me with a pack of lawyers. I explained how I'd mistaken Ben for a burglar, and they somehow convinced Ben to drop the charges. I suspect the Sanctum intervened."

She gave a shaky sigh. "You'd really have sacrificed your career and freedom for Henry?"

Simon inspected his pallid fingers, splayed out on the tabletop in front of him, then smiled at nothing. "Hadn't I done that already? But yes, I would have, because he's all I've got."

"But, Simon." The tone of her voice made him raise his head, even though he didn't want to. "Maybe it *is* too dangerous. It sounds like I was lucky. And maybe you've been, too."

"One incident in nearly three decades," he said sharply, shaking his head. "And Ben broke the rules. I have no idea why you weren't properly briefed; Salverson usually takes care of it at his welcome interview. B302 is strictly off-limits—everyone knows it. It's why I'm lax about locking up: we're shunned like the plague."

Artemis looked thoughtful. "Salverson was ill when I arrived. Peter Hastings gave me the spiel."

"Well, somebody messed up somewhere."

"But back to the original point," she said. "From some things he's said, I have a feeling Ben's forgiven you. He may be a bit eager, but he's kind. I think it's worth trying to start again."

"I'll think about it," Simon said, just to get her off his back.

He could only just about tolerate Artemis' pity, but the thought of *Ben's* was sickening, made him want to see his nose broken a second time.

∽

SOON AFTERWARD ARTIE AND SIMON got down to work. They were assigning each virus signature a set of criteria, a multivariate numerical description: the GPS coordinates of the pet's home address, date isolated, percentage of mutations in each of the three genes, all of the rest of the information that Simon thought would be important to represent the variation and spread of Artie's viruses through the space-time of Kent. Many hours of careful molecular research, all condensed into a set of numbers: it seemed more like witchcraft than science to Artie, especially as the process was far from black-and-white. Sometimes they had to make subjective decisions, which bothered her in exactly the same way that filing did, having to commit irrevocably to one route when another seemed equally appropriate.

But Simon was relaxed and comfortable with these painfully arbitrary choices, assigning the borderline cases with the careless ease of a mental coin-toss. And this was odd, because he had seemed so cold and mathematical and she, so warm and intuitive. When it came to his craft, Artie was starting to realize, Simon was anything but rigid. *It will all cancel out in the end, Artemis*, he kept saying. *Trust me.*

And she did, even though she was still unnerved by their earlier conversation, unable to get the what-if out of her mind. What if she had tapped Henry on the shoulder like Ben had? Of course she could defend herself in theory, but Henry was huge, and potentially electrified with abnormal energy. And an attack was the last thing she would have been expecting. And then, if the lights had gone out, if she'd struck her head...Simon had been on the roof, so nobody would have been there to shine a torch, to frighten him away, to keep him from—what? It was impossible to say from what. It was impossible to know his limits. She thought about the way he'd looked calculatingly at her legs, and felt cold sweat spring up under her arms, across her belly.

She'd read Henry as a gentle soul, and she'd been wrong. This error in judgement was the most disconcerting of all.

∽

SEVERAL HOURS LATER, SIMON SCROLLED down the directory list of Artie's external drive and the cursor arrested at the bottom.

"Is that all?" he asked.

She blinked at the inventory in her notebook, becoming aware again of the office, her body, the ache in her back and neck.

"Yes, up until last week," she said. "We've just received some particularly interesting samples... is it okay to proceed before we've got those sequenced?"

"Of course," he said. "These models are very flexible. In fact, they're designed to be ongoing, to respond to new data—more like a movie than a snapshot. The time dimension is crucial for analysis."

"Okay... what's next?"

Simon stretched in his chair, looked at his watch. "Let's run the La Fontayne and the Meyerhof-Hernsley in parallel—there ought to be time for a quick look."

Artie leaned back in her chair and rubbed her neck while Simon turned back to the keyboard and began to work, entering keystrokes, pulling down menus and opening and closing windows so quickly that she couldn't begin to follow. Simon muttered a few things which Artie knew she was not meant to respond to—about the analysis queue, about the "cluster," about Fourier transforms, about Henry's mammoth avian flu simulation, which apparently was a nuisance because it was making everything else run sluggishly.

And then something was rotating on the screen: a green, three-dimensional shape like a squashed ball, or a very flat donut with a slightly filled-in hole, Artie thought. It didn't look anything like Henry's avian flu epidemic, with its graceful lily-like bell spinning about the Y-axis.

"This is the Meyerhof-Hernsley," Simon said. "It's a much more simplistic algorithm, so it doesn't take as long to calculate. We use it mostly for bioterrorism modeling, not for natural outbreaks—which is why Henry favoring it makes no sense."

"Does it look right?" Artie inspected the shape anxiously. She'd done a bit of reading about the two algorithms, but she hadn't been able to penetrate most of the mathematical descriptions she'd read.

He met her eye for a moment. "You should probably stop thinking in terms of right and wrong, Artemis. This is entirely theoretical."

"So what terms should I be thinking in, then?"

"Probable and improbable," he said, shrugging.

"What do the axes represent?"

"Okay," he said. "X and Y are just geographical coordinates, so you can think of the oval shape as the simple distribution of viruses all over the radius of your collection area. The program is displaying this as a perfect oval, since we're looking at averages here, but it could just as well have been projected onto a scale map of Kent. In fact..." He clicked a few buttons and semi-transparent satellite map appeared over the donut, a blur of greens and greys intersected by a tracery of roads and railway lines. With another click, small red dots sprouted up across the space. "Those are the precise spots where each cat was located."

"Got it," Artie said, as Simon removed the dots and the map with another tap at the keyboard. "And the Z-axis...the height of the oval?"

"That's the trend of variation," he said. "How much the different mutants are distributed in the cat population, and how infectious the model thinks they are. It's flat now because this timepoint is 2010... the beginning of your study. You didn't have that many different signatures then."

"We've run out of axes," Artie said. "How do we compare over time?"

"Time is our fourth dimension... like a video, from the past to the present. Watch."

He clicked a few keys, and then the donut began to wave and wiggle. But the movements were minor, and by the end of the video, which took only about ten seconds, the overall shape was not much changed from the original.

"Hmmm. Not what I would expect from a mutable virus, even if your theory wasn't true." Simon ran the video again, then a third and fourth time. Then he gave each snapshot in time its own color, and superimposed the lot. It almost perfectly overlapped.

"Well?"

"Nothing's really happening," he said. "No evidence of mini-epidemic spread over what's entrenched... no evidence of much significant variation at all. I'd have to run the calculations, but I doubt those fluctuations are statistically significant."

Artie felt the beginnings of a huge wave-crash of disappointment cresting overhead.

"This had all been a huge waste of your time, hasn't it?" she said.

He looked at her, surprised. "We've only just started. And I never thought this particular algorithm was going to be useful anyway, remember? It's just to make Henry happy."

"I'm sorry. It's just... I have absolutely no idea what any of this means. I'm not used to not being in control." Feeling the shame of a star pupil caught out not doing her homework, she resolved to take another stab at digesting those impenetrable articles about the two algorithms until everything made sense.

"Mathematics has that effect on a lot of people," he said. "Just relax and let me do the driving."

"I'll try."

There was a beep from the computer.

"The La Fontayne is finished," he said. Artie thought she could hear excitement under his matter-of-fact tone. "Let me split the screen and we can look at the two models side by side."

A few seconds later, there were two donuts rotating in space, the green on the right and a new, red one on the left.

"They look the same," she said, utterly deflated.

"Not surprising, as this is the starting point," he said. "2010. Both algorithms will display an identical time zero. The changes you're predicting can only be seen through time—and this is where the algorithms differ. Let me run the fourth dimension."

And the two donuts were off, rippling and wobbling as before. But something happened immediately to the red shape on the left: small domes began to sprout all over its top surface like goose bumps. The domes grew taller over the course of the video, so that by the end, the donut resembled a hilly landscape. A few of the domes were much taller than all the others, starting to flatten out like buttes.

"Well, well," Simon said. He ran the video again, watched the bumps grow from the donut, then hit a few keys that made the video run much slower. "Very interesting."

"What? What are those protrusions?" She was transfixed.

"They look like the beginnings of small epidemics," he said. He clicked a square around one of the larger domes and blew it up to about ten times its size, watched it twirl idly in space. At this magnification, Artie could see that it resembled an hour-glass more than a butte.

"But like no epidemic I've modeled before," he said. "Epidemics look like up-turned cones with algorithms like this."

"Like the lily shape of Henry's avian flu simulation," she said.

"Exactly. But maybe the underlying incidence of chronic infection is constraining the spread, altering the typical pattern."

"Are you saying my theory may be right?"

He zapped away the blow-up, then performed the keystrokes that would give each snapshot its own color. Tilting his head, he studied the resulting superimposition.

"I'm saying," he said, "that your theory, based on the data you've given me, and within the limitations of the La Fontayne model... is fairly *probable*."

"That's good, isn't it?" There was that feeling again—she was as green and ignorant as a new PhD student.

"I can't say for certain," he warned her. "Not before doing a lot of statistical calculations. And I can already see places where I ought to custom-refine the algorithm."

"You mean, fudge it?"

"Of course not." He frowned. "Any idiot can plug numbers into a model. The art comes from tailoring the program to the unique nature of the situation—and then using this to accurately predict future events. That's what takes the time and energy." He sighed. "And thanks to Henry, I've got to do precisely the same with the Meyerhof-Hernsley as well."

"So this is still just the beginning?"

He nodded. "And then I'll have to compare this shape to published patterns of other pathogens, run statistical comparisons on them. And we're going to need to plug in a lot more signatures... the more data, and the longer the time span, the better. And once we're happy, we can try to project forward in time... to predict what will happen next."

Artie thought about giving him more details about her new Minster mutants, which might very well serve as the icing on top of the proverbial donut, then decided it would better to wait until Fiona's sequencing confirmed what was going on.

"But yes," Simon summed up. "In answer to your initial question, I'd say it's looking very good indeed."

Artie felt the first stirrings of triumph. Already casting aside Simon's sober caveats, her thoughts were running ahead to publications, to conferences, to the look on Bud Fisher's face when she presented the final proof of her theorem to an astonished audience.

Simon had turned back to the screen in the meantime, and Artie watched as his hands moved on the keyboard and mouse, inspecting the La Fontayne donut from all angles, checking numbers, zipping back and forth from graph to spreadsheet. He seemed to have forgotten that she was there. This reminded her of the instinctive way he'd made those difficult decisions when they were assigning each virus a number, and of further back, when he'd filled page after page in an almost trance-like concentration during their first chat.

"Simon," she said. "Assigning the multivariates to each virus... even choosing the proper starting algorithm... there's an art to that, too, isn't there? I mean, not any idiot could do that properly either."

Even though his gaze remained on the screen, his profile took on a distinctly smug cast.

"No," he said. "They couldn't."

She suddenly realized, with a stir of uneasiness, what she'd just implied about Henry.

❧

IT WAS AROUND MIDNIGHT WHEN Simon escorted her through the main computer room of the warren.

"You'll get home all right?" he asked.

"I'll have to include a taxi section in the budget of my next grant," Artie joked, just as Henry turned around ponderously in his chair.

"Good evening, Professor Marshall," he said.

Artie replied in kind, realizing that her stance had altered subtly into a defensive posture. But Henry's rumble contained its usual mildness, and his eyes, when she took a quick glance, seemed calm and inquisitive, just as they'd been on the evening of their first exchange. One incident in decades, she reminded herself. And Ben had broken the rules.

"Have you found Simon's help to be adequate for your needs?" Henry asked, courteous and friendly. Beside her, Artie could sense Simon stiffening, his anger blooming up like a pulse of infrared.

"Very," Artie said, with extra emphasis. "I am thoroughly satisfied."

"Good." Henry nodded. "And the Meyerhof-Hernsley... how is it looking?"

Artie waited for Simon to step in, but he didn't. She turned her head slightly to meet Simon's eye, but his expression was too complex to interpret, and there was no guidance there. *Thanks a lot*, she thought with disgust.

"Actually, the La Fontayne seems more promising at the moment," she said recklessly.

Henry's left hand twitched and flopped as its owner gave another nod.

"And by what means do you conclude that?" Measured and reasonable, like a normal scientist engaged in a normal scientific conversation. Why, then, did his words feel like a trap?

"Well..." Artie looked at Simon again, but he was staring at the floor with the focus of someone trying to recite the alphabet in reverse: no help whatsoever. "His preliminary La Fontayne model projected evidence of the mini-epidemics predicted by my theory."

"And is it good practice to assume that the model fitting your favored outcome must therefore be the correct one?" Flop and twitch, twitch and flop. "Isn't it equally likely that your hypothesis is incorrect, and the Meyerhof-Hernsley is telling you so?"

"I suppose it is," Artie said.

He was absolutely right, of course. She felt ashamed, as if she were that fresh PhD student back in Boston, and Jasper was having a go at her for letting her irrepressible enthusiasm get in the way of proper methodology.

Simon cleared his throat.

"The Meyerhof-Hernsley is suspect, Professor, because it did not respond realistically in the time dimension," he said diffidently. "The Y-axis alterations seemed more reminiscent of a stable agent—which feline leukemia virus is not, regardless of her theory's soundness. I'm sure the comparative statistics will back up my initial impression."

"I want you to leave now," Henry said, in a tone so impossible to ignore that Artie, mesmerized, took a step towards the door before she realized she'd done so.

"Not you, Professor," the rumble clarified pointedly.

Silence fell then, until Simon ventured, "Surely it would be more effective for me to hear how you want us to proceed."

"Professor Marshall can brief you later."

Simon clearly wanted to protest further, but Artie knew he wasn't allowed to.

"I'd rather he stay as well," she said, flustered. Too flustered to lay on the charm as she should have done. "I don't have the vocabulary to transmit all your instructions."

"You'll manage," Henry said pleasantly.

"I'll be in my office," Simon said, looking at Artie significantly as he started towards the inner door.

"No," Henry said. "I want you to leave us completely."

"But..." Then he clamped his mouth closed, but not before fury and surrender had spilled over. And fear, Artie saw. He was afraid for her safety, and she wanted to reassure him, tell her she could defend herself—but at the same time, she longed to grab his skinny arm and whisper *Don't leave me alone with this crazy man!*

"I'll be fine," Artie said instead, and Simon left the room, with only a stiff caricature of his normal gait. A few seconds later, the door to B302 clicked shut, and Henry and Artie were alone.

Artie sank down onto one of the chairs at a monitor, the one furthest away from Henry's. It wasn't terribly far—maybe two meters. Yet again she had neglected to bring along her mobile phone—what on earth was wrong with her lately?

Seconds expanded into nearly a minute, all without Henry saying anything.

"Would you care to inspect the two models?" she finally blurted out, desperate to infuse some everyday briskness into the stagnant air of the room. "He's left them up on the screen in his office."

"I don't need to see the screen," Henry said.

"But you aren't even familiar with the data set," she said.

"Oh, but I am." Henry waved a hand behind him at his own screen, and Artie realized with a start that it displayed a copy of the spreadsheet that she and Simon had just spent hours so painstakingly filling in.

How long had he been monitoring their activities from his terminal? And just how aware was he when he was ostensibly "absent"? Artie found herself unable to speak.

"I do agree," he said, unexpectedly, "that the dynamics of the prototype La Fontayne currently appear more probable than those of the other model. But it would be premature to retire the Meyerhof-Hernsley without customizing its algorithm further."

"Simon explained that to me already," she said, stretching the truth somewhat. "He's being very cautious, truly."

"You don't know him like I do," he said. "He's clearly already decided that the Meyerhof-Hernsley is inappropriate, and I am worried that this bias will color all future manipulations of your valuable data set, Professor Marshall. Which would be a shame. After all, we only want to know the truth, do we not?"

This was sensible, Artie thought. And Henry was intimately familiar with Simon's intellectual behavior, so he was bound to know his weaknesses better than anyone.

"What do you recommend?" she said.

"Don't allow him to become lax with the Meyerhof-Hernsley. Insist on rigor— the same rigorous attention he will lavish on the La Fontayne. The same rigor that you have applied to all your own work in the past."

She nodded. How could it hurt? After all, Henry was far more experienced than Simon.

"I will, Professor," she said, starting to relax. Then, eagerly, "What did you make of those spikes in the La Fontayne?"

"They have a very intriguing shape," he conceded immediately.

Could he really picture those bumps from the raw data without having run the actual program? *Could* a human brain visualize something that complicated? Weren't some Asperger's patients also mathematical savants, like those famous "calculators" who could instantly tell you the day of the week of a date from the Middle Ages or tally up the number of bricks in a buildings in once glance? Or was it just simple genius—genius, and years of experience?

"Intriguing how?" She risked a quick glance at his eyes, which were still bright. He seemed to be thinking very hard.

"More I cannot say without seeing the effect of the boy's future customization. I will only step in as a last resort—he needs to learn."

"I understand," she said, not letting her own annoyance show.

"You must forgive him," Henry said. "He's very young and still has a long way to go. He's only been with me a short while, you know."

Henry has no concept of time, Simon had told her.

"There's nothing to forgive," Artie said. "I was the one plugging for a particular outcome. And Simon did caution me that it's too soon to know one way or the other."

"Very young," he said, as if she hadn't spoken. "At first I was convinced it was going to work out, but sometimes I worry he's not dedicated enough to finish his PhD thesis."

"He seems very dedicated to me," Artie said, hiding her shock. Simon would have finished his PhD ages ago, while she was still at Oxford. His title was *Dr.* on the Heatherfields directory, and Ben had also referred to him completing his doctorate.

"I've advised him not to spend so much time with her," he said. "But he has been resisting me."

"With whom?" Artie said slowly.

"With whom," Henry said, in an odd tone of voice. Odd, in a way that made Artie's skin contract. "With whom, with whom, with *whom*."

And then, just like that, a dullness crept over his stone-colored eyes, and after a few more seconds, he rotated back to his computer screen.

❧

ARTIE LET HERSELF OUT OF B302 into the empty corridor, slammed by nine layers of silent building pressing down on her. Dizzy, in fact, with a pressure in her ears that would be ringing if there were any component of sound in the sensation. But not panicked, thankfully. Just... unsettled.

With whom, with whom, with whom.

She found Simon sitting at her desk, dark head bowed and staring at his hands. When she opened the door he looked up, relief in a rush across his face.

"Thank goodness," he murmured. "Are you all right?"

"I'm fine, Simon." She came and dumped her stack of books onto one of the chairs, sat down on another.

"Well, at least it was quick," he said.

Was it? She felt as if she'd been in there for hours.

"I'm sorry, Simon. I should've tried harder to make him let you stay."

"No, I'm sorry," he said, indigo eyes solemn and uncertain. "I never dreamed he'd want to see you alone."

"Uncharted territory?"

He nodded. "Maybe you ought to stop coming. Now that I've got the bulk of the numbers, we can do quite a lot by email."

"No!" she said. "Not my style, Simon. I want a flesh-and-blood collaboration. There's no danger at all—he just wanted to talk, and I followed all the rules."

He slumped a bit in the chair. "What did he say about me?"

"Oh, Simon..."

"Let me guess." Anger played around his eyes, a cool blue fire. "He's warned you that I'm inexperienced, and that if I'm not watched carefully, I'll shirk on the Meyerhof-Hernsley."

Artie didn't reply—she didn't need to.

Simon smiled bitterly, shaking his head. "And you believed him, didn't you? You're going to side with him against me, aren't you?"

"It's not a question of belief, or sides..." she said, rather lamely.

"I knew it," he said, more to himself than to her. "You trusted me before, but it only took *two minutes* for him to turn you against me. And to think I was worried about you in there!"

"Simon, please just let me—"

"Let me tell you something, *Professor*," he said, shooting to his feet. "For the past decade, while Henry has been fiddling around with his hypothetical situations and his mathematical abstractions, I have almost single-handedly shouldered the burden of hundreds of important practical projects. Projects that work with real data, real situations, real dangers. Even though everyone assumes Henry's masterminding it, he isn't. Half the time he doesn't even register what's passed through my in-tray. I'm quite confident that I know far more about real-life epidemics that he ever will!"

"I don't doubt that," she said, starting to get annoyed herself. "Really. But look at this from my perspective. I don't have enough information to begin to take sides."

Furious, he came around the desk and headed for the door.

"I've had enough of this," he spat out.

Artie raised her voice. "He's a mentally-ill oddball who's under the delusion that you're still writing your thesis, and you're a bitter, anti-social man who's afraid to leave his room! How in hell am I *supposed* to make the right choice?"

Simon froze with his hand outstretched towards the handle. Then slowly, he turned to face her.

"What did you say?" he said.

Artie stood up, crossed her arms and glared at him.

"You heard me. Just leave, Simon. We can talk about it tomorrow when I'm not quite so pissed off."

He dropped his hand, a look of intense concentration on his face.

"The part about the thesis," he said. "Did Henry actually say that?"

"He thinks you've just arrived in B302—you weren't joking when you said he doesn't understand time!"

"I meant clock time," Simon said, voice strained. "Minutes, hours. There's nothing wrong with his long-term memory."

"You're wrong, Simon. He thinks you're still a twenty-something student who spends too much time chasing girls."

"Girls?" He almost wilted against the wall, looking completely disoriented. In a low, urgent voice, he managed, "Did he say something... about *her*?"

"Just get out," she said, exasperated.

As soon as he was out the door, Artie regretted her behavior. She chased after him, intercepted him halfway to his room and took his arm. He shied away from her touch, but she kept her grip powerful and resolute. Skinny or no, his muscles felt surprisingly well-developed.

"Wait, please," she said. "I'm sorry."

He didn't say a word as she shoved him back to her office, impelled him into a chair, pawed through a desk drawer until she'd found the bottle.

"I don't drink," he said dully, finally noticing what she was doing.

"You do tonight," she said, splashing the single-malt into a coffee mug. She pushed it on him, stood over him like an administrating nurse watching a patient take his meds. He took a gulp and shuddered, took another, knocking it back like water. Satisfied, Artie refilled his cup, poured herself a more civilized finger and perched on her desk, watching him closely.

"It must've been a misunderstanding," he said at last, wiping his mouth with distaste. "He must've said that I'm as unreliable as I was *when* I was a student, writing up my thesis."

"There's nothing wrong with *my* memory."

"Amnesia isn't an Asperger's quality," he said stubbornly.

"Then there's something else going on, Simon," she said. "Be reasonable. He's aging. Maybe he's..."

"What?"

"Deteriorating in some other fashion."

"Deteriorating?"

"Losing it. Going senile."

He took another slug of drink and shook his head before looking down at the floor.

"Impossible," he muttered.

"He did something odd just before he switched off," Artie persisted. "He parroted back something I said in a completely nonsensical way. It was creepy."

She had still not put her finger on precisely why it was so creepy. It was part of the thing about Henry that she could not place.

Simon's head drifted up, reluctant to look her in the eye. "He's been doing that with me as well."

"You already told me his judgement is deviating from yours. Any other changes recently?"

He nodded grudgingly. "Some bizarre behaviors—nothing major, but nothing I've ever seen from him before."

"And talking to me in the first place—it could be related."

"Yes, I suppose." He put the cup unsteadily on the floor. "But it could very well be nothing, Artemis. Stress, or..."

"Maybe he needs a medical check-up."

"Maybe." This seemed to remind him of something, and he looked at his watch. "I've got to get Henry home."

"Simon—what about this woman? What was Henry talking about, and why were you so upset?"

He got heavily to his feet, put a hand against the wall. The alcohol appeared to have hit him hard.

"It was a long time ago," he said.

"Tell me."

"I'm late, Artemis."

"Was it a girlfriend?"

His face began to slide, a long, slow transformation until not a millimeter of emotion remained.

"Fiancée," he said.

Artie found that she was holding her breath and let it go.

"What happened to her?"

He just shook his head and stumbled out, leaving her with a feeling of tremendous foreboding. She sat at her desk long after he'd gone, hand on the telephone to ring a cab and unable to find the energy to raise it to her ear.

ARTIE LAY IN BED LATER that night, long since slid from linear thought into the tangled back-and-forth, remembering-and-forgetting storyline of waking dreams. From the repeated playback of the unsettling episode with Henry, and the subsequent argument with his protégé, she had segued into the sheer unfathomability of Simon Renquist having ever been engaged to anyone. And from this, it was probably inevitable: she found her own memories pressing in of that first night at the Beehive: the jolt when Calvin had looked up from his vodka tonic, eyes widening at the sight of her.

There he was, preserved inside her head as solidly as a deformed embryo in form-aldehyde: crimson tie loosened, white collar in disarray, silver cuff-links unhinged, hair ever so slightly mussed. He was dressed in a way she would normally despise, like a man who dealt with money for a living, yet his cavalier off-duty desecration of the expensive suit struck her as almost bohemian in effect. Even then, how could she have missed the edge of alcohol that lubricated the entire persona? Calvin the professor, the philosopher, the charming and reassuring clinician, still in control most evenings—this was the man who had wooed her as she sat down next to him, heart pounding inside her ribcage and entirely unprepared for what was to come next.

"What a lovely name," Calvin said—the post-introduction salvo. There was some-thing feral about the curve of his smile that Artie had found more sexy than perilous, back then. "But is it apt?"

"You tell me."

She sipped her pint, trying to calm herself. The two of them seemed to be an-chored in a bubble of sudden seclusion against the pub noise raging around them.

"Physically, no," he replied. "Most artists render Artemis as boyish, with hard lines. Leochares' Diana of Versailles in marble; Houdon's bronze; Titian's painted representation with Callisto—none are even remotely like you." He tilted his head, continuing the inspection. "Really, they ought to have called you Aphrodite."

"Psychiatrists shouldn't make the mistake of judging people by their appearance, should they?"

"I beg to differ: one begins outside and moves inward, one layer at a time."

"With respect, what good are even starting assumptions based on the superficial?"

He regarded her sudden anger with interest. "How you look will sculpt how the world responds to you, which will in turn influence how you react to the world. What you wear, for example, will speak volumes about the message you are trying to transmit."

Artie became aware of her oversized T-shirt and sloppy jeans, her unwashed hair. She somehow knew that he would be able to interpolate her curves despite the smokescreen, that all men could. The only person she was fooling was herself.

"Most research scientists dress like this," she said.

Another smile. "I know, I have to deal with them at committee meetings. But I am not convinced that your profession completely explains your sartorial choices."

"Well, go on. Enlighten me."

He downed the last of the vodka and swirled the ice in the bottom of his glass.

"This is only an educated guess, based on a snap assessment," he said, looking up from his glass to meet her eye. "But I suspect that you don't like the fact that you are beautiful and are trying as hard as you can to cover it up."

As heat flooded her face, he added, more softly, "But it's entirely futile, you know. Your disheveled façade only emphasizes how gorgeous you are. If you were made up, coiffed, coordinated, you wouldn't come across as half so raw and desirable. You look as if you've just been ravished—speaking as a professional, of course."

She had to laugh, when actually she was having difficulty breathing. "You could probably get struck off for a comment like that—if I were one of your patients."

"Then it's a bloody good thing you aren't," he said. "That was, by the way, quite an Artemisian response. You don't want to admit that I'm right, so you've gone on the offensive."

"It was either that or turn you into a stag."

"I do hope that you aren't as chaste as your namesake, though."

He was too quick for her—the perfect retort failed to materialize.

"Although if you are," he added, "the world's a safer place. I somehow doubt there is much defense that any red-blooded man could mount against your silver bow."

"Are you one of those?" she asked. "Red-blooded?"

He laughed. "In my spare time. I've just been promoted to head of the Department of Clinical Psychiatry, and nothing dampens the libido like a mind-numbing avalanche of bureaucracy."

Artie suspected that his libido was probably coping just fine despite the onslaught. At least, she very much hoped so.

"I'm still just a post-doc," she said. "But I plan on securing a permanent position by the end of the year."

The slant of his brow was skeptical. "You look a bit young for that—how long since your PhD?"

"Four years and a bit."

"I wouldn't get your hopes up, Artemis. The job market is fierce—you'll be competing against people who've been in the game for much longer."

"I'm not at all worried."

He nodded. "Yes, I can see that the goddess is undaunted." His eyes, a light shade of hazel, went thoughtful. "You're all guns blazing... superficially. But what's underneath?"

As he examined her, Artie got the feeling that her secret fears had floated up to the surface like a cloud of hawks responding to their handler's whistle. But it was strange: although she was speechless yet again, she didn't feel threatened by his insights. For someone with demons, what could be more comforting than the regard of someone who vanquished them for a living?

"We need more information," Calvin said, more to himself than to her. Then, seeing something over her shoulder, "Ah, the very thing!"

That evening, the pub had hired an attractive handwriting expert to amuse the clientele, circulating amongst them and analyzing samples of their script. Calvin waved her over, clearly delighted, as if she was a colleague at a psychiatric symposium instead of a thinly glossed fortune-teller.

"My friend here," he proclaimed, with that easy smile that could coax a gracious meal from the surliest of waitresses, "would like your learned prognosis of her temperament."

The woman proffered her Artie her clipboard, asking in her gentle Edinburgh lilt to write a sentence about how she was feeling precisely at that moment. There was something about the ethereal grey of the woman's eyes and the intensity of the last few minutes that had thrown Artie off balance: she gripped the pen, blocked by embarrassment.

"I don't know what to write." She looked imploringly at the analyst so that she wouldn't have to look at Calvin, this complete stranger who so quickly had got the upper hand. But before she could respond, he leaned close, warm breath vibrating the delicate hairs inside her ear: "Let go, Artemis. Don't think of anything: just write the first thing that comes into your head."

"But I—"

"You think too much. You need to listen to your subconscious."

Slowly, as if possessed, she watched in astonishment as the lines of ink unspooled beneath her hand:

I am falling.

She stared at the full stop: a point receding into the distance. As the analyst retrieved her clipboard and studied the sample, lips moving with some rehearsed platitude, Artie felt Calvin's palms, shockingly warm, slide around her waist, his lips brush her neck, the bloom of desire submerge her.

"Don't worry," he said. "I'll catch you."

CHAPTER 6
Jaunts, Ruses, Confessions and Confusions, Assorted

THE NEXT MORNING, THE PHONE'S jangle dislodged Artie from a fug of sweating, restless nightmares.

"I didn't mean to wake you," Mary said. Her cheerful tone conjured up an image of the veterinary surgery: sun blazing through the window onto a pleasantly messy desk, a tranquil day with nothing more than a docket full of dogs, cats, birds and rabbits to look forward to. Discrete little furry or feathery problems and a minimum of trauma. No abusive husbands, no dark basements, no crazy domineering mathematical wizards or twisted apprentices arrested in development—just real life, comfortably mundane.

For the first time in years, Artie did not look forward to going to work.

"I should've been at the lab by now," she told Mary, squinting suspiciously at the alarm clock. Had it failed to go off, or had she beaten it into submission while still unconscious?

Over the phone, she heard something that sounded like a squawking parrot, then a glissando of female laughter in the background.

"I'm calling because there have been a few more suspicious cat deaths on Sheppey. Same clinical signs, same neighborhood."

Artie sat up, fully awake. "How many?"

"Five," Mary said. "All ELISA-negative like the first ones. Freddie's got his hands full."

Still clutching the phone, Artie kicked off the sheets, padded into the kitchen and started fussing one-handed with the kettle, all the while carefully listening to Mary's detailed account of each case. Suddenly she had an idea.

"Do you have plans for your half-day today?" Artie said.

"Actually, no. What do you have in mind?"

"Can I come visit? I want to see this for myself... and meet Freddie-the-vet, if possible. I could pick up the new samples, which would save you a trip... and we may have some preliminary results by this afternoon that I can share with you both."

"I'd love to see you—provided that white wine and a sunny terrace are part of the package. I can't speak for Freddie, but I'll give him a ring. I'm off at one—you can meet me at the surgery."

After Artie hung up, she made a cup of coffee and rang the office.

"Marshall lab," Mark said, and Artie experienced a little thrill. How many years had she answered the phone using the same convention, wondering how it would feel to hear her own name coming out of someone else's mouth?

"I must be late, if you're in already."

"Artie," he said, snapping out of his indolent drawl. "Everything all right?"

"Fantastic," she said. "Listen, Mark, how do you fancy a little trip this afternoon?"

SIMON OPENED HIS EMAIL AND was confronted by a message from Artemis Marshall. He saw that it had been sent about ten minutes after he'd slunk out of her office the night before, dull with embarrassment and the effects of that vile liquor—effects he was still feeling like a nauseous fog. He felt like deleting the message without even bothering to open it, but that was the sort of strong, vindictive thing that diarist-Simon would do. The real Simon had no sense of self-preservation, couldn't resist any opportunity for yet more humiliation. She was going to pry now, manipulate the sordid details out of him, and he wasn't going to be able to resist.

But the message was a lot more succinct than he had expected:

Dear Simon,

I apologize for those terrible things I said about you. It was wrong of me. And I wanted you to know that I do trust you.

-A.

Well. She was the consummate opportunist, he thought. Keeping her options open, playing both sides until she got the data she needed for her project. He had made the mistake of trusting her, and he wasn't going to do it again. It was only the alcohol, and his uneasiness about Henry's health, that had made him say what he'd said. From now on, he would ensure that science was the sole topic under discussion.

The third phone rang then. Simon almost considered not answering: the thought of speaking with Brees with a hangover was utterly unappealing.

"What is it," he said irritably into the receiver.

"Has the Professor had a chance to review our initial report?"

"Yes," Simon lied.

"Good, because it's spreading, Dr. Renquist. Three more patients reported ill, and the first case is in a critical condition. Initial indications from the associated lesions suggest foot-and-mouth disease. No doubt you saw it on the evening news last night."

"No," Simon said. "I must have missed it." In fact, he never bothered to keep abreast of the petty concerns of the outside world. "FMD virus doesn't cause serious symptoms in humans, does it?"

"Not natural foot-and-mouth, no, and these people haven't been anywhere near livestock. Plus there haven't been any afflicted animals in the UK for over a year—that's why we're concerned."

"I understand." Simon was already reaching for the code apparatus.

"There's been some recent chatter on monitored Islamic social media channels about a bioterrorist attack planned for somewhere in South East England," Brees said. "We've got lots of people on this, but perhaps you could ask the Professor to focus on Mother Nature."

Mother Nature—their patented suite of algorithms designed to determine, based on epidemiological characteristics, whether an outbreak was natural or manmade. It happened to be one of the specialities of Renquist and Manfield. Far more Renquist than Manfield, as it happens—not that Henry would admit, or anyone else would believe.

"You're going to need far more than four cases to—"

But Brees had already hung up.

Simon sighed, heartily sick of dealing with idiots who didn't understand mathematics.

∿

ARTIE DRAGGED HERSELF INTO THE institute by half past ten and found Mark and Fiona in the lab, huddled over Fi's desk in the corner.

"Plotting my overthrow?" Artie said. They looked around, and she caught a glimpse of a DNA sequencing report spread all over the desk. "Please tell me the news is good."

"Good… and weird," Mark said, inspecting her closely. "Another late-night rendezvous?"

"Yes," Artie said, giving him an *I'll-brief-you-later* look. "What've you got?"

"Feline leukemia virus," Mark said. "Indisputably. There's only one major dominant provirus integrated in all of the samples, and we've assembled perfectly clean sequence from the Pol gene. And we know why the Gag primer pair gave that extra-large band."

"An insertion? What is it, a direct repeat or something?"

Fiona pushed a sheaf of papers at her. She didn't look happy. "It's bizarre, Artie. There's a bit of feline immunodeficiency virus stuck in there."

"Come again?" Artie blinked down at the report, which was a routine sequence comparison, chains of nucleotide base pairs lined up in rows. "What do you mean?"

"Here," Mark said, pointing out a place highlighted with yellow pen. "This is a hefty chunk of the FIV Gag gene, inserted into the FeLV Gag gene… you can even see a short stretch of homology at the junctions that probably facilitated the swap."

"Weird is right," Artie said. "What do you reckon, Mark?"

"I vote for lab contamination," he said, giving Fiona an apologetic look. "Then a recombination during the PCR itself. Fiona used the FIV Petaluma strain plasmid as a control in the same experiment, so it could have made its way into some of the other tubes."

"No way," Fiona said sullenly. "My stuff is *clean*. I've never had a PCR contamination in my life."

Artie looked at Mark. "Have you ever heard of a PCR polymerase jumping onto junctions this short?"

"No," he admitted. "But it's the most likely explanation."

"Whereas FeLV," she said, "has been reported to have picked loads of foreign genes with stretches of sequence this limited, or even shorter."

"No one has ever reported a natural hybrid recombinant between FeLV and FIV before," Mark said. "If it were possible, you'd think it would have happened before now."

"There has to be a first time for everything, Mark. FIV and FeLV often infect the same cat, and they'd both be replicating in T-cells, with the potential to swap parts..." Her mind was already racing, thinking of Mary's description of the unusually virulent nature of the Minster virus. "Besides, I could buy a PCR jumping incident in one tube, but we saw the same insertion in all three, didn't we? What are the odds of that?"

"Billion to one, I'd say." Fiona said, looking pointedly at Mark, who shrugged. "What should we do next?"

"Just to be sure, let's redo the Gag region with different primers, see if it's an exact match with the Petaluma control."

"Right," she said. "Bet you twenty quid it isn't, Mark."

"You're on."

"And," Artie said, "while you're working on sequencing the entire virus, do some PCRs to see if you can find any evidence of FIV lab contamination in the original cat preps—or in your stock solutions."

"No problem," she said.

"And if there isn't?" Mark said.

"There won't be," Fiona said, glaring at him.

"Then the story just became a lot more interesting." Artie paused, thought of something. "What about the case of the missing Envelope gene? Have you sequenced through there as well?"

"It was a real mess," Fiona said, handing her one of the printouts. "Most of the primers don't seem to have recognized the template, and our most downstream forward primer that did was too far away—only just cleared the splice acceptor. The old machine upstairs isn't that brilliant for getting long sequences. I had to order new primers... we won't know until next week."

"Did you manage to get any PCR clones?" Artie asked.

"Yup—lots of colonies today. I'll work them up as quickly as I can, but I doubt my mate will fast-track us again on the sequencing so soon. I don't want to push it—but hopefully we'll have some results early-ish next week."

Mark followed Artie into the office.

"You really think it's bona fide recombination between FeLV and FIV?" he asked.

"I don't know, Mark. I do agree it's unprecedented—but then, this virus is nasty."

She felt a stir of uneasiness. *Freddie's got his hands full,* Mary had said. And a few days ago: *the man's got endless enthusiasm when it comes to poking around the innards of a dead cat.* But then she pushed this irrational fear aside—there were no known cases of any human getting naturally infected with either FeLV or FIV, and those few cases of lab accidents reported had not resulted in any disease.

❧

ARTIE HAD ASSUMED THAT SHE and Mark would be taking the train to Gillingham, but Mark disappeared before lunchtime and returned with a surprise.

"Will it offend your principles to be chauffeured around in this baby?" Mark patted the roof of the Fiat 1500 convertible. "And by a man, no less?"

"Hell, no." Artie put on a proper show of feminine admiration as Mark unlocked the doors, less ironic than she wanted to admit to herself. "It's beautiful, Mark. And a road trip is precisely what I need."

He didn't know the half of it. On top of her initial reluctance to come to work and her unorthodox decision to skive off half the day, the sight of Heatherfields' brooding bulk on the hillside had inspired a strange sensation of dread.

"Feeling restless?" Mark met her eye before they swung inside.

"Claustrophobic, more like."

Mark jetted out the exit, heading for the M25. It was wonderful to feel the air blast through her hair, buffet her skin and pull at her clothing. She dug her sunglasses out of her backpack and wished she had a scarf to wrap glamorously around her head like in the old Hollywood films.

"Any particular reason?" he asked eventually, voice raised to be heard over the wind.

"It's the batty epidemiologists—they're starting to get to me."

"Really, how?"

"They're just so... abnormal. It sort of intensifies my own insecurities."

This bit came out before she even knew she felt that way, but as soon as she said it, she knew it was true. Being around Henry and Simon was as troublesome, in its own way, as being around Calvin. Simon's dark oppression and Henry's odd behavior: she didn't know which was worse.

"It's got to the point," she said, "that hanging out with you, on the road in broad daylight...it's a relief."

"Are you sure it's worth the trauma? They're not the only mathematicians in the world."

"Of course I'm—*shit*." Artie put a hand to her forehead. "I can't believe I forgot to tell you the first result of our modeling!"

"You've got a result already?" Mark took a quick glance at her before refocusing on the road.

"I'm such a donkey," she said. "It was late last night, but then I overslept, and Mary told me about the new cases, and I came in to news of the possible FIV recombination..."

"I understand," he said quickly. "Just tell me now and all is forgiven."

As Artie launched into the story of the La Fontayne, her heart filled with renewed excitement, a buzz that synergized with the sunshine, the warm wind, the feel of the powerful little engine and the prospect of a Friday afternoon off. The basement now seemed like a distant nightmare.

After she'd finished speaking, Mark was quiet for a while, thinking, as they sailed over the QE2 bridge. To the right, they'd left the grey outskirts of London far behind, and to the left the Thames swept eastward, looping toward the Estuary region through industrial wastes and docklands. In the distance, the North Downs were dark purple smudges behind a summer haze, but the rest of the sky was clear. The weather had been beautiful for weeks, breaking all sorts of records.

"The X and Y axes are map coordinates, did you say?" he finally asked.

"More or less."

"And some of the spikes were much bigger than the others?"

"That's right. I should've asked for a printout."

Mark drummed fingers on steering wheel. "Maybe you ought to have found out exactly where those bigger spikes were located. Could one of them have been centered over..."

"Sheppey?" Artie said slowly. "Mark, you're a genius. Why didn't I think of that? He even superimposed a map over the top for a few moments, but I didn't think to ask."

"Maybe because I'm not juggling fifteen million other items in my head at the same time. To say nothing of trying to conquer the universe."

"Mmmm." Artie was distracted, playing with the idea for a while before tossing the ball back to the driver's seat. "What if this hypothetical Minster mini-epidemic has an unstable characteristic?"

"What do you mean, unstable?"

"You know, like being particularly prone to recombination."

"Prone how?" he said, looking into the rear-view mirror before overtaking a line of cars. Mark was one of those drivers who maneuvered so smoothly and carefully that it wasn't easy to tell how fast the car was actually going. Artie was elated by the speed, by the rush of acceleration pressing her against the seat. She kept catching glimpses of the muscles of Mark's arms flexing with the driving, the veins twisted like cord across the muscled surface of his skin.

"Well," she said. "Say there's a subpopulation of viruses with a mutation in the Reverse Transcription gene... a mutation that makes the protein more sloppy, more likely to jump around during replication, recombine with the wrong templates. Like a messed-up copy machine that spits out defective copies."

"Have you heard of that sort of mutation before?"

"I seem to recall reading something about HIV... but anyway, just say, for the sake of argument."

"Okay, go on."

"When Fiona sequenced our new samples, did she see any unusual mutations in RT?"

"I can't recall exactly." Mark thought for a moment. "The sequence generally matched pretty closely to the FeLV-A/Glasgow strain, but now that I think about it, I'm pretty sure she didn't get that far into it. We weren't trying to get a full stretch, you know... just far enough to confirm it was really FeLV."

"OK. But that could be easily done. I don't suppose you remember if any of our older Sheppey samples had Snip signature mutations in the RT gene?"

"No, I don't," he said. "I can check the database once we're back in the lab, but I suspect Snips wouldn't be thorough enough—we'd have to finish the detailed sequencing of our older samples to see if you're right."

"But if I am... it would be a great way to explain this whole Minster outbreak," she said. "A swarm of viruses infecting cats on Sheppey evolve a mutation that makes replication more sloppy... this leads to lots more mutated viruses, which might confer an advantage, allowing them to escape the immune system, get access to more cats..."

"Which starts to register as a spike of spreading variation in the computer model..."

"And then—*zap*, one of these variants, which is particularly prone to recombining with alien sequences, picks up a bit of FIV and co-opts it into its own genome. And this turns out to be a particularly favorable but nasty combination—"

"And the Minster epidemic is born," Mark said, "inside one particularly unlucky cat."

"Cat Zero!"

"Who then spreads it onward to every other cat it encounters," Mark finished.

Artie fished her mobile out of her backpack. "I can't relax until I find out if one of those big spikes is centered on Sheppey. Let me call Simon..." But then she dwindled off. "Damn, I still don't know his number."

Mark started to laugh. "Forget it, Art. Later's soon enough—don't let them spoil our adventure."

"You're absolutely right," she said, putting away the phone and reaching over to turn up the music. "No more talk of batty epidemiologists for the rest of the day."

◠

MARK, MARY AND ARTIE STOOD in the car park of the veterinary surgery, heat radiating from the asphalt.

"I can't believe I'm about to waste my half-day obsessing about feline leukemia with the pair of you," Mary said. But she didn't look at all put out, Artie thought—in fact, she looked almost too pleased.

"You're probably the only person I know small enough to fit in the back of the Fiat," Mark said.

Mary cast a longing glance at the little red car. "I've got a professional get-together in Canterbury this evening—completely the opposite direction. Better if we make our way to Sheerness in two cars."

"It's absolutely no problem," Mark said. "I love any excuse to drive. We can drop you wherever—unless Artie's in a hurry to get home."

"Definitely not," Artie said, thinking of her empty house.

"Then you'll be able to drink at your bash—take a cab home," Mark said.

"Actually," Mary said, "I was sort of hoping to cajole Freddie into accompanying me to the party."

"Two cars it is," Mark said. "Far be it for me to stand in the way of vets on the prowl."

"Why didn't you tell me about this before?" Artie asked Mary when Mark was out of earshot, checking something under the bonnet.

"Nothing to tell," she said placidly. "*Yet*. But he's charming, and we get on well. He's just a bit shy."

"Can't wait to meet him," Artie said.

"We were lucky he agreed to bunk off early," Mary said. "He's a workaholic. It was the prospect of meeting you that did it, Art—he's read all your papers."

"Don't worry, Mare, I'll steer well clear."

Soon Artie and Mark were following Mary's Toyota down the A2.

"She drives like my granny," Mark grumbled, braking yet again. "A woman heading for a rendezvous with her beloved shouldn't be doing *under* the speed limit."

"Don't tease her about him when he's around, Mark."

"Give me credit for a bit of subtlety."

"Unlike Mary's colleagues... did you see how they were fawning over you during the surgery tour?"

He made a face. "Not my type."

"What is your type, Mark?"

She looked over and saw that he was now smiling, eyes fixed on the road ahead.

"Trade secret," he said. "Isn't that our turn-off?"

They lapsed into silence as the two cars turned onto the A249 toward the Isle of Sheppey. Artie had never been in the area before, and though she'd expected the desolate stretches of industrial wasteland, much of the land spread before them still retained the flavor of Kent—green fields and gently curved hills rolling off into the haze. It was an unsettling combination, she thought. The wind had become much fiercer and tasted of the sea as it buffeted the car, flattened the rippling fields of grass, buttercup and clover.

"Is that the bridge onto the island?" Mark said, lifting a finger from the steering wheel, "or a very poorly executed Communist monument?"

"Don't be such a snob," Artie said, taking in the stark concrete monstrosity which flanked another, more modern-looking bridge. "I think it's got... character."

Mark emerged from his contemplative mood then and began to poke gentle but relentless fun at various details of local color, making Artie laugh and then feel guilty for doing so. They followed Mary's car across the bridge and up into the hills, until the shops and terrace rows began to take on a shabby, run-down appearance. Soon they were parking at a small vet surgery in the outskirts of Sheerness.

"I thought you wanted an al fresco lunch," Artie said to Mary as she locked her car, and Mark took in the surroundings with interest.

"That plan went out the window when Freddie insisted on showing you his lab," Mary said. "As you may have noticed, Sheppey's not big on terrace culture."

"No shortage of bait and tackle shops, though," Mark murmured.

"Behave, Mark." Artie elbowed him as a smiling man emerged from the surgery: Freddie-the-Vet himself. He looked like a farmer: blue denim shirt, big hands, windburnt face, sun-bleached brown hair. And healthy—no evidence of any virulent infections. Which would be impossible anyway, she reminded herself sternly.

"Lovely to see you, Mary," the man said, leaning down to give her a kiss. Mark took his turn to dig an elbow into Artie's side, and she stepped firmly on his toe.

"And *very* pleased to meet you at last, Artemis." Freddie stuck out his hand. She expected a laborer's chapped skin to go with the rest of the look, but of course she contacted only smooth professionalism. She introduced Mark, and then Freddie's eyes fixed back on hers with keen energy. "You've no idea how thrilled I am that you're taking an interest in our little outbreak."

"We're the ones who should be thanking you," Artie said. "For the samples. And for today—are you sure you can spare the time?"

"It's been slow," he said. "Kamini can handle the last few cases. But do please come in, and let me show you my lab... I've been worried my facilities are too primitive to have preserved the samples properly..."

"Don't believe a word he says," Mary said. "Just you wait."

"The samples were perfect," Artie said, and Freddie's sudden anxiety flitted back into a smile. Artie could see then what Mary saw in him: there was something very appealing about the intensity of his attention, about the way his emotions were so close to the surface.

Freddie ushered them enthusiastically through the main entrance. Through a door to the side, Artie saw a waiting room populated by an elderly lady clutching a birdcage and a man with a dog sprawled listlessly on his lap. A tortoiseshell cat suddenly appeared, leaping up with effortless fluidity onto a side table heaped with well-thumbed magazines. Whether patient or surgery mascot, Artie couldn't tell, but the animal was clearly in peak physical condition.

Freddie gestured for the group to precede him to the reception desk at the other end of the foyer, where a woman was looking up from her computer with a smile.

"This is Kamini Banga," Freddie said. "My partner in the business."

"Freddie has talked of nothing else but you for the past week," Kamini said after everyone had been introduced. Her hand rested with easy grace on a formidable pile of paperwork. "Have you solved the mystery yet?"

"Not exactly," Artie said. "But we do have some clues."

"Good," Kamini said, "because he's going to be absolutely useless until you've sorted it."

Freddie led them into another room behind the desk, and Artie stopped short when the scene hit her: a veritable arsenal of high-tech laboratory equipment glittering softly under the fluorescent lights.

"Hey, cool," Mark said, crowding in behind her.

Freddie looked about, half proud, half apologetic. "I pick up stuff cheap when small start-up biotech companies go out of business," he explained. "Two in the nearby bioscience park in Sittingbourne have folded in the last six months alone. If you're alert, you can even score freebies."

"Is that legal?" Artie asked, amused.

Freddie shrugged. "Disgruntled ex-employees are happy to spread the wealth when the bickering shareholders are distracted with more important things, like trying to murder one another... especially consumables, which are almost impossible to trace."

"Not sure why you bothered sending the material to us," Mark said, sticking his nose into an open Sorvall centrifuge, giving its shiny rotor a spin. "Some of these models are swankier than ours."

"Well... I don't have a PCR machine yet. I'm saving up, mind..."

"Now I know what to get you for Christmas," Mary said.

"Nor sequencing, of course. I'd have to contract out, and that would get pricey."

"Freddie," Artie said. "Do you by any chance have any plasmid DNA in this lab? Say, FIV plasmid? Anything that might have contaminated those latest samples Mary brought us?"

"Oh, goodness no," he said. "I can't afford to do much molecular work here. Sometimes I type genomic provirus using Southern blot and non-radioactive detection methods, though. It's a little hobby of mine."

"Southern blots?" Mark said. "That's so retro it's almost cool again."

"How do you probe your Southerns without plasmids?" Artie asked.

"My mate in America sent me some short probes when he asked me to troubleshoot his new kit. FIV, and FeLV as a control."

"Have you typed the samples you sent us?" Mark asked, running an envious finger over one of the stainless steel digital water-baths.

"Yes." Freddie hesitated. "But I seem to have had a few technical problems."

"What do you mean?" Artie said.

"Well, when the FeLV and FIV tests both came up negative on the ELISA strips, I thought I'd confirm it by Southern blot," he said. "But the thing was... they came up positive for both."

"It's not so unusual to find cat infected with both viruses," Mary said.

"Yes, but the patterns were all wrong," Freddie said. "And the same funny pattern in the first three cases and the next five dead cats—the ones you haven't looked at yet. It must be some stupid mistake I'm making."

Mark and Artie exchanged glances.

"Show us," she said, keeping her voice calm.

"Really, Artemis, it's not likely to..." He dwindled off and started rummaging in a filing cabinet until he'd pulled out a few translucent grey X-ray films.

"You got an X-ray film developer in this place?" Mark said incredulously. "We have to go up five flights of stairs!"

"Pets do break bones," Mary reminded him.

Freddie snapped on a wall-mounted light box and clipped a film on.

"Here's an old Southern signature I did on some routine Sheerness cases that were co-infected with FIV and FeLV," he said. "Note the pattern. Now compare to the Minster strain..." He clipped a few more films on, and pointed out how the arrangement of black bands was completely different.

"And these fragments your mate sent you as a probe," Artie said, "what were they?"

"Well, the Gag gene, of course, to match the test."

Mark put a finger on one of the superfluous black bands. "How much bigger would you say this band is from the Sheerness cases?"

"I can't afford decent size standards, but after five years of doing this, I don't need them," he said. "It's about five hundred base pairs too large."

"I rest my case, ma'am," Mark said, looking at Artie.

"Don't tell me my probes have contaminated all your samples!" Freddie said. "I was so careful!"

"No, not at all," Artie said. "You've just backed up our initial findings. The Minster virus appears to be a new hybrid recombinant between FeLV and FIV. That might explain why it's so virulent. We could be witnessing the birth of an entire new species."

"A new species..." Freddie trailed off, entranced.

Artie noticed that Mark was still studying the films with a frown.

"What is it, Mark?"

"I'm just wondering what's going on in the Envelope gene," he said, pushing the Sheerness film closer to one of the Minster films and squinting at the bands.

"I was wondering that as well," Freddie said. "Although I've probed for Gag, with the enzyme I've used to cut, you can work out the size of Envelope from the partially digested DNA up here. And it's completely wrong—have you found that too?"

"Actually, we haven't been able to PCR up or sequence the Env at all, so you're way ahead of us," Mark said. "It's funny—Southern blotting is so passé, you forget how useful it can be in certain situations."

"When you say the wrong size," Artie said, "do you mean bigger or smaller?"

"Bigger," Freddie said, showing them which band to compare. "It's huge, at least two kilobases longer than it ought to be."

Mark met Artie's eye. "I wonder what's inserted in there?"

"Did you save the actual blots?" she asked Freddie.

"Oh yes, they're in the freezer."

"Can we borrow them? We can re-probe them with a more extensive battery of fragments back at Heatherfields, see if we can figure out what's going on in the Env region."

"By all means," Freddie said. "I'll package them up with the new blood samples when you leave."

⌒

IT TOOK THE GROUP ABOUT an hour to exchange information and hammer out a future strategy. While Artie's team was busy dissecting the mysterious sequence changes in the Minster strain, Freddie and Mary proposed to broaden their sampling, checking in with more vets in the area to find out how far the new virus may have spread and alerting them to be on the lookout for the unusual symptoms.

"I've got a contact in Sittingbourne," Freddie said, "so we can see if it's got off the island yet."

"And we might want to consider contracting the Department for Environment, Food and Rural Affairs to see if they think it's worth posting a surveillance bulletin," Mary said.

"Might have better luck lower down with the Animal and Plant Health Agency," Freddie said. "DEFRA is a bureaucratic nightmare to deal with."

Mary looked at her watch. "I've got to run soon—that party in Canterbury. Are you coming, Freddie? I can give you a lift."

"Well, vet society socials aren't normally my thing," he mumbled. "Besides, it seems rude to abandon Artemis and Mark after coming such a long way. I was going to take them out to dinner."

"Actually, Freddie," Artie said. "It's very kind of you, but I've got to get back to the lab—a very important experiment I need to finish off."

"You're sure?" he said.

"How about it, Freddie?" Mary said.

When he hesitated, Artie ventured, "Sounds like an ideal opportunity to chat to an unusually high concentration of local vets. Get the word out about the Minster outbreak—widen our net."

His eyes widened. "You're absolutely right! Let me just box up those samples." As he scurried off towards the main part of the surgery, Mary threw Artie a look of thanks.

Five minutes later, Mark and Artie were zooming off down the hill, a polystyrene container full of frozen cat blood wedged into the back of the Fiat.

"I'm not really driving you back to the lab, am I?" he said.

"No, you're driving me off this god-forsaken island to a place with a proper restaurant." Artie paused. "That is, if you want to, and don't have other plans."

He started to laugh. "It's an eye-opener watching you in action, Artemis Marshall."

"What do you mean?"

"The way you mold the world to suit you."

"I was just doing a friend a good turn," she said, a bit stung. "And I suspect he secretly wanted to go with her, but was too shy."

"It wasn't a criticism, Art—and dinner sounds great," he said. "How about Rochester?"

"Very civilized," she said. "Any town with a cathedral is bound to offer more than kebabs for tea."

"Or bait," he said. "I know just the place, actually."

She looked over at him. "I didn't realize you were familiar with this area."

"I spent some time in Kent when I was younger."

"Where are you from, anyway? Your accent is all over the place."

"I moved around quite a bit," he said. "Is French cuisine acceptable?"

MARK'S RESTAURANT OF CHOICE WAS deckside of a boat moored in the River Medway. A fresh breeze came up as the sun angled downward, and staff circulated around lighting candles in glass globes. Almost in concert, streetlights on the shore flicked on, and passing boats lit up red and green. There was sensuous pleasure in the color of the dusk sky, the taste of grilled plaice and its accompanying fresh tarragon and rosemary, the tart Chardonnay in its cloudy-moist crystal glass. She was unusually aware of the heft of heavy cutlery and the fall of cloth napkin across her thighs, of the feel of her hair, wild from the open-topped journey and pushed back from her forehead with sunglasses, of Mark's hands, manipulating knife and fork like precision instruments. The background was alive with sounds: the tinkles and pops of ice melting in the water glasses, the flapping of flags, the scolding of seagulls, the creaking of the timbers beneath her chair, the shouting of men in the dockyards.

Mark kept refilling her wineglass and asking questions about her experiences in Boston and Edinburgh, about Philip Cox, about why she had become a scientist.

Whenever she tried to probe him in turn, she found that before she realized what had happened, he had tickled the focus squarely back onto herself. For a woman who spent most of her time quizzing colleagues about their specialities, it was a rare pleasure to finally give in and just prattle on about her own life for a change. And Mark was so laid-back—his laughter came readily, generously, with no hidden points to score or harsh lessons to impart as had so often been the case with Calvin.

It was nearly dark by the time they got on their way. As they were settling into the car, Artie felt a little niggle of sadness. She knew she'd have a lab of ten people or more one day—because she couldn't imagine her success curve ever waning—but there was something satisfying about the smallness of the operation now, something cozy and uncomplicated. Lab outings like this would never be so intimate or spontaneous in the future.

When they were crossing the bridge over the Medway, Mark said, "Are you in a hurry to get home?"

"Not at all." Artie stretched her legs out, feeling dreamy and content with the effects of the food and wine. "Why?"

"There's a great stretch of road out Cliffe way with some views over the Estuary."

"Sounds good to me." She was similarly reluctant for the evening to end, aware that it wasn't as simple as not wanting to be alone. "Can we go very fast?"

"That was the idea," he said, revving the motor to make her laugh.

When they'd turned north toward Cliffe, Mark sped up even more, and the air flowing over them became chilly.

"Cold?" he said, reading her mind.

"No, I'm fine."

"Are you sure?" He snaked his left arm around the back of his seat and produced a blanket. "There'll be no need for this, then."

"Well, maybe a little cold."

"You don't always have to act so tough, you know."

"I wasn't." She wrapped herself gratefully in the blanket. "The truth is, I didn't want to complain and force you to feel all gentlemanly and have to put the top up— which would be a crime on such a gorgeous night."

"That it would," he said. "I miss real driving. I used to tear down this very road when I first got my license."

The song on the radio ended, and the local news came on—something about a person who'd contracted a novel form of foot-and-mouth disease in the area. Mark reached over and switched it off.

"Where were you living?" she asked.

"In Higham." He jutted a thumb westward, then threw fingers toward the front. "The marshes were a great place to wander about wallowing in late teenage Dickensian angst—and this road didn't have speed cameras back then, of course."

"Not that they appear to be much of a deterrent now."

"A fine would be worth every penny tonight."

Studying him with peripheral discretion, she sensed an unusual joy in him then: his concentration was fully on the road, and the car flew under his hands, utterly controlled but somehow wildly reckless at the same time.

"If I hadn't been drinking," she said. "I would've asked you for a chance at the wheel."

"Next time," he said, and they fell silent.

The main road eventually ended, and Mark turned them into a small street, and then another, finally pulling into an empty car park fringed with dense brush. It looked like a point of departure for walkers and bird watchers; she could make out a rustic lavatory, a bulletin board and map, a wooden donation box in the gloom.

"Would you look at that," Mark said softly, turning off the engine to silence. "It's beautiful."

Following where his finger pointed, she saw it too: a bloated moon just over the Thames. A vast, orange, ominous moon, sending a smear of pale gold over the water; almost, she thought, as if time were unraveling and the sunset was rising in reverse. It was an incitement to mania and violence: a madman's moon. Secretly horrified, she registered a pressure behind her inner ears and, through it, the awareness that their surroundings weren't as silent as she'd originally thought. She could hear rustlings and twig-snappings, crickets and other insects, birds, occasional frog song, all leaching out from the shadowy blackness. Sounds that big city living had rendered astonishing and strange; sounds that reinforced the absence of human life.

Artie shrank against the leather upholstery, trying to will away her disquiet.

"Still cold?" Mark said.

"No... just feeling a bit lonely all of a sudden."

"Relax," he said. "You're with me, remember?"

He put his arm around her, and it didn't seem wrong at all to undo the seatbelt and move against him. And the not-feeling-wrong part confused her even more, because this time there wasn't the convenient excuse of tears to justify the contact, to allow her to file the episode under "Comfort, Collegial" and carry on as if nothing had changed.

Whatever was happening, she wasn't in control of it—and Artemis Marshall did not like relinquishing control. For the moment, the heaviness of his arm and the warmth of his body served as mere solace, but all that was needed was a breath, a particular word, a stray movement on either side for arousal to flare to life. This time, she wasn't sure she wanted to brush it aside.

"What are you thinking about?" She found her tongue at last, the words coming out almost defensively.

"I'm trying to remember the last time I saw a moon like this." A pause. "How about you?"

A ghostly birdcall floated out of the darkness, some solitary wader in search of companionship, or contemplating a border skirmish.

"Let me guess," he said, when she didn't reply. "You're trying to work out exactly what's going on here."

The glib answer she should have given wouldn't come. Instead, she felt her breathing speed up, intertwining with the forlorn birdsong as it pierced the night in staccato bursts.

"Or more accurately," he said, "your mind is frantically weighing dozens of different hypotheses and trying to come up with some sort of cunning strategy."

"That's not fair."

"I wasn't trying to be unkind—it's just the way you are." He gave her a squeeze. "It's one of the many things I like about you."

"Does this mean you aren't wondering what's going on?"

"No," he said. "In fact, you're doing my head in. But the difference between you and me is that I don't particularly mind being in that state."

She tried with force of will to tame her heartbeat, to squelch the flames—but it all ran on ahead of her, a stream of fear and desire bleeding out into the desolate night.

"I want you to tell me what's happening, Mark. Please. Because I haven't a clue."

His free hand came round and clasped her right hand; the contact made her realize it was shaking. He smoothed it palm down against her thigh, a simple movement that made her suddenly want to cry.

"You're going through a hard time," he said. "You're feeling vulnerable. We get along exceptionally well, and we find each other physically attractive. It's the most natural thing in the world—you don't have to feel afraid."

"I don't feel anything," she said. "The thought of being with anyone makes me ill, after Calvin. It's as if my heart is numb, but my body somehow missed the briefing."

"Just accept it, Art. They've got two different agendas at the moment. One day, with time, they'll merge again."

She hated this calm description of herself as being split down the middle, body from heart. How could he speak so calmly of being mutilated? But then she remembered that he was a man who didn't love: he was permanently mutilated. His own scar would be barely discernible. Or maybe it was more like a birth defect: effortlessly deformed from day one.

She let out a shuddering breath. "In what way am I doing your head in?"

He pressed his fingers between hers: an advance party, she suspected, of physical apology.

"You're sending out very contradictory signals," he said. "Unintentionally, I think."

"What sort of signals?" It was not the first time she had heard this accusation.

"Where do I start?" he said. "You're dripping in femininity, but you'd rather die than be treated like a woman. You act like you're invincible, but somewhere underneath, you're pleading for help—it eats at me until I can't help wanting to protect you. And this is hard on me, because I'm not usually one to intervene. And worse, when I try to help, you slap me down."

"Calvin used to hate me for just that."

"Please don't make assumptions," he said. "You think it's a crime not to be perfect—and maybe Calvin did too. But I actually like you far better for being mixed up."

"Mixed up... God, I don't know what's got into me. I don't want to be the type of lab head who preys on her employees. I swear to you that I never intended..."

"This isn't you being a *type*," he said. "This is very specific."

"Specific how?"

The bird's lonely song pierced the air again, refraining its ballad of love or hate, and Mark paused to listen before carrying on.

"I knew within five minutes of meeting you that we were going to be unusually close. Tonight's conversation was always going to happen in one form or another."

There was something so truthful about this that Artie felt herself relax against the seat, against him, letting go of a tension that she had been holding since he turned off the engine.

"And no one could accuse either of us of preying," he said. "Some things just happen."

"But I can't just let it happen, Mark. It wouldn't be right."

"Why not?"

"We're colleagues. I'm supposed to be your manager."

"Who's judging you, Artie? Salverson? The Inner Sanctum? Tavistock? Feminism as a whole?"

"Nobody." She sighed. "But it will all end in disaster. We'll quarrel. You'll quit— and probably Fiona as well, if it gets bad enough."

"Do you really think that's likely?"

"I don't know." The truth was that she found quarreling with Mark almost impossible to picture, but she couldn't bring herself to admit it.

"Maybe it would help to look at things from my perspective," he said. "My relationships with women have always settled somewhere on a long continuum of friendship. Unlike love affairs, friendships don't tend to end in disaster. If they end at all, it's a natural fadeout."

"I thought you'd been breaking hearts, Mark."

"Only those few who didn't understand the limitations of the relationship from the outset. Believe me, I wouldn't be taking this position if I didn't have a healthy respect for your powers of understanding."

"It just seems rash: we've been talking about a permanent scientific partnership. Do you really want to risk all that for a bit of meaningless sex?"

"Who said anything about meaningless?" His hand tightened around hers. "Just because I'm not in love doesn't mean I don't care."

"Sex changes things," she said, stubbornly. "Bonds start to form whether you want them to or not."

"It's too late: we already have a bond. Sex would only hasten the inevitable." He sighed. "Anyway, I wasn't necessarily proposing sex. The point is that there are no rules. If you just feel like being kept company, or looked after... or if you need a hand with the divorce, I'd like to help you."

"I'm absolutely fine on my own." She disentangled her hand and looked away, but found herself unable to look the moon in the eye.

"How far did you actually get on that paperwork the other night?"

She stared straight ahead, feeling pig-headed. "I opened the envelope, all right?"

Mark began to chuckle, and Artie joined in, shaking her head and running fingers through her hopelessly tangled hair.

"Here's what I think," he said. "Your fear of being alone makes you afraid to follow through with the divorce, but the connection with Calvin is feeding your fear. This could perpetuate forever—you've got to break the cycle."

"How?"

"Use me as a placeholder," he said. "I can keep you company while you do what you have to do. And later..."

"What? What happens later, Mark?"

"You'll heal, move on, fall in love with someone, and I won't be offended. Promise." His fondness was so apparent that she felt like weeping again, just for a short second. "We'll be friends for life."

A grey moth fluttered past her face. She saw it as a contradictory signal, a testimony to the impermanence of things. In a few hours, it would be dead.

"It can't possibly be that simple," she said.

"It can. You just *make* it be, with the same ferociousness you apply to everything else in your life."

It was madness, and they both knew it. Yet Artie found herself mesmerized by the sensible brownness of his eyes. With a funny twist to his smile, he reached over and put his palm, briefly, on the side of her face. She closed her eyes, and in the few seconds before his fingers slid away again, she realized how much her body had been starving for physical tenderness. It wasn't desire; it was something else: she felt light, released. It was nothing like being in love, but she felt almost as close to him as if she were.

There are no rules. Thinking there were had only been a form of self-oppression, and Artie wouldn't tolerate oppression from anyone. Mark wanted to help her for his own unfathomable reasons, so she might as well use him to overcome Calvin, just as she used everything else that fell her way. And why shouldn't she? Who knew— maybe with him in her arsenal, she could even defeat her solitary demons altogether.

When she remembered herself and opened her eyes, she found Mark wearing his usual lazy grin.

"I'll take that as a yes," he said.

"A *conditional* yes—I still think sex would be a bad idea."

"Well, you could always go for the upgrade later."

Tucked under his arm, she could feel a rumble of unvoiced laughter in his chest. But underneath, his longing for her was a faint glow of radiation off his skin. It was as patient and measured as the man himself, yet with a layer of undeniable force underneath.

"I still don't really understand why you want this," Artie said. "If you don't mind me saying so, it's a little odd."

"I don't understand either," he confessed. "But I'm not going to think too hard about it."

Over his shoulder, the monstrous moon still floated there, perfectly patient. After all, it had been waiting for millennia.

Artie closed her eyes again and blotted it out.

CHAPTER 7
Cracks, Ones That Expand When You're Not Looking

SIMON COULD NOT BRING HIMSELF to go inside. He couldn't remember the last time he had failed to switch off his reading lamp and close his eyes precisely at half past midnight, and here it was, nearly two in the morning and he was still sitting in the back garden, staring at the sky. Something had got into him. The moon, perhaps. It filled him with a savage joy, the way it had changed color as it rose, shedding its blood-orange veneer for custard yellow, settling finally onto its present dusky grey. A fine mist, felt more than seen, hovered around his ankles and cloaked the shrubbery, and the grass was wet. He knew this because he had removed his shoes and socks and rolled up his trousers to the knee—another unorthodox activity. The grass was slick and cold and he thought he could detect tiny insects traversing the pale slabs of his bare shins, even though every time he reached down to brush them aside he found nothing there.

It must be the moon that made him want to do something crazy, like visit the corner shop, buy a bottle of whisky and drink the entire thing down. As unpleasant as he'd found Artemis' cupful of poison at the time, he could not deny the strong appeal of the blunted edges that had resulted, an appeal that had been lingering suggestively behind the focus of his work ever since.

Or maybe it wasn't the moon at all. Maybe it was the thought of her snide voice in his head: *What's the matter—past your bedtime?* He could hear her as clearly as if she were lounging on the grass in front of him, swishing her tail and preening her fur, using the same tone as when she'd said, *Aren't you allowed out into the corridors until after dark?*

And yet.

Despite his irritation at her provocations, he also felt a parallel triumph: this hotshot professor with her *Nature* papers and her independent existence *needed* him. The other night at the computer, she had trusted his judgement over her own, had deferred to his decisions with respect. Her limitations emphasized his strengths, and this gave him an indescribable feeling of power. There was no way that his competence could be confused with Henry's—not in that situation, when Henry wasn't directly involved. She was perfect, yet she had been hanging on his every word. The sensation felt dark and intoxicating in his bloodstream, like the anger had mutated into something else, something related but much more potent.

But the scornful flipside of her opinions couldn't be mathematically canceled out by her admiration, not completely. The one thing he'd always had over Henry was his mental health. But now he wasn't so sure. He'd known he was weak and insignificant, but Artemis had forced him see himself in an even harsher light: he was no less strange than Henry, perhaps even worse because he had no genetic excuse. Because it was self-inflicted.

Something had been set loose in his mind now, and Simon could tell that it could never be recalled.

ARTIE AND MARK HADN'T SPOKEN much on the journey home, and she was drowsy and content, wrapped in the warmth of the blanket with Mark's hand resting on her thigh when he wasn't changing gears. She began to register unease as soon as they left the M25, but she didn't know she'd tensed up until he shook her leg.

"What's wrong, am I going too fast?" His fingers explored her clenched quadriceps as if it were a new toy for the lab. "I'd hate to meet this leg in a dark alley."

"Stop... that tickles."

His palm went flat again. "Well?"

"I don't want the evening to end."

Mark took a glance at the dashboard. "Shall we find a 24-hour petrol station and keep going?"

He was serious, she realized. The scope and significance of this bizarre new alliance were only beginning to dawn on her.

"It's got nothing to do with the driving," she said.

They hit a traffic light, superfluous red with not another car in sight. When it flicked from amber back to green he said, "Come home with me, then."

"Is that a good idea?"

"No rules, remember?" When she didn't reply, he said, "Or we could go to yours, but Muswell Hill is marginally closer at this stage. You've got about three minutes before you have to decide."

It took her about three seconds. "Okay... back to yours." And just like that, the unease was gone. Shouldn't she be frightened by this facile cause and effect? Shouldn't...

"Your thoughts are churning again, Art. I can practically hear them."

"I'm afraid I'll become dependent on you."

"So be dependent for once. It won't kill you."

"I might become a nuisance, though."

He smiled. "I very much doubt that."

Mark's flat was tidy, with high ceilings, hardwood floor and minimal furnishings in deep browns and reds. Nice, though: calm and undemanding, exactly the sort of home she would have expected. She caught a glimpse of herself in a mirror: sunburnt face, hair wildly unkempt. *What in hell are you doing here?* the baffled green eyes wanted to know.

While Mark was in the kitchen stashing Freddie's samples in the freezer and making tea, Artie fell asleep on the sofa, and the next thing she knew he was helping her to a bed in a dark room before slipping out and shutting the door. Only half conscious, she removed her top and jeans with dozy fingers and burrowed into the bedclothes. After what seemed like a second or two later, she opened her eyes to sunlight, birdsong and a flow of cool air through an open window. Light cotton curtains billowed. It was early, she knew—her normal seven o'clock.

The unfamiliarity of the room and the absence of the sounds of human activity ought to have disturbed her, but she felt a simple peace, a peace that had not visited her for some time. A peace, perhaps, like most people experienced as a matter of course—the ability to be alone without being afraid.

She rose, pulled on her clothing, moved silently down the corridor. The door to the adjacent room was ajar; peering in, she made out stray bits of a largely invisible Mark in the sea of duvet—half a head, an elbow, a foot protruding out the bottom. She found the bathroom, and the face in the mirror did not cast aspersions this time. Control was fully restored.

Trying to make as little noise as possible, she moved aside a coffee table and slipped into the rhythm of her daily karate regimen. It only took a few minutes to forget the strangeness of the room and the restriction of her inappropriate clothing, and then she was gone, lost in a blur of kick-punch-block, *ichi-ni-san*, the blood pumping, heart beating, mind-clearing cycles of *kata*. Sole against wood, forearm against hard air, invisible foes falling like splinters—until a floorboard creaked and she whirled to respond, arm in strike position, and came face to face with Mark shirtless in the doorway, taking a hasty step backwards.

"Hey!" he said. "I come in peace."

"God, I'm sorry." She lowered her arm, panting with exertion and the restoration of reality as the adrenaline and endorphins rained down. "You startled me."

"I should've realized I'd be watching at my own peril," he said. "You were in another world."

Embarrassed, she wiped sweat from her eyes with fingers still buzzing from accelerated blood pressure. "How long have you been standing there?"

"Maybe five minutes? You're magnificent, Art."

"I woke you up, didn't I?"

He came over and put his arms around her, smelling pleasantly of maleness and sleep.

"Don't worry about it," he said. "It's not every morning a beautiful woman tries to kill me in my own home."

She leaned into him, blissfully happy. "I'm ravenous, Mark. Can we cook something spectacularly unhealthy?"

ON MONDAY MORNING, ARTIE EMERGED from Mill Hill East station and set off on the short walk to Heatherfields with her usual enthusiasm. When she thought back to her dread and hesitation of the previous week, she could not recapture the sensation. *Dread, hesitation*: they were empty words that held no weight. Of course Simon and Henry were a bit eccentric in their own way, but at the moment she wasn't sure how or why she could have let herself get so worked up about them. Exhaustion due to overwork, undoubtedly, and those late nights necessitated by the epidemiologists' asocial hours.

In fact, this past weekend was the first since her professorial appointment that she had failed to turn up at the lab. She had been intending to, of course, but when Mark had suggested a drive to the Chilterns after breakfast on Saturday, she found herself acquiescing without a second thought. She loved walking, but had not indulged since a trip to the Pentlands last autumn when she and Calvin had spent most of the walk bickering and had decided to cut the outing short. Since then, the rapid deterioration of the marriage had only reinforced her natural tendency to bury herself in her research.

She and Mark had walked for six hours, alternating between filling the air with conversation and just moving in comfortable silence, absorbing the unfurling green meadows, the chalk streams rushing in the sunlight, the sky in its haze of lavender-blue. Afterwards, they ended up lingering in a country pub for dinner and returning to London late again.

"Tired of me yet?" she'd asked as Mark approached the intersection where the routes to their respective homes diverged. Even games with no rules must have some sort of inherent limitations, and she was still groping around in the dark.

"Not even remotely. I was about to ask you the same question, though."

So she'd invited him back to Hampstead, where they downloaded a film and stayed up getting quite silly over a bottle of wine. Halfway through it, Artie's mobile chirped and coughed up a text message from Mary: *Success Fri with F proves gloriously reproducible, will call you when up for air for proper lowdown!*

Artie howled with laugher, face buried in Mark's chest as he suggested appropriately salacious replies. Every so often she would worry about how weird the situation was: they were two grown adults behaving like children, or playing house, or acting out a fantasy. Then she would rebound, scolding herself for being insecure enough to care what anyone else might think.

The next morning, after another big breakfast, Artie had kicked Mark out good-naturedly, feeling focused and clear-minded and eager to start work on a major grant application at her laptop in the kitchen and catch up on her scientific reading in the garden. When the evening arrived with no shades of ill-ease, she went to bed alone, congratulating herself on her first battle won. It had almost seemed too easy, but she didn't allow this impression to mar her triumph.

She keyed her way into the basement's side entrance, the musty smell of the place almost sweet as she strode down the corridor, greeting colleagues on the left and right. She was determined to wring every last bit of information she could out of Simon and Henry. First, she popped her head into the lab.

"You're looking cheerful, Artie." Fiona looked up briefly from her PCR tubes. "Nice weekend?"

Artie realized that she and Mark had failed to get their story straight. He would be discreet, wouldn't he?

"Very relaxing," she said. "Just to warn you that we collected some more bloods, and a few old Southern blots that need to be re-probed. I can help if it's too much."

"Southern blots?" Fiona said. "Seriously? I've only read about them in textbooks."

"One for the old folks, then. Hopefully I can borrow a fluorescent kit from upstairs—didn't Bakerman's group mention doing some genomic probing in their last seminar?"

"I can go up and nose around for you, Artie. And do the bloods, obviously—where are the samples?"

Artie paused. "I think Mark took them home—we got back late on Friday."

Next, she went to B302 and knocked, but nobody answered. Looking around to confirm the corridor was empty, she tried the door, but it was locked. She sent Simon a terse email:

I'm going to knock again at 10, if you'd be so kind as to open up this time. And I'm going to knock for as long as it takes, H.'s peace be damned. It's urgent.

About five minutes later, there was a tap on the glass of her office door, and she almost choked on her tea when she registered Simon standing there in the bright light of the corridor as if he were a normal human being. She waved him in with a smile.

"What's the big urgency, Artemis? I'm swamped today."

His voice was curt, defiant. She took a closer look at him; in one way he seemed stronger, more confident than she had ever seen him, but at the same time, she noted that he was unusually disheveled, with several days' growth of beard and an almost desperate glint in his eye.

"Sit down, Simon. You look awful—let me make you a cup of tea."

He looked physically torn, poised like a sacrifice about to be drawn and quartered. The horses were pawing the earth, the ropes were taut—and then he collapsed into a chair.

"Actually, I could really use a cup right now. Why shouldn't I?" This last bit was muttered more to himself than to her.

She eyed him warily as she flipped on the kettle.

"Are you all right?" she asked.

"Perfectly."

"Are you still angry with me about the other night? I'm sorry I was so horrible."

"You didn't say anything that wasn't true," he said. "And I *was* angry... but not anymore."

"Good. I get carried away sometimes. You mustn't take it personally."

He looked up, and the deep blue of his eyes hinted at cryptic conflicts.

"I'll try not to. But it's difficult, the thought of Henry badmouthing me behind my back after I've spent so many years helping him."

"I know." She bowed her head to escape his stare, pouring hot water over the tea bag. She was afraid to disturb their fragile truce by asking whether he had talked to a doctor about Henry's possible degeneration. Instead, she passed him the mug and said, "I know you think I'm taking his side, Simon. But it's simply not true."

He waved aside this comment, impatience restored. "Tell me why you wanted to see me."

"I've got some interesting news from the field," she said. "But first I need to know—"

The office door opened and Mark stepped in, came to an abrupt stop.

"Sorry," he said. "Is this a bad moment?"

Artie watched Simon stiffen in his chair before forcibly relaxing. Simultaneously, she felt Mark's gaze settle on her, and though she didn't meet his eye, a bloom of warmth moved in over her heart like a summer high.

"No, it's perfect timing," she said. "Mark, I'd like you to meet our epidemiological wizard."

She performed introductions, experiencing a rapid mixture of sensations: relief that, despite everything, she still felt like the boss and Mark, like the employee; fascination as Simon stood up immediately to clasp Mark's hand, sealing the masculine encounter with the ancient ritual; irritation as she remembered that Simon had never once felt the urge to shake her own.

The men sat down, looking each other over in no doubt primitive, ritual ways that only they could understand.

"I was just about to ask Simon," she said, "whether any of the larger La Fontayne spikes happened to be pinpointed over our area of interest."

"I've done some preliminary customization of the algorithm over the weekend," Simon said. "A few of the spikes became even more prominent as a result. If you'll allow me to access my account from your computer, I can get you the GPS coordinates right now."

She stood up from her desk and beckoned him to take her chair. While Simon was busy with keyboard and mouse, Mark murmured, "I've given Fi the bloods and suggested what primers to use. She says you volunteered for Southern blot duty."

"I think she was still in primary school when I did my last one."

"I can start them for you now if you're busy."

He was giving her another chance to be alone with Simon, she realized, with his usual tact.

"No," she said. "I want you to hear this."

"Thank, Art. I appreciate it."

She felt the urge to reach over and initiate some form of physical contact like she'd been doing all weekend—a hand to his shoulder, a pat on his forearm. How quickly strange new things could become natural impulses.

Simon cleared his throat. "If you'd care to have a look?"

Artie and Mark went over to the desk and peered at the laptop's screen, where the flat donut lay trampled.

"I've already explained the basics to Mark," she told Simon.

"Good," he said. "Then let's cut straight to the time dimension."

He clicked the mouse and the bumps began to sprout. Even Artie's inexperienced eye could see that the resulting protrusions were subtly different than those of Thursday evening. A few of the spikes became much more elongated until by the end of the video, one in particular towered over the others.

Mark emitted a soft whistle. "Very cool."

Simon blew up the biggest bump. "One of the things I noticed after customization was that the shape of this largest spike had begun to deviate significantly from the smaller ones. What I'm showing you now is a projection into the future. A forecast, if you will."

"How far into the future?" Mark said.

"One month—though the time-scale isn't that finely resolved with the sporadic nature of your sampling."

"It's really starting to spread at the top," Artie said. "Like a bell."

"Like a *bona fide* epidemic... but with a twist," Simon said. "It's as if in this sub-population, the variation has accelerated: the mutation rate has perceptibly increased, and these mutants are accessing more cats."

Artie looked over at Mark, who was smiling.

"That's exactly what you'd expect," Mark said, "if Artie's new theory were correct."

"What theory?" Simon demanded.

"That's why I contacted you this morning," she soothed. "I needed your expert opinion on this idea I came up with on Friday."

She saw the corner of Mark's mouth twitch.

"Tell me about it," Simon said, hand relentlessly busy with the mouse, exploring the shape from dozens of angles.

"I was thinking," Artie said. "The viral reverse transcriptase protein—RT—is already a sloppy copier by nature, but if it developed a mutation in a key region, it might become even more error-prone. Then it would start to spawn even more mutants."

"We might be able to see that," Simon said slowly. "I can repeat the La Fontayne using only the relevant RT signatures, see if we can see a geographical bias with that as the sole variation parameter."

"But only if our Snips happen to pick up the key mutation," Artie said. "It's a pretty crude snapshot."

"If you gave me a full DNA sequence, I could come up with an appropriate numerical descriptor and run it through," Simon offered.

"Our database is fairly limited for actual sequence in that particular gene, but I'll see what we've accumulated."

"Let's try the Snips approach first," Mark said, excited. "Can you do it right now?"

"Oh, no," Simon said. "I can only run the generating program off our private cluster server. I'd have to get back to you on that."

"I nearly forgot," Artie said. "The geographical location of the major spike?"

"Oh, yes," Simon said. He pulled down a menu and clicked into a control panel. After ticking a few boxes, tiny numbers appeared all over the bumpy donut. "The biggest one... let me connect to the GPS server..."

A few seconds passed, and then the location flashed onto the screen.

"Minster," he read out. "The Isle of Sheppey."

There was a moment of shocked silence, so intense that Simon stopped his relentless fiddling and turned his head to stare at Mark and Artie. She registered that she'd crossed the room and whirled back around without even realizing it.

"What's wrong?" Simon asked.

Mark slapped him on the back. "Don't worry, mate—that's a pretty muted reaction by Artie's standards."

"Is there something wrong with that geographical location?" he asked, clearly startled by Mark's collegial assault—but not necessarily displeased.

"Wrong?" Artie broke into a huge grin. "This is brilliant, Simon. Your algorithm has just predicted a genuine field phenomenon."

"What do you mean?"

"I *mean*," she said, "that we've recently stumbled on what looks to be an emergent epidemic of a new, highly virulent feline leukemia virus in Minster. I was just about to tell you about it—it's killing cats like arsenic!"

"Sheppey..." Simon looked suddenly thoughtful. "Sheppey directly borders on Faversham, doesn't it?"

"Not exactly," Mark said. "It really is an island... the Swale comes between them. To say nothing of acres of marshland."

"I wonder... is there a bridge there?"

Mark frowned. "I don't think so. There might be a ferry service."

"Why do you ask, Simon?" Artie said.

"Never mind, it's not important." He shook his head. "Have you characterized the mutations in this new virus? How soon can you give me more signatures from the Minster area?"

As they lapsed into technical talk, Artie noticed that Simon seemed animated and almost entirely altered from how he'd been at the outset. The news that the virus was a recombination between two different species seemed to strike him as particularly significant, although he refused to explain his reaction. From that point on, he became distracted, still involved in the conversation but clearly processing something else at the same time.

"What time is it?" he said eventually, feeling for a watch that wasn't there, and then looking at his bare wrist in bewilderment.

"Nearly eleven," Mark said, glancing at his own high-tech contraption. After Saturday's walk, Artie knew that it even contained a compass.

Simon leaped to his feet. "I've got to get back—Henry might be wondering where I am."

"When can we meet again?" Artie called over as he was slipping out the door.

"Um... I'll email you later."

And then he was gone.

Artie and Mark both collapsed into their respective chairs.

"This is fantastic!" she said. "Entirely too much excitement for a Monday—I need some coffee."

"Don't look at me—that's woman's work."

Artie clouted him on the shoulder on her way to the kettle.

"Ouch," he said. "Looks like your theory about RT instability is becoming more plausible."

"You were the one who thought of checking where the spikes were in the first place, don't forget."

"So we're both geniuses," Mark said.

"We're a good team, Reynolds." She fiddled with the cafetière, overflowing with the triumph of the moment.

"So are you going to reveal how you finally coaxed the turtle out his shell, or is it a female secret?"

"Ha! He'd run in the other direction if I played the girl card. No, I threatened to make a huge scene outside B302."

"Brute force, then." He grinned.

"What did you make of him?"

"Weird," he said promptly. "I understand now why his company was getting a bit oppressive. All *sorts* of things going on there."

"Like what?"

"Well, he obviously felt threatened by me for starters."

"He's not used to being around people, that's all."

"I think there's more to it than that."

"No way," she said. "It's impossible: he's almost worse than Hastings in the misogyny department."

"I didn't mean he was jealous of me sexually," he said. "He acted more like a favored sibling who suddenly wasn't getting all the attention from Mum."

She poured coffee into the glass container, smothered it with hot water and breathed in the resulting aroma. Everything had been smelling and tasting especially intense for the past few days.

"Well, I have to put up with him because he's so sharp with the mathematics."

"That he definitely seems to be," he conceded. "But we don't want any potential hostility interfering with the science. That's why I offered up a bit of male bonding."

"Ah... the matey back-slapping episode. I thought he was going to have a heart attack."

"That was just veneer, Art. The subtle thing was the comment about you."

"Which was very cheeky and bordered on insubordination, I'd like to point out."

"And which was also cleverly designed to impart to Simon, from one rational male to the other, that the female of the species might be a bit less so." Mark looked at her fondly. "Sometimes we just have to put up with their quirks."

"You are one clever bastard."

He shrugged. "You were playing him too, if I recall correctly."

"Like I said, a good team," Artie said.

"Next time *you* get to be good cop."

"Hmmm. So what else was wrong with him?"

"Well, he's clearly on the edge."

"Yes, but he's always like that, Mark—stressed out, tired, fed up with Henry yanking his chain."

"I don't mean chronically," he said. "I mean acutely. It looks to me like he could snap at any time—I recognize the signs. Although..."

"What?"

"Now that I've seen you in action, I don't think it's anything you can't handle. Not that I'm not still worried, mind."

Artie paused halfway through plunging the cafetière. "Shit—that's something else I forgot to tell you. About Fiona's rumor..."

She quickly explained what Simon had told her about the attack on Ben.

"Have you checked up on his story?" Mark said, after thinking over what she'd said.

"Well, no. If Ben's really got amnesia, there aren't any other witnesses."

"You're forgetting someone," he said. "Henry. He talks to you now."

Artie felt a quiver of disquiet pass over her skin, took a quick sip of coffee to cover it up. "I don't think it would be prudent to bring up the topic, somehow."

Her desk obscured to any passing colleagues the fact that Mark had put a gentle hand on her knee. She allowed it to soothe her; she had been craving his touch ever since he came into the office. Ever since she had woken up alone, to be entirely honest with herself.

"You're the best judge of that," he said. "But in the absence of an independent corroboration, you might just want to maintain a healthy suspicion of Simon's version."

"You really think he's lying?"

"Not necessarily. I only think there's a possibility—especially when I clocked the look in his eye earlier. And if he is violent, you still need to be on full alert when you're around him. You don't want to be so busy watching Henry that you turn your back on the wrong man."

She nodded. "Okay. I'll be careful."

"From you that's a pretty big concession."

"I am adaptable, you know. I'm really trying not to be so tough around you."

"I've noticed. Just don't get soft with anyone else—it would break my heart if you took me too literally."

⌒◡

23 June

Full moon on Saturday. I didn't sleep at all that night, only a few hours last night. Could not stop thinking about issues arisen from my fight with A. on Thursday. She left me alone on Friday after the email. I came in today all prepared to hate her, and she did it to me again: we had a meeting and I ended up forgetting I was supposed to dislike her. Met her post-doc Reynolds—seemed v. sensible, is probably keeping her in line. He seemed to like me as well. It felt v. strange when it turned out the La Fontayne had predicted their outbreak—everyone was so happy, and I felt like I was part of it. Desperately wished H. was around to see it and hope that A. brings it up next time she's at ours—much more effective than if I do. V. strange to watch how A. interacts with Reynolds—more equals and friends than boss/subordinate. Have no idea how that would feel. Something strange about their outbreak, probably a coincidence...

Simon put down his pen, reminded again of the fact that Faversham was so close to Minster. He stood up and went to check on Henry—still completely out—then returned to his office, shut the door and picked up the phone.

"Mr. Brees office, Tanya speaking."

"I need to speak with Mr. Brees."

"And you are..." Her tone was infuriatingly dubious. Simon had no idea what Brees' PA looked like, but he was certain she bore more than a passing resemblance to Artemis Marshall—with a frontal lobotomy, that is.

"Dr. Renquist at Heatherfields."

"He's in a meeting. I can take down a message."

He sighed. "Okay. Could you just ask him if there have been reports of epizootic activity surrounding the Faversham outbreak."

"Epi... could you spell that, Mr. Renquist?"

"Afflicted animals," he said impatiently.

"Afflicted?"

"Sick! Sick animals! Ask him if there've been any sick animals in Faversham, with similar symptoms to the human disease—especially cats."

"Cats?" she said in bewilderment.

He remembered that he'd forgotten to ask Artemis what the precise symptoms of the Minster virus were. "Killing like arsenic" was hardly informative.

About two minutes later, Brees returned his call. So much for his "meeting," thought Simon. He just didn't want to speak to Simon unless it suited him. He had his attention now, though.

"What's this about epizootics?" Brees said. "Did Tanya misunderstand you?"

"No," Simon said. *Miraculously enough.*

"Is this something Professor Manfield has predicted with Mother Nature? That terrorists might be using infected cats?"

If Brees understood anything about mathematics, Simon thought, he would realize how amazingly asinine that question was.

"Something like that," Simon said vaguely.

"Well we've not heard of any, but I could initiate a small investigation." Brees sounded almost helpful.

"I... the Professor would appreciate being kept closely informed of any findings."

"Certainly."

"And another thing, Mr. Brees... have you by chance had any affected people on the Isle of Sheppey?"

"Why do you ask?"

"The Professor is trying to determine the direction of spread," he improvised. "The R_0 factor is suggestive of a delta-zed maximum approaching the omega asymptote, and—"

"No," Brees said hastily, and Simon smiled to himself. *Dolt.* "No new cases since the last update."

After Simon put down the phone, he stared into space for a moment. One of the potential hallmarks of a bioterrorist attack was a rash of unexplainable animal deaths. But then, the Minster virus wasn't unexplainable: his algorithm (*not Henry's!*) had predicted an epidemic arising from the natural pattern of disease brewing in the area for the last several years. And Artemis had clearly stated that FeLV caused AIDS, cancer or occasionally anemia, not the telltale blisters of foot-and-mouth. It had to be a coincidence.

ARTIE SOON FORGOT ABOUT MARK'S disturbing suspicions, immersed as she was in the day's experiments. Working at the bench was a rare pleasure now that she was responsible for the administrative tasks of keeping a lab running and funded— even routine chores such as the Southern blots currently spread out in front of her had their charm when you didn't do them every day. Despite the others' teasing, Artie was highly skilled at experimental manipulation and was nowhere near losing the touch that had been partially responsible for her successful career. Scientists could be big on ideas and poor at execution, or vice versa, but the most successful ones excelled at both. And she loved lab culture—being holed up in an office was not nearly as entertaining, she was starting to realize.

"Coping okay with that labeling?" Mark called over, not taking his eyes off his gel apparatus. "Give us a shout if you need help."

"I think I can just about manage, Reynolds."

In fact, she was amazed at the way the memory of the classic procedure still seemed to be encoded into the muscles of her hands. In the old days, though, the probes were radioactive, so it seemed wrong not to have a Geiger counter lurking on the bench, emitting warning ticks like sprays of sinister static.

"Which probes are you going to use on those blots?" Mark asked.

"The entire Envelope gene of FIV Petaluma. Might as well cut to the chase. And as there are duplicate blots, I'm going to test FeLV Env as well." She paused. "Hey, Mark... do you remember when we used to have to pour our own Sepharose columns to separate the probes?"

"God, not this again," Fiona said. "Please."

"It's all fancy spin-columns nowadays," Mark said. "You're spoiled, Fi. I used to make my own out of stripettes. How about you, Art?"

"It's bad enough when it's just Mark," Fiona pleaded, "but with both of you in here you only encourage one another."

"Stripettes, hmmm?" Artie said. "That's quite clever... I used to use a syringe barrel."

"And what about these fancy new ready-made solutions?" Mark said, winking at Artie over Fiona's head.

"Don't *start* with the whole ready-made thing!"

"Yes," Artie said. "Poor Fiona's never had the pleasure of handling herring sperm DNA personally."

Fiona got up and turned up the music to a nearly unbearable volume.

"Kids these days!" Mark shouted. "They just don't understand!"

The phone rang.

"Mary for you, Artie!" Fiona yelled.

Artie peeled off her gloves and tossed them into the bin.

"What on earth is that racket?" Mary said.

Artie reached over to turn down the volume, checking the playlist on the screen as she did so.

"Nobody you'd know, dear. So tell me!"

"Thanks again for tricking Freddie into coming to Canterbury," Mary said. "I didn't make it back to Gillingham until Sunday night."

"You sly devil," Artie said, giving Mark a thumbs up, to which he mouthed *on a scale of one to ten...?* "How on earth did you overcome that paralytic shyness?"

"I got him drunk," Mary said smugly.

"God, you're getting subtle in your old age, Mare. How was... it?"

"Exquisite," she said dreamily. Artie put the phone under her chin and held up ten fingers to Mark, who started to laugh uncontrollably, practically dipping his hair into his buffer tank as he bent double.

"What's that laughing?" Mary asked suspiciously.

"Just Mark sniffing the solvents again," Artie said. "Freddie seemed really nice. I approve."

"I thought you might. I'm just glad I managed to distract him from his intellectual crush on *you*."

"If that hadn't worked, you could've just told him I was a lesbian," Artie said cheerfully, which set Mark off again.

"Did you and Mark manage to find a decent place to eat? I felt guilty for abandoning you."

Artie was suddenly embarrassed. "Yes, it was fine. Listen, I'm up to my elbows in cat genes. Can I ring you tonight?"

"I'll be at Freddie's, so try my mobile... but I'm warning you in advance that I probably won't answer. Let's get together this week for sure."

Artie hung up and returned to her probe, feeling oddly deflated.

When Fiona left the room to borrow some enzyme from the labs upstairs, Mark asked her what was wrong.

"Nothing," she said. After a short pause, she said, "Do you have plans this evening?"

"I was hoping to spend it with you."

She kept her eyes on the open tube between her fingers, feeling again that warming sensation of a sudden sunlight.

༄

THAT AFTERNOON, ARTIE ASKED MARK to take over the next step in her Southern blot experiment, pretending that she had a phone call to make. Instead, she took the stairs up to the library and went straight to her usual carrel. This time, she didn't have an armful of books to deposit on its surface.

Artie had not come to read.

She dropped her head into her hands, rubbed the tips of her fingers over her eyebrows and through the roots of her hair, letting the suppressed desire highjack her body at last: racing heart, electrified skin and that familiar ache. Mary's news of sexual conquest and Mark's comment about wanting to be with her had synergized in an unexpectedly potent way.

She knew now that she had been in denial. How could the act of deciding to have a non-sexual friendship actually eliminate the impulses underneath? He had not once attempted to cross this line, of course, and until this moment, the experiment had seemed workable. True, there had been a number of incidents over the weekend when the sight, smell or feel of him had aroused her, but it hadn't been difficult to ignore at the time. Besides, sexual tension, she'd thought, was a small price to pay for security and peace of mind. But now she was losing control, and calamity prickled just beyond her conscious awareness.

"Are you all right, dear?' The voice was low voice as per library etiquette, but still managed to sound strident.

Artie jumped and raised her flushed face, momentarily dazzled by the vast Celtic knot that confronted her at eye level, worked in silver against crimson silk.

Susan Tavistock stood before her, hand gripping the filigreed top of the carrel in such a way that easy escape was blocked.

"I'm fine," Artie said, after clearing her throat.

"Are you sure?" Susan inspected her shrewdly. "Indulging in a little cry away from watchful male eyes? I personally prefer the toilets—access to cold water afterwards to eliminate the swollen eyelids. Can't afford to relax appearances for a moment, you know—it's fatal."

"I'm not crying," she said. "I'm thinking."

"What about?"

About how it would feel if my post-doc backed me against the lab freezers, ran his hands underneath my blouse, bit my neck, pushed his knee up between my legs—she would probably organize a lynch mob.

"About fevers and rampant epidemics," Artie said. "Did you want something, Susan?"

The arm that was not boxing her in produced a sheaf of papers.

"As a matter of fact, I do. There's to be a new Associate Professor in Evolutionary Development, and we've started a petition to get the female candidate appointed. You'll sign, of course?"

Artie frowned. "Is she the best choice?"

"Actually, yes."

"Then why do you need a petition in the first place?"

"Wake up, Artemis. This is Heatherfields, remember?"

Artie rose to her feet. "Sorry, but I'm not going to support a candidate I know nothing about."

"So inform yourself! I've got all the CVs right here."

"This is a really bad time—excuse me, please." Artie was never this rude. It must be hormones, something Susan probably believed did not exist.

The older woman dropped her arm.

"Women like you are almost worse than men," she said, her tone more thoughtful than hostile.

Artie fled the library, almost grateful to Susan for having uprooted her. It had done more harm than good to dwell on things; what she needed was to focus on work.

But Ben Crombie intercepted her on the way back and asked for a quick word in his office.

"It's about Henry and Rennie," he said without preamble. "Heard you've initiated a collaboration after all."

"He prefers to be called Simon, you know."

"I'm not sure you're aware of the... safety issues."

She paused. "It's fine, Ben. I know all about your broken nose."

"Oh." Red blotches began to appear on his face and neck. "Who told you?"

"Simon."

Ben blinked. "Right. Okay. And you feel comfortable being in there by yourself?"

"Perfectly," she said, standing up. "It's sweet of you to be concerned, though."

"Would you have a drink with me sometime?" His words came out in a desperate tumble, as if they'd been composed and rehearsed in a miasma of fear.

God, what next? "Oh, Ben... I don't think that's a good idea."

He bowed his head, twisted his fingers together. After a moment of heated silence, he said, "More or less what I expected you to say. Someone like you would never be interested in someone like me."

"I'm in the middle of a messy divorce," she said. "So I'm not interested in anyone at the moment. Besides, we're co-workers."

She did not sound convincing even to herself, and he raised his head to meet her eye.

"You can just admit that you don't like me that way, Artie. Less humiliating than being fobbed off."

She got up and left without another word, aware of a growing sense of shame. She'd handled that about as proficiently as a pubescent teenager—but then, he had forced her into a difficult position. She was meant to be an academic, concerned with abstract intellectual pursuits, but everything around her seemed to have something to do with sex: Ben's crush, Mark's so-called friendship, Calvin's predatory stalking, Tavistock's pressure tactics, Hastings' machinations, Simon's disparagement, Fiona being harassed. And all she really wanted was to do her job, to make amazing discoveries and coast off the dizzy highs they provided.

She went back to the office, determined to push everything else out of her mind and finish another section of her grant. She felt Mark's eyes inspecting her as she sat down, and was grateful that he didn't comment.

There was an email from Freddie in her Inbox:

Hi Artemis. Sorry it took so long to get back to you about the local vets.

"And why might that be?" she murmured.

"What's that?" Mark said.

"Nothing."

But the word on the street is that nobody's seen any evidence of our scourge, including my mate in Sittingbourne. So as far as we know, it hasn't managed to get off the island, which is good news for our feline friends. I'll keep my ears open, though.

"Hmmm. No sign of our recombinant on the mainland, Mark."

"Says who?"

"Lover boy."

Artie expected an amusing comment, but Mark just grunted and went back to his reading. There was a definite awkwardness to the air, making her fingers clumsy on the keys, so she soon abandoned her grant and went to the lab. The rest of the day was busy enough to keep her distracted, and it was nearly eight by the time she and Mark had finished.

"Are we still doing something tonight?" he asked when they were locking up the office.

She was surprised by the diffidence in his voice. "Of course. What gave you the idea we weren't?"

"Just checking," he said, which was no answer at all. "I drove today, by the way."

"Why?"

After a pause: "This morning the idea of whisking you off to someplace nice seemed like more of a good idea."

"Actually, Mark... I am rather tired. Can we just go back to yours?"

He nodded, seemingly resigned to something that was still inscrutable to her.

They didn't speak much on the way, and Mark kept both hands on the wheel. When Artie sat down on the sofa, she expected him to put his arm around her, but he just settled next to her with a good few feet between them. The sun was just setting, piercing the Victorian bay window and firing up its smudges and smears into a hundred little glassy haloes: the one thing that Mark's tidiness had apparently overlooked. Steam rose from the cup of tea she hadn't really wanted, the faint plume roiling uncertainly over its milky surface.

"So tell me," Mark finally said. "What happened this afternoon?"

She shook her head, miserably inarticulate.

"Was it something Mary said?" he persisted. "That's when you changed—like a circuit going dead. It's heart-rending when your light goes out, Art."

She watched him through the fading glow of the room, the way his hands rested on his knees, perfectly composed and prepared for whatever might come next. She felt disembodied, hyperaware. They were on stage, surrounded by paper walls and angled just so on prop furniture as the audience waited for the trite resolution.

"I don't think you actually want to hear whatever it is that doesn't want to come out of my mouth," she said.

"You don't have to be afraid to be honest with me," he said. "If you think this has all been a big mistake, it's not too late to go back to the way we were before Friday."

There was her cue. The audience held its collective breath, waiting for her to deliver the crushing blow. Instead, she veered wildly off-script: "Talking to Mary made me jealous."

"Really?" Then his eyes widened. "Jealous because she bagged Freddie?"

She couldn't help smiling. "No, I didn't think his equipment was *that* nice."

"Just as well," he said. "The poor man isn't suited for the full Artemis Marshall experience. He'd probably vaporize on the spot."

She felt a fluttering warmth spread in her belly, then: the lust again, patiently waiting its turn. She wasn't an actor on stage after all; she was a marionette, being passed from hand to hand and strings and limbs all entangled.

"I was jealous," she said, "because I wanted *us* to have spent all weekend in bed having ten-out-of-ten sex."

"Oh." He paused. "Is that what this is all about? And here I was thinking you'd gone off me altogether."

"No, that's what I'm trying to say. It's..."

"Though I do feel a bit short-changed," he said. "A meagre scale of ten, with our sexual chemistry?"

"It's not funny, Mark. Just shut up and listen to me."

"I'm sorry, Artie. I'm listening, truly I am. But it sounds as if you aren't listening to yourself."

He was, she saw, gallantly suppressing further amusement, confident and composed and the perfect opposite of her heart-slamming, befuddled state. Later, she wasn't sure precisely who had made the first move. Had she wordlessly green-lighted, with an intuitive cant of shoulder or tilt of head, the approach of his hands, hands that slid around her waist and lifted her onto his lap as if she weighed nothing at all? Had she fallen backwards against the sofa, pulling him down on top of her, or had he twisted her there himself in one fluid movement? Whatever the motive force, she found herself beneath him with their legs entangled, light-headed and weak with desire. And at that moment at peace, too, with what was certain to happen next.

"Forgive me," she whispered, even as her fingers slid over the bristly angle of his jaw and down his neck. "I'm..."

"It's okay, Artie. It's a lot more fun than doing your Southern blots."

She could feel laughter rippling though his throat and chest, but when she tried to join in, a sudden vacuum blocked her lungs, and she was astounded when sobs came up instead, and tears began seeping out through her closed eyelids.

"Artie?" His arms tightened around her and she felt him kiss her wet cheek, her forehead, her nose. She couldn't seem to open her eyes. "What's wrong?"

It was the oddest thing—although his touch still ignited her, the kisses themselves felt innocently comforting. He'd long since stopped laughing, but his earlier humor remained somehow infused in his lips, landing on her passive, upturned face like rain. It was an act of tenderness that twisted the shard of sadness even deeper.

"Oh, God, I'm..." She couldn't speak either—she could scarcely breathe. She was unraveling.

"Artemis, sweetheart, I know this is all very strange, but I promise everything will be all right." A kiss brushed against her ear, her chin.

"I'm terrified I'll grow to like you too much, Mark." She had to gasp through the sobs. "I'm terrified..."

"I know... I understand," he said. "I didn't before, but I do now. We won't do anything you don't want to do. Just cry, sweetheart, and we can work it out later."

❧

THE ROOM HAD LONG SINCE fallen into a bluey darkness. Artie felt depleted, collapsed there in Mark's arms. Her swollen face was finally starting to cool, only an occasional shudder moving through her chest. A few weeks ago she'd been poised to conquer the universe, and now she was reduced to this.

"I didn't mean to hurt you, I swear to God." His first words for a long time: she had never heard him sound so shaken. "I felt certain there was no danger, and I only wanted to help."

"It's not your fault." Her own voice was dull to her ears, dull and oppressed.

"Are you sure you even need to worry?"

A pause.

"I'm sure."

Artie felt his response to this pathetic confession as a movement against her chest. He was drawing in his breath, she realized. As the air came out again, he said, "I'm not questioning your judgement, but I can't see someone like you ever falling for someone as defective as me."

"Please don't make me spell out how wonderful you are," she said. "Anyway, even if it's only a remote possibility, it seems foolish take the risk." Remote—who was she kidding?

"You're probably right," he said. "You know, I don't think that holding back from the sex is going to make a jot of difference."

"You're right. It's all or nothing."

The quietness of the room gathered around them.

"So what's it going to be?" he said.

CHAPTER 8
Symptoms, Those Leading To Misleading Diagnoses

ARTIE'S BODY CLOCK ROUSED HER about five minutes before her alarm would normally go off. She felt stiff, exhausted. Her heart was trembling from lack of sleep: only about an hour, if she was right about the time, but even that short dream period had swum with sex. Eyes still closed, she extended an arm to home in on his body warmth, an automatic touchstone against the demons. She felt the desire gather again, nowhere near depleted after the long night of sweaty exertion, sweat that had dried along the length of her naked body and made her skin feel gritty against the cotton.

When her hand found only duvet, she opened her eyes and remembered afresh, as she so often had to do, that she and Calvin were separated. A triangle of sunlight highlighted the emptiness of her bed like a primitive punctuation mark. More memories returned: her humiliating loss of control on Mark's sofa. His gentle acceptance of her decision to return to their former professional relationship, and the silence between them as he'd driven her home.

She had gone straight to bed but was still so aroused that she'd had to take matters into her own hands once, twice, three times before she could finally think clearly. And it wasn't Mark she imagined for this purpose, but Calvin. Since she'd expelled him from the house he'd preyed on her in ways he never had when they were together, in ways she'd never dreamed he wanted. Last time he'd bullied and tricked her, managing to restrain her before she knew what was happening and, once she was helpless, he'd brutalized her in a manner she was horrified to find she half enjoyed. And as she lay there alone in bed after Mark dropped her off, she relived the sharp pleasure and shame again and again, even embellished it, crying out in the dark like a wounded animal until the desire was finally wrung from her body and mind.

And when it was, the demons had slithered back like reptiles, bellies low to the floor and especially virulent. She particularly hated the times when the fear manifested as *sound*, her running mental dialogue transformed into a shouting match that left her wanting to cower against a wall with hands over ears.

So she'd risen in the dark, put on her *shihan gi* and fought imaginary assailants in her moonlit lounge until dawn, blocking her thoughts as she blocked shadowy arms and legs. Self-defense: a particularly appropriate term. She carried on for hours longer than any sane *sensei* would have deemed appropriate, until she was weak and dizzy and fell asleep as soon as she'd collapsed onto the bed.

Artie sat up, loathing the smell of her own body. She felt too tired to go to work, but it seemed imperative to force things back to normality as soon as possible before anything had time to fester. She simply had to regain control.

In the shower, she imagined her lust and all its affiliated danger sluicing off her and spiraling into the drain with the suds of shampoo and mats of clumped hair and flecks of shed skin. On the way to the kitchen, she looked away from the dining room table where the divorce petition was still spread out on one end, untouched since the evening on Parliament Hill last week. She remembered the way Mark had noticed it on Saturday night and had failed to comment—then pushed him out of her mind.

The walk to the tube station revived her somewhat, human life surging around her as she moved up the hill. Behind plate glass lay displays of beautiful feminine accoutrement: a coyly stepping snakeskin stiletto, a fall of lace-edged stocking artfully discarded on a velvet pillar as if during an act of passion, a sheath dress of black silk on a headless mannequin. Everything looked expensive and deadly this morning, and in the foreground, her own reflection floated over it all like a haggard voyeur.

She keyed her way into the basement and passed Ben's office. Pausing, she backtracked and tapped on the open door. He waved her in, face expressionless—until her appearance registered.

"I wanted to apologize," Artie said. "I thought I was being kind, but really, I was just making it easier for myself."

His freckled hands slowly closed the immunology journal he was reading.

"I feel bad, too," he said. "How could I possibly understand what a divorce feels like? Last thing you need is more pressure."

She felt the sting of tears in her eyes, but they were no match for Artemis Marshall: she'd been battered, but the new improved version was back and stronger than ever.

"We can have that drink sometime," she said. "God knows I could use one."

He smiled, and she was astonished by his poise.

"I'll keep that in mind," he said.

After she unlocked the office and deposited her things, she had a thought. Why not clear the decks completely?

Susan Tavistock was frowning at a spreadsheet in an office even smaller than her own—about one-third the size of Ben's, who was only an Associate Professor.

"What can I do for you, Artemis?" Her eyes were surprised but free of rancor—but then, she was a political animal.

"I want to apologize for my surly behavior. Yesterday... and in general."

There was a pause.

"Sit," Susan said, pushing away from the computer and removing her reading glasses.

Artie sat, feeling like she'd been called before the head teacher.

"I'll tell you right now," Artie said, "that I don't fully agree with your approach and I probably never will. But I'm sure we can find some sort of middle ground."

"Undoubtedly," she replied, eyes keenly amused. "What did you have in mind?"

"Tell me more about this candidate for the Evo Devo position."

Susan raised an eyebrow before opening up a file on her desk and passing over a CV.

"She's hot, Artemis. Younger than the others—thirty-eight, but has far more publications. And her stuff is fresh—Graves down in Evo Devo told me she's shaping up to be one of the brightest minds in the field, and he's never effusive about anything except snails." A pause. "She reminds me of you, to be honest."

Artie slowly paged through the CV, a sense of shame growing as she absorbed all the impressive details. She could not deny that when Susan had said the words "female candidate" before, Artie had conjured up an automatic, stereotyped image in her mind, an image whose main component was mediocrity. Was Susan right? *Was* Artie worse than a man for making the same assumptions—for refusing to give a hand up to others once she'd managed to scrabble aboard ship?

Artie raised her head. "I don't understand why you need a petition for this person. The CV speaks for itself."

Susan tapped her chin with a pen. "Hastings is on the selection advisory committee, and the Sanctum prefer unanimous agreement. I've already heard he's going to vote no."

"Do you have the CV of his top choice?"

Susan extracted another sheaf, and Artie scanned it.

"But this is ridiculous—there's no comparison whatsoever!"

"Precisely my point," Susan said. Then she sighed. "Anyway, it's probably moot: she's already got offers from Oxford and Yale, and during the interview she confided to me that she'd rather be someplace with more women."

Artie felt her anger rise at the thought of Hastings' repellent eyes.

"Why do you even bother, Susan?"

"Because," she said, "moot or not, it's important not to let things just *happen*."

"I'll sign the petition," Artie said suddenly. "With pleasure."

After she'd scrawled her name with its bold irrepressible swoops, she asked, "Did you pass around one of these for me?"

"Of course."

"Can I... can I ask how many people signed?"

Susan leaned back in her chair, fingering the lapis bauble pinned to her collar. "Every last woman in the Institute, down to the rawest PhD student. And from what I hear so far, you haven't disappointed us."

Artie felt the tears again, made herself blink them back.

"Susan," she said. "Do you know why Hastings hates me? Aside from the fact that I've got tits, I mean... there's something in particular, isn't there?"

The older woman nodded. "You probably don't know this, but Hastings was part of your selection committee as well."

"But..." Artie stared at her. "You said it had to be unanimous!"

"No," she replied. "I said the Sanctum *prefer* unanimity. Yours was the first case in about twenty years where a negative vote was overlooked. The Sanctum... intervened."

"Was it down to your petition?"

Artie felt a sudden awe for the power of the sisterhood, rapidly followed by guilt for having underestimated it until Susan started laughing, a deep, throaty, chain-smoker's laugh.

"Goodness no, dear, the idea! If only..." Her humor faded, and she shrugged. "The truth is that the Sanctum wanted you, and the Sanctum got you, Hastings be damned."

"Why? I'm only thirty-two. I'm..." She didn't have to remind Susan of her gender.

"Who can say? But Hastings is the Head of your department, and the Sanctum is notorious for shuffling Heads at a moment's notice—especially to reflect unusually impressive academic scholarship."

Artemis Marshall, Head of Virology... it had a definite sweetness to it.

"He's got nothing to worry about," Artie said flatly. "I'm working on a very obscure little problem, and he's a big knob doing big influenza research."

"I shouldn't wonder if the size of his knob isn't half the problem," Susan said. "He's bound to be deficient in that area—men like him often are."

"Ha! Still, you can't argue with his academic reputation."

"The Sanctum doesn't think in terms of big being better. And I'm no virologist, but I've heard his research is rather pedantic and predictable."

Artie privately agreed, but just said, "Not to judge by his grants."

"Again," Susan said, "there's not much of a correlation between grant-winning ability and what the Sanctum, historically, have found important."

"If they thought I had so much potential, then why did they stash me in the basement?"

Susan frowned. "That I can't tell you, Artemis. Perhaps it was a backhanded apology to Hastings to keep the peace. Or perhaps it was to protect you from him. I'd keep your eye on him at any rate, dear. The man, as we say in Ecology, is unadulterated pond scum."

When Artie got back to the office, Mark's laptop was set up on his desk and a half-empty coffee mug rested beside it. This, too, needed action. But first, she rang up Calvin's solicitor, apologizing sincerely for having missed the last appointment and arranging a new one in a few days' time. She couldn't bring herself to speak to Cal in person, but she did send him a text, giving him a brief, embroidered update about her progress on the divorce papers. Finally, then, she went into the lab, feeling unexpectedly at peace. Mark and Fiona looked up from their work at her entrance: her smile, she found, came naturally. Mark opened his mouth, clearly shocked by her physical condition, but then managed to answer her good morning in a normal tone of voice.

"Are you ill, Artie?" Fiona asked with concern, clearly not constrained by similar propriety. "You look as if you've been hit by a train."

"I'm just a bit tired," she said. "Catch-up meeting in my office in five minutes, okay?"

~

24 June

Brees called; the Faversham cases have expanded and virology reports show that the agent is not foot-and-mouth after all. Similar blisters, but the FMD virus has not been found in the lesions. They are currently checking other leads. No evidence of epizootics, in cats or anything else. Symptoms include acute gastritis, no fatalities thus far and certainly no immunodeficiency. If this is bioterrorism, they are rank amateurs, trying to bring Britain to its knees with a poorly infectious stomach bug—I don't know what all the fuss is about. But the truth is, it doesn't feel entirely natural to me either. We simply need more information.

❧

LATER, IN THE OFFICE, FIONA said, "I'm warning you in advance that I've got something strange."

Artie glanced at Mark, saw by his demeanor that he had already been briefed. Saw, too, when he was distracted finding a pen in his pocket, that he hadn't slept well either.

"Show me, Fi."

"I know Freddie's experiments already proved that I hadn't contaminated those cat samples with FIV from the lab," she said, pointedly not looking at Mark.

"Did Mark cough up that twenty quid yet?" Artie said.

Fiona nodded smugly as she slid a photo across Artie's desk. "But I'd already started those checks you wanted me to run, so I thought I might as well finish."

"Good." Artie nodded, picking up the image and studying it.

"No evidence of FIV in the samples with any other primer set, see here and here, so it's not likely to be a Petaluma lab contamination.

"Agreed."

Fiona pulled out a sequence comparison and passed it over, a neutral expression on her face. "But I got back the complete sequencing results on the FIV gag insertion just now, and it's almost a perfect match with Petaluma."

Artie stared at Fiona, and then at Mark, who leaned forward, pointing out the scant handful of mismatches.

"I was as surprised as you," he said, "so Fi and I re-checked the traces pretty carefully. It's really similar—six minor mutations between the three cats, but it's clearly only recently evolved."

"This can't be right," Artie protested.

Fiona nodded. " I know—Mark's already explained to me that Petaluma is an ancient California isolate."

"Not to mention," Artie said, "that it's a rather weak strain that should never be able to compete in the wild. It makes a great lab tool, but its performance is pretty disappointing in actual cats compared with most of the heavies out there."

Mark shrugged. "It must be competing just fine on Sheppey. Maybe all the local strains are on the dole and too busy watching daytime TV."

Artie frowned at the printout. "Mark, remind me to call Sidney Sheppard after this, ask him to check his database. He still does lots of FIV sampling in the UK, doesn't he?"

"Mostly in Scotland, but it's worth a check."

"So maybe a Petaluma-like strain is more common than we think."

"It must be."

"What about the Envelope, Fiona? Do we know yet whether it's from FIV as well, and if so if it's also Petaluma-like?"

"Not yet," she said. "Still sequencing delays. Your Southern results will come first."

"We won't have them until tomorrow," Artie said. "Unfortunately the first attempt was a total mess, possibly because the strip reaction wasn't stringent enough."

"I thought those old membranes looked too dry when you unwrapped them," Mark said. "Freddie must not have stored them properly."

"Anyway," Artie said, "I'm nuking them right now and will start over with the hybridization shortly."

"There's something else," Mark said, opening his notebook and showing her a photo. "These are the Gag PCRs on the five new cats we got from Freddie last Friday. As he already suspected, they've also got the same FIV insertion signature."

"Right. So this strain, whatever it is, is spreading."

"And I had a look at our database," he said. "To see whether there were any useful Snip signatures in the RT. And it turns out all eight Minster cats have got the same mutation—but this signature doesn't appear in any of your other cats, anywhere, even as far back as 2010."

"Very interesting."

"It could be a coincidence," he said.

"True. To prove our instability theory, we're going to need a functional assay. Fiona's short clones will be useful, but we really ought to isolate a full-length version to test its behavior."

"I volunteer," Mark said promptly. "In my previous lab, I was pulling out full-length avian proviruses with my eyes closed, using long-range PCR. Piece of cake."

"Show-off." Artie smiled at him. "Remember when we used to have to screen libraries using lambda cloning? It could take months!"

"Don't even start," Fiona said, fleeing the office.

MARK STARTED TAPPING AT HIS computer.

She watched him for a few moments, then said, "You're allowed to ask me how I am, you know."

He stopped typing and raised his head, eyes grave.

"I was trying to respect your privacy."

"Don't be a dope, Mark. You never did that before."

"I was hoping you don't feel as bad as you look."

"I probably don't. How about you?"

"I've been so stupid—I don't know what I was thinking. I told myself I was helping you, but the truth was I was just being selfish."

"No, I'm the one with the problem," she said. "I didn't realize how much this divorce had messed me up."

"Which is exactly why I ought to have kept well clear." His eyes searched hers, looking for something that was impossible to define. "My cure was worse than the original disease."

"No, it wasn't. I don't want you to think you've done wrong. I don't want to offend you."

His smile was strangely bitter. "You worrying about liking me too much is about the most inoffensive thing I can possibly imagine. Do you have any idea how good it made me feel? I lay awake all night trying to get my head around it."

She felt that tightness in her chest again. "I should've asked you this last night. I'll ask you now, if you don't mind."

"I half wish you wouldn't," he said. "But you'd better get it over with."

"This is all hypothetical at this stage, but I need to know."

"Just say it."

Regaining control, she reminded herself. Control at all costs.

"I know you said you don't fall in love," she said. "But could you see yourself, one day, falling in love with me?"

"No," he said sadly. It was not something he even had to consider. "I'm sorry, Art. As much as I'd want to, it's simply impossible."

She felt several things: a kick in the stomach, an ache in the throat, a rush of relief. But at the same time, there were other things she could no longer feel at all.

"Then we've definitely done the right thing," she said. "Thanks for being honest."

He nodded. "Friends?"

"Friends. And scientific partners, too. I don't want to conquer the feline virus world without you."

"I'm glad." A pause. "I'm still worried about you, though, how you'll cope alone."

"I'll cope, Mark. I'll be fine. Besides, you're not entirely off the hook. I fully expect you to help me drown my sorrows down at the Victoria Arms on a regular basis."

And that seemed to be that, the closing of another sad chapter in an even more painful year.

She rang up Sidney Sheppard's office, but the line was engaged, so she left a message on his voicemail.

AFTER LUNCH, ARTIE KNOCKED SOFTLY on B302 without an appointment, but to her surprise Simon came to the door immediately.

"Hi," he said, almost like a normal person uttering a normal greeting. "I was just about to come find you."

"Should we go elsewhere?"

He glanced back at the inner room. "No, he just zoned out five minutes ago, so he'll never notice. Come to my office."

They passed through Henry's twilight world; in the brief glance she got of his screen, the avian flu lily seemed to be overblown, past its prime, about to start dropping its petals. It was, she thought, a particularly ominous pattern. She pressed her hand involuntarily over her trouser pocket where the phone rode over her hip. In this strange journey she seemed to be undergoing, nothing could be taken for granted any more.

"When will Henry's avian flu simulation be finished?" she asked Simon once they were safely tucked into his office. *Safely...* she caught herself, remembering Mark's warning about turning her back on the wrong man. And thanks to last night's marathon karate effort, she could scarcely lift her arms.

His smile was a cryptic twist. "Finished? Finishing isn't the point. It will never be *finished*. There are billions of variables and permutations, and he seems bent on trying them all."

"Why?"

"That's just what he does, Artemis." Simon seemed impatient, clearly not keen to dwell on Henry. "Have you looked into the RT question?"

"Yes," Artie said. "Mark has confirmed that all the Minster viruses have the same Snip signature, but it's not present in cats from any other geographical regions, or from earlier times. So this Minster strain seems to have come up out of nowhere."

"Nothing comes from nowhere, epidemiologically speaking," Simon said. "The Snip signature is a crude measure, like you said. You might see evidence of the change already evolving years ago in the area, if only you used a finer comb."

"Sequencing, you mean. There are thousands of DNA clones, and my budget is in the red as it is. Obviously I can rejig some priorities if you think it's worth doing, though."

"Maybe we could help out," he said. "Our research spending is frugal, and we're dripping in MoD money. We could cover the sequencing costs."

"Really?" Artie came out of her slouch. "No offense, Simon, but what's in it for you?"

In answer, he called up the La Fontayne on his screen, a magnified view of the Minster spike. "I can't get this shape out of my mind," he said. "Last night I even dreamt about it. There's something going on here... something important, I'm convinced. This pattern: it's not entirely natural, but at the same time, it all fits in. I want us to find out what it is."

❧

WHEN SIMON WAS ESCORTING HER back through the main computer room, she nearly jumped when Henry swiveled around to face them. It reminded her of a creature coming to life after its mad scientist creator had thrown a lever. It would be almost comical if it didn't feel quite so sinister.

"How are you this evening, Professor?" Henry inquired in an unusually gentle rumble. There was something odd about his expression that took Artie a few moments to work out: he was *concerned for her wellbeing*.

"Is something amiss?" he persisted.

She exchanged a quick glance with Simon and saw that he was similarly puzzled. Asperger's Syndrome manifested in a number of ways, but one of its key features was a complete inability to empathize. Henry had no business asking her that question—it must be a formulaic thing, an imitative thing, a snippet he'd heard on the radio. But why, then, did Simon seem so uncomfortable?

"I'm fine," she said.

"You are lying," he said.

She took an involuntary step backward, her heart beginning to take an interest in the possibility of preparing for action. It was one in the afternoon, she reminded herself—a scream would muster a healthy response. But then her collaboration would be over forever, and the Minster spike would remain a mystery. She had to talk her way out of this.

"Professor Marshall was just leaving," Simon said, taking her arm and starting to hustle her toward the door. She could feel the tensed charge of his scrawny fingers.

"Don't you agree, Simon?" Henry said, louder. "She looks awful. Take a closer look, lad."

Simon stopped walking and turned to face her, shy and reluctant and awkward. She saw apology in the way his lips pressed together, the usual anger for Henry and the rest of the universe flickering just underneath. She felt deeply uncomfortable—even violated—but tried not to show it as his indigo eyes searched her face.

"She does look tired," he finally admitted.

"She looks traumatized," Henry corrected. "What has happened to you, child?"

She couldn't help it; she was too naturally curious not to look directly at him for a moment. His eyes burned at her across the room, seeming to see everything inside that she did not want to reveal. She found herself both attracted and repelled by this familiarity.

"My personal life is none of your concern," she said.

He bobbed his head in accord. "Nevertheless, I would very much like to know, if you would entrust me with your confidence."

She slid her gaze toward Simon—*what in hell am I meant to do?* He responded with an almost imperceptible shrug—utterly useless as usual.

Well, Henry had asked politely, and anyway, Simon and Henry were probably the last two people in the basement who didn't know.

"I'm in the process of a divorce," she said. "It's gone a bit messy, and sometimes I can't sleep."

Simon's brows slanted—it was clearly not what he had expected her to say.

"I am sorry to hear that," Henry said. "How long were you married?"

She couldn't help it; he sounded genuinely regretful, and this made her feel expansive.

"Ten months," she said. When he nodded again, without a trace of the poorly hidden scorn she sometimes encountered after this admission, she felt herself relax further.

"And who has initiated the divorce?"

"I have."

Still no censure, only sympathy.

"Why?" he said.

Her gaze was drawn to his again, drawn with a magnetism she couldn't resist. She saw inquisitiveness there, and commiseration, and a wisdom that felt ancient; at the same time, it was like she was looking at her own eyes in a mirror, as if he were a blank surface reflecting back everything she wanted to see. She felt a dozen different responses to his question queuing up behind her lips—and then she came to herself, to the room, to Simon's anxious spectator fascination; she broke the forbidden eye contact and the charmed feeling immediately vaporized.

She had to get out of this room.

"If you wouldn't mind terribly, Professor," she said, covering her violent uneasiness with a tone of the smoothest honey, "I am expected elsewhere."

"Very well," he said after a moment. "We can speak more about it on another occasion."

He turned to face his screen—not zoned out, just finished with her. He tapped a few keys, and the lily began to spin.

"I need a word with you in my office," she murmured to Simon as he was opening the door for her.

"Okay, but he's still awake, so I can only be away a moment," he whispered back.

As they walked down the corridor together, Artie saw two of her colleagues glance at them, one with a troubled expression, the other carefully neutral.

Mark looked up when Artie slammed into the room.

"Do you want me to leave?" he asked.

"No need," Artie said, then turned on Simon, fiercer than she'd intended. "What was *that* all about?"

He pressed himself back against the closed door, paler than usual.

"I have no idea, Artemis. I've never seen anything like it—but I'm truly sorry, that you had to..."

Artie could feel Mark's curiosity and willed him to keep silent—there wasn't enough time to explain. "I don't need to tell *you* that was atypical Asperger's behavior."

"I can't explain it," he said, bewildered.

"Where did he find the compassion to register my condition in the first place? Even *you* didn't notice."

"I'm sorry... it wasn't because... that is, I'm not very..."

"Could he have picked up a stereotyped discussion from the television or radio?"

Simon shook his head. "Henry doesn't have either in his flat. I can't imagine where he could have been exposed to it. Besides, it didn't sound like simple parroting to me. It was all very... pertinent, wasn't it?"

"What's going on?" Mark said.

"In a minute," she said. Then to Simon, "There's no way I'm going to tell him any more—it's out of the question. So what will happen if I refuse to answer him a second time?"

"I don't recommend crossing him."

"These rules of yours," she said, "Who wrote them?"

"I did."

"Based on what? Psychological advice?"

He shook his head. "Trial and error in the past, Artemis. Twenty-five years of close, careful experimentation."

"And what happened when you broke them? In the past?"

His reluctance slouched in his shoulders. "He got angry."

"Violent?"

"No! Just loud... verbally loud."

She knew exactly what Mark's face would look like, and wouldn't let herself turn to check.

"Well, not all your rules seem to apply to me," she said. "He doesn't mind when I make eye contact, for example. He doesn't stay switched off when I'm in the room. How can we rely on any of the others?"

"They're all we've got," he said. "I'm sorry, but I've really got to get back."

"We need to discuss this further," she said as he was letting himself out. "Come by tonight when he zones out."

When the door swung shut, Artie sank down into her chair and rested her forehead in her hands. She was happy it was daytime, that Mark was there. There was no question that something about Henry's scrutiny brought the dark things closer.

"What's he done to you, Artie?" Mark demanded.

She explained what had happened, omitting the peculiar feeling she'd received from Henry's attentions. Now that the moment was over, she almost wasn't sure it had really happened.

"I don't like it," he said. "Surely there's no need for you to go in there anymore, now that Simon's being more accessible."

"It's fine," she said. "I know how to handle him."

"For Christ's sake, Art—why do you put yourself through so much unnecessary torture? Is it some sort of macho thing?"

"And why do *you* have to be so bloody over-protective?"

"I wouldn't have to if you actually had an ounce of sense!"

They glared at each other for a few moments.

"I *have* been keeping your warnings in mind," she said. "But now more than ever, it's important for me to be strong and not let things get the better of me. It's how I cope."

"You can be strong without actually walking on hot coals."

"It's just the way I am, Mark. I thought you liked it."

He slumped back in his seat. "I like it in theory. It's the practical consequences that worry me."

"It's all part of the same package."

"I know," he said. A smile crept in, decidedly grudging. "That's why it's so fucking annoying. You drive me crazy, Artemis Marshall."

"As long as I don't scare you away."

"Not a chance in hell," he said. "I can handle the likes of you."

The phone rang.

"Sidney!" she said into the phone, delighted. "Thanks for returning my call—I'm going to put you on speakerphone so Mark can hear too..."

"Mark Reynolds, isn't it?" Sidney's voice boomed into the office. "I heard you'd abandoned your chickens for superior pastures... what do you miss the most?"

"Their lovely aroma," Mark said.

"Is Artie running a reign of terror down there?"

"Artie is eating out of my hand," Mark said.

"You're deluded, lad... she just wants you to think you are. So how goes it in the unfashionable backwaters of feline leukemia?"

"Don't scoff until you've heard the latest, Sid," Artie said. "Our worlds are merging: we've stumbled onto an FIV/FeLV hybrid virus."

"Have you, by Jove? Replication competent?"

"We don't know that yet. But it's spreading in the wild, so it must be a competitive genotype."

"Well, you've come to the right place—I'm flattered you chose to contact me over Parke-Mayhim."

"Parke-Mayhim tried to put his hand up my skirt at the last European Retrovirus Meeting."

"Well, you can't blame a bloke for trying," Sid said. Mark grinned, and Artie stuck her tongue out at him.

"Anyway," Artie said, "I called because I was hoping you'd look at our FIV insertion and see if you could find the closest match in your database of British isolates."

"Whereabouts is the wee new beastie lurking?"

"Estuary Kent."

"Well, my students have done a bit of sampling down Dover way recently," Sidney said. "Email it over and I'd be delighted to blast it through."

"I'm warning you in advance that it looks a lot like Petaluma," she said.

There was a staticky pause.

"That's impossible," he said.

Artie met Mark's eye.

"Evidently not," she replied.

"That's like finding a polar bear on the Costa del Sol, lass. Perhaps your technician has been drooling into the PCR tubes?"

"It's not a lab contamination," she said haughtily. "Maybe Parke-Mayhim would be more interested..."

"No! Send it over, damn your beautiful green eyes. We'll get to the bottom of this shortly."

Artie put the phone down, disgruntled. "That wasn't at all what I was hoping to hear."

ALONE IN HER OFFICE THAT evening, Artie tried to catch up on her outstanding correspondence, but the chat with Sidney had left her too charged and distracted. Instead, she initiated a barrage of new contacts, asking every FIV expert in the world—even the odious Alistair Parke-Mayhim—whether they'd ever seen evidence of a Petaluma-like virus signature doing well in their respective necks of the wood. Then she broadened her queries to specialists in other related viruses such as HIV, seeking any indication whatsoever of the resurgence of old lab strains into the wild, of any formerly weak signatures coming and going in cycles. Business as usual: that was the plan, but somewhere behind the barrage of bright words on the screen she could feel the pressure of the empty building, bearing down on her frenzy of correspondence with even more weight than usual.

You're not alone, she reminded herself. *Room B302 is fully occupied.* At this time of night, such an anemic substitute for proper human companionship was more comforting than she might have expected. Looking at her watch, she saw it was long past the time that Simon normally managed to escape—what was keeping him? She wanted to grill him more about the Minster spike, feed him more virus signature data, anything to keep the buzz of her project between herself and the great surrounding silence.

Artie stood up with the intent of ferreting him out, only to be walloped by a wave of dizziness. She grabbed at the chair back with both hands as the shadows crowded in and pixelated her vision into a collage of brightness and muted greys. Staring into the funneling maw that yawned open before her, she became doused in naked terror: she was a tiny planet, lost in an empty galaxy, orbiting around a sea of nothingness.

The next few minutes were a blur. Somehow she must have managed to regain her seat, because that's where she found herself when her vision cleared. Hands trembling, she reached for her phone, slick with sweat, and pressed a few buttons until Calvin's number came up. Horrified, then, to see his name on the screen: the default, subconscious solution to all her problems. She stabbed the "cancel" button and stared, devoid of inspiration, at the main menu. That's when she remembered the yellow piece of paper with Mark's number on it, still folded in her wallet. *It doesn't matter how late,* he'd said.

She got as far as entering and saving the digits into the phone before she decided that calling Mark was the last thing she should do. His prior intervention, no matter how kindly intended, had only increased her instability: running to him at the slightest hint of fear would just make things worse. Hadn't he shot her that look of concern as he'd taken his leave earlier that evening? Somewhere underneath her disappointment that he didn't propose going out for a drink (which she would have declined, of course) was the irritation that he was treating her like some fragile ornament that only he could stop from shattering.

And anyway, she was absolutely fine, now that she'd managed to catch her breath. Logic reasserted itself: it hadn't been an anxiety attack, a symptom of some deeper problem; it had been her lack of sleep, compounded by a skipped breakfast and insufficient lunch. She'd visit the vending machine, then knock on B302.

The phone rang in her hand and she cried out with surprise: *Mary.*

"You okay, Artie? You sound weird."

"I'm fine," she replied, though the pumping of her heart seemed to roar in her ears. "It's so good to hear from you."

"Sorry for the short notice, but I'm in town. Fancy a drink near London Bridge before I hop on the train home?"

An hour or so later, Artie waited outside the Underground station exit on the Borough Market side, watching the flow of people emerge from the depths before fanning out in dozens of different directions when they hit street level. Such an astonishing mass of humanity: jostling, lighting cigarettes, jabbering into phones, hailing taxis, running for buses. She tried to imagine what they would look like on one of Henry's models, whether anyone would ever develop mathematics powerful enough to predict, based solely on such patterns, who was likely to head left instead of right, or right instead of left—or to return home to find their partner in bed with a work colleague.

But no, she wouldn't think about Henry, or Calvin. She would focus on the life around her, on the glorious absence of absence. It was another hot, sultry night and beyond the station's entrance the pavements were full of revelers spilling out of the Market Porter and other bars along Stoney Street. She let the scene cleanse her of her recent nightmarish evening, determined to regain complete normality by the time Mary arrived.

In vain: Mary came up the steps, face flushed and happy, only to take one look at Artie and reach out hands in concern.

"I knew something was up." She squeezed Artie shoulders before pulling her in for a pair of breezy kisses. "You're a wreck, Art. It's Calvin again, isn't it?"

"No. It's nothing, honestly."

Mary crossed her arms. "Don't give me that bullshit. You're unhappy, and you're going to tell me why. And if you refuse, I'm back down those stairs and off to Gillingham."

"But I wanted to hear all about Freddie," she protested weakly.

"Freddie, as lovely as he is, can wait." Mary took her arm and hustled her around the corner and into the nearest tapas bar. "Two glasses of Grenache," she told the waiter, "as large as they come. Wait, make that a bottle. And—" she grabbed his arm as he was moving away—"Bring us some tortilla and a plate of *calamares*—my friend's about to pass out."

"Mary, quit fussing."

"Now, what's he done? And when are you going to get a restraining order? I've been looking into it for you, and actually it's not too—"

"It's not Calvin," Artie said. "It's... Mark."

"Mark?" Her eyes grew large. "He hasn't... I mean, you haven't... *have* you?"

Artie put a hand over her eyes, having no idea where to begin, and Mary said, "Oh, dear. I had my suspicions, the way the pair of you were acting last Friday."

The hand dropped in indignation. "Nothing was going on Friday!"

"Please, Artie. You were like a couple of teenagers on a school outing."

"We were perfectly professional! We get on well, is all."

"Okay, if that's really true, then what's this all about? What happened *after* Friday?"

The drinks arrived, and Artie downed half a glass before starting at the beginning: Calvin's unannounced visit to the lab and the subsequent picnic with Mark on Hampstead Heath. Mary was familiar with Artie's phobia, although she had no idea about the presumed underlying cause. Calvin was the only person she'd ever revealed that to, and that had resulted only solidified her resolve never to make the same mistake again. But the phobia was surely enough—more than enough—to explain her motivations. The pent-up words tumbled out and sped up, and Mary listened without comment, astonished and sympathetic, until Artie finally disgorged the details of the embrace on Mark's sofa and her subsequent breakdown. Strange how something so vivid and intense, which had seemed to last forever, could come across so banal and predictable in words: *he pulled me against him; we nearly kissed; I cried.* Especially as she still couldn't think about it without being consumed by a relentless bloom of fire.

"Don't waste your breath telling me it's a bad idea, because I've already cut it off," Artie finished. Belligerent, as if an offensive strike could possibly hide her embarrassment.

"What makes you think I was going to say that?"

"We're work colleagues, Mare! This is the part where you're supposed to despise me for dallying with my own staff."

Mary put down her cutlery, the faintest of smiles on her lips.

"The first time I met Mark, I thought you'd be perfect together," she said. "He's an angel, Art. And no offense, but he's also more than enough of a man to actually handle someone like you."

"I don't want to be *handled*."

"There's handling and then there's handling. But it's really sad if what you say is true."

"Yeah, well." Artie attempted a forkful of tortilla, but it stuck halfway down, so she knocked back some more wine. Her lips were already starting to go a bit numb.

"I'm not sure I completely understand, though," Mary mused. "It seems a bit too pat, *not being able* to fall in love. How do you know that he doesn't experience similar feelings, but calls them something else?"

"He seems very sure of himself, Mary. It's not something I'd feel comfortable questioning. Even if it was relevant to me."

"And is it?"

Artie pushed a glistening olive around the glazed azure dish with a toothpick; try as she might, she could not penetrate its skin, and she was too stubborn to just pick it up with her fingers. "Not now, I don't think. But... possible, I would say." Admitting this to Mary was not easy. "Okay, *highly* possible, if I were to let it develop."

Mary thought about this for a moment. "I can't help wondering... are you sure it would really be such a bad thing?"

"Being pulled under by someone who can't love me back? In some ways that feels more twisted than Calvin."

"But actions speak louder than words. You said he'd like a long-term relationship one day, even children. You say you've got great sexual chemistry."

"It's not enough."

"But the fizz tends to fade from most couples anyway. Couldn't this be sort of like cutting to the chase?"

"You need to live through the romantic obsession, and then the peace at the end is something you've *earned*."

"Did you pick that up from a Barbara Cartland novel?"

"Fuck off, Mare. I want a grand romance—passion, fire, the works. Calvin didn't work out, but I don't need to settle for something suboptimal at my age."

"'Suboptimal' is about the last word I'd use to describe Mark Reynolds."

Her disapproval hung between them, making her feel ashamed.

"He's a wonderful friend," Artie said. "And that's enough for me."

"What about just enjoying yourself on a temporary basis? I bet he's unbelievable in bed. And it doesn't sound as if he'll hold it against you when you move on."

"Because." Artie played with her wineglass, watching its ruby-colored reflection shimmer on the white linen tablecloth. "The fears are getting worse. More intense. This thing with Mark... in some ways it helps when he's around, but in others, the feelings that he brings out in me—it synergizes, somehow. I'm more on edge now than ever before."

"Oh, Artie. I thought things had been a lot better since the separation."

"So did I... but I was wrong."

There: she'd confessed that as well. Hiding and self-delusion were a weakness, and she was determined to cut out all inner traces of it from her like the brown bruises on an apple.

"And I suppose there's no point in me begging you, yet again, to get some professional help?"

"I've had enough of shrinks for a lifetime."

"*He* doesn't count, not even remotely! How many times do I have to—"

"I can't. I've got to do this on my own. I've got to find the right way and stick to it."

Mary just shook her head, disgusted.

"Hard work," Artie said, giving her words a confident veneer they did not truly possess. "That's the key. Hard work, with no time left for brooding."

∽

24 June—later

The strangest thing happened today. H. spoke to Artemis as if he had feelings, as if he empathized with her bad mood. I have never before seen this happen. It was v. embarrassing, as it turns out the reason for her mood was a recently failed marriage, and H. made her say it out loud. Funny how someone like her could have those sorts of problems—hard to believe I thought her life was perfect at first. But that is not what is important: what is important is Henry's peculiar behavior and what it all means. I should tell Samantha, or ring up Caruthers, but it seems too premature. I don't want them to think that H. is slipping; I have no idea what they might do in response. Almost wish I hadn't told Samantha those other things last week, though nothing seems to have come of it in the end. The dozy bitch probably forgot to tell Caruthers altogether—I should be grateful for her stupidity.

Artemis asked me to stop by after hours, but when Henry switched off, her office and lab were dark. I was v. angry for a few minutes. I see this as typical female unreliability—she has allowed her emotional problems to interfere with work, which I cannot respect.

Simon banged the notebook shut, a startling disruption of the kitchen's quiet. He imagined the sound waves flying in all directions, rattling against the grimy refrigerator and tangling in the corners where he never had time to hoover out the cobwebs. The truth was that he'd been just as disappointed as angry to find that Artemis had deserted him, though he didn't want to admit as much to the faceless, timeless audience that haunted his journal. And he actually doubted it had anything to do with her blues; no doubt she had some shiny social engagement she'd forgotten about earlier. Despite all his bluster, despite the fact that he didn't really even *like* her, their collaboration had become the thing he looked forward to, the sole brightness that broke up the hours and days of his blur of a life: the data point that did not fit on the curve, and so, by its existence, called into question the entire model. Which in a way was deadly—before, it hadn't been so painfully clear what he'd been missing.

Suddenly, Simon felt trapped, trapped and stifled, with an uncharacteristic anxiety that made him want to throw something. The clock over the door said twenty past midnight: time to brush his teeth and go to bed.

Halfway to the bathroom, he turned back around, laced on his running shoes and slipped out into the dark.

CHAPTER 9
Secrets, Those Unprofessional To Foster

ARTIE WENT INTO THE LAB the next morning to check on Fiona. Music blared and the tissue culture hood was switched on, but the woman herself was absent. Probably upstairs, braving the taunts of Hastings' barbarian male post-docs aping their master as if by doing so some of his success might rub off on them.

Artie nudged down the music and turned to face the room. Standing in the middle of her own laboratory was a sweetness she had not yet become accustomed to; sometimes she thought she never would. Completely at odds with the aging décor in the rest of the basement, the space had been redesigned with care and fitted out with new bench surfaces and equipment in honor of her arrival. It was very small, but still perfect. As the years went by, she knew that the gleam of brushed steel and the smooth expanses of white fridges and freezers would age under the onslaught of the many itinerant scientists passing through her care. But for now, the cleanliness and order gave her a fierce, quiet joy, as if her mind could somehow align with it and take up some of its restful perfection.

She ducked into the tissue culture alcove and put on a pair of gloves. Inspecting the troops: the boss's prerogative. Swinging open the door to the incubator, she breathed in as the moist warm air brushed against her face—watched her reflected face in the stainless steel back panel smile in response. Within, she found a full house: on the top shelf, Fiona's obsessively neat stacks of round dishes and flasks, each row separated by a precise column of empty space that could have been measured with a ruler. And on the bottom shelf, Mark's domain: the containers thrown in chaotic disarray and their marker pen scrawls too messy to decipher. Artie knew that Fiona longed to have her own private incubator, but as Mark had never once suffered contamination from mold or bacteria in his cells, Artie had vetoed such an extravagant purchase.

Idly curious, Artie reached for a plastic culture plate on Mark's shelf, a flat, rectangular box with six wells in a two-by-three array, each well about the size of a fifty-pence piece. The lab didn't usually use plates like that. Whereas she knew exactly what her technician was up to, she suspected that Mark had a number of small experiments on the go that he only told her about after the fact. Which was fair enough: he was a very experienced post-doc, and more than entitled to his independence.

Artie studied the writing on the plate, but couldn't make it out. She put it under the small microscope anyway, careful not to slosh its pink fluid. Fiona never overfilled her wells like that.

She flicked on the light source and small glowing spheres appeared down the eyepiece: feline white blood cells, swimming in space, gently swaying back and forth and tumbling as she pushed the plate around and adjusted the focus.

"Gorgeous," she murmured out loud. There was nothing more beautiful to Artie than cat leukocytes, bright and fat with vitality.

She nudged the plate along to the next well, where a different story was in progress. The cells were oversized, bloated and sending out balloon-like protrusions: a sea of soap bubbles, clinging together in complex, desperate patterns.

Correction: there was nothing more beautiful to Artie than cat leukocytes being devastated by an acutely pathogenic strain of feline leukemia virus. She smiled to herself again, wondering exactly what Mark was up to. It must be infected with one of the zoo of control nasties she'd imported from Edinburgh.

"I feel positively violated," the man himself said, just behind her. Artie jumped away from the microscope, and Mark laughed at the look on her face.

"Red-handed," Artie said. "Sorry, but I miss cell culture—it doesn't feel like the day has started properly unless I've checked out something under the microscope."

"I know what you mean," he said, putting his notebook on the bench beside her. "Feel free to gawp at my plates anytime you like. Better still, feel free to maintain all my cells for me while I go off to the pub and catch up on my reading."

"Nice try, Reynolds."

Their interaction was perfectly amiable, as if the preceding week had never occurred. Artie couldn't stop probing herself for minute fissures, but fortunately, everything about her felt intact. Blurting everything out to Mary seemed to have brought her some semblance of closure.

Mark looked at her a moment, as if equally aware of her self-diagnostics. But his expression was as non-judgmental as always, and then he was turning to glance more closely at the plate, still resting under the microscope.

"You picked a spectacularly dull sample to satiate your vicarious urges, Art. It's a negative control—shouldn't be anything going on in that one."

"If so, you must be losing that famous touch. Check out well A2—have you notified their next-of-kin?"

"What?" Mark went completely serious, nudging her aside to look down the scope. He pushed the plate around, peering down the oculars. "That's impossible."

"Relax, Mark, You probably just swapped your virus tubes or something. Happens to the best of us."

He looked up at her slowly.

"You don't understand," he said. "These aren't cat cells. They're *human* T-cells—I borrowed them from Ian, up in Hastings' lab."

"And what have you put on them?" She kept her voice level as a pellet of coldness began to dissolve in her belly.

"The Minster virus." His voice, too, was steady, but Artie could see contradictory evidence in the tiny lines around his mouth.

"You isolated the full-length clone already?"

"No, it's just a quick-and-dirty chimera I started last week." He quickly explained how he'd managed to use PCR to coax out the business end of the Minster virus using the crude sequencing information Fiona had cobbled together, coupled with some guesswork about the regions that were still in the dark.

"You're sure it's the right beast?"

"Positive." He opened up his notebook and showed her the PCRs. "It's the right size, and it's not amplified by our normal primers. So then I just spliced it into our normal lab strain of FeLV to reconstruct a whole, zapped them into cells yesterday."

"But why into human cells?"

"I've done the cat cells too, on another plate, but—rather ironically as it's turned out—I wanted to include some controls where I wouldn't see any pathogenic effect..."

There was a long moment of silence, then Artie said, "Please tell me you haven't tried to reconstitute a live Minster virus using normal FeLV helper virus."

The look on his face said it all. Both Artie and Mark looked down at Mark's bare hands as they rested on the microscope's control knobs. He seemed almost mesmerized.

"Go wash your hands," she said, with authoritarian crispness. "Now." As he nodded and dashed to the sink, she added, "Has Fiona been exposed?"

"No, she doesn't even know I've been testing it."

"Exposed to what?" Fiona demanded, coming in. "Has Mark given us a bloody yeast infection at last?"

"Fiona," Artie said. "Sorry about this, but could you go get a coffee? We've got a situation here."

She opened her mouth, closed it. Then: "If there's a situation in *my* tissue culture room, then I'm helping."

"Okay," Artie said—there wasn't time to argue, even though time itself had taken on a strangely elastic consistency in the past few seconds. "Protect yourself first—coat, double gloves and a mask—"

"A *mask*?"

"Yes, please," she said, as Mark grabbed his own coat and snapped on gloves.

"You haven't gone and made a replication-competent Minster virus, have you, Mark?" Fiona's voice was rich with disgust. "Of all the idiotic stunts!"

"Now is not the time to bicker," Artie said, tone sharper than she'd intended.

"Sorry, boss." Fiona went into high gear, whipping on the protective garb as Artie washed her hands at the sink: one, two, three rounds of disinfectant soap and water so hot it scalded. She hadn't opened the dish: true, the wells were too full, but she was almost certain that no pink liquid had sloshed onto the outer sides. She felt a mask go around her nose and mouth—Mark, adjusting the band around her head, gloved fingers smooth and rubbery-cool against her scalp. She dried her hands, then gloved and gowned up herself.

"Why don't you two empty the incubator and wipe it down? And the scope?" Mark said, voice muffled through the mask. "I'll do the plate—it was my stupid mistake in the first place. Actually, there are two—let me just grab the other one in there..."

Mark transported the contaminated plates gingerly into the sterile hood and sat down before it, while Fiona took the first stack from the incubator, saying, "Should I wipe all these down with ethanol, put them back after we've cleaned inside?"

Artie hesitated. "I'm really sorry, guys, but I'm afraid we're going to have to bin everything. We can't take any chances. Try to avoid any splashes."

"I don't believe this," Fiona said, glaring Mark's way. "Some of my assays have been running for over a fortnight!"

Artie handed Mark a squirt bottle of bleach.

"Thanks," he said, voice tight. "You read my mind." Artie watched as he forced a stream of caustic liquid into the pink broth in each well, turning it instantly yellow. A brand-new virus obliterated—a brand-new virus that could decimate human cells. As much as she was frightened at that moment, she couldn't suppress a tinge of regret that they were stopping the experiment, that they couldn't run a barrage of tests immediately to find out what was going on. It could be the most important retroviral discovery of the decade.

"It's pretty much impossible that any virus could have escaped that plate," Artie said, trying to ease the fierce look on Mark's masked profile. "Dumping everything is just a precaution. And if you've been working properly, there's no way you could have been exposed to any aerosols."

"I can't believe I didn't put on gloves before I touched that plate," Mark said. "I *never* forget to do that. And I can't believe I put my lab mates at risk."

"Shall I double-bag this, Artie?" Fiona said, coming up to them with a bulging yellow plastic biohazard sack.

"Triple," she replied.

"Wait," Mark said, "let me put these bleached plates in before you seal it up."

"And if one of you could chuck it into an autoclave straight away? I don't want it sitting around on the floor for the staff to deal with later."

"I'll do it," Fiona said. "The incubator's clean now. But somebody should nuke the hood too."

After she left, holding the bag at arm's length, Artie sank into a seat and watched Mark spray down the inside of the hood repeatedly, rub the steel surfaces angrily with wads of paper towel.

"Shall we call in the equipment guys and have this officially decontaminated?" Mark finally asked, in an uncharacteristically subdued tone.

"I don't think that will be necessary," she said. "Until we know what we're dealing with, I think it would be sensible to treat Minster virus as Hazard Group 3—but even then, it's not like we need to use moon suits. This isn't Ebola by any stretch."

"But we can't do any more Minster work in this lab, can we?"

"I'm afraid not. We'll have to negotiate with Hastings for Containment Level 3 hood time upstairs with all the pandemic flu guys—not a prospect I relish. And I know it's a pain for you. The company, more than the stairs."

"I've never used a glove box before," Mark said. "At least it's something new and interesting for my CV. But how do you know it's only Hazard Group 3?"

He had paused his relentless wiping and was looking at her over his shoulder. *How indeed?*

She thought about it, shook her head. "There's never been a retrovirus classified as Group 4; they're just not equipped to be that pathogenic. All the preliminary tests suggest we're dealing with a particularly unusual recombination between FeLV and

FIV: nasty, but not life-threatening. I understand why you're spooked, but let's try to keep things in perspective."

"I just don't understand how you can be so sure about something this important."

"Listen, Mark. There have been nine reported cases in Minster thus far, and probably loads more that we don't know about. If this cat virus was so dangerous, we'd have heard about human casualties by now."

Mark slowly nodded, visibly relieved. "That's true."

"And we don't know if what you just caused in that plate could happen in real life. Just because you put Minster together with normal FeLV in a dish full of cells and they managed to cobble together a functional bad-boy doesn't mean it's easy, or even possible, in the wild. I could give you a dozen examples right now."

"Also true." He stripped off his gloves, ripped the mask from his face and swiveled his chair to face her. "Thanks for not being furious, Art."

"You didn't do anything I wouldn't have at least thought about doing myself," she said. "And I want you to repeat that exact experiment again—once we've sorted out hood access with Hastings. I hate to say it, but he'll take the request much better from you than me, since he's trying to poach you. Conveniently, as it turns out."

"Consider it done."

"We're onto something mammoth here, Mark. You realize that, don't you?"

Finally, his face relaxed—not actually a smile, but it was a start. "I'd say your plan to conquer the universe has just received a significant boost."

WHILE MARK AND FIONA RETREATED to the freshly sterilized tissue culture room to re-start all their lost cell cultures, still not completely on speaking terms, Artie went into her office, looked up a number and dialed.

"Cable Street Practice," a wary female voice answered.

"Can I speak to Freddie Preston, please?"

"I'm afraid he's quite busy at the moment—can I ask who's calling?"

"It's Artemis Marshall, over at Heatherfields."

"Oh! Why didn't you say earlier? It's Kamini here, our receptionist's popped out for a fag. Only you sounded just like the Chihuahua Lady."

"I did?"

"She's been ringing every five minutes for updates about her precious Prince Albert, so I jumped to conclusions."

"Nothing terminal, I hope?"

"Well, I suppose it wouldn't be too much of a breach of patient confidentiality to say that the problem lies almost entirely with the chocolate diet she's got the poor thing on. Oh, here's Freddie."

"Artemis? Good to hear from you!"

"You sound funny."

"Just congested—I've been a bit under the weather recently. What can I do for you?"

Artie wanted to ask him what his symptoms were, then told herself she was being ridiculous. His immune system was probably just shattered from too many sleepless nights having mad sex.

"Listen, I need to let you know something potentially important about the Minster virus. Mark's done some preliminary tests, and it looks as if the virus can kill human T-cells."

There was a pause. "Really? Well, that's... remarkable." She could tell by his tone that she didn't need to spell out the implications. "Are you saying it's actually contagious?"

"We don't know that yet. But even if it's replication-defective, we have to assume that there are a lot of normal FeLV helper viruses around to mix and match with working parts. This doesn't mean the virus would have a human-specific envelope, or even that it could pass cat-to-human, but it's certainly possible."

"Well, I always wear gloves when I take samples, and am scrupulously cautious throughout—I've got two cats myself, don't want to risk taking anything home. And I never let Mary or Kamini anywhere near the samples until the box is taped up. But I might start wearing a mask."

"I was going to suggest that. But it's not just the dead ones I'm worried about. If any more of these sick cats are brought in for you or Kamini to see..."

"Understood. We'll be careful."

"It's just a precaution."

"Artemis... you don't think I should stop studying this, do you?" His voice was anxious—not a man frightened of disease, but more like a little boy, afraid someone was going to confiscate his toy.

"Oh, no. If this thing were dangerous, we'd know by now."

There was that doubt again: she was the FeLV expert, and a number of people were depending on her professional opinion; didn't she bear ultimate responsibility if anything went wrong? But then she remembered that Freddie had performed those necropsies long before they'd started officially collaborating; if anything had happened, it was already well out of her control.

"I *could*..." Freddie voice dwindled off.

"What?"

"Well, it's not outside the realm of normal professional courtesy to make follow-up calls. I could just double check that all the owners of those afflicted cats are still..."

"Alive?" she said. "Better be careful how you phrase it; if someone panics and rings up the *Daily Mirror*, *it* wouldn't look good."

"Not a problem, Artemis. I'll be discreet. And if they've had so much as a sniffle, I'll let you know."

"Okay, thanks. That would ease my mind a bit."

She cradled the phone, stared into space and then picked it up again and dialed her former post-doc supervisor in Edinburgh.

"Cox," Philip answered curtly, as he always did. "Make it quick, the next batsman's nearly at the crease."

"One of these days it's going to be someone important, like the Queen, and you'll regret your cavalier manner."

"Artemis! Lovely to hear from you. And Her Majesty knows full well that I follow the cricket, would never dream of interrupting me at such a crucial time."

Knowing Phil's status, he might not be joking.

"I need your advice," she said, sketching out the entire story of the Minster recombinant and Mark's most recent results. "Do you think I'm putting people at risk? What if this virus is actually dangerous?"

"Hogwash," Phil said. "FeLV is a pussy-cat, if you'll pardon the pun, never mind how sharp its claws may have become. In fact, I think you're playing it too safe."

"Really?"

"I can't believe you let Reynolds bleach those wells before taking off a supernatant sample for filtration and analysis! Don't you *want* to know if it's replication-competent?"

"Of course I do. But there are rules..."

"Don't get me started about Health and Safety! They're making our lives a living hell up here, practically can't walk one end of the corridor to the other without filling out three forms and giving a urine specimen. In my day, retrovirologists were real men—figuratively speaking of course, my dear. We didn't wear gloves or have sterile hoods, let alone fret about a little bit of healthy pathogenicity. The more the deadly the better, we thought. Whoops, there goes the ball—"

She smiled as the dial tone resounded in her ear. Exactly what she had needed to hear.

ARTIE SLIPPED OUT OF THE fourth-floor communal equipment room, squinting at the tantalizing marks on the printout in her hand. In all the excitement of the morning's incident, she'd completely forgotten that her second attempt at the Southern blots was ready to be processed. And now, having captured the results under the digital imager, she felt that familiar post-experiment feeling, the half-disappointment, half-excitement when an outcome didn't entirely make sense—which was most of the time, if she thought about it objectively. Disappointment, because an unambiguous answer would have led more quickly to the next step; but excitement, because the unexpected always holds the promise of something unforeseen that could be even better than the original hypothesis. Especially in this case.

She was walking slowly down the corridor towards the stairwell, still puzzling over the printout, when her gaze was caught by tan trousers and a pair of brown brogues planted on the floor below, obstructing her passage.

"How charming to see you doing such trivial tasks personally," Peter Hastings said. Backlit against the lurid magenta stained-glass window behind him, he looked positively Satanic. "It's such a pity that the Sanctum did not deem your research program ambitious enough to warrant funding a few more technicians."

Fuckwit. She gave him a sweet smile, said, "Well, you know how it is after your latest *Nature* paper. The experimental angles seem to expand exponentially."

Unlike Artie, Peter Hastings had not been blessed with such an honor for many years; in some quarters, the rumors had it that the big American labs were leaving him in the dust. As he visibly regrouped, she added, "Besides, it's good to keep your hand in, don't you think? I wouldn't want to go soft behind a desk."

"I've heard all about your little *outbreak* this morning," he riposted, "and have half a mind to report you to Salverson for reckless lab practice."

"No need," she said. "I appreciate your concern, but I've already been in touch with him myself."

Hastings opened his mouth, but Artie cut him off: "He agrees that given the surprising nature of the experimental outcome, we handled it in textbook fashion. And he's as excited as we are about the implications. I take it Mark has approached you about our new Containment Level 3 needs?"

"He has," Hastings said, with a frosty smile. "I've given my permission—for him alone, do you understand? Not that... *female* tech in your employ. She doesn't seem serious enough to understand the risks and responsibilities."

She bit down her anger. "That's very kind of you, Peter."

"And I've warned him that he has to work completely around my people, who will have priority at all times—even if that means the graveyard shift."

"Naturally," Artie said, knowing that none of his post-docs would ever be rude enough to be that unaccommodating—their treatment of the lowly Fiona notwithstanding. Science was a communal endeavor, and post-docs stuck together with a fierce loyalty that went far beyond laboratory boundaries. "We certainly do appreciate your hospitality."

Afterwards, she flew down the stairs, blood singing with outrage and looking forward to relating the whole episode to Mark over a few chuckles. But she stopped flat just outside her office door, taking in the strange tableau visible through its glass window: Fiona shrunk against one corner with a print-out in her hand, staring suspiciously at Simon Renquist, who was flattened against the opposite wall looking equally uncomfortable, and Mark sitting at his desk in the center, utterly unperturbed as always. Simon must have come in after Fiona—she knew instinctively that she would not have entered if "Rennie" were already there. Though having said that, she was surprised that Simon would have entered in Fiona's presence. It must be important.

All three looked up at her breathless entrance with universal relief.

"Hastings is a toad," she said cheerfully, "but even a toad has his uses if he happens to possess a few fancy biosafety cabinets. Nice to see you, Simon. What's up?"

"I came to tell you about my analysis of those RT Snip signatures we were talking about before," he said diffidently. "I only had a small window, but Reynolds was here, so I..."

"That's fine," she said. "What did I miss?"

"Nothing yet," Mark said, "because I've just briefed him about our recombinant, and Fiona's just got some sequencing results back, which we were discussing."

She felt a small twinge of irritation at being the last to know, but mentally waved it aside as paranoid.

"Who first?"

"Me, " Fiona said. "I've got to get back to the lab." And indeed, she looked like she was ready to run a marathon. "The short answer is that there isn't much to discuss: we still don't know what sequences are in the Envelope region. The sequences start off okay, then degenerate into nonsense."

"Let me see." Fiona passed over the sheaf of traces, and Artie scanned them. "God, that's ugly. Any ideas?"

"I've seen something like that before," Mark said. "When you get certain regions of DNA that are rich in guanine and cytosine repeats, normal sequencing conditions can't cut through the secondary structure. It happens frequently in some avian viruses."

"FeLV doesn't have any problem regions like that," Artie said thoughtfully. "At least not normal strains. So the GC stretch must be in the swapped-in part."

"So I'm going to repeat with the high-stringency protocol," Fiona said impatiently. "Can I go now?"

At Artie's wave, she slipped away.

"Are those your Southern blot results?" Mark asked, indicating the printout she'd forgot she was holding.

"You've got time, Simon?"

He nodded. She placed the paper onto her desk and they all crowded around.

"We've sorted out the origin of the Gag and polymerase genes," Artie explained, "but the nature of its Envelope gene has remained elusive, other than us knowing it's about 2000 bases longer than it ought to be."

"And that it isn't recognized by our standard Envelope primers," Mark said.

Artie said to Simon: "Because the Envelope protein mediates virus attachment to cells, it dictates what cell types—and species—can be initially infected."

Simon nodded. "In that respect, it would be a key epidemiological factor, a main governor of spread. Something we need to get a handle on as soon as possible."

"Our vet colleague on Sheppey took these DNAs from cats infected with the Minster virus. At the time he was working under the hypothesis that it was FIV, because it had come up negative on his standard FeLV kit, and normally cat AIDS is caused by one or the other. But his FIV test came up negative as well. So we retested them with a variety of our standard probes."

Mark was looking at the films with narrowed eyes. "And it's not looking good, is it?"

"Depends on your perspective," Artie said.

"I don't understand this read-out," Simon said. "Can someone explain?"

"Sorry, Simon. The punchline is that the Minster cats are negative for both FeLV and FIV envelopes. We have no idea what gene has taken its place." Artie filled him in on the technique and pointed out the black bands missing from the afflicted cats, bands that were present in control infected tissue that Artie had probed in parallel.

Simon blinked. "Is commandeering other genes a normal behavior for this virus?"

"Yes," Mark said. "A lot of the cancer genes we know about today were discovered because retroviruses isolated from tumors had picked up stray bits of their hosts' DNA."

"Major recombinations don't really harm the fitness of virus any more than the minor mutations do," Artie said. "Because there are always plenty of normal viruses around to take up the slack, and package their defective signatures into healthy particles, even variants with very large stretches of alien DNA can perpetuate."

"Interesting." Simon stared at the rectangles, looking as if he were processing several things simultaneously. "So not only do we have to deal with simple mutations, but we also have to factor in wholesale swaps and recombinations with other species. That certainly complicates the mathematics."

"Does this make any sense in light of your Snip analysis?" Artie asked.

"May I?"

As before, Simon called up his account on Artie's laptop and produced the familiar flattened doughnut. "I repeated the La Fontayne using only the relevant RT signatures to see if a similar geographical bias comes up, and..."

The doughnut did its usual dance, sprouting its spines and peaks. "This is Minster," Simon said, tapping a pencil, eraser end forward, against the largest peak with its inverted bell top.

"It looks similar to the last one, doesn't it?" Mark said.

"Yes. Which is very strange, when you think about it." He hit a few keys, and a ghostly grey spiky doughnut of similar proportions was superimposed over the top. "This is just a representation of the original La Fontayne created from the entire genome, emphasizing the similarity in pattern."

"Why is it strange?" Artie said. "They're all from the same cats, the same viruses."

"Well, most of the variation in your data set is in the Env gene," Simon said.

"That's normal, "Mark said. "Env is always the most unstable."

"Yes, but I would have thought that restricting the analysis to the RT region would have muted the phenomenon, smoothed down the spikes, or at least changed it in some way. Yet as you can see, if anything the Minster epidemic is more prominent. This strongly supports your idea that mutations in RT may actually be driving this whole thing."

"That's fantastic!" Artie said.

"But as I've mentioned before, raw sequence data would be more accurate."

"That's my cue." Mark pulled open a drawer, rummaged around and drew out a flash drive. "Artie asked me to assemble this for you, Simon—it's all the sequences we have, as far back as 2010. Nowhere near as extensive as our Snip database, but..."

Simon nodded his thanks as he took the drive, looking about as pleased as he ever got. "Perhaps not. But instead of looking at an entire jigsaw puzzle made from an out-of-focus image, this will be like having fewer pieces at much higher resolution—little details may become apparent that the blurry big picture could not provide, which we can extrapolate to the whole."

"We can't wait to see your results," Artie said. "Not to pressure you, but how soon?"

"How soon..." Simon's gaze flew to his scarecrow wrist. "Is that the time? Sorry, but we'll have to talk about this later."

Silence filled in his hasty wake, then Mark said, "I'm afraid he doesn't get any less weird on second glance, Art. Did you notice the way his hands were shaking?"

"But those Snip results!" She leapt to her feet, started pacing. "It's so promising—we need to work out what mutations in RT are causing all this. We need to make chimeras, test them in culture. Check the databases, see if it's evolved elsewhere, maybe make a recombinant protein version, do some in vitro RT assays? Then we need to—"

"Hey." Mark held up a hand. "Easy there, Prof. You need to save some experiments for *next* decade."

She halted by the plastic palm, shadowboxed its fronds and watched tiny motes of dust float outward under the harsh fluorescence. "God, it's so frustrating. Imagine if we had a lab the size of Hastings', and the money from all his grants!"

"It wouldn't make a jot of difference," he said. "You'd still come up with a hundred more angles that we wouldn't have the resources to cover. That's not a criticism," he added, as she made a face.

"I worry sometimes that I've more or less bullied you away from independent research. You came here with a fellowship plan, remember?" Artie realized with a pang of guilt that it was the first time she'd even thought about Mark's immunodeficiency project in at least a week.

"Don't worry about it—we're a team, and Minster is a thousand times more interesting. Besides..." His look was sly. "I still have a few things up my sleeve."

ABOUT HALF AN HOUR LATER, during a stretch of studious silence in the joint office, Mark's mobile went off. Artie, who was standing waiting for the kettle, watched Mark glance up from his article, annoyed until he saw the number on his phone's screen.

"*Hey!* It's about time you returned my calls." His grin emerged, more vibrant than usual. "Uh huh, nice try... No, I was not! In fact, I was going to say the same thing about—ha, please, you wish. I... yeah... of course we're still on for tonight, *chez* Reynolds all right with you? Good... isn't it your turn to cook?"

As he stood up and wandered out of the office, Artie could just about make out the tone of a female voice issuing from the phone during his pauses in speech. As the door clicked shut behind him, Mark emitted an appreciative laugh that echoed down the corridor.

The kettle boiled over and clicked off, and Artie registered that the sensation in her gut was jealousy.

Don't be an idiot, she scolded herself as she prepared the tea, one cup instead of two. She hadn't been interested in sleeping with him on his terms, so he'd moved on. Not only was it no big deal, but it was the best thing that could happen to either of them. Once he was safely entangled with someone else—or as entangled as he ever got—they could get on with the business of being colleagues without all the underlying tension. And she could wean herself from any remaining traces of dependence on his support. Still, her hands were trembling slightly as she picked up the mug, and she burnt her tongue on the first fierce sip.

A tap on the office glass, then: Simon, face drawn into unusually anxious lines. She was not pleased to see him back so soon, in her present mood, but waved him in.

He only stuck his head around the door, said softly, "Henry would like to see you."

"What, you mean *now*?"

"Yes, now, if you wouldn't mind."

"What if I'm busy?" He looked dispassionately at her tea mug, which she put down, too late.

"Are you? I don't want to go back empty-handed, and if you're actually free—"

"All right, all right." Trying not to make a big deal of it, Artie grabbed her phone and shoved it in her jeans pocket as she followed him out. "This is a bit unusual, though, isn't it?"

"It's unprecedented." He lowered his voice further, even though the corridor was empty. "He's not normally so coherent this time of the day, either."

They went into B302, through the blind office and into the inner room. But Henry wasn't hulked at his computer, back to the door and tending to his lily; he was sitting at the table in the room's center, waiting expectantly for their entrance. Looking sideways at Simon, Artie could see that he was equally surprised at this transposition.

"Ah, Professor," Henry said, rising to his feet like a Victorian gentleman. "Thank you for attending to me on such short notice; I do hope I haven't inconvenienced you?"

"I was just having some tea," Artie said—the first thing that popped into her head. She was distracted by the way he looked; expression pleasantly composed, shaggy brows relaxed, granite lips sculpted into a smile. And the eyes—which she'd looked at before she remembered not to—were mild and lacking in that edgy, alien element that had so unbalanced her in the past. Eyes so convincingly personable that it would be rude not to meet them. If she had seen him now for the first time, she would never have guessed he was abnormal in any way.

"Simon, would you be so good as to prepare the Professor another cup?"

"Really, that's not necessary."

"I insist. Simon?"

Simon blasted her with an untranslatable look before stalking off out the door towards his office. She heartily hoped he would be quick about it.

Henry sank back into his chair as Artie settled in opposite.

"Actually," he said softly, "the tea was just a ruse. I wanted a word with you... in private."

"Oh?" she said. Her body was busy finding its center; her feet, weighing the solidity the floor in case she had to leap into action. If this was more prying about her divorce, she was out the door, Simon's rules be damned. "Concerning what?"

"The project," he said, drawing his fingers into a tidy cage between them. "I have been following your progress at a distance"—a hand waved back towards his monitor before returning to its cage—"and I understand that the La Fontayne continues to produce a beautiful and intriguing pattern of natural spread, consistent with actual activity in the field."

"That's correct."

"But I've been tinkering with the Meyerhof-Hernsley quite a bit myself, just out of my own interest. Recently I've customized it more thoroughly, and something equally interesting has arisen."

"It sounds fascinating." She covered her surprise as best she could. But underneath the thought that Simon would be furious if he found out was a deep, quickening curiosity to know what the great man had discovered. "Do elaborate."

"There's no time for details now," Henry said, looking over his shoulder towards where Simon had vanished. "Let us just say, for the moment, that what is happening in Minster does not, to me, seem entirely natural."

"What do you mean? Do you mean because cats are largely domesticated?"

"Not at all." He waved a hand. "I am referring to human intervention. Specifically... to bioterrorism."

Artie felt the first shimmer of adrenalin washing over her. Suddenly, she was willing Simon to dawdle over the chore, to break a mug, have to search for the teabags, anything to prevent him from cutting off this conversation. Her virus, a manmade entity? Ludicrous! And yet... this was the famous Henry Manfield before her.

"What makes you think that?" She kept her tone even, courteous: not a trace of skepticism.

"The MoD has alerted us to a human incident occurring in a similar geographical area even as we speak, and the profile bears some resemblance to your Minster outbreak. Furthermore, the shape of your Minster spike is not entirely natural, even in the La Fontayne."

Hadn't Simon said as much himself?

"But Professor, why don't you want Simon to know about all this?"

He nodded. "A fair question. Simon is very good, but his true calling is shaping up to be natural epidemics. Artificial ones, on the other hand, are undeniably my speciality. I don't want to undermine him, however—I fear in recent months I've been getting under his collar a bit. If my model comes to nothing, he need never know."

Artie was not too bemused by the scientific implications to miss how strange it was that Henry was both aware of his effect on his protégé, and also genuinely regretful. Two attributes that ought to have been impossible for someone with his condition.

The door opened and Simon scuttled back in, placing a chipped mug before her. She made a show of murmuring her thanks and sampling it, though the water had obviously not boiled properly, the brew was weak and he'd added far too much sugar. The sickly concoction sat uneasily in her stomach as the full implications of Henry's theory became clear. As remarkable as a bioterrorist angle would be, it would also signal the end of her glorious theory. No matter how unscientific the impulse, she simply did not want it to be true.

"I was just asking Professor Marshall for a progress report on the collaboration," Henry said, looking up at Simon, whose entire frame seemed braced for a shockwave. Returning his gaze to Artemis, he actually winked. "She has assured me that you are doing an excellent job and that the research is advancing to her satisfaction."

"Oh." Simon blinked. "Good, that was precisely my opinion as well."

"I have therefore decided that your proposal to spend some of our research funds on outsourcing her sequencing needs is entirely appropriate."

"Ah—that's good news, Professor," Simon stammered. Why, Artie wondered, did he look so shocked?

"See to it that you provide Professor Marshall with the appropriate funding code."

"I... yes, of course. Straightaway."

"Splendid," Henry said. "If there are no further questions, Professor Marshall, then I will regretfully ask you to leave us; we have a very busy afternoon ahead."

A pause ensued, with each party seeming to eye the other with multiple layers of hidden motives.

"I have no further questions," Artie finally said, snapping out of the spell. "Thank you, Professor."

She stood up, gave a sort of funny bow that she immediately regretted, and felt their gazes deflect off her stiff back as she made her way out of B302c

—and straight across the corridor into the toilets. Opening a stall, she slammed the rattling metal door, locked herself inside and leaned against the cool tiled wall, still reeling from the strange exchange. Terrorists, using feline viruses as a weapon? It was too preposterous to be true. Various vets had been in direct contact with the virus, and they were fine. And surely if Britain were currently under attack, it would have been all over the news—even the MoD couldn't keep something so important secret for long. Henry must be going senile; this was the most likely explanation.

Yet this didn't jibe at all with Henry's performance: if he was only acting like a sane, reasonable and unimpaired human being, he was one hell of a performer. And anyway, how did she know the virus did no harm? Because Freddie was still unaffect-ed? Scientifically, she knew this wasn't adequate proof. The MoD had sick people on their hands, Henry had implied, sick enough to have drawn their attention—if she could believe what he said. And the Minster virus might not be the source of the attack—it might merely be a spin-off, a virus strain that had mutated beyond its original engineered form and that was now in the process of adapting to its new environment—just as retroviruses had done for millennia.

But her theory about the natural evolution of the Minster epidemic being entirely incorrect was only one implication she now needed to consider. Henry Manfield was asking her to hide crucial experimental information from a scientific collaborator. How could she do such a thing? How could she continue to feed Simon virus signa-tures, discuss the work, bounce off ideas if she knew in her heart that an alternative hypothesis was looming just off-stage? Come to think of it, this entire complication could make telling even Mark problematic. Henry did not want Simon to know, but Mark would never allow her to get away with keeping him in the dark. So the con-clusion was inescapable: she couldn't tell Mark either. It was going to be a dirty little secret, just between her and Henry.

She shivered. Damn him for putting her in this quandary in the first place. He must be losing it: it was the explanation that most suited all the facts at hand.

Then Artie paused, thinking of something. It should be possible to fact-check a bit of Henry's wild story—via Simon, if she did it skillfully enough.

She unbolted the door and went back to reality.

❧

LATER THAT AFTERNOON, ARTIE WAS sitting at her bench in the otherwise empty lab, jotting up the most recent experiments in her lab notebook. Most data were electronic these days, but Phil Cox had instilled in her a deep reverence for committing the details in ink on paper nevertheless: a strict account of the messy real-life narrative, no matter how shiny and inevitable the final product might appear when published in a scientific journal. And she took solace in the soothing ritual, these days more than ever.

At the sound of the door opening, Artie looked up to see a woman about her age, tanned and smiling with a head full of blustery brown curls, wide eyes seeming just on the verge of laughter. Big-boned and athletic, attired in jeans, a forest-green T-shirt and sensible sandals, she looked like a hillwalking enthusiast, the sort that rises at 5 AM to make the most of the day. There was something very familiar about her expression. Almost reflexively, Artie found herself smiling back.

"Any idea where Mark Reynolds has got to?" the woman asked. "Sorry to barge in, but the man on the door didn't seem to interested in calling anyone, just left me to fend for myself. And Mark wasn't answering his mobile."

"That's okay," Artie said. Was this Mark's mysterious dinner date? If so, she had to give him some credit. "He's at a seminar, I'm afraid—the sort where you can't really creep out without causing a fuss." She checked her watch. "I'd give him half an hour."

"He's always getting the times wrong," the woman said. A pause. "You're Artemis, aren't you? I can tell, even though his description doesn't remotely do you justice."

"And you are...?"

"Sorry, I'm always ten steps ahead of myself." She came into the room and stuck out her hand. "I'm Rebecca—Mark's sister. I've heard a lot about you."

"Call me Artie," she said, marveling at the resemblance, now utterly apparent, as the woman's hand gave hers a firm squeeze. Aware, too, somewhere underneath, of relief that the voice who'd so delighted him earlier on the phone was not a romantic prospect. Aware, and then just as quickly dismissive of such a ridiculous notion.

"Is there any place around here where I can park myself in the interim?" she asked. Her regional accent, like her brother's, was utterly unplaceable. "I promise I'll keep well out of trouble."

"Do you fancy a coffee instead?" Artie asked, on impulse.

As Artie led her upstairs to the Senior Common Room under a cover of casual chatter, she remembered what Mark had said about his sister's abusive ex-husband. She wondered what sort of twisted soul would want to hit such a lovely person; it seemed like something that could only happen in a parallel universe.

"Such an impressive space," Rebecca said, gazing upward at the high ceilings and chandeliers.

"I hardly ever come in here," Artie said. "Professors and their guests only, and I hate all that elitist shit. But the coffee is a lot better than the stuff in the staff canteen."

Soon they were settled into two velvet wing-backed chairs in a dark corner, silent until the waiter had poured the steaming cups from the silver urn and melted away.

"I'm so glad to finally meet you," Rebecca said, leaning forward. "Mark hasn't stopped raving about you since he started here. He was pretty miserable in Bristol, but now he's back to his former self—which must be down to you."

"I don't know," Artie said, embarrassed. "It always struck me that happy was his default state."

"Yes and no," the other woman said. "He told me he's told you about his particu-lar...problem. The relationship that went wrong in Bristol was especially difficult for him. Maybe the worst yet."

"I'm not sure he'd want me to be..." Artie felt distinctly uncomfortable at this frontal assault. Just how much detail had Mark been disseminating about her?

Rebecca rapped knuckles against her head. "Sorry, I'm getting ahead of myself again! I always forget that other people don't..." She paused, taking a deep breath. "Mark and I are close, like twins, even though he's three years older. We share ev-erything, always have done. It's down to our childhood—has he told you we were fostered?"

"No." Artie sat back, deciding just to shut up and learn a few things.

"Well, it's not a secret and he wouldn't mind me mentioning it. There were five of us, four brothers and me. The elder three were quite a bit older and were placed separately, but Social Services did their best to keep me and Mark together, through multiple placements. Mark remembers our original family, though he doesn't like to talk about it—but I was too little. For as far back as I can remember, he always tried to protect me, look after me. If it wasn't for him, I never would have turned out sane."

Artie was silent, struck by the image of Mark as a little boy, having to be an adult. She knew exactly what that felt like.

"I'm really sorry about spilling all this out," Rebecca hastened. "It's just that I feel like I already know you, from all that Mark has told me. He's always nagging me not to be so forward."

"It's okay," Artie said with a faint smile. "Has he told you... everything?"

"I'm afraid so." Rebecca reached over, put an unexpected hand on hers. "And are you all right? Do you understand his limitations in the relationship department?"

"Yes," she said, feeing naked before the other woman's luminous gaze. "Well, per-haps not entirely."

"I know it's difficult," Rebecca replied, after a few moments. "I just wish—you know, it doesn't make him a bad person, or less worthy of finding happiness."

"I don't think any less of him." Artie could scarcely get her voice above a whisper.

Rebecca looked at her more carefully. "I can see now why he's so wildly attracted to you. You're not his normal type—but there's something about you that fits perfect-ly. I only wish..."

"We work together, Rebecca, and I think we're going to be close colleagues and friends for a long time. It's all settled."

"I know." She shrugged, smiled. "I just want everything to be perfect for him."

"Me, too. But I don't think I'm the one who can give him what he needs. I'm pretty messed up myself at the moment, anyway."

"Yes, he told me all about your *husband*." Her voice seemed to darken. "You've done well to get out. Don't *ever* let anyone—" She paused to get herself under con-trol. "Sorry. Whenever I think about men like that, I want to strangle something. Preferably something with a penis."

"It's all right, I understand. And I'm glad you got out, too."

"That was all down to Mark, knocking sense into me," she said briskly. "I know you've been resisting, but you should let him help you too, Artie—he's brilliant at that sort of thing. Listen, speaking of help, and as I've already completely violated your privacy, do you mind if I make one last foray?"

"Why not?" She threw up her hands: there was something about this woman that made it impossible to be offended. What would it be like to live with such a soul of transparent glass, open for anyone to look in? "Might as well make it a thorough pillage."

"I don't know if Mark mentioned it, but I'm an occupational therapist. Mark was telling me about your phobia."

"This is so unfair," Artie said, starting to laugh. "All I wanted was a coffee."

"I know, I know! But listen—I've got this mate at Guy's Hospital, where I used to work before I moved to Birmingham? He's brilliant—specializes in phobias. I'm sure if I put in a word, he'd love to have lunch. Especially with someone as gorgeous as you."

"I'm not so sure."

"Come on, Artie, aren't you even curious? This guy, Augustus Faber's the name, is practically the world's *expert*. Don't you want to know if there's something that can be done? Mark says that your fear is the one thing about yourself that you hate the most. Imagine if you could be rid of it!"

"Is he a shrink?" Artie asked, interested despite herself.

"Well, he's a psychiatrist, but he's very academic. Not a lot of one-on-one patients, just scholarly stuff, case studies, clinical trials—that sort of thing. But I'm sure that doesn't mean he wouldn't be—"

"In that case, put us in touch," Artie said quickly. "Why not? I'm interested to hear what he has to say."

WHEN THE WOMEN RETURNED TO Artie's office, Mark stood up hastily.

"Becky, I'm so sorry I was tied up. I thought today was tomorrow."

"I'm not sorry," Rebecca said. "I got to have a lovely chat with this amazing professor I ran into. Have you met her yet?"

Mark's eyes narrowed. "Artie, I apologize if she'd been a complete pain in the arse."

"Not at all," Artie said. "I found it quite... informative."

He groaned. "I don't even want to know. Artie, is it okay if I bunk off a bit early?"

"Not before you go back down into the coal pits and reach your ten-ton quota. No, of course it's okay, you idiot."

"Great, thanks."

"Can I just dash to the Ladies' first?" Rebecca asked.

After she'd been pointed in the right direction, Artie sank into her seat, a bit exhausted. Mark perched uncertainly on her desk, looking out the door where his sister had vanished.

"I was serious about that apology, Art."

"Don't be. I had a nice time."

"Did she...?"

"Of course she did. But it was... a relief, to be honest. And she's amazing, Mark."

He turned to her then. "I'm so glad you like her. I can tell she likes you, too. With Becky, it's all or nothing—but you obviously passed." He paused. "You're not pissed off at me for being so indiscreet?"

Artie passed a hand over her eyes. "Of course not. It's your life, to share as you see fit. To be honest, I'm envious. I would have loved to have had a sibling, someone to talk to about anything and everything."

"It can be annoying sometimes, believe me. There are certain things you just want to keep to yourself, say to retain a little manly dignity—but with her, it's impossible."

"I can imagine."

He grinned. "The benefits outweigh the annoyance. Most days."

"And you never have to be alone."

"True." He looked at her a moment, as if wanting to say something more, but then scooted off the desk and collected his things without another word.

After the siblings departed in a wave of cheerful laughter, Artie felt the silence press in. Somewhere upstairs, she could sense the setting sun, bathing the upper floors with rose-colored light, hear the building slowly depopulate as, one by one, the scientists of Heatherfields headed home. Opening up her computer under the harsh fluorescent lights, she searched for Augustus Faber's name, put her nose close to the screen and began to read.

CHAPTER 10
Episodes, Subtle Differences Between

THE NEXT MORNING ARTIE WAS drinking a cup of coffee at the kitchen table and flipping through a copy of *Science* when her mobile went off: Calvin. Remembering her new policy of confronting things head on, she answered on the second ring, not taking her eyes from the paragraph she was reading.

"Artie," he said, sounding distinctly surprised. Good, she thought: keeping him off-guard.

"What can I do for you, Cal?" She studied the colorful diagram of a swarm of influenza virus particles—a particularly interesting news item on the potential spread of bird flu—and wondered what Henry Manfield would make of it.

He cleared his throat. "My solicitor let me know you'd rescheduled for tomor-row—I wanted to thank you."

"Of course I rescheduled," she said, flipping a few pages forward in the journal to find the original research article on which the news piece was based. "I'd just dou-ble-booked myself the other day, is all."

"Yes, so I'd heard."

"I'm in a bit of a rush, Cal. Was that all?"

"Actually, no."

In the silence of his pause, Artie could make out what sounded like a running shower. She doubted he was still fucking his secretary, but was happy to realize that she didn't, actually, care who her replacement was any more.

"I wanted to arrange a time, preferably over a weekend, when I could come by and box up the rest of my things. I'll hire a van."

It sounded like a challenge.

"Fine," Artie said. "This weekend is good, actually. If the weather stays fine, I'll be out in the garden and out of your way."

"It's—" He cleared his throat. "I was thinking that this act—the removal of pos-sessions—is rather symbolic, even more so than the paperwork. Are you sure your mind is completely made up?"

"About the divorce?" She was so surprised that she finally dredged herself out of the scientific sentences beneath her fingertips. "Yes, quite."

Down the line, the shower went dead.

"Fine," he said. "Shall we say Saturday at two?"

ARTIE HESITATED IN FRONT OF B302 on the way in to work, willing her knuckles to rap on the glass. She needed to charm some information from Simon about possible human infections in the Sheppey area, but dreaded the possibility of rousing Henry. Unfortunately, what she wanted to know required advanced tactics that could not be deployed via email, and she didn't want to risk Mark being around guessing that she was up to something. But her post-doc had rung earlier asking for the morning off to be with Rebecca, so she needed to make her move as soon as possible.

When did you become such a coward? she chided herself. Executing a few soft but firm knocks on the cool surface, she thought she could make out a flicker of shifting light and shadow from within the muted glow of the inner room. But after several more attempts to arouse the more benign of its two inhabitants, she gave up and went to the office.

Her office phone began ringing as she unlocked the door. Dumping her backpack on the floor, she grabbed the receiver and emitted a breathless hello.

"Sidney Sheppard here." The stout Scot's voice boomed out, no less impressive for being squashed by the receiver's tinny speakers.

"Wonderful to hear from you, Sid. What news?"

"Well, I'll cut to the chase: it's a right pickle. Your wee hybrid specimen is like nothing else we've seen anywhere on these fair green isles."

"I was afraid of that. What do you make of it?"

"I agree it looks like Petaluma, but one of my students has taken the liberty of analyzing the drift, and it's definitely mutating in a highly natural pattern."

"Meaning, it's not a lab contamination?"

"Oh, assuredly not. It's been skulking out there in the wild for a few months, minimum, accumulating the usual point mutations. I can't tell you exactly how long, mind—the rate is always too slow for precise calculations."

"What do you mean, 'usual'?"

"Well." His voice took on a sly coyness. "I can't go into too much detail: Leonardo is just writing this up for the *Journal of Virology*."

"For goodness' sake, Sid, I'm hardly likely to scoop you. I can't go into detail about our hybrid either, but let's just say that natural variation in FIV is not currently on our radar. And if you help us out, we can include your observations in the paper with you and Leonardo as co-authors." She paused strategically. "We're thinking *Nature* at the moment."

"Well! In that case, those are... er, acceptable terms. Scout's honor, lass?"

"Absolutely." Artie's heart had started to flutter.

"Well, your beastie is doing a good job of arming itself for combat. Seven out of eight of our new determinants of infectious spread have been beefed up by point mutation. We're no' looking at some backwater strain: this bird wants to fly."

Artie released a pent-up breath. "That's great news. But where did it come from?"

"Must be convergent evolution," he said. "And the chances of being Petaluma-like by chance must be higher than we previously thought."

"I suppose none of those early papers worked out exactly why Petaluma was on the weaker end of the FIV spectrum. It could have been a mutation anywhere—and probably the Env gene was the culprit, not Gag."

"Exactly. Leonardo's already in raptures about the possibilities—I'll need to rein him in. These Italians are so excitable."

"You'll keep us informed of anything else he comes up with?"

"Oh, aye. And likewise, any more signatures you can send our way, we're happy to add them to the mix. The lab has a bet going on how long it will take for the eighth switch to flip. I've got a bottle of twenty-five year old Laphroaig on the line!"

Artie set the receiver in its cradle, palm resting briefly on its warmth. She had not seriously believed that Fiona had contaminated the samples after their own experiments appeared to rule it out, but this further proof of natural variation was a relief nonetheless. And the suggestion of a competitive genotype was even more satisfying: it all fit in with her main theory. She would let the offer of authorship on a prospective *Nature* paper sink in for a day or so, then sweet-talk Sidney and Leonardo into sharing their entire database of the relevant FIV isolates so that Simon could run a complete comparison.

Did the natural pattern of variation rule out Henry's wild idea about bioterrorism? Reluctantly, she decided that it didn't. After all, if the "agent" had been released a few months previously, it would still have started drifting in the wild much like any other native virus. For about the hundredth time since Henry had dropped his dirty bomb on her project, she burned to know the details of his evidence.

Artie dealt with a few of the most pressing email messages in her inbox before emailing Simon, asking him to stop by as a matter of urgency. She'd lure him in with Sidney's news, then start probing him for information; with any luck she'd have what she wanted before Mark came in for the afternoon. She was just preparing to get up and track down Fiona when a new message popped onto the screen—from Augustus Faber.

"God," she said out loud, sinking back into her seat. She'd been half-convinced he wouldn't reply: what sort of a nutcase must he think her, Rebecca's reassurances aside?

Thank you for getting in touch. I'd be delighted to meet for lunch—I've always been curious about Heatherfields, would be fascinated to hear the inside story from one of the few women who've managed to battle their way in. I'm swamped for the next few weeks, but a cancellation has come up for tomorrow, if you could make it down to Guy's for about 1 PM? I know a quiet little place on Tooley Street...

"Oh you do, do you?" Artie murmured. If he'd found her on Heatherfield's website, he would have seen exactly what she looked like.

"What's that?"

It was Fiona, hesitating on the threshold.

Artie smiled. "Just hoping a male colleague doesn't have any non-collegial ideas about our lunch date."

"I find that a large club comes in useful. Look, can I show you something?"

"Sure, come on in."

Fiona perched on the desk, holding out a handful of reports. "I've had a closer look at my most recent sequencing results."

"I thought you said they're too messy to read?"

"Yes and no." She pointed to a stretch near the bottom of the page. "It *is* a dog's breakfast, but I thought I might try to search for stretches of homology anyway. And I hit something."

"Show me, Fi." Artie squinted, trying to makes sense of the multicolored swoops on the page. Many years had passed since manual sequencing, with its quaint scattering of horizontal black marks on X-ray film, had been the norm in labs, and sometimes Artie missed its more intuitive readout—though certainly not the arduous way it had been produced.

"Rabies," Fiona said, pulling a sheet of paper from the stack showing lines of code neatly aligned.

"I beg your pardon?"

"Rhabdovirus—a fifty-two per cent match."

"That's very unlikely," Artie said.

"I did some research," she said, stubbornly. "Rabies infects cats."

"In Britain?" Artie shook her head. "I'm no expert, but with the draconian quarantine systems in place, I doubt there are any active infections. Even if one or two manky rats managed to slip in, say through the Channel Tunnel, the odds of these infecting cats that are simultaneously infected with our precursor virus are practically impossible."

"I didn't think of that." Fiona looked sheepish. "I was looking on American websites."

"And this fifty per cent match—can I see your line-ups?"

Fiona handed over the sheet, and Artie studied it. Despite the ultimate futility of the gesture, she was pleased that her technician had had the initiative to even try to make sense of suboptimal data, and didn't want to discourage her from further independent thought.

"I admit that in the absence of remembering that Britain doesn't have a rabies problem, this doesn't look half bad," Artie conceded. "But the sequence you have is so spotty—this is probably just random noise."

"You're right, Artie. I just thought I should take a stab at it."

"And I'm glad you did. How soon till your next attempt with the high-stringency cocktail gets processed?"

She shook her head. "I sent the reactions off, but we've still got a serious backlog upstairs. I thought about outsourcing it, but you mentioned that our budget is running a bit thin this month."

"No, you're right. We can't afford any unnecessary waste until my next grant is funded." Artie remembered Henry's promise to pay for their sequencing, and resolved to prod Simon on that front as well. Maybe they could splash out on an express service. "A few extra days won't make a difference."

∽

SIMON PICKED UP THE RINGING MoD phone—typically, Brees had chosen to pester him right in the middle of a crucial calculation. As the Minster spike hovered like a mushroom cloud over the Isle of Sheppey, his irritation slowly heated to outrage as Brees' horsey voice issued through the receiver.

"A *fatality*, Dr. Renquist," he repeated. "Do you understand?"

"Of course," Simon said, tamping down his rage. *Patronizing twat.* "But have you actually ascertained the cause of death?"

"Still with the forensic pathologist," Brees said. "But I should have thought that was mere formality."

How, Simon wondered, could anyone in Brees' lofty position be so stupid about basic statistics? People dropped dead all the time for a large variety of reasons, particularly the elderly. Just because they happened to be infected with a weird stomach bug at the same time—a bug that had thus far shown itself to be relatively harmless—was no reason to assume a causal relationship. In fact, if he did the mathematics he could probably show that the chances of one of the patients *not* dropping dead was a lot more remote. Not that there was any point.

"We have Professor Manfield to thank for finding this latest victim, you know."

"Really?" Simon said. "How so?"

"That tip-off of his you passed along, about a possible spread to the Isle of Sheppey region? It was spot-on."

"I beg your pardon?"

Simon had sprung fully upright in his chair: in the reflection of his computer screen, superimposed over the Minster spike, he could see his own ghostly face, mouth hanging half open.

"Yes, the fatality was from the outskirts of Sheerness. Little old granny in a bungalow by the sea—not the sort of person we'd ever have found without having put out the word to the local NHS Trust and GP surgeries."

"Did she..." Simon paused, cleared his throat. "Did she, by any chance, happen to own a cat, Mr. Brees?"

"A cat? We didn't ask."

Simon closed his eyes, started to count down the prime numbers backwards from 577.

"But you do remember my...the Professor's query about epizootics?"

"Oh, *that* whole thing—seemed to come to nothing, as I recall. Is he still interested?"

"Very much so," Simon said tightly: *547, 541, 523...* "Mother Nature is still throwing up a few interesting predictions about a possible feline vector."

"In that case, I'll make some enquiries and get back to you."

The phone went dead in his hand and he slammed it down, so hard that machinery inside echoed a shimmering harmonic.

ARTIE SAT IN THE SHADE of the towering lime tree in front of the institute's main entrance, picking over the remains of her brie and tomato sandwich. The graceful lawn was dotted with a few other scientists, but most had long since brushed the crumbs from their clothing and been swallowed back into the brooding hulk of the building. She had her back to Heatherfields, resting against the tree's warm bark. The valley below was deep green and dotted with trees and rooftops shrinking into the distant lilac haze. Beneath her the ground was crawling with ants, lumpy with half-submerged roots and unevenly baked mud. The air stirred with a sporadic breeze, heavy with the scent of the jasmine and wisteria that crawled all over Heatherfield's brickwork and twined around its baleful windows.

Old Flemmingsworth was puttering in the Institute's prize-winning rose garden, shirtsleeves rolled up, Einstein hair fired platinum-white in the sunshine. Artie watched as he stooped his emaciated frame nearly double and murmured to himself, applying a spray from an old-fashioned brass pumping device. Occasionally he would flap an irate arm and a wood pigeon would explode from the beds, hurling upwards in a blur of grey (and only to settle again behind the man a few moments later). Flemmingsworth had been a fixture of the Institute as long as anyone could remember, according to Ben, and God help anyone who attempted to steal blooms to brighten up their office.

If you wouldn't mind, as a little exercise to get us going—try to remember the first time you experienced your phobia, and come armed with a few examples of incidents when it has been particularly intense.

Augustus Faber's email postscript had been preoccupying her mind all morning. *The first time.* She didn't know if it was truly the first, but it was the first episode that she could recall, and she'd told the same story to Calvin when he asked. How old had she been: Five? Six? Certainly it was the first time her mother had had to stay overnight in hospital. Artie was being looked after by the goth-pale, desultory girl who lived next door. At the time—what was her name, Hannah—had seemed worldly and sophisticated, with her black clothing and purple lipstick, but she must have only been in her mid-teens, still a child herself.

Hannah had been in the next room, listening to Radio 1. Music that still cropped up occasionally in the lab now, semi-ironically, and which never failed to immerse Artie in the particular melancholy of those years, grainy electro-recollections in the minor key.

The child Artie stood in the kitchen, unpleasantly hyper-aware of the song lyrics snaking around the corner. She was too young to truly understand what any of them meant, beyond their surface impression—it always felt like this thing known as *sex* roiled beneath all of them, black and suggestive and shameful. But on this evening, as light faded though the green and pink cotton curtains and the worn lino grew cold beneath her bare feet, the words from the song gradually became louder, more emphatic, pummeling themselves against her brain as if she was *thinking* the songs at top volume, thinking like shouting, with a brassy flatness that was somehow horrifying. Her heart began to race, hot flushes in the coldness of the kitchen, the red digital clock on the cooker pulsating in time, and as the weight of fear bore down, she found herself in Hannah's arms without knowing how she'd got there, crying uncontrollably. *You left me alone. Don't leave me alone. Where's my mum? Why did she go away?*

Artie shivered, brushing an ant from her hot shin a universe ahead in the future. The air seemed to waver with the soporific lull of bees. It was funny: although it was a very long time ago, she was almost positive that her younger self, even in the midst of the episode, was somehow aware that she was acting like a child, far younger than her normally mature self. Was aware, and despised it, even as she couldn't stop her tears or her silly baby questions.

"Why was your mother in hospital?" Calvin had asked, predictably enough. They'd been sitting on a porch swing at a colleague's house in Virginia on a hot, breathy night. Their first and only long-haul trip together, she to an international virus symposium in D.C. and he to visit a collaborator at Georgetown, with that weekend in the suburbs tacked on at the last second. It was meant to be romantic, but already the fissures were starting to show.

Artie turned her head to check, but their hosts were still bustling around in the kitchen, laughing over the washing-up in an easy way that she and Calvin somehow failed to achieve, most nights.

"They diagnosed her as manic-depressive, that visit," Artie finally said. "But now you'd call it bipolar."

The swing creaked with the slight rocking motion as Calvin applied the toe of his shoe against the weathered wood floor. The night beyond the insect-screened porch was moonless black, singing with cicadas, the fenceless American houses so far apart that their lights glowed like distant campfires.

"Oh Artie... I didn't know." Under his sympathy, she could feel his clinical interest quicken. "Both manic and depressed... so, bipolar I?"

"Yes, definitely."

"How did it present that time?"

She was quiet a while, trying to stifle a sense of betrayal that the focus of his professional probing had shifted so easily from wife to deceased mother-in-law.

"Apparently she went on a spending spree," she said, "until she hit the limit on her credit card. Later, they found her on the roof of our apartment building, laughing and singing. She'd climbed up the side—it was five stories. They had to call the fire brigade. I remember that—she was still laughing and flirting with the men as they carried her down, as if it were some game. I thought I would die of shame."

"Feelings of indestructibility," he said, nodding. "Euphoria. Did she talk a lot? Full of elaborate plans?"

"Yes. She wrote, too—filled up stacks of journals with wild ideas. I looked through them a few years ago when I was clearing out the house for sale; they were well-written but seriously grandiose."

"Like mother like daughter, perhaps?"

Artie stiffened, removed herself from deadweight of his arm.

"Fuck you."

"It was only a joke." Calvin, smelling faintly of sweat, after-shave and gin, looked her over in the dark, a calculating look of awareness slowly replacing the expression of mock-outrage. His eyes, unblinking, glittered like a serpent's.

In Artie's collection of *first times*, this was also one to remember.

INSTEAD OF GOING BACK IN by main entrance, Artie wandered the long way around the building, through the avenue of white birch, leaves trembling in the wind and fragments of shells crunching under her sandals. She cut through the car park, with its fairground-mirror heat warp, and was heading toward the basement door when it opened: Simon, blinking in the sunlight like a troglodyte. She studied him as he leaned, head bowed against the brick wall and breathing deeply, and found herself willing his scrawny sprung-taut shoulders to relax.

"Didn't you get my message?" she called out.

His head jolted up then, and when he raised his hand to shade his eyes, his expression was completely obscured by a purplish slash of shadow.

"Of course," he said. "Henry was alert for longer than usual. I looked for you a few minutes ago, actually."

"Well, never mind, I've got you now. Do you have a few minutes?"

"A few," he conceded, retreating a few feet into the shade cast by the eaves, and she joined him there in the snowfall of spent cigarette butts. "But if this is about Mark's sequences, I'm afraid I haven't finished processing them yet."

"No—I've got some more news about the Minster virus," she said, then filled him in on Sidney's information.

"You're right: that's very interesting," Simon said, with the modest nod that passed for gushing enthusiasm for him. "We really need to take a look at their entire FIV dataset, though."

"I'm working on that. Listen, that reminds me: can we go ahead and start some sequencing runs using your MoD funding code?"

A look of disquiet passed over Simon's face.

"I needed to ask you something about that," he said. "Yesterday, when I was making the tea and left you two alone—did you mention the sequencing to Henry? Or did he bring it up out of the blue? From context, it sounded like the latter."

Artie ran a hand through her hair, shuffling through her memories of that uncomfortable episode. "No, we definitely didn't speak of it until you came back."

"So there is no way he could have known about our plans from you."

"What are you getting at, Simon? He said you asked him."

"No. He said that my *proposal* was appropriate. But I hadn't submitted any proposals, or mentioned it in conversation."

"You must have, Simon. How else could he have known?"

He stared slightly off to one side, pupils like tiny pinpricks in the milky blue of his eyes. "I have been asking myself that same question for the past twenty-four hours. And there is only one answer: he must be spying on us."

Artie laughed. "Really, Simon. Double-oh-seven, Henry ain't."

"I'm serious." He scowled at her. "You and I spoke of the sequencing in my office just before leaving, but when we came out he was switched off, so there is no way he could have eavesdropped and then got back into his chair without us knowing."

"Okay," Artie said slowly. "All your MoD support doesn't extend to bugging, I assume?"

"If we are under surveillance, I'm sure Henry would be the last to know. But I did make a note of the sequencing idea in my work diary, so I'd remember to check the budget codes. I never need to run anything like that by him for approval."

"So he's been going through your desk: case closed."

"No, my work diary is online," Simon said. "Password protected. But I was thinking he might somehow have spied via his terminal while I had it open, over our closed network."

"Hang on." Artie felt a blip of unease. "That first time he made you leave us alone—he mentioned the La Fontayne as if he had actually seen it. Had you showed it to him?"

"No!" Simon stared at her. "And he couldn't have submitted the computation without me knowing about it—I've got all the logs and check them regularly."

"Maybe you just missed it?"

"I can assure you I would have noticed *that*. It takes a massive chunk out of the cluster time."

"And he couldn't have somehow just…visualized it from the raw data on your shared server?"

He just stared at her, scornful.

"Okay," she said. "So maybe he is able to access your screen. Does it really matter? I mean, it's not as if we have anything to hide."

"But why would he bother?" Simon slammed a fist against the wall. "It's just completely out of character for him."

Artie thought about Henry, about how even now he might be poking and prodding her dataset looking for nefarious intent—with her full knowledge and collusion—and felt a flush of uneasiness at her betrayal. At the same time, the thought of Henry watching over their larger activities like some dark cyber-voyeur was definitely creepy.

"I'd better get back," Simon said. "I'll email that code straight away."

"Thanks. Would you mind if we splurged on expedited service?"

"Be my guest," he said, flailing an arm as he strode towards the door. "Just save copies of all the invoices for me."

"Wait, Simon. Just one quick thing?"

"Yes, go on." He was practically twitching.

"When Mark and Fiona briefed you about the recombinant virus back in my office, before I got there, did they mention the human cell infectivity we'd just discovered in tissue culture?"

His hand slipped off the door handle as he turned to face her. She already knew the answer, because she and Mark had agreed to keep it to themselves until he'd confirmed the observation properly with filtered virus. But why was Simon reacting so strongly?

"No, this was not mentioned."

"Really sorry," she said breezily. "It's all happening so quickly, it's hard to keep track of everything in my own head. It's early days, but I just thought you might want to know that Minster might be able to spread via humans, in case you want to factor that into your models."

"I see." His voice was scarcely audible.

"What is it, Simon? Is there something you're not telling me?" She took a little risk: "Something to do with the MoD?"

"No—no, of course not!"

"Come on, Simon, you're obviously—"

"Excuse me, please."

He shook off her hand on his arm and slipped into the building without another word.

Artie expelled her breath and sagged against the hot brickwork. She had not truly expected her exploratory arrow to hit dead center.

⌒∽

ARTIE HAD JUST STEPPED INTO the office—still no sign of Mark—when her mobile went off.

"This grant is destined never to get written," she said to herself, digging the phone out of her pocket. "Mary, how nice to hear from you."

"Something terrible has happened. Can you come straight down?"

"Down? Down, as in to Gillingham? What's wrong?"

"No, to Sheppey, to meet me and Freddie. One of Freddie's clients is dead, and we're worried it was her cat."

Artie sank into her chair. "Are you sure?"

"I don't have all the details, but Freddie can fill us in. Are you free?"

"Hell yes. Just give me a few hours to get there—I'll ring when I'm in the general vicinity."

Heart pounding, she went into the lab, but Fiona wasn't around. She scribbled a hasty note and stuck it to the glass screen of the tissue culture hood. After checking the train times online, she grabbed her backpack and locked up the office. She rang up Mark as she strode down the corridor, but it went straight to voicemail.

"Shit," she said into the phone, after the beep. Then, more coherently, she told him where she was off to and why. What a time for Mark to be AWOL—she was looking at a train journey with several changes as it was. And frankly, she needed his support.

She half walked, half ran to Mill Hill Broadway rail station and threw herself into the first southbound train to St Pancras International, face flushed and entire body drenched in sweat from the afternoon heat. It wasn't until she was sitting in the sticky seat with the countryside rolling past her that it really started to sink in. The Minster virus—her virus—might have killed someone. *Killed someone.* For all she knew, it was a hand-crafted weapon of terror, a slow-burner to be sure, but possibly now coming into its own.

This bird wants to fly.

Freddie might be infected—even herself and Mark, for all she knew. Why on earth hadn't she acted more sensibly when Mark's experiment went so terribly wrong? Why had she allowed Philip's laissez-faire attitude to cool her concerns? After all, Henry had alerted her to the human cases yesterday: she should have told him what she knew straight away so he could contact the MoD and transmit what might be vital information in stopping further infections. Further fatalities. She should have leveled with Simon earlier, admitted that Henry had given the game away. She pulled out her phone, then remembered for the umpteenth time that the men in B302 could not be contacted by that mechanism.

It rang in her hand.

"Mark, thank God."

"Where are you, Artie?" His voice was taut.

She looked out the window. "Just coming into Cricklewood. You?"

"I'm in the car, on the way to pick you up. Just name the station."

∽

"IT'S NOT FAR," FREDDIE SAID, nosing the Ford tentatively into the column of traffic crawling westward along the seafront.

Artie stared at the back of Mark's head over the passenger seat up front; even in the seriousness of the situation, she could sense his impatience at Freddie's driving. Next to her in the back seat, Mary had said nothing of substance since they'd all met up at the surgery a few minutes before, instead giving off an uncharacteristic unease. Out of the window, the North Sea was a flat, burnished blue expanse dabbed with flecks of foamy relief. Rabid, she thought. As the car accelerated unevenly, Artie swallowed a surge of motion sickness.

"Can you tell us everything you know about Mrs. Morris and her cat?" Artie asked, voice raised against the engine's noise. Back in the car park, as they'd hurriedly reshuffled themselves into Freddie's sedan, there hadn't been time to say much.

Freddie caught her eye briefly in the rear-view mirror. She thought he looked sheepish.

"Kamini took the call. She—"

"This was when?" Mark asked.

"Yesterday."

"*Yesterday?*" Artie said. "Why didn't you let us know sooner?"

"I thought about it," Freddie admitted. "But at the time, we didn't want to cause any unnecessary panic over what was probably just a heart attack or something. But when I woke, I wasn't so sure."

Artie looked over at Mary, who pointedly avoided eye contact.

"You should have rung," she told her friend, who just shrugged. "Anyway, it doesn't matter—carry on."

"Mrs. Morris was in a bit of a state—her tabby was very ill, she said, but Kamini thought Mrs. Morris herself sounded very... off."

"Off how?" Artie said.

"Confused, mostly—and she never normally is, despite her age."

"How old?"

"Eighty-two—but still quite mobile and mentally sharp. Lives... lived alone. She never asked for house calls, always brought Mackenzie—that's the tabby—for check-ups by cab. We'd drop by the flea medication as a courtesy, but she insisted she was perfectly capable of attending check-ups. Lovely woman."

Freddie faltered, busied himself with easing the car into a right-turn-only lane at the next light.

"So what happened next?" Mark said, gently.

"When Mrs. Morris didn't show up for her appointment, I went round. It's on my way home, and her appointment had been so late in the day that I thought I might as well. But she wasn't in. I knocked for ages, rang her phone. I could hear it ringing inside, but nobody answered."

"What did you do?"

"At that point, I just assumed she was out—maybe she'd got a late start, and the cab was stuck in traffic on the way to the surgery. Kamini had gone home, so I was just thinking of going back to the office in case Mrs. Morris was waiting—and that's when Mrs. Seville tapped me on the shoulder."

"Nosy neighbor?" Mark asked.

"Exactly. Told me she was worried about Mrs. Morris, who'd been feeling 'poorly,' and was wondering if I'd seen her today. Confirmed that no cabs had shown up, and that Mrs. Morris hadn't left the house. Mrs. Seville likes to sit in her kitchen, said she would have noticed any comings and goings."

Freddie steered the car into the smaller road, heading straight seaward. On their left and right, small bungalows were lined up in neat rows, weather-beaten but most tidily kept with little front gardens: yellow flowering gorse, tough-looking roses, the sorts of plants that can flourish in windy, salty conditions. Freddie braked as a black streak whizzed across the road: a cat, Artie saw, looking up at them with impassive green eyes from the opposite shoulder before vanishing into a row of stunted privet.

"So you called the police?" Artie guessed.

"That's right. Minster's a small town, so I'm on a first-name basis with the officers at the nearest station—dog owners to the last. They sent someone out straightaway."

"Did they have to smash the door in?" Mark asked.

"Oh, heavens no. Mrs. Seville has a spare key."

Mary stirred, for the first time. "Freddie, did you actually... see her?"

"No," he said, turning the car into a close and decelerating. "I wasn't allowed in. Then I heard she was dead and it looked as if nothing was going to be happening for a very long time." Artie saw him shrug. "More cop cars showed up. They said there was no sign of the cat inside, so I got permission to search the grounds, but he was nowhere to be found—there's a cat flap, and he's a pretty flighty individual. So then I went home, because I was clearly in the way. I'm hoping he's come back by now, if he's actually..."

Artie said what they were all thinking: "You do know that if Mackenzie is still alive..."

"Oh, yes," Freddie said grimly, pulling into a drive. "I've brought barbiturates. But if he's in the same state as the others, it will be a mercy."

The house seemed deserted. Artie noticed a fragment of yellow police tape tangled and flapping in one of the buddleia bushes lining the front walk, and some of the border flowers looked trampled, but other than that, no evidence of yesterday's incident remained.

Freddie switched off the engine, and in the silence, Mark said: "We probably need to be extremely careful if we do find him."

"Yes," Freddie said. "I want all of you to stay well clear. I've got protective gear, and have been trained to handle dangerous animals. Before I set up the surgery, I did a few years up at the London Zoo, wrangling in the big cat house."

"You mustn't put yourself to any unnecessary risk," Mary said anxiously, as they were all getting out of the car. "I still think we should have let DEFRA handle this."

"I'll be fine," he said, fishing behind the seat for a leather case, which he snapped open on the bonnet of the Ford. "We can't afford to wade through their nightmarish bureaucracy while Mackenzie might be out infecting every cat in the village." Out came a white smock, a packet of latex gloves, goggles and a mask, a few syringes and a small casket of glass vials: Artie's estimation for the man was steadily increasing. "Let's spread out, but please try not to scare him away. Just call for me if you spot him, and I'll take over."

"What does he look like?" Mark said.

"Middle-aged silver tabby, but he might be extremely emaciated. Could someone open this?"

He had retrieved a small circular tin and an opener.

"Tuna?" Mark said incredulously.

"You've obviously never owned a cat," Mary said. "Here, give it to me. Freddie, promise you'll be careful?"

"I promise," he said, leaning over to give her a kiss. The look in his eye was so potent that Artie had to glance away. "Let's go."

Artie and Mark headed around the right side of the house while Freddie and Mary took the left.

"I don't like this," Mark said, swatting down to peer behind a hebe bush in full bloom. "We know absolutely nothing about the route of transmission. Freddie's taking a hell of a risk."

Artie stood up on tiptoe to peer over the fence into the neighbor's side garden: no felines, tabby or otherwise, just a swarm of sparrows and tits around a bird feeder.

"Well, he's already been exposed," Artie said. "All those sick and dead animals he's seen in the surgery. I still think we have to assume that it's not highly contagious."

"Assumptions are dangerous," Mark said—his favorite maxim—as he stood back up to face her.

Artie sighed. "I know. But Mark—if Mackenzie is still alive and shedding live virus, we've got to stop him as soon as possible. I don't fancy Freddie's chances trying to convince DEFRA that this is an emergency—you know what the Government is like, and we don't really have a lot of evidence. Besides..."

"What?"

Artie had been about the mention that the MoD was probably already acquainted with what was happening on the island, but remembered just in time that it was a secret.

"Freddie knows what he's doing," she said instead.

"That does appear to be the case," Mark said, surrendering. "But what Mary said to Freddie applies equally to you: no heroics, okay?"

"I promise," she said. For the first time, she realized exactly where his whole overly cautious approach might stem from. Despite herself, she felt a little flutter of warmth at the thought—which didn't even come close to touching the primitive, chilling feeling that the last thing on earth she wanted to do was to go anywhere near a terrified and cornered cat infected with the Minster virus.

"Don't move," Mark murmured, touching her arm lightly. Following his gaze, Artie saw it too: the tip of a striped, trembling tail, grey and deep brown in color, emerging from behind a tower of clay flower pots stacked neatly by the side of the house.

"You keep him in sight," Mark whispered. "I'll circle round the front and get the others."

The seconds ticked by. An airplane droned overhead, and a fly kept landing on her bare arm, oblivious to her attempts to brush it away. She was grateful for the shade cast by the house; despite the fresh sea breeze, it was hot, the sun mercilessly intense and causing her eyes to ache. She caught her breath when the tail slid back slightly behind the pots, but after a few more seconds, it looked as if Mackenzie was in no hurry to vacate his safe haven.

Hearing whispering behind her, Artie glanced briefly back before refocusing on the tail: Freddie passed her, fully smocked up and looking resolute and inscrutable behind mask and goggles. In one gloved hand he held a syringe and in another, the open tin of tuna. Mark and Mary stopped beside Artie to watch, Mary throttling a plastic cat carrier with both hands until Mark pried the handle out of her clutches and set the box down on the grass.

Slowly Freddie approached the pots. Squatting down, he put the tin just in front of the pots, but the animal did not stir.

"He must be really ill," Mary said softly. "After a certain point, they just stop wanting food. But at least that means he's unlikely to have the strength to run far either."

Freddie must have reached the same conclusion, because he leaned forward and reached a hand behind the pots. There was a hissing noise, and Freddie extracted the limp cat by the scruff of his neck and restrained him at arm's length in the grass in front of him.

"My God," Artie said. The animal was just a sack of bones, the collar dangling around his thin neck. His hiss had clearly been just a reflex: if there had ever been any fight in him, it was long gone.

"If I had to guess," Mary said, "I'd say the end-stage of one of the severest forms of immunodeficiency. I'm surprised Mrs. Morris waited until yesterday to ring the vet's."

"She always got in touch at the slightest sign of trouble," Freddie said. "The onset must have been very rapid, just like all the others." He paused, smoothing Mackenzie's matted fur with his free hand; his yellow eyes were dull and unresponsive. "Mary, this animal is nearly dead and is suffering incredibly. Is it your professional inclination to agree with my decision to put him down here and now?"

"Absolutely," she said. "If any relatives complain, I'll back you up."

He nodded and ran one hand gently over the gaunt skull a few times. It seemed to Artie that the cat tried to raise his head to respond but couldn't bear the weight, chin sagging back down onto the ground.

"You're all right, mate," he told the cat kindly, administering one final stroke before shooting a dose of barbiturates into one of his wasted legs. "Easy now."

Next to her, Artie could sense Mary finally letting go of her tension as the animal sagged and then moved no more.

"Now what?" This from Mark.

Freddie looked up at them. "There's a sheet and a pack of plastic body bags in the boot. I'll package him up in three layers and stash him in our chest fridge in the surgery until we decide what, if anything, we need to do. I'll take a few samples for analysis... carefully," he added, seeing the look on Mary's face. "I doubt it will be any different than the other eight animals, but best to be sure."

"Agreed," Artie said. "We can have the viral DNA sequenced when you're ready. After that confirmation, we can decide exactly who to tell, and how to go about it."

"We shouldn't delay too long," Mark said. "Someone might cremate the old lady before they realize we need to test for the virus."

"Good point," Artie said. And longed, but dared not, confess that the body was highly unlikely to be released before a very large battery of tests was performed. "We'll move quickly."

Mary fetched the items from the Ford and everyone watched in silence as Mackenzie's corpse was packaged away into the carrier box. Freddie stripped off his gear and bagged that up too, finally completing his ablutions with copious applications of disinfectant gel. The box was stowed in the boot and everyone was just getting into the car when a woman walked by the drive with a carrier bag of groceries. When she saw them, she backtracked and rushed towards them.

"Mr. Preston," she cried out. "I've been trying to raise you at the surgery."

"Mrs. Seville," Freddie said. "What can I do for you?"

When Mark had spoken of a nosy neighbor, Artie had not conjured up this sleek, silver-haired woman in jeans and a fashionable blue linen T-shirt, sunglasses up on her cropped hair and eyes glimmering with intelligence. Probably only just retired— early sixties, she guessed.

"Sue, please. Did you come for poor Mackenzie? Bill tried to lure him in last night for a bite to eat, but he was terrified."

Freddie nodded. "We've got him—I'm afraid he's dead."

"I'm not surprised, the way he looked last night." She paused. "Mr. Preston, the reason I was calling—I need to tell you something about June Morris, if you have a moment. Something... a bit weird." Her gaze flicked hesitantly at Artie and the others.

"They're professional colleagues," Freddie said.

She paused a moment longer, then nodded. "You'd all better come inside, then."

"JUNE FELL ILL A FEW days ago," Sue Seville said. Sunlight blazed into the kitchen, glinting off the tea as she poured it into china cups. Despite the breeze, the little kitchen—with its clear view of Mrs. Morris's front garden—was baking with trapped heat.

"What sort of illness?" Freddie asked.

"She was feeling a bit faint, she said. And mentioned she was having problems keeping food down—wondered if Meals on Wheels had left her a dodgy sandwich."

Artie met Mark's and Freddie's gazes across the table; next to her, she could sense Mary concentrating overly hard on pouring milk into her cup.

"I offered to drive her to the local surgery," the woman continued, "but she waved me off, said it was nothing and she'd wait and see. Yesterday she was much more poorly, confined to bed with what looked like a pretty bad summer cold. I brought her some supplies first thing in the morning, but she refused again to be taken to the GP. She was completely fixated on Mackenzie's illness."

Silence, punctuated only by the tinkle of teaspoons on porcelain, and then Sue shook her head. "I really should have done something, shouldn't I have? Called an ambulance, or Social Services at the least. If I had..."

At that moment, a plump white cat jumped up from nowhere into Mrs. Seville's lap, tail high and purring loudly as the woman absently ran her hand along the back of its head. Despite its glossy fur and good spirits, Artie resisted the urge to edge back in her chair as her heart rate ticked up a notch. Had this cat have been in contact with Mackenzie or any of the other victims?

"Listen, we don't know why she died," Freddie was saying, gently. "She was quite elderly, wasn't she?"

"That's what Bill's been saying, too," she said. "And I had just about convinced myself—until early this morning."

"The weirdness, I assume?" Freddie said.

She nodded, slender fingers pressed briefly against her lips. "It must have been about three in the morning—not yet starting to lighten, though I didn't look at the clock. We were awakened by the crunch of gravel outside. It had been mad over there yesterday, cops and ambulances and I don't know what all, but everyone had vanished by about eleven that night. We'd assumed they'd done their investigations, cleared out... the body, and that was that."

Artie was starting to get a tingling sensation along her shoulder blades.

"It was a very large white van—unmarked," Sue said, staring out the window as if she could still see its ghostly form parked on Mrs. Morris' drive. "And four men got out, two from the cab and two from the back. They were completely silent, not a word spoken, and dressed all in white. "

"White?" Mark said.

"Yes, rather like hospital gear. Covered head to toe, gloves and masks. Some of the police yesterday evening were dressed a bit like that—forensics people, I guess—but not quite so heavily covered. Bill and I..."

"Go on," Freddie said, with a voice that had probably soothed a thousand distressed pet owners.

"We wanted to challenge them, but it seemed wrong. They were calm, confident, knew exactly what they were doing. They brought out a stretcher from the back of the van, had keys to the house. They must have been with the police, we thought, despite that funny van."

"I would have thought the same," Freddie assured her.

"Really?" she said. "Things sometimes seem so confusing in the middle of the night. But they surely didn't have the look of burglars, which had been my initial fear: word gets out an old lady has died, you might expect some opportunists to show up and try their luck."

"What happened next?" Artie said, hardly able to get the words out.

"They were inside maybe five minutes—ten at the most. They didn't turn on any of the lights, which was strange. And then out they came with something on the stretcher, obviously very heavy, wrapped in white but—not exactly a sheet. More like plastic. Body-shaped—well, I suppose it must have been *her*, that she had been in there all along. Bundled her into the van and drove off, discreet as you like. They'd been ever so *quiet*. After they left, it was almost as if we'd dreamt the whole thing."

The silence around the table was absolute.

"How very peculiar," Freddie finally said, with the bemusement of the honestly confused. Artie, meanwhile, was staring at the tablecloth, desperately trying to keep her own face politely puzzled despite the cold clench of her sudden inner certainty. When she looked up, she found Mark gazing at her intensely.

She recognized the slight narrowing of the eyes, the set of his mouth. It was the expression that gripped him in lab meetings when he was trying to work out which of a handful of competing scientific theories was the most plausible.

CHAPTER 11
Truths, Those That Don't Want to Be Recognized

ARTIE TOOK THE WRONG EXIT at London Bridge Station and ended up wandering halfway around its sprawling bulk, already five minutes late for her date with Augustus Faber. Contrails melted across the acid-blue sky, and beneath it the city pressed in from all angles: tourists queuing for dubious attractions, double-decker buses belching diesel fumes, black cabs disgorging fares and swallowing others, cars sounding their horns in the bottlenecks of dusty road works. Hundreds of people streamed through the Joiner Street underpass: Northern Europeans in Birkenstocks, Americans with shorts and white trainers, Asians in expensive tailoring, Londoners in drab lunch break understatement. Heat bloomed from the pavements and sun lanced off steel and glass—Artie longed for the fresh breeze of the Thames, sensed but not seen just behind the towers of Guy's Hospital.

On the long Underground journey south, she'd been preoccupied with the previous day's events. Only sheer luck had prevented Mark from grilling her about her reaction to news of the corpse's midnight removal: Mary had needed a ride back to London to visit her father, so the conversation in the car was thankfully restricted. When they hit the M25, Mark asked whether Artie needed to go back to the lab. Although she'd originally planned to do a few things in the office, she knew that Mark would probably try to join her, so took the opportunity of bailing out at Stratford to take the overground train back to Hampstead while the other two carried on to a station more convenient for Mary. And today, she'd worked at home before coming straight to town. She knew the reprieve was only temporary, but she simply wasn't prepared to withstand Mark's probing without a bit of mental fortification.

There was no doubt in her mind that the white van had been associated with the MoD; as far as she was concerned, Simon's lousy poker face had as good as confirmed Henry's wild story. It didn't, she thought, actually *prove* that the Minster virus was artificial, but it did suggest that the MoD suspected it was, and had said as much to the Theoretical Epidemiology team at Heatherfields. And if that was true, it followed that the MoD suspected June Morris of being infected with the Minster virus—the latest victim of a bioterrorist plot. There were a lot of *ifs* in this chain, but Mackenzie's symptoms certainly suggested that he had been in contact with the virus. Although she still needed the blood test results to be sure, both Freddie and Mary had seemed convinced that the physical appearance of the animal was consistent with all the other feline victims on the island.

But one thing niggled her especially: why had Mackenzie been left behind for her and her friends to find? Surely if the MoD were talking with Simon, they would know enough to be on the urgent lookout for infected cats. She refused to believe that Simon would not have made that connection by now, as a formal possibility at least; despite his apparent surprise at her news of human cell infectivity, the geographical coincidence was far too suspicious. But she and Mark had easily found Mackenzie just inches from the house, and in no state to stray much further. If the MoD had wanted the cat, the men in the white suits would not have left the grounds until they'd secured him as well. But Mrs. Seville said they had not searched the garden at all—they'd gone straight into the house and straight out again. Any idiot looking for a cat would have noticed the cat flap. This omission, she thought, made no sense.

Then Artie thought of something else: maybe Simon wasn't fully in the loop with the Government after all. What was it Henry had said? *Simon is very good, but his true calling is shaping up to be natural epidemics. Artificial ones, on the other hand, are undeniably my speciality.* Despite Ben's claim that only Simon communicated with the outside world, Henry had known about the MoD's involvement in Minster. Of course he might merely have been spying on Simon's online activities as he had with the diary earlier. But the other possibility was that the MoD, for whatever reason, had sidestepped Simon to consult with Henry directly on this issue—or vice versa. Could the rift that Henry and Simon were experiencing over modeling her dataset—the La Fontayne versus the Meyerhof-Hernsley—have propelled Henry to conclude that Simon was not fit to have sole control over the consultation about a suspected man-made epidemic? Had he overcome all natural repugnance to direct communication to approach the MoD personally?

And if so, was that really so surprising, considering that he had broken a lifetime's silence to talk to *her*?

TAKING ONE LAST GLANCE AT the map on her phone, she looked up and finally saw the restaurant ahead—and was hit by a sudden flurry of nerves. She squelched them with deliberate physical acts as she walked: the blotting of sweat with her sleeve; the training of damp hair around her ears, the stashing away of phone into handbag. Taking a defiant breath, she pushed open the glass door and paused inside the threshold, disoriented by the cool air and sudden relative darkness.

A waiter materialized from the gloom and led her to a small table near the back. A middle-aged man already waited, occupied with a stack of printouts—scientific papers by the look of them. With one hand he held a glass of ice water, arrested a few inches from his mouth, and with the other he was scribbling furiously with a beautiful old fountain pen, a faint smile on his lips. *A man after my own heart*, Artie thought.

"Professor Faber?" She held out her hand.

"Oh dear, is it one o'clock already?" Light glanced off his specs in startled counter-point as he looked up. "Time flies when you're immersed in the latest on quantitative psychophysiological reactivity!"

He put down the glass and made a move to shake her hand before stopping short to inspect the moisture on his palm. "I beg your pardon—condensation!"

"It's fine," she said, sitting down with a chuckle. "Handshakes are dead in academia, anyway. Can I chuck formality completely out the window and call you Augustus?"

"Gus, please." Faber looked her over as he wiped his hands with his napkin and stowed his articles into a briefcase by his chair. He was a trim, angular man—late fifties, she guessed, with a neat greying beard and purple-rimmed spectacles, their trendy rectangular lenses amplifying pale green eyes. His voice had the faintest trace of a foreign accent, but Artie couldn't place it.

"Thank you for agreeing to meet up," Artie said. "This all seems rather...irregular. I really don't want to waste your time." She couldn't bring herself to say what she was really worried about: that it seemed wrong to talk about her mental health without going through the proper NHS channels. Was he even allowed to be doing this?

"You mustn't fret!" Faber said. "We are colleagues in science. Do you like talking about your cat virus work with other interested, intelligent people?"

"Oh yes, more than anything. But—"

"It's the same with me." He held up a palm. "Phobias are my life's work, and I can think of no more pleasant way to spend an hour than with someone who is obviously articulate and scientific enough to talk about her experiences in a way that is sure to be enlightening—entirely off-the-record, of course."

"I'm not really sure this is—"

"I empathize with your concerns," he said, eyes glimmering with humor. "But think of it this way: it would be the same as you finding a cat who could communicate what its infection *feels* like. It is helpful, but also..." He paused, tapping his glass with an absent fingernail: *shave and a haircut.* "Incredibly stimulating."

He shot her a boyish smile, and she couldn't help smiling back. Yes, he knew this was naughty, but he didn't give a fuck. That suddenly suited her just fine.

"Well, if you put it like that..."

"Splendid! I suggest we order—the sea bass here is excellent—and then we dive right in, and have no further feelings of guilt or discomfort, yes?"

As they munched on breadsticks, he asked her a little bit about her research, which Artie decided was his way of both putting her at ease and getting a sense of her personality. Perhaps not surprisingly, Faber was a good listener, but he also had a dry sense of humor that soon had her feeling expansive. After the waiter had taken their orders, Faber leaned forward.

"I have been trying to guess what your phobia is, but confess that I am stumped." She laughed. "Party trick?"

"Ha! Yes, sometimes my wife makes me do this. But I have a wretched track record." He tilted his head, considering. "You don't, if it's worth anything, look like the type who would run shrieking from the room on discovering a spider."

"True enough." She waited for Faber to crack another joke, but realized that he had fallen silent and was waiting for her to come clean.

"It's basically an agoraphobia sort of thing," she finally said. "I hate being alone."

He nodded, eyes neutral through the spectacles.

"I assume that the word 'hate' is an understatement? Go on."

Artie gave him the basics: how the phobia had been with her since childhood, though she had never allowed it to interfere with her life or career. How the severity of the fears mirrored the stability of her general outlook on life at any given time. How if she could sense companions around her, either somewhere nearby or present virtually in correspondence or broadcasted through a radio or television, she could keep the fears to a tolerable level, but how this was not always effective—especially in recent months.

"And these fears, how do they manifest?"

A small black notebook had appeared discreetly by Faber's plate, she saw, and the old Waterman pen was back. Artie took a few moments: he wanted precision—he wanted a patient who could describe with a scientist's eye for detail. She wanted to give useful answers, to make this meeting worth his while. And hers: as in the lab, bad starting materials would lead to inconclusive experimental results. Despite how irrational it probably was, she was secretly hoping that this conversation might lead to a *cure*. Ideally, a cure she could deal with on her own, without resorting to shrinks or prescriptions.

"It depends. For milder attacks, just generalized anxiety: my heart rate accelerates, I sweat more and feel a bit clammy. Just typical adrenalin, I guess."

He nodded. "That's very common. And for the more severe episodes?" He peered at her more closely. "What is it, my dear?"

"I'm almost afraid to say it. I don't want you to think I'm nuts."

He smiled. "I have only known you for about five minutes, Artemis, but I can assure you that your sanity is not in question. Do go on."

"My thoughts," she said. "They get... loud. Insistent. Impossible to shut down or block out."

Faber leaned forward. "Can you be more specific?"

"I think something, but it sounds like shouting. Of course I can't actually *hear* anything," she added hastily. "It's not voices."

He was holding up that placating palm again. "I understand: they are not telling you to jump off Waterloo Bridge. Please, try to relax."

"Okay, yes. Sorry."

"Can you describe the sound of the thoughts? The mental sound, if that is the right way of putting it?"

"The sound..." Artie looked off in middle distance for a moment, trying to re-member, to recreate the sensation in her mind. But it was so difficult, like trying to recapture the fear of a nightmare after waking. "Robotic. Dispassionate, despite the underlying violence. Almost... metallic."

"*Metallic*—wonderful." Faber nodded, made a few more scribbles into the notebook.

"And every thought-word feels... too precise. Too sharp. Like a physical blow. It increases in intensity until it becomes really quite unpleasant—and after a while, say fifteen or twenty minutes, it wanes."

The pen scratched on paper. "It sounds most distressing. Any other manifestations?"

"Well, sometimes I get panic attacks, but this is the exception, not the rule. I don't need to describe them—they're absolutely textbook."

After cross-examining her for another ten minutes or so, he said, "Would you mind terribly, sometime at your convenience, filling out a few online questionnaires about these attacks? The metallic thoughts angle is compelling—I'd like to get an idea of your basic rankings with the standard diagnoses."

"Sure, my pleasure."

"Good—I can send you the links later." Faber poised his pen again. "So tell me now about the treatments you have undertaken. I'm interested to hear which regimens you have found most effective, and in what way. It could..."

But Artie was shaking her head. "I have never... officially been seen for this."

He raised an eyebrow. "Not even when you were a child? Your parents didn't send you to a GP, get you referred?"

"My father ran off when I was a baby, and my mother was... quite chronically ill. She had bigger things to worry about, basically."

"Teachers, then? Close relatives?"

"I learned to hide it pretty well. I was ashamed."

"I see." His eyes appraised her. "This is understandable. But as an adult? You've got a deeply curious mind and the ways and means of assessing the scientific literature, so you must know there are treatments. Agoraphobia is, of course, a lot trickier than fear of tangible things like spiders, but many patients find cognitive behavioral therapy, neurolinguistic programming or even certain drugs quite helpful."

"I don't know," Artie said. "I realize it's irrational, but I feel as if seeking help somehow... codifies the problem. Makes it something major."

He nodded. "This is a very human reaction. Especially for someone like you—exceptionally intelligent, hyper-ambitious and highly achieving."

When she didn't answer, he went on: "But surely you also realize that it already *is* major. It is affecting the quality of your life; it is casting a pall over what otherwise seems like a blessed existence: youth, fine physical fettle, a prestigious and stimulating career. It is not healthy to paper over such deep cracks and just pretend they do not exist."

"I know." Suddenly, she wanted out of this place, away from the reasonable tones of this too-knowledgeable man, out into the bright afternoon before he asked her the question she knew was about to come. What on earth had she been thinking, opening this secret box to a stranger, and in public no less? Her heart began beating faster.

"Many phobias," he said, "as you probably know, are precipitated by a significant traumatic event in early life. Do you have any idea what might have instigated yours?"

MARK LOOKED UP AS ARTIE entered the office.

"How was lunch?"

"Very...stimulating," Artie said, remembering Faber's word choice with a little shiver. "Everything under control on the home front?"

"Fiona's dispatched all those sequencing reactions to the express service you arranged with Simon."

"So we might get to the bottom of the mystery of the envelope swap as early as tomorrow!"

"It's Friday," he reminded her gently. "Monday at the absolutely earliest, if all goes well."

"Ah... OK. Good."

As Artie settled into her chair and plugged in her laptop, she could sense the expectant silence gathering.

"Is everything okay with you, Artie?" he finally asked. She looked over and saw the internal struggle on his face.

"Sure. Why?"

"I've been getting the feeling that you're avoiding me recently—that there's something you're not telling me."

"I'm just a bit preoccupied," Artie said. "Worried about Freddie and all those people on Sheppey."

"Right." He looked at her a big longer. "You would..."

"What, Mark?"

"You'd tell me, wouldn't you, if something important came up in B302, about the project?"

She laughed, hoping it would cover up the surge of shame. "Of course I would. We're a team."

He nodded, slowly. "Good. I'm glad to hear it."

Her email beeped: a one-liner from Simon, asking her to stop by.

"In fact, that's the hunchback now, requesting my presence in the bell tower." She took a calculated risk that he didn't have time to call her bluff: "Want to come along?"

At last, a smile. "Thanks, but I'm due upstairs at Hastings' lab for my hood slot in about twenty minutes."

"Oh, that's great. Are you going to repeat the killer experiment?"

"Already have, yesterday. It's a bit early, but I'm hoping I might already be able to see something nasty happening to the cells. If so, I'm going to make purified virus and see how far I can push it."

"Fabulous!" Despite the subterfuge, Artie could still feel her mammoth sense of curiosity trumping all other considerations. *Her* virus, about to be reincarnated in the lab, imbued with animation and possibly deadly intent. "Let me know the moment you have something."

"Will do, boss."

As Artie was transferring her mobile phone from handbag to jeans pocket, she felt the business card that Faber had handed her before they stood up from the lunch table. He'd scribbled onto the back of it before passing it over; at the time she had assumed he was just supplying an alternative number or email address. She'd been flushed, still, from a sense of reprieve, yet proud of how she'd managed to look him in the eye and tell him with a clear voice that she hadn't the slightest idea what might have kicked off her phobia. In the flurry of getting her things together, there hadn't been time to look at the card. Pulling it out now, she flipped it over and saw words, scrawled out in delicate ink from the Waterman pen:

When you are ready to tell me all about it, I will be here.

☙

188 | Jennifer Rohn

SIMON CAME TO THE DOOR when Artie knocked on B302. But instead of letting her in, he stepped into the corridor and murmured: "We must speak entirely in private. Is your office free?"

Artie shook her head. "What about the roof?"

"I never go up there in the daytime," he said. "It's not actually permitted."

"Do you care?"

He grimaced. "I don't want anyone on the eighth floor to notice and blow the whistle. They might install locks on that stairwell."

"Outside, then?"

He hesitated, then a peculiar look passed over his face. "I know just the place."

He led her out the basement door and through the car park towards the back of the building, where Artie had never explored, and squeezed through a gap in the privet hedge ringing the concrete lot. Artie followed, the rough twigs scraping at her bare arms. The wide back lawn stretched before them, impeccably manicured: all it needed was Sir Rupert and his entire acquaintance in period dress, whacking balls around with wooden mallets. Actually, there wasn't another soul on the grass, but when she glanced over her shoulder at the nine floors towering above, she cringed at the sight of a hundred windows reflecting back anonymous daylight.

"Could you have chosen any place more conspicuous?" she said. The thought of someone mistaking this for a romantic tryst was not a pleasant one.

"Researchers are too busy to look out windows," he said shortly. He was, she saw, heading for the ha-ha at the back, and a small copse of trees on its left hand side. "Besides, most of those panes are stained glass—statistically, there are very few places where one can actually see anything."

Which was, she thought, a very odd thing for him to have noticed and filed away. But he was right: as the angles lengthened and the sun's glare lessened, she saw that whoever had designed the back of Heatherfields had prioritized aesthetics over functionality. The colored windows were of various shapes and sizes and arrayed in sweeping circular patterns, vaguely mathematical or astronomical, that had little regard for the linear boundaries of floors. In fact, an independent observer would be hard pressed to guess which windows were on which floors: it was a surprisingly disconcerting architectural effect.

As they entered the stand of oaks and beeches, the temperature dipped. Artie became aware of the trickling of running water. Simon paused on the periphery, his back tensed even more than usual, then stepped onto a gravel path leading to a small creek. An ornate bench came into view, overlooking a waterfall pulsing sluggishly over mossy stones. Simon sat with unreadable emotions flitting across his face as his gaze razed the surroundings.

"Come here often?" Artie joked, sitting down too.

"Not for twenty years," he said, as if the question had been straight. "But it looks exactly the same. I don't have much time, actually."

"What did you want to tell me?"

"It's about your epidemic," he said. "There's something I've been keeping from you."

Artie leaned forward, summertime languor dissipated.

"Go on."

"This is entirely classified information—I could get into serious trouble."

"You can trust me," she said.

He looked her over calculatingly. "Before I say a word: that question you asked me yesterday, about the MoD. Was this an idea you picked up from Henry?"

"No!" The lie felt especially contemptible.

"Because you were entirely right," he said. "And I was wondering how you guessed."

Artie watched the dappled shadows play over his pale face.

"I just put two and two together, like any good scientist would," she said. "You've made no secret that you work with the Government on stuff like this, and you reacted too strongly to my news about the human cell infectivity."

He considered this for a few moments before nodding. "I'm not used to talking to third parties about my work—I guess I've never had to be discreet before."

"So, I gather there have been human cases of some unexplained virus?"

"Yes, a handful in Faversham, and now one on the Isle of Sheppey."

Artie made the decision without realizing she had: "Old woman, by the sea in Minster? Died yesterday?"

His eyes widened. "How did you know?"

Artie explained everything, words coming out in a tumble: Freddie's house call, finding and putting down Mackenzie, the neighbor's story about the white van. There was, she realized with great relief, no reason to have to tell Simon about Henry. She had enough data all on her own side to make everything plausible.

"A sick cat," he said, voice tense. "You're absolutely sure it had your recombinant virus?"

"You didn't *know* about the cat?" Artie said. "I assumed you'd be up on—"

"Believe me, I've tried," Simon said, bitterly. "The contact I'm dealing with hasn't been taking the feline angle seriously."

"So that's why they didn't nab Mackenzie," she said. "I couldn't work it out."

"I'm really glad you managed to get a sample," he said. "It's become incredibly important to see whether that woman was actually infected with the Minster virus."

"We'll have the test finished later this afternoon. But I'll bet you anything that it was positive. Will they tell you the dead woman's results?"

"Eventually, I hope." He scowled. "Everything's been moving glacially. After the first few cases, they were convinced it was some weird variant of foot-and-mouth—and did lots of specific tests that led nowhere."

"Foot-and-mouth? Why?"

"The symptoms, primarily. Well, at least some of the symptoms: blisters around the mouth."

"How odd." She mulled it over for a few moments, but it didn't really make sense for feline leukemia. And someone as thorough as Freddie would definitely have noticed blisters if any of the sick cats had presented with them.

"And now, apparently, they're finally branching out into tests for a broad panel of illnesses, but I gather there's been a lot of red tape and inter-departmental bickering. The unit I deal with is just a side-shoot of the main operation, and most of the terrorism money is going towards ferreting out suspected cells and bomb plots."

"I would have thought a bioterrorist angle would get more attention."

"But that's just it. The evidence is simply not compelling—I don't blame the MoD big shots for giving this entire thing a low priority."

"So you're not convinced the Minster virus is a manmade agent?"

"On balance, no." Simon said. "It is poorly infectious, and minimally pathogenic."

"What about the dead woman?"

"Chances are it was natural causes—or she was particularly susceptible because of her age. None of the other patients were more than mildly inconvenienced. Also, there haven't been many cases, and the patterns are all wrong."

"But your models of how my virus is spreading in cats—you said yourself it doesn't seem entirely natural."

"I know I did. But bioterrorist attacks have particular hallmarks, and we're just not seeing most of those."

"Maybe it was a botched job?"

"That doesn't quite fit either."

"Please don't take this the wrong way," she said. "But have you considered letting Henry know what's going on?"—the last part lamely, in a rush—"Maybe three heads might be better than two?"

Unexpectedly, a tired dip of his head. "Don't think I haven't been considering it. Because it's a lot worse than you think."

"What do you mean?"

Simon took a folded piece of paper out of his back pocket. Artie expected him to open it up and show her, but he just gripped it, forearm rigid.

"My contact at the MoD," he said, "is an idiot called Brees. Lord knows I'm no expert on office politics, but my impression from his behavior is that he's in a relatively powerless position and is desperate to make his mark with this little outbreak. So desperate that he's not terribly interested in listening to my scientific advice."

"Hence the ignored cat angle."

"Yes. He's so stupid that he doesn't even realize that a parallel animal outbreak would actually bolster the case for bioterrorism—that's one of the hallmarks. But I get the feeling his bosses just aren't interested."

"I don't understand," Artie said. "If it's not bioterrorism, it still could be an emerging virus that needs urgent attention."

"Yes, but that's not in the MoD's jurisdiction. The Department of Health already knows about the human cases, of course, and has a team looking into it. But so far, it's pretty low priority, as it's obviously fairly mild."

"I take it," Artie said, awareness dawning, "that they'd be more interested if June Morris and her cat were found to have had the same virus?"

"Yes! But the Department of Health wouldn't want to talk to me. And actually, I think that would violate the Official Secrets Act I signed with the MoD—I couldn't have known about all this without you and your vet colleagues."

"Well, I haven't signed anything," Artie said. "Mark's about to find out if the Minster virus is transmissible in human cells, and we should have the old woman's cat sample worked up soon. All we need is the old lady's sequences, and if there's a match I can ring up one of my old Oxford colleagues—several of them went into public health."

"Really?" Simon blinked. "Just like that?"

"Just like that," Artie said briskly. "You just need to ask this Brees person for the results of the old lady's microbiology work-up when it's ready. This virus is entirely new, but they're likely to hit some of its familiar parts with routine PCR—the retroviral repeats, for example. Eventually they'll have enough clues to sequence the entire virus."

Simon considered. "I can probably come up with some mathematical nonsense for why I might need such information. But how will you explain to your colleague how you got them, without getting me into serious trouble?"

But despite the anxious lines creasing his forehead, he looked almost cheered.

"I'll think of something. Are you going to show me what's on that paper now?"

"Oh!" He looked down, surprised, before slowly unfolding it. "Brees just sent me this, from the BBC News website—it's about the arrest of some activist based in Faversham. He's convinced there's a link."

Artie skimmed the story: twenty-year-old University drop-out, British Muslim, well-known in the London area for organizing protests about the UK's involvement in the Middle East—the last one of which had led to a bit of a scuffle in Parliament Square. The youth, Abdul Farah, was alleged to have struck a police officer but had been released under caution soon after being brought in.

"And the link is...?" Artie was baffled.

"Faversham," Simon said.

"Hang on—that's it?"

"Quite. Brees told me that Farah has suspected terrorist ties, but honestly—it would be very difficult to find a British town where you wouldn't find at least one suspect, these days."

"Are you sure that's all they've got on him?"

"Well, Brees also said that one of Farah's Muslim friends is doing a degree in biotechnology—but there are thousands of biology undergraduates in this country, so again, the chances of being friends with one is high. I tried to explain to him about coincidences, about statistics, but it was futile."

Artie gazed, a bit unfocused, at the ferns dipping into the pool at the base of the waterfall: the chaotic roiling of the water gave the fronds a frantic animation. She had to tread extremely carefully now. But she had too many secrets from too many people, and was desperate to consolidate at least some of them.

"So why you don't want to bring Henry in on this? If things are getting political—if innocent people are being made into scapegoats..."

Simon took the printout from her, began to shred it unconsciously in neat strips. "That's exactly what I'm afraid of," he said. "In recent months, Henry has become more... suspicious about the epidemics we've been modeling."

"Suspicious? How do you mean?"

"Perhaps a better word might be 'paranoid.' Given a scenario, he's been more likely to choose modeling techniques tailored to bioterrorism rather than natural epidemics. The whole argument about the Meyerhof-Hernsley, for example—that was a prime example. He looked at your dataset, seemed to make a snap judgment that something untoward was behind it, and chose an algorithm more appropriate for artificial scenarios. Whereas to me, as a hopefully objective observer, it seemed better not to make assumptions of that sort without having more of a good reason."

Artie was silent a moment. "This paranoia—have you seen it manifesting outside of the mathematics?"

"That is an interesting question. I'd not..." He considered. "Well, if he's spying on my activities, that could qualify, I suppose."

And if he's gone to the MoD behind your back, Artie thought, that would be a dead giveaway. But had he? And how could she find out?

"This could all be related to his other behavioral changes of late," she suggested.

"Which is precisely why I'm wary of bringing him in now. If he gets one whiff that Brees is suspecting foul play, I fear he'll happily drum up the epidemiological support required."

"Would Brees' superiors take Henry's opinion over yours?"

Simon just stared at her, then looked away. "As far as he's concerned, I'm just the messenger—the disseminator of Henry's sacred knowledge." He emphasized the last two words with distaste.

"What are you saying?" Artie was shocked. "You're not actually passing off your advice as Henry's, are you?"

"There's no other way," he said, shoulders curling up defensively. "That's how it's always been—it started out as a workaround, just to make things less convoluted, and solidified many years ago as standard operating procedure."

"God. So if Henry wades in now with a contrary opinion, starts throwing around his reputation and gravitas with the big bosses..."

"Exactly. That would be it. And imagine: this Farah person is obviously a bit of a hothead, but what if he got falsely accused and ended up behind bars because of erroneous scientific advice?"

She sighed. "OK, we keep it between ourselves for now. And we do our utmost to prove that this outbreak is natural—and possibly worthy of closer scrutiny by the Department of Health, if it's truly an animal virus that's jumped into humans."

He nodded, not very convinced.

"Everything's going to be fine," she said. "Trust me."

∾

As Artie was walking past the lab on her way back, she heard laughter rise like a wave over the music emanating from within. Backtracking, she went in to find Ben and Raisa leaning against a lab bench, chatting to Fiona, whose hands were moving non-stop over a microtiter plate as she added purple buffer to each well, all the while shaking her head in mock-horror.

Raisa's eyes brightened when she saw Artie, waving the clipboard in her hand for emphasis. "Another potential victim!"

"I don't like the sound of this," Artie said.

Ben looked her over appraisingly. "I reckon she's got a good arm."

"Artie, tell them about your childhood car accident," Fiona advised.

"My what?"

"You know, the one where the doctors told you you'd never be able to play sport again."

"What's this all about?"

"The Heatherfield's summer cricket tournament," Raisa explained. "Each floor makes up a team to compete at the annual picnic."

"Truth be told, the basement hasn't managed to muster a big enough group in living memory," Ben said. "No interest."

"Imagine that," Fiona murmured.

"But now you lot are here!" Raisa said. "Three *normal* people—it might just make up the numbers."

"Count our lab in," Artie said. And when Fiona made a face, "*All* of us. I'm crap at things like that, but we can't let the honor of the Basement lay uncontested. And I suspect Mark could actually do some damage."

"Wonderful—thanks, Artie!" Raisa started scribbling on her pad, and then Mark himself burst into the room, radiating fury. The loss of his normal serenity was so unexpected that all four of them just stared at him; even Fiona stopped pipetting.

"I don't *fucking* believe it," he said, slamming his notebook down onto the closest bench.

Artie knew immediately that whatever had gone wrong, it had nothing to do with science. Mark faced all experimental set-backs with the same equanimity he applied to the rest of his life.

"Another fun-filled afternoon of brotherly love up in the Hastings lab?" Fiona asked.

"My experiment from yesterday," he said. "All ruined."

"Ruined?" Artie said, spirits plummeting.

"Yeast contamination," he said. "In every single well. I had to chuck the whole thing away, but didn't have enough hood time to even set up the experiment again. And there isn't another free slot until late this evening."

"Serves you right for being so messy," Fiona observed.

"It wasn't my fault," Mark said. He was, Artie saw, making great efforts to keep his voice under control. "It was sabotage. Someone in Hastings' lab has it in for me."

"Surely not!" Ben said, while Raisa let out a small gasp.

"That's a pretty serious accusation," Artie said. One that he would not have made lightly, she knew. "In hot weather like this, yeast can be very difficult to control, even with the best sterile technique in the world."

"You don't understand," Mark said. "Just before lunch, I went upstairs to see if I needed to fetch some more culture media for this afternoon's session. While I was in there checking the fridge, I had a quick look at a few of my plates. They were crystal clear. Five minutes ago, there was so much yeast that the medium was cloudy yellow and I couldn't even see my cells."

Fiona looked thoughtful. "That sort of an infestation would take a day or so to accumulate."

"Exactly."

"Just what are you suggesting happened?" Ben said slowly.

"I'm suggesting," Mark said, still with that dangerous edge to his voice, "that someone pipetted heavily yeast-infected medium into my plates while I was at lunch, thinking that I wouldn't have checked them since my last session yesterday morning."

There was a tense silence.

"Probably just a practical joke got out of hand," Ben said, but his voice trailed off in an unconvincing question mark.

"*Nobody* would do that," Raisa burst out. "Jokes are one thing, but to interfere with someone's experiment—it's just not done."

"Who was signed up just before you in the hood?" Artie asked. She, too, was struggling to keep her tone level. She didn't know which was more potent, her sudden flare of angry suspicion or her disappointment at yet more delays in finding out the truth about the Minster virus.

"Nobody," he replied. "When I checked my cells, Barbara had just cleared up and was turning on the UV lights. This was twenty minutes before my slot, so there wasn't time for anyone else to sign up and do anything productive."

"Well, somebody could have snuck in while everyone else was at lunch," Artie said.

Fiona, who had been drumming gloved fingers against the grey surface of the lab bench, deep in thought, looked up.

"What is it, Fi?" Artie said.

"There might be something." She hesitated, blue gaze flicking uncertainly to Mark and the others before settling back to Artie. "Only I popped in over lunch to fetch my tubes from the ultracentrifuge. The lab was empty—except I passed Hastings on his way out. He gave me a more than unusually ugly smirk."

"Out of the question," Ben exclaimed. "And it's the man's own lab—chances of finding him in it are pretty high, aren't they?"

"Hastings spends almost all of his time in his office," Mark said. There was a storm brewing in the set of his stubbly jaw. "Even his own people joke at how out of touch he is."

"The man's obviously slimy," Artie said, "and doesn't think too highly of my lab. But would he really cross a line like that?" She paused, then said, "I'd appreciate it if you could all keep this to yourselves while I look into it."

As Ben was following Raisa out the door, he paused.

"Really sorry about this," he said, eyes troubled. "Heatherfields is a friendly place—never in all my years here have I heard of such a thing. Shocked that this has happened to you—shocked, and baffled."

"Thank you," she said, patting his arm. "I'm sure it was just a one-off."

But the moment they'd gone, Artie shut the door and faced the others.

"Right: this means war."

"If you really plan to do something about this," Fiona said, "then you didn't hear it from me, right?"

"Don't worry, Fi. We can't do anything without more evidence, anyway."

"I'm more worried about the experiments, Art. How on earth can I get anything done if someone's going to fuck around with my plates? It's not like I can guard them day and night."

"Good point." Artie thought for a moment. "There is a solution, but it's one hell of an inconvenience."

"If it's not as inconvenient as fungus in my T-cells," Mark said, "then I'm all ears."

"I've got a mate in the flu labs down at the Camden Institute," Artie said. "She's on the WHO Asia surveillance team. She might be able to get you some regular hood time."

"That's a twenty minute tube journey from here!" Fiona said.

Mark brightened. "I wouldn't mind. In fact, Ben was telling me there are a few bicycles available for staff—it can't be more than 45 minutes, and the hills would be great exercise. A million times more pleasant than having to work in that godforsaken snake pit."

"Okay, I'll ring her up in a moment. But do we want to do anything else about this? Broach the matter with Salverson?"

"I say if your mate comes through for us, we let it lie," Mark said, and Fiona nodded vigorously.

"But if you stop using his hoods, it will be him scoring a victory."

"Not ultimately," Mark said. "He thinks he's got sole control of the Containment 3 facility. By finding away around this, we're outwitting him. Which will make it all the sweeter when this work finally appears in *Nature*."

Artie laughed. "OK, fair enough. We won't rise to his childish behavior."

But when she went back to her office, she had to breathe deeply to control her fury. She balled up her fist and aimed a precisely rotating karate punch at one of the plastic palm's fronds. The man was unmitigated evil, and the incident had rattled her thoroughly. What on earth was Hastings' agenda? Whatever it was, there was no way the jealous, self-righteous prick was going to intimidate her. When she was Head of Virology, she'd find some way to oust him one and for all.

THE REST OF THE AFTERNOON passed in a rush. Artie managed to just make her four o'clock appointment with Cal's solicitor, whose Islington offices were so grand that she could only assume he'd chosen to intimidate. She survived the exchange by assigning only a fraction of her attention to the other woman's pomposity, mumbling apologies when her efforts on the forms were criticized, signing where she was told to sign, nodding or shaking her head when it seemed appropriate. But the bulk of her thoughts were with the Minster virus: experiments, theories, possible outcomes. Science as escape; there was no tactic more effective in Artie's arsenal.

"Am I correct in saying that your period of marriage before separation was only ten months?" The lawyer arched a perfectly plucked brow, managing to imbue the act with equal parts professional scorn and haughty feminine pity.

By the time Artie left the building it was rush hour, so she didn't get back to the labs until after seven. Walking through the silent main corridor of the basement, she hunched her shoulders against the weight of solitude. The lab and offices were dark, their rectangular panes of glass reflecting her form as she passed —except a flicker of blue light sensed rather than seen as she walked by B302. She never would have come back if she'd had the sense to bring her laptop with her to Islington—but the pre-application of yet another grant was due the following day and she still had a lot to do.

Later—after minutes or hours, Artie wasn't sure which—a tap at the door roused her from her writing. Simon, she assumed automatically, come to give her a preliminary report at last of how he'd got on with Mark's data. With a tingle of reprieve and anticipation, she extracted herself from the sentence she was dawdling over—only to be confronted by a wholly unexpected face at the window of her office door.

It was Henry Manfield, peering in through the glass with academic curiosity as if she were an exotic fish.

Many things happened simultaneously: her heart gave a primitive lurch, sweat sprung up beneath her arms, and a quick pat of her pocket confirmed that her mobile phone, yet again, was not in its accustomed place. In the lab, she recalled, next to the freezer, where she'd placed it during a break earlier after consigning a few samples to deep storage.

Artie stood, motioning Henry to enter. When he just stood there, face still pleasantly composed, she realized he probably hadn't understood the hand gesture. Coming from around the safe barrier of her desk, she walked over to let him in.

"Good evening, Professor," he said, in his usual dark-chocolate tones. "Apologies for the intrusion, but may I come in?"

"Of course." She forced herself not to shrink away as he ambled inside. "Please, have a seat."

She was relieved that he followed her suggestion without complaint and allowed her to retreat to the relative safety of the big oak desk between them.

"What can I do for you, Professor Manfield?" Brisk, businesslike. Just a normal collegial interaction with a scientific collaborator.

But he was looking around her office now, hands folded on his lap, as if he had never seen anything quite so fascinating. Gone was that twitch that usually accompanied his bouts of awareness; his eyes again, like the last time they'd spoken, seemed mild and normal. Artie and Mark hadn't done much to the space yet, but there were a few framed images on the walls: a group shot of Mark's departmental football team in Bristol, celebrating after a victory; an issue of *Science* featuring Artie's research findings on its cover; a humorous cancer charity calendar of naked post-docs of both sexes, the pertinent bits obscured by pieces of lab equipment. She noticed that he was fixated on Dr. June—a smiling redhead posed behind a strategically placed microscope.

As the silence lengthened with no sign of an opening gambit, Artie's nervousness gradually morphed into exasperation. The man was obviously not in a threatening mood, and he was interrupting her work. She might as well try to sculpt the intrusion to her advantage.

"How is the Meyerhof-Hernsley simulation playing out?" Artie asked in a loud, pointed tone. "Does my epidemic still resemble a bioterrorist plot?"

The words sounded ridiculous even to her own ears.

Henry turned to face her obligingly. "Yes, indeed. And those recent sequences you supplied to Simon only bolster the model's conclusion."

"You've tried the new sequences?" She kept the shock from her voice—Simon himself obviously hadn't had a chance to finish his own analysis. "How did you get hold of them?"

"He copied them onto the main data server," he said. "Standard procedure. He won't know I've sampled them, don't worry."

"Still trying to protect his feelings, then?"

"Oh, yes. His recent increase in stress shows no sign of subsiding. I think it would behoove both of us to tread carefully with him."

Artie studied his craggy face for any signs of irony, but his expression was perfectly composed.

"Bolster the model how, exactly?"

"Your older sequences, from 2010 and later. They confirm the fact that no statistically significant mutations affecting spread have arisen until very recently. And then, when the changes do begin—earlier this year—the patterns that result bear close similarity to the profile of artificial agents that are newly released into the wild *en masse* at one sole location."

"But Professor," Artie said. "Mutations did accrue in the dataset before this year. If you inspect the raw sequences, you can clearly see they are littered with them."

He nodded. "Yet these are not the mutations that matter, that affect spread, according to the algorithm. It is only in early March that we see the expansion. This is also the month in which the Ministry of Defence first reported problems with human health. I believe that this outcome is most consistent with a manmade release near the epicenter of feline—and human—illness."

"Tell me," Artie said, striving to keep her tone casual. "Have you mentioned my dataset to the MoD yet, spelled out the implications?"

He paused. "I am afraid that I am not at liberty to discuss our dealings with the Government in any further detail, even the logistics. In truth, I have already disclosed too much. But then, I know that I can trust you."

"Why?"

"Why? Because you are a kindred spirit." His grey eyes played over her face, intense but not uncomfortable. "I have read all of your papers. The way you think, the way you theorize—I find that it sits very well with my own methods and philosophies, far more than Simon's efforts have in the past few years. In fact, I have high hopes that our collaboration now is only the beginning."

Artie battled with a mixture of feelings: bewilderment, disbelief, revulsion, fear—but also gratification. Did one of the greatest living infectious disease theorists really rate her that highly?

"Thank you, Professor, that's very kind of you to say." She paused. "But if you can trust me, if you believe our collaboration to be that long-lived—then why can't you tell me a bit more about your MoD involvement? On this particular matter, is Simon taking care of the correspondence as usual, or have you stepped in personally?"

"Why do these logistical machinations matter to you?" he asked. "It suffices to reassure you that the important information is being disseminated."

"Does that information include details about my feline leukemia virus dataset?"

"It would be a breach of my Official Secrets Act statement to disclose more at this time," Henry said. Though his tone was impeccably polite, Artie sensed again that implacable rock at its core. Further pressing might lead to an unwanted reaction. Although most of Simon's "rules" seemed to have become irrelevant, she could never completely forget about the attack on Ben.

"At any rate," he said, "I did not come to discuss the project with you."

"Did you not? Then why are you here, exactly?"

Maybe it was her exhaustion, but this whole chat was so surreal that she found the change in subject completely fitting. *Bring it on.*

Henry's hand—still perfectly steady—went to his throat, stroking the veiny coarse flesh above his collarbone. She watched as his fingers slid to the first button on his worn tweed waistcoat, began to worry it. It was attached by only a few threads, she saw: she willed him, without psychic success, to stop playing with it before it popped off.

"I realized this evening," he said, "that something important is happening to me. Something very important. And yet—I have no one to whom I can reveal it." His voice had taken on a strange soft urgency. "Around me, there is no one who matters. No one at all."

Artie was glad that Simon was not in earshot of this unexpected confession. She didn't know how to begin formulate a response, but fortunately Henry did not seem to be expecting one.

"And then I remembered you, and I felt, somehow, that you were the right person."

He gave a little nod as he continued to stare in the general vicinity of her desk, fingers pushing the loose button around in a wobbly orbit.

"My life thus far has felt like one long dream," he said. "I spend most of my life in B302, existing amongst numbers. My memories of life before B302 are hazy at best: sometimes I doubt I existed before, though logic dictates I must have. There are other, less significant times, too: in my apartment, when I sleep, when meals are prepared by some caretaker or another—the faces change, but they might as well be the same entity. And then there are shadowy moments in between, when Simon walks me to and from. It feels that this has been going on since the beginning of time; or rather, as if there is no time at all, no time axis—merely the static images overlaid one on top of the other, all time compressed into one present moment: a model shape that never moves, never changes, that forecasts no significant event."

The hum of the fluorescent lights overhead seemed to press in around them like clay, molded around her ears, her skin, her entire body.

"But in the past few weeks," he went on, "I have felt, now and again, that I am waking up from this dream. I look around with surprise and see that there is an entire world outside of the space in B302, a world that did not previously exist. There is color, there is sound, there is light. There is conversation—other people. That evening you came to B302 and spoke to me, I suddenly thought, why not reply? *Why not?*"

He looked up from his desk, met her eye with unerring candor. "I would be frightened, except that it is not unpleasant. Not at all. It is only unpleasant when I feel the old dream trying to reclaim me, as it always does. And then I am angry, because I don't want to go back. But I always do go back—I can't fight the dream. Every day now, I surface—and every day it pulls me back down sooner or later."

Artie cleared her throat, said the first random thing that occurred to her. "Have you spoken to your doctor about this?"

"Spoken?" He gave her a thin smile. "I am the man who does not speak. I do not know how to even begin. And besides, the doctors—and there have been many, also interchangeable—I fear are all on the side of the dream. They have never really cared about me. I do not think they would support my efforts to become something other. I feel it would be safer to hide it."

He leaned forward. "You must tell this to no one, child. Especially not to Simon. He is on the side of the doctors, of the dreams, too. I don't trust him not to betray my secrets—not to try to collude with them to take away my newly born reality forever."

"But Simon has been looking after your interests for something like twenty-five years! He has sacrificed everything for you. You are like a father to him."

"You do not know him as I do," he said. "Perhaps it was once as you say. But not now—not for many years."

Artie raised her voice more than was probably prudent. "I've had Simon in that very chair, telling me he was worried sick about you. You do him a grave disservice, Professor."

He studied her. "I have no doubt that he is worried about a change in the status quo. He has a very comfortable position here in the Institute—I have no doubt he would worry about my health inasmuch as it impacts on his own affiliation. If I were to go, I doubt the Sanctum would keep him on. And without an independent research career, who would have him?"

Comfortable? Artie could not imagine a description so at odds with the reality of Simon's situation. And yet, from Henry's fractured, otherworldly perspective, perhaps it did appear relatively normal—even enviable.

"I really think you ought to seek some medical advice, nonetheless," Artie said. "Perhaps someone new, someone unfamiliar with your history, so suitably objective? Perhaps I could have a word with..." She opened up her email contacts, started scanning the list. She had at least two acquaintances from Oxford who had gone into clinical cognitive neuroscience fields—what were their names again?

But something about the silence made her look up. Henry was slumped in his chair, eyes open but utterly absent.

"Professor?" Artie spoke sharply. No response. She stood up, went around the desk and waved a hand in front of his face. Nothing. She couldn't quite bring herself to touch him, to shake his shoulder. He looked exactly like the man she had first encountered coming out of the lavatory—was it really only a month ago? It seemed like years since she had become embroiled with this strange man and his suffocating dream world.

What on earth was she supposed to do now?

Fortunately, that decision was taken from her. Without changing his expression, Henry rose magisterially to his feet. Artie gave an involuntary squeak and jumped away, but he was still completely absent. He turned around and, perhaps seeing nothing familiar—if "seeing" was the right way of phrasing it—stared at the door.

Instinctively, Artie went over and opened it wide for him, exposing his blank stare to a corridor that she hoped would trigger the appropriate visual recognition. Sure enough, he started to move, drifting out the door, diagonally across the scuffed lino flooring and over to B302. A moment later, the door was closing behind him.

Artie's own door, in the meantime, finished its lazy arc back homeward and clicked into place with a magnetic finality, sealing her inside with the deafening silence. Backing away from it, Artie felt something lumpy underneath her shoe.

Bending down, she picked up the worn beige button.

CHAPTER 12
Surprises, Those Not Entirely Welcome

A RTIE WASN'T SURE WHAT HAD made her change her mind.
When Calvin had first arrived with his armfuls of cardboard boxes flattened into neat stacks, she mumbled a few words of greeting and retreated to the garden.

She'd been dreading his visit all morning. Despite her absolute certainty about wanting the divorce, there was still something deeply troubling at the thought of all his possessions vanishing from the house, tendrils of him that had wormed their way into her life hacked back like some invasive species. In many ways, the ambivalence was the worst feeling of all. Although most of the time she thought she hated Calvin, there was an edge of tragedy about the ending of their relationship, an edge that she could not reason away. Some core remained, like the cooling heart of a dying star, terminal yet still capable of giving off heat, of exerting gravitational attraction. A thousand subsequent cruelties could not negate the previous closeness and intensity they had shared. Artie realized that to deny she had ever loved him was pointless: for she had, abjectly so. And this was what hurt: feeling the death of that, re-experiencing it in little shockwaves of memory and denial.

Artie stared, uncomprehending, at the stack of papers—graphs, charts, images of cells and virus particles, the dry technical sentences of her profession—before her on the wooden garden table, splashed with dappled shadow as the cherry tree cast its shade. It was another hot, flawless day; magpies scolded, blackbirds shot endless questions back and forth; the air was heavy with the scent of honeysuckle and cottage roses. Beneath her bare feet, the grass felt cool and soft. She ran the pads of her fingers over the smooth, printed surfaces before her: sometimes, all of this knowledge seemed so abstract, as flat and lifeless as the paper on which it was rendered; insignificant, compared to the vital rawness of the real world.

He had been absolutely right: moving out was highly symbolic.

She went inside to top up her glass of ice water. On the way back from the kitchen, she peeked into the lounge to check on his progress and was taken aback by the sudden holes in the bookshelves, random gaps like mortal wounds. Would it mend, when she pushed her own books together after he left? Or would there always be a scar, a ghostly memory of absence? She experienced, too, a flutter of silly panic at the loss of all those psychiatry textbooks. Although she rarely consulted them these days, their presence alone had exerted a soothing influence, as if such symbols of scholarship and rationality could battle off the demons by their sheer gravitas.

Calvin came back into the room with yet another armful of flat-pack boxes, gave her a tired smile.

"Do you need a hand?" Artie asked, impulsively.

He paused. "Sure. That would be great, actually. If you could tape up these boxes while I fill the ones I've already done?"

They worked together in silence for a while, just the ripping of tape and the thumping of tomes. It was awkward yet comforting, all at the same time. Then Artie said: "While I've got you here, can I ask you a professional question?"

His paused in the act of pulling a massive leather-bound book from the shelves. Glanced at her.

"Certainly. What about?"

"It's this colleague of mine at work. He's quite an interesting case."

"Really?"

She could hear his interest quicken, just as she hoped it would. She explained about Henry's condition, and how he'd been for all the many years before she'd joined the Institute.

"That's remarkable," Calvin said. "To be able to achieve such a scholarly reputation with such social impediments is quite a testimony. Not speaking isn't so unusual, but to at the same time be so ferociously vociferous in print truly is. I know of quite a few high-functioning Asperger's cases, and that's extreme."

"'Extreme' is pretty apt," Artie said. "But something even stranger has happened to him recently, and I'm wondering if you have any ideas."

"You know me too well—carry on. I'm hooked."

"It seems to me as if he's deteriorating, but on the other hand, it's like he's...improving." She shook her head. "Sorry, that's completely contradictory."

"Why don't you break his behavior down in each category," he suggested—Calvin in patient professor mode. "How he's slipping, then how he's gaining ground? It's quite common for patients to fluctuate on different axes."

So she told him everything, describing Henry Manfield as a disinterested observer might—leaving out the fact that it was she alone to whom he was responding. That she had probably catalyzed the whole affair. She mentioned the deterioration: paranoia, memory loss, nonsensical word repetition. The sense that he might be noticing female colleagues in an inappropriate fashion.

"Leering down your cleavage, is he?" he said, grinning. "I'm not sure that's in any way abnormal for your average bloke."

"It is for *him*."

"I know, Artie. Can't an ex-husband at least tease?"

She gave him a relenting smile, grateful that they seemed to be having a civil, sober conversation for a change. But then, it was just past three in the afternoon, and he'd only helped himself to one beer from her fridge so far.

"Cal—it's like he's losing his autism at the same time."

"That's impossible." Calvin put down the book he'd been weighing indecisively in his hand, glanced at her. The sun shafting through the blinds made his brown eyes a strange shade of amber. Despite everything, she still found him attractive. "Perhaps it's just different symptoms, manifesting as something else?"

"Maybe," Artie said. "But he's started to notice other people's emotional states—quite accurately, as it turns out. Comment on them. Trying to act in ways that protect other's feelings, even."

Calvin frowned. "That is rather strange. Anything else?"

"We had this conversation last night. He was very... meta about his illness."

"That's not unusual. Most Asperger's patients know exactly what they are."

"No, but I mean—he was talking about his condition as something he had recently started to periodically escape. As something he was desperate to avoid." She described what Henry had told her.

"Waking from a dream?" Calvin had abandoned all pretense at packing. "Waking from... hang on, how old is this man?"

"I'm not sure." Henry, to her, always seemed timeless. "Late fifties? Early sixties, max?"

Artie watched his face as the diagnosis slowly crystallized inside his head.

"Frontal lobe dementia," he said, with that crisp authoritarian confidence she had used to adore. "FLD, on a background of Asperger's. It all fits."

"Are you sure?"

"Well, obviously not, without a proper examination and tests. But the personality change is a giveaway—and it seems to be dominant over the autism. That's not outside the realm of possibility; I'd have to check the literature, but I reckon we'd find other examples. If we don't, I've got half a dozen colleagues who'd be desperate to do the honors. Do you think he'd be up for being featured in a case study?"

"Hmm... I sort of doubt it. So he's just going senile, then?"

"I hate that term," Cal said. "FLD is a very specific disorder. The personality change would be one of the first thing that happens—the increased emotional awareness, the inappropriate attention to women, the paranoia, all would be consistent. After that, he wouldn't necessarily lose his memory in a major way, as is the case with Alzheimer's, but the intellect would be bound to suffer. Any sign of that so far?"

Artie thought about how quickly he'd pounced on and processed Mark's data. "He's still churning out the research. But according to a colleague, his thinking has become more... rigid of late. Less open to subtleties and alternate hypotheses."

"That all fits—but will get much worse, possibly rather quickly. It would be the death of his scientific career, that's for sure."

"Is there any cure?"

"No. It's a good thing he's just a theoretician—he can't do that much harm with the odd misguided premise, and eventually he'll get put quietly out to pasture. To be frank, it happens more than you think in academia."

After Calvin finally left, the house seemed especially quiet. Following their conversation, he had ruined the spell of civilized interaction by propositioning her as he was leaving, spouting some shrink crap about "the importance of closure." Fortunately he hadn't pressed the issue when she declined, but the aftermath was a terse and awkward silence, and he was soon out the door, squealing away in the hire van.

The episode left Artie feeling depressed—and then, swiftly, assailed by loneliness. She poured herself a glass of white wine and stepped out into the twilight garden, drawn to the comforting laughter of a party on the other side of the fence. The scent of charcoal and singed meat mingled with the moist earth smell of a heavy dewfall, and the wine was sharp and cold in her mouth. She pretended that she was a guest at the party, and had just stepped away from the group to gather her thoughts.

Can't do much harm. Artie wondered if Simon would continue to resist getting Henry's doctors on the case. But he must get regular check-ups—someone was bound to notice sooner or later. Or would Henry, in this bid to preserve his strange new awareness, be clever enough to hide the evidence? And if he could keep up the charade for long enough, what ill-fated advice might he pass along to the MoD?

And what might happen as a result?

ON MONDAY MORNING, ARTIE TRUDGED up the road towards the underground station. She was tired after a long Sunday reading stacks of scientific papers, and feeling, more than usual, that start-of-the-week longing to be re-immersed into the bustle, distraction and companionship of lab life. But instead, she joined the rush-hour throng of commuters heading southbound into Central London to make her appointment with her old university friend Lisa Owusu at the Camden Institute.

"I can't believe," Lisa said, "that you've been working just five miles away for months and haven't got in touch until now!"

"I know, it's scandalous, isn't it?"

Lisa looked good, Artie thought: hair shaved close to her delicate skull, dangling silver loops in her ears, dark skin and eyes set off by a white polo shirt. Relaxed and easy-going as always—which set her apart from many of the scientists around them. Casting her gaze along the tables of the institute canteen, Artie saw a blur of tired people, clutching their hot drinks like life buoys, collective morning conversation a subdued murmur compared to the brash pandemonium of the Heatherfield's refectory at breakfast. Not a few of the younger scientists had that rumpled, "I've been here since last night" look about them. This, she thought, was one of the hallmarks of more traditional, high-powered biomedical research institutes that she certainly did not miss.

"You've chosen a good time to pester me, though—the big epidemic in Guangdong has waned, so hopefully we'll have a few weeks of peace and quiet."

"Has it been really bad?"

Lisa took a sip of coffee. "Well, I thank my lucky stars I'm not on the vaccine team—they're practically freebasing over-the-counter caffeine products. It's all still basic research for me, so these epidemics just mean plenty of samples and fodder for new ideas."

"So it's definitely not a problem to accommodate Mark?"

She shook her head, making the silver loops jingle. "In fact, it's great timing—my senior post-doc just eloped with a rather voluptuous biomedical supplies sales rep."

"She must have been quite persuasive!"

Lisa emitted a throaty laugh. "I was almost relieved when they finally got it together—all of that underlying tension was causing him to order far too many high-priced reagents from her company—loads of stuff we didn't strictly need. In the end I had to take away his purchasing privileges."

"And who says sex doesn't sell?"

"Quite. Anyway, he's taking an extended leave of absence to trek around India with her. I'm afraid I can't offer more than three hours a day, though. And he'll have to be indoctrinated by Personnel as a Visiting Scientist—which means we'll have to invent some sort of 'collaboration.' Leave that part to me."

"Fantastic! Three hours is more than Hastings was giving us, that's for sure."

"You really need to watch your back," Lisa said. "I've known him for quite a few years, and it's common knowledge that he can be downright cutthroat to people who get in his way."

Artie nodded, deciding again that it would be indiscreet to admit there was a reason other than scheduling difficulties that had led to this particular request. Instead, she said: "Lisa, while I've got you here... do you know if anyone in our year went into forensics?"

"Sure, a few—why do you ask?"

"Oh, just one of my colleagues—she's..." Artie thought fast. "She's tired of the academic conveyer belt, is considering a career change and wants to talk to various people doing alternative things."

"Can't say I blame her, some days," Lisa said. "Infectious diseases, I assume?"

"Yeah. You know anyone she might be able to chat to?"

"Remember Johnny? Johnny Ingsall?"

"Oh... tall chap... from up North, always trying to speak with a fake Oxbridge accent?"

"That's the one." She chuckled. "Only slipped back into his natural persona when he was plastered. He got his PhD at Reading, but decided he didn't want to post-doc and went on to get trained as a crime scene investigator for the Crown. We exchanged emails last year—I'm sure I can dig it out and forward you his contact details. He's based in Portsmouth, but your friend could at least ring him up."

"AND I THOUGHT I WAS LATE," Mark said, looking up as Artie came into the office. "My slacker post-doc lifestyle must be contagious."

"I'll have you know I've been busy arranging your Containment 3 hood time, smart-arse."

"Really?" He sat up straight.

"All sorted." She gave him the details, told him he could head over after lunch and get registered with the Camden Institute's HR person. "You could be communing with our Minster monster by teatime."

"Art, you are an absolute star." His gaze was frankly admiring. "Is there anything you can't finagle?"

"Well, I once failed spectacularly getting a table at Nobu Berkeley."

"Please—don't shatter my idealism."

"Any word on those express sequences?"

"No," Mark said, "but we're expecting the email before lunchtime."

"Damn, the suspense is killing me. What else are we waiting for?"

Mark tapped absent fingers against the top of his laptop. "Well, I was hoping Simon might have had a chance to run his model with our detailed dataset by now."

"Oh, yes." She remembered Henry's thoughtless commandeering of those very sequences, and what he thought they proved. "I'll see if I can't get him in here to brief us."

Just then there was a tap at the door, and Mary poked her head in.

"Hey, you!" Artie said. Then, noticed the polystyrene box she was carrying: "Is that what I think it is?"

She nodded. "Tissue samples from Mackenzie, as promised."

Artie was relieved to see that the strange pall the incident had cast over her friend seemed to have worn off.

"This is brilliant," Mark said, taking the box from her. "We'll have this worked up in no time. Thanks so much."

"Be careful," she called out to him as he left the room.

"I promise, Auntie Mary!" came the reply floating up the corridor, and both women chuckled.

"I hope it wasn't too much of an inconvenience, dropping this round," Artie said.

"Not at all—there's a networking luncheon and afternoon workshop on today at the Royal College. Freddie would have come here too, but he's got a few things on that he needs to settle back at the surgery."

"It's a long slog up here from town, nonetheless."

"I don't mind," Mary said. "It's nice to see you—although I do have something to tell you."

"Time for a cup of tea?"

"Definitely."

Mary fussed with the collar of her pea-green linen suit while Artie put the kettle on.

"Anything wrong?" Artie asked.

"Just some strange news." Mary shrugged. "I'm not really sure what to make of it, to be honest."

"Tell me."

"Last night, Freddie received a phone call. We were just about to turn in—around 11 PM. It was a man, claiming to be with the police and wanting to know if Freddie had ever treated June Morris's cat."

"No—seriously?"

"Freddie was a bit suspicious because the man didn't sound convincing—and plus it was practically midnight on a Sunday evening. He thought it might be an over-enthusiastic journalist from the local rag, trying to sniff out an exclusive on Mrs. Morris's death. Asked him for his badge number. The man apparently mumbled something and hung up."

"How odd."

"Then, when I was on the train, Freddie rang me up to say that Kamini had had some visitors at the surgery this morning, soon after opening, when he was out on a call."

"Cops?"

"No, just two men dressed normally—suits. They apparently were quite friendly and well-spoken, said they were detectives and asked for Freddie. When Kamini said he wasn't there, they wanted to know about Mrs. Morris' cat—whether he had been ill and whether the surgery had treated him. And if so, did they have any samples?"

"Wow. What did she say?"

"Well, Freddie hasn't told Kamini anything about Mackenzie—she knows there's a cat plague, of course, and has seen some of the affected cats, but he's been keeping the more recent stuff to himself. So she told them, honestly, that yes, Mackenzie was on their register but that Mrs Morris hadn't shown up for the appointment, she'd heard about the death and that was all she knew."

Artie clutched her hot mug, pondered this. "Did Kamini ask to see any identification?"

Mary frowned. "I'm not sure. Well, at least, Freddie didn't mention that—and I think he would have. Are you thinking they might not actually be detectives?"

"Well, on TV they always show badges, don't they, and give names and contact details. And taking this together with that neighbor's story about the unmarked van..."

"Yes. I thought there might be connected as well. But Art, maybe this is important. I was wondering if we ought to ring someone up and tell them we actually do have all the tissues and bloods. But who on earth would we call? If they are spooks, it's not as if you can just look them up in the Yellow Pages."

"Hmmm." Artie stared into space. "Well, if they're really serious about finding out about the cat, I suppose they'll be in touch again. I don't see any reason for Freddie to hide this. After all, we were discussing the futility of interesting the Government in a very sketchy animal-to-human outbreak anyway, so perhaps these people might be able to help. But in the meantime, it also can't hurt for us to work up Mackenzie's viral sequences while we've got them."

Mary let out a breath of air. "I suppose you're right. Actually, whoever they are would probably be grateful for any light we could shed on the causative agent—makes their job that much easier."

Both women started around when Mark burst into the office.

"Good news—our sequencing results have finally arrived! Would you two like to join us at Fi's computer for the results?"

"Fantastic," Artie said, leaping to her feet, and to Mary: "Hopefully this is the answer to the mystery of what gene the Minster virus has swapped in to replace its own envelope. Do you have a few more minutes?"

"Wouldn't miss it for the world," she said.

Soon everyone was crowded around Fiona's terminal in the lab as she clicked open the files.

"Well, it looks as if the high-stringency cocktail did the trick," Fiona said as the first sequence file opened, revealing a long string of nucleotide code. "Roughly eight-hundred base-pairs of reliable read, not great but certainly loads better than what I was able to manage before."

"We can definitely get an ID with that much sequence," Mark said. "It's nowhere near the total predicted length, but we should have the bulk of the intruder sequences from this."

"Is more than one cat represented in this set of results?" Artie asked.

"Yes, both direct sequencing of provirus amplified straight from the samples, as well as all of my clones," Fiona said. "I've already checked—the viral sequences from all the different Minster cats are all roughly the same. I can do you a proper alignment of each in a bit."

"Look," Artie said, pointing at the sheet. "Loads of Gs and Cs—probably why you couldn't cut through with the normal cocktail, Fi."

Meanwhile, Fiona had submitted the code for identification. "Here we go," she said, scrolling down. "Lots of hits coming in."

"And the winner is..." Mark said.

"Vesicular stomatitis virus." A general chorus, with Artie's contribution ending on an upturned querying tone.

"VSV glycoprotein G," Fiona echoed, a bit uncertainly, scrolling further down. "It's hitting lots of different strains of the same thing."

"Looks like I owe you an apology, Fiona," Artie said, "when I dismissed your rabies theory. VSV is a prominent member of that family of viruses."

"It's a solid match," Mark said. "A few mutations, but it looks to be VSV-G itself, not just something similar to it."

There was a little silence, and then Mary said: "It's a bit weird, isn't it? VSV is a disease of horses and cattle... and occasionally, of swine. And a very rare one in Britain, at that—though it's on the list of notifiable diseases. We seldom hear about it, except in the context of it being mistaken for a foot-and-mouth scare. I've never heard of it infecting house cats."

"What do you mean, mistaken for foot-and-mouth?" Artie experienced a niggle of adrenalin, a strange counterpart to the sense of unreality that was slowly enveloping her at the same time.

"The clinical disease caused by vesicular stomatitis is indistinguishable from that of foot-and-mouth," Mary explained. "Blisters on the mouth, teats and hooves. Sophisticated tests are needed to tell them apart. It causes no end of problems when there is an outbreak—DEFRA tends to get really skittish, assuming the worst."

"Does it infect people?" Mark asked.

"No idea," Mary said. "Sick people are not my forte, but I'm sure you could find out on the internet."

"Why have we also hit all these vectors?" Fiona asked. Sensible and thorough to the last, she had continued to scroll down the list of positive matches from the search. Artie saw that, sure enough, the Minster insert was also related to a whole host of artificial DNA constructs.

And then, suddenly, she realized why. The implications hit her with an almost physical force, but she managed to keep her words even.

"VSV-G protein is what allows the virus to stick to and enter a cell it wants to infect," she said. "It turns out to be incredibly good at this—so much so that labs around the world exploit it to package up foreign DNA for delivery into human cells. It's also being trialed in gene therapy."

"If I recall correctly," Mark said, "VSV-G is capable of entering even resting T-cells—which is why it's handy for HIV vaccine work. I could check this pretty easily with my home-made virus."

"It's my understanding that VSV-G is so promiscuous that it can get into literally any cell, any species." Artie was thinking aloud, trying to shoehorn the Minster virus back into the realm of the natural by sheer force of will. "Cat cells would be no exception. So there would be a strong selection pressure for feline leukemia virus to pick this gene up, right?"

"It doesn't make sense," Mark said, "when you think about it. Sure, it would be an advantage, but Mary says it's not normally a cat disease. How could the two viruses have ever encountered one another in the wild long enough to recombine and merge their genetic identities?"

"It only takes one event, no matter how rare," Artie countered. "Natural selection could do the rest." How foolish she felt, uttering these words: foolish and desperate.

"Well, I suppose it must have," Mark said, but he still sounded dubious. Then he brightened a bit. "But the fact that it's so unlikely is bound to make it more scientifically interesting. And think about it—this beast is comprised of *three* different viruses. It's a great story."

He met her eye, and she knew he was expecting her usual rampant display of enthusiasm. But she just couldn't find the energy to put on an act.

"We should probably consult a rabies virologist, find out what we can about circulating strains in England," Artie said, instead. "Pin this insertion down to something that's known to be out there."

It still was theoretically possible, she told herself stubbornly. At its heart, being a good scientist meant following every lead and ruling out all alternatives, no matter how unlikely. Privately, she resolved to do a bit of parallel research on the currently favored strain of VSV-G used in labs for artificial delivery and gene therapy.

"And meanwhile we can walk along this sequence, finish it off and see how the virus ends," Mark said. "We already know it's probably missing the crucial long terminal repeat."

"What does that mean?" Mary asked. "That it can't replicate on its own?"

"Yes—but it would be good to confirm that."

"Still, with that VSV-G protein helping out, it's probably safe to assume it can infect human cells once it's been packaged inside the hybrid viruses," Artie said.

"Does that mean it can definitely pass from cat to human?" Fiona asked.

"Not necessarily," Artie said. "It takes more to establish a live infection than just the ability to enter the target cells. Cross-species transmission requires a whole set of hurdles to be overcome—it's got to get past a person's immune defenses, to the right place, first. And once inside the cell, it's got to be able to replicate efficiently. That's not a given either."

"Some strains of animal viruses already have the right kit to infect human cells in culture," Mark added, "but still hardly ever pass to people. Bird flu is a great example.

People do get sick from it, but rarely. And those who do don't usually pass it on to other people."

"So as far as I'm concerned," Artie said, "June Morris's death notwithstanding, we have to assume that the jury is still out on cat-to-human transmission."

"Which doesn't mean that you all shouldn't be incredibly careful." Mary's tone was severe.

"Agreed," Artie said. "The virus particles in Mackenzie's frozen tissue and blood are probably well inactivated, but treat it as ultra-hazardous just to be safe."

After Mary left, Mark and Artie went back to the office.

"You're not happy, are you?" Mark said, studying her face with neutral brown eyes.

She sighed. "It just seems wrong, doesn't it?"

"It's certainly unusual, I'll give you that. But I'm not sure why you're being so pessimistic, Art—it's not like you."

"I was expecting a big juicy cancer gene, to be honest—preferably one no one's yet discovered. Or in my wilder hopes, some key bit of some other cat pathogen. But not this."

"I have to confess I don't know anything about VSV, apart from its use in the lab," Mark said.

"Me neither."

"I volunteer to bone up on the essentials," he said. "I know you've still got that grant to conquer. I can have it ready for the next lab meeting."

"Thanks—that's exactly what we need. More information."

"Maybe I'll uncover something about VSV that makes sense in this context."

"Let's hope so."

HOLDING HIS BREATH, SIMON PUSHED open the door to the central server area of B302. With any luck, his master would still be lost to the world. As Simon's eyes adjusted to the dimness, he caught a flicker of movement in Henry's direction and turned his head just as something seemed to disappear from the older man's screen: a confused microsecond memory of blood-red lines tangled in an electric blue grid. Had Henry just closed a window on his computer screen? But no: Simon blinked and saw that the terminal displayed only its usual bird flu simulation—a pastel basket of lazy lines. And the older man himself manifested no more conscious awareness than he'd demonstrated when Simon had passed on his way out to the canteen. Simon decided that he must have imagined seeing a projection of his own Meyerhof-Hernseley simulation: it was a trick of the light; a reflection from motion of the glass pane in the door.

Simon placed the wrapped sandwich and bottle of water to the left of Henry's keyboard. Still no response. Relieved, he crept onward through the room and then into his own office, easing the door closed behind him with the quietest of clicks. Henry had been "awake" this past week far more frequently than Simon could ever recall—and unusually demanding too, during those periods of sentience. In fact, it had been hard to cobble together more than a few uninterrupted hours to work on the new set of virus sequences Mark had provided. He prided himself on his efficiency and didn't want Artemis to think him lazy or unreliable. With any luck, he could use this quiet spell to finish off the analysis before Henry's imperious commands started issuing forth.

Predictably, the MoD phone rang at that precise moment, sounding as shrill as a fire alarm. Simon ripped the receiver from its cradle, almost surprised himself by the volcanic eruption of molten anger. As Brees spoke, he choked it down with effort.

"Some new developments, Dr. Renquist. We've established a link between the dead woman in Minster and the terrorist suspect Abdul Farah."

"Really?"

"Yes, it turns out her grandson lives in Faversham and they share a few mutual friends."

Simon felt a rare headache prickle up between his eyes, and kneaded the area fiercely with finger and thumb.

"With respect, Mr. Brees, is that really a very robust connection? It's a pretty small village, as I understand it."

"I suggest you stick to the mathematics and leave the rest of the business to the experts."

"Fine." Simon practically bit down on the word. "Any news yet on what killed the woman?"

"Nothing conclusive. It wasn't a heart attack or stroke—it looks as if she may have had multiple organ failure, presumably from the illness she was suffering at the time—brought on, as we suspect, by an artificial agent."

"Have you made any progress identifying this... agent?" Simon carefully filtered the scorn and sarcasm from his question. Artemis was counting on him to obtain the information they needed to prove her virus was natural, so he needed to tread carefully.

"No." Brees sounded reluctant. "We know what it isn't: anthrax, smallpox, plague, botulinum or ricin. But if it's something entirely new, it's very difficult to test for."

As Simon took this in, he was hit by an idea, so perfect that he didn't even pause to think through what he said next.

"If I might offer a suggestion: the spreading patterns that the Professor is seeing in his models are reminiscent of... a retroviral signature."

"Retroviral?" The other man dropped his bored, superior attitude. "You mean like HIV?"

"Yes, or something related to it." Simon didn't want to give away his privileged knowledge completely, and the fact that he'd broken the Official Secrets Act by collaborating with a third party on MoD business. But felt he needed to put Brees onto the right track—a track that would vindicate this Farah idiot—as closely as he dared.

"Well, we could certainly order a few tests and see what comes up," Brees said. "Please thank the Professor for these insights. I'm only surprised he didn't mention this on Friday."

It was only after Simon hung up that he realized that he hadn't spoken with Brees last Friday; checking his diary, he confirmed that their phone call had been the day before. And Brees had said "he," not "you." But then, Brees always spoke about Simon as if he were an extension of Henry, and Simon decided Brees had probably just mis-remembered the day.

∿

AFTER FINALIZING THE COSTING SECTION of her grant application and catch-ing up on her correspondence—including firing off a message to a rabies specialist in Nottingham and the forensic scientist Johnny Ingsall in Portsmouth—Artie felt unusually restless. Mark had headed off to the Camden Institute with his live cultures cradled in plastic boxes and Fiona was busy with cat tissue in the lab. She felt entirely surplus to requirements. To make matters more frustrating, an email message and a spate of soft knocking had failed to invoke Simon from B302. She stood indecisively in the corridor. What she really ought to do was to return to her computer and com-pare Fiona's latest sequencing results to the common laboratory strains of VSV-G in more detail. But her reluctance to prove Henry right—and to kill her glorious theory once and for all—was so strong that she finally grabbed her handbag and left the building.

Half an hour later she was sitting at a corner table in the Victoria Arms, picking over the remains of her chicken salad. Although the indoor space was practical-ly empty, the window offered a view of the back terrace, which was teeming with chatting, happy people under parasols, enjoying the sunshine, a pint or two and the spectacular prospect of the valley below. How she envied their carefree existence. She recognized quite a few people from Heatherfields in their number, but she was content to skulk in the relative darkness and obscurity and try to sort out the mess of secrets and lies that had grown up around her, almost without her realizing it.

When had everything become so complicated? Artie was feeling, keenly now, the tactical error of keeping Mark ignorant of the entire MoD subplot in this increasingly farcical chain of events. How could they freely discuss the implications of the VSV-G insert when Artie was withholding such crucial information? True, Simon's involve-ment with the Government was not hers to share; he had already broken rules just by talking to her. She knew that she could trust Mark to be discreet, but the problem was that it was now too late to confess that she'd been holding back on the bioterrorism theory, on the other human cases—especially after he'd specifically asked her, and she had looked him in the eye and lied about it. And if she confessed about this, she'd also have to tell him about her clandestine meetings with Henry—and how she was keeping secret his presumably key information about the Meyerhof-Hernsley from Simon as well.

And then there was this business of Henry's deterioration/improvement; she really needed to have a frank discussion with Simon about what Calvin suspected his symptoms meant, especially if he was now in the position to influence the MoD. But as Henry had chosen her to confess his awakening, she felt it would be a personal betrayal to go running to Simon with this information. He had, in fact, specifically told her not to. And did she really want to be the one responsible for him getting eased out of Heatherfields, put in a home, possibly drugged up into oblivion? And what about Simon's career? Henry was probably correct in assuming that Henry's departure would precipitate Simon's dismissal—and that he'd be hard pressed to find a position elsewhere.

Finally, there was the Minster virus itself. Surely now it was patently irresponsible that she had not reported the incident to DEFRA or another official body. At least this was one oversight that could now finally be rectified, with the sequencing largely completed—and she tried to convince herself that it was entirely justifiable to have waited until its identity was firmly pinned down. Artie resolved to ring up Mary as soon as she got back to the office and arrange a tactical meeting.

"Is everything all right, dear?"

Artie surfaced from her turmoil to find Susan Tavistock standing by her table, a quizzical look on her face.

She returned the older woman's gaze, found herself confessing, "Things have been better, to be honest."

"I've got about twenty minutes before I need to meet with a PhD student," Susan said. "Can I sit for a moment?"

Artie waved a hand, trying to work out why she wasn't annoyed by the intrusion.

"How are things in the basement?" Susan asked. "You getting much flak?"

"Not at all," Artie said. "It seems to be a bit of an exception to the rule down there."

"You're lucky," Susan conceded. "Ben Crombie is a genuinely decent guy, and between you and me, the others are so... weird that gender politics are probably the last thing on their mind."

Artie laughed softly. "True."

"Although... are you really collaborating with Simon Renquist?"

"I am—although it took some doing."

"If I may say so, that's quite a coup," Susan said, "considering his tendencies. I've never spoken with the man, but I understand he's a textbook chauvinist."

"The nice thing about Simon is that, although he assumes all women are dolts from first principles, he is adaptable enough to revise this hypothesis in the face of evidence to the contrary. Unlike some."

"How *is* it going with Hastings? I've heard your post-doc has had to make arrangements to work off-site."

Artie met her eye squarely. "I won't deny there's been some turbulence. But I decided it would be better just to sort out something independently."

"It was a master stroke, dear. The Sanctum like it when people avoid conflict and don't complain, even when they are well within their rights. I hear that Peter is positively belching flames."

"Good." The pair smiled at one another, and then Artie ventured: "Susan, do you ever keep information from certain members of your group?"

Susan eyed her curiously, shrugged. Her hand, meanwhile, had strayed into the inside pocket of her navy blue jacket, pulled out a pack of cigarettes—then realized what it was doing and pushed it back.

"I'm finished here," Artie said. "If you need a smoke, I'll walk you back to the Institute."

"Yes, that would be great."

Artie left some notes on the table and the two women headed out into the blinding sunshine.

"Of course I do," Susan said, lighting up and taking a long pull. "You know, it's difficult to make the transition from post-doc to group leader—and I believe this is largely because academic science is such an egalitarian profession. We are conditioned to think of the lab as a flat structure, where everyone has a say and scientific truths are the only law of the land."

"But in a way, isn't that how it should be?"

"I'm not so sure," Susan said. "No matter how brashly they might act, PhD students and technicians, deep down, crave leadership and direction. Of course it's more difficult with post-docs—the lines are a lot more blurred—but at the end of the day, you are the one bringing in the research funding and it's you who needs to keep track of the big picture. You must be the boss of your kingdom—not just on paper, but in how you behave."

Artie thought about this for a few moments as they trudged uphill on the hot pavement, her calve muscles pulling slightly against the grade. Ahead of them, Heatherfields loomed like a gothic B-movie apparition.

"Were you, for example, au fait with everything that Philip Cox was up to?"

"Of course not," Artie said. "But that's different... he's..."

"What?" Susan shot her a sideways smile. "Old? A big shot? A *man*?"

"A former President of the Royal Society," Artie said defensively.

"Immaterial." Susan took another toke on the cigarette, unperturbed. "Listen, it's clear that Dr. Reynolds is a very enlightened individual, and I think you're lucky to have secured him. But the fact that he's slightly older, and slightly more experienced, is bound to influence your feelings of authority."

"Mark has never once made me feel threatened," she protested.

"Without knowing the details of whatever is so obviously troubling you, I can only speculate," she said. "But it sounds to me as if you are feeing pressure from him, no matter how well-intentioned. Or perhaps it's more indirect, in that you're worried about his future reactions to something you want to do. And I'm telling you that you are well within your rights to run your laboratory as you see fit, wholly without reference to what he might think."

They completed the journey to Heatherfield's main reception in silence and, at the vertical divergence point of the grand staircase, Artie said: "Thanks, Susan. I feel a lot better."

"Any time, dear." She paused, patted Artie's hand where it rested on the mahogany railing. "You know, it really doesn't matter what I say. If you're anything like I was, you'll ignore all well-meaning advice and learn through disastrous mistakes anyway. Just think of your career as one mammoth, overly ambitious experiment and you'll be fine."

❧

ARTIE WAS JUST GETTING SETTLED back at her desk when there was a tap on the door.

"Sorry I couldn't come earlier," Simon muttered, barely audible, as he poked his head inside.

Something about his posture, Artie thought, poised half in and out of the room, resembled kinetic energy personified: a still object bristling with the desire to hurtle itself across the room. This was in contrast to the dullness of his eyes, sunken as they were in the purple shadows surrounding them.

"God, Simon—aren't you sleeping? Here, let me make you some tea."

"No!"

The sharpness of his tone arrested her, halfway from leaving the chair.

"No tea, no pleasantries, not a single second wasted," he said, coming inside and sitting down. "Henry has been awake far more than he should be, and I need to get back as soon as I can."

She sank back into her seat. "OK—fine." She made her voice gentle, as if placating a threatening dog. "Are you here to show me the new results?"

"Yes." He pulled up a chair next to her laptop, started typing and clicking at rapid speed until the now-familiar La Fontayne grid appeared on her screen, in green. Another click, and the grid was cloned in red, two side by side.

"On the left, our model based on all the earlier Snip data—you've seen this before. On the right, the model after having fed in and integrated all the detailed sequencing fragments that we have."

He pressed a key and the doughnuts did their usual dance, sprouting hives and protrusions. It all played out faster than Artie could process, but it was clear that the endpoint—the ominous Minster spike—was very similar in both.

"A superimposition," he said, clicking a few more keys. The left grid slid into the right and enlarged to fill the screen, with the many overlapping threads colored yellow. "It is all highly consistent—statistically, the outcomes here are very robust. Your detailed data wholly corroborate your shortcut Snip signature data."

"That's good news, isn't it? It means that we can rely on the more extensive Snip data, even though the sequencing coverage we have over the years is patchy."

"Exactly. You should feel very confident that your unstable RT variant arose entirely naturally, and that its existence was presaged earlier."

"Earlier than what?"

"Earlier than the human cases were first reported—almost two years earlier, if we go to the limits of the p-values."

"Which would rather argue against the bioterrorism theory."

"Quite."

"Can you show me exactly when?"

In response, he made the model play backwards, very slowly. Artie watched, fascinated, as the Minster spike lost its flat top and then started to shrink—down, down until it was no more than a large goose bump in geographical plane. Simon clicked a button and the projection froze.

"Any further back and I can't be confident, statistically, that this bump is meaningfully greater than background noise."

"It's clearly still centered on the Isle of Sheppey," Artie said, "as it hasn't shifted on the X–Y axis. But *when* is that?"

Simon pulled down a menu and selected an item; a dialogue box popped up: *November, 2015.*

"Wow," Artie said. "That's great, Simon."

"We do need to keep in mind that this is solely based on the feline leukemia virus elements," he said. "To be thorough, we really ought to have a look at what's happened to the FIV insert in time, compared to known circulating isolates of that virus. Have you managed to obtain those data yet?"

"No—but I'll give Sidney a prod today." She paused, coming back to reality. For about a minute there, she had utterly forgotten how her glorious theory had been abruptly grounded. "And I'm afraid the situation has just become more complex with the new sequencing results—we now know what's taken the place of the Env gene."

"Tell me." Glanced at his watch. "But briefly, if you don't mind, because there's one more thing I need to show you before I go."

Artie sketched the specifics, finishing with: "As you can imagine, I'm rather alarmed to discover that this virus contains precisely the sort of attachment protein that one would consider as a top candidate for artificially introducing foreign DNA into humans. As a vector delivery method, it doesn't get much more efficient than VSV-G. At least, if I were designing a DNA-based weapon, it would be up there in my top three."

"You do say that there have been VSV outbreaks in this country, though?"

"I think so, since it's on DEFRA's hit list. We're still looking into it, but a bigger problem is that I'm almost positive it doesn't naturally infect cats."

"I thought you said that VSV-G could get into any cell," Simon said. "How sure are you that it can't infect cats?"

"I have no doubt it could be done in the lab—VSV would definitely be able to at least enter cat cells," she said. "But in order to recombine, different viruses need to infect the same cell at the same time, out in the wild, so that their RNA genomes can intermingle and get packaged into the same particle. It just seems highly improbable that FeLV, FIV and VSV could all have ended up in the same animal."

"You mean in *cats*. But what about in the VSV hosts—cows, pigs, horses? Could your cat viruses have jumped to any of these, then got passed back? Say on a farm?"

"Hmmm." She tapped a pen against her chin. "It's a good question. I don't know about FIV, but the FeLV strain that Minster most resembles has a strict host range of feline cells. True, we don't know anything about the envelope it lost when the VSV sequences invaded, but I'd say it was pretty unlikely."

"But this makes no *sense*." Simon slammed his fist onto the desk, causing her tea mug to rattle in response. "Let's think about this logically. A, you are telling me that the chances of this recombination happening naturally is vanishing small. Which supports the theory that it could be man-made. But B, although your mutant may have an efficient attachment protein in VSV-G, the rest of it makes no sense for a weapons-grade agent: it doesn't seem to be spreading well in humans, and it certainly doesn't seem to be causing much morbidity and mortality. And C, this variant has been fermenting for the past eighteen months—long before any reported illnesses in Faversham."

"Could it have been a failed attempt—someone releasing something in 2015—and this is just the remnants we're seeing?"

He shook his head. "The profile of your Minster expansion doesn't support a sudden introduction, whether recently or two years previously. You saw yourself how smoothly the spike develops. And it still doesn't answer the question why any terrorist would have selected these relatively benign—and almost ludicrously obscure—cat virus genes to do the job."

"And there's another thing," Artie said. "Mary has done plenty of sampling in areas around Kent—Faversham, Sittingbourne, Rainham, Gillingham and further afield. There's no sign of the Minster virus DNA signature anywhere off the Isle of Sheppey. No reported feline cases matching the symptoms either, if my vet colleague's recent informal survey is correct. Yet the first human cases were in Faversham. The *only* cases, if June Morris died of natural causes. This doesn't jibe with the Minster virus being the manmade agent that the MoD is seeking, either."

They both were quiet for a little while, then Simon seemed to shake himself. "I should go, but I'd like to show you some of my forecasts first, using the more robust sequence model."

"Forecasts?"

"What's likely to happen with your virus epidemic based on previous behavior. I've got two scenarios."

He pulled down a menu and changed some parameters. "The first projection is based on the infectivity and rate of change that we're currently seeing."

With the click of a button, the Minster spike continued to flatten out, the top of its hourglass shape spreading, and then eventually stopping. Slowly, then, the bulge began to shrink, melt, merge back into the bumpy background.

"What's happened?" she said, strangely disappointed.

"The epidemic has run its course," he said. He clicked a few places, and a map of Kent appeared underneath the grid. "The Minster virus is confined to the island, which has a limited number of cats. All the infected animals die. Eventually other strains of feline leukemia re-establish dominance and the profile returns to what it resembled in 2015."

He fiddled with a few more buttons and menus. "But I was curious to see what might happen if one of the infected or carrier cats managed to get off the island—under its own steam via the A249 Sheppey Crossing or the Kingsferry Bridge—or even just someone taking their cat on a trip off-island, say to leave it with relatives or kennel it."

He restored the model to its present day spike. "I have to change the scale here—you'll see why in a minute." A few clicks, and the Minster spike, and all its surrounding court of minor variant bumps, shrank to a small, postage-stamp-sized rectangle in the lower-right corner of the screen.

"Now," he said, with a click of the mouse.

Artie watched, horrified, as the Minster bulge began to flatten out and spread, sending out red tendrils and establishing new bumps. These pioneer bumps spread too, and merged with one another until the entire screen was covered. Simon overlaid the map, revealing that all of England, Wales and Scotland lay underneath.

"My God," she said. "And that's just one cat getting loose?"

"Yes," he said. "And surviving long enough to pass it on to cats in a relatively dense population area. For all we know, it might already have happened."

"It could be a disaster," she said.

"I want to stress that some of this is guesswork—we don't know the incubation period, for example, or how many cats are carriers versus symptomatics. But I'm hoping that it's a pretty improbable scenario, a cat leaving the island. I've already checked—Sheppey had several boarding catteries of its own, and the Swale and its associated marshlands and mudflats are an awful long way from most of the centers of habitation. Domestic cats don't range too far from sources of food, I gather."

"If this thing could infect humans—even if it didn't cause symptoms—I suppose people could easily spread it to cats off the island as well."

"Yes. If that's the case, I think we'd have to assume it's pretty likely that the cat population of Great Britain is under serious threat. And of course, if any mutations arise that make it more virulent in humans..."

After Simon left, Artie stared at the red scourge on the screen of her laptop for the longest time. Then she picked up the phone and called Mary.

CHAPTER 13
Deceptions, One Fewer To Worry About

MARK CALLED BACK ABOUT FIVE minutes after Artie left a message on his mobile, asking if he'd be free to meet with Mary and Freddie once their workshop had finished: "We need a proper War Cabinet on this. State of the art on the science, a discussion on whom to notify and via what channels, et cetera. And they both happen to be in town."

"Sure, that sounds like a great idea," he said. "I spent a few hours before lunch downloading and reading a bunch of VSV articles—I'll bring them along."

Something obvious occurred to Artie then—something that cheered her considerably. Mark and the others might actually raise the possibility of the virus being man-made of their own accord, merely based on the evidence at hand. And then once it was out in the open, they could discuss it along with all the other theories, without Artie having to betray any other confidences.

"Will you be done at a reasonable hour?" she asked.

"Yeah, I've already seeded all my cultures—I was worried the heat of the afternoon might have fried them on the journey over, but they seem to be settling in nicely. I'm going to get started on the big experiment in a few minutes."

"So you're all set over there? How is it?"

"The facilities are amazing, Art. Makes Hastings' gig look like a children's sandpit. And Lisa's really great. Did you know she has a thing for filthy lab limericks? *There once was a chemist from Bucks...*"

"I had a feeling you two would hit it off." She suppressed the stupid little flare-up of jealousy. "You're not going to like it *too* much over there, I hope?"

"Don't be daft. Pandemic influenza has nothing on our nifty cat plague. I'll see you in a few hours."

No sooner had she set down the phone than it rang again.

"Professor Marshall?" It was a woman with a southern American accent. "This is Lucy Greenswold, from Zack Johnson's lab up in Nottingham. I understand you emailed him with a rhabdovirus query?"

"Yes! Please, call me Artie."

"I'm a post-doc in the lab—Zack suggested I get in touch because I'm the main person here working on vesicular stomatitis." She paused. "To be honest, he was a bit lukewarm until he looked y'all up on PubMed and saw how many *Science* and *Nature* papers you have—I mean, cats and all that, when we work on cattle."

"I'm so glad you called. Let me tell you a little bit about it."

Artie explained in very general terms about the recombinant virus.

"It's kinda strange," Lucy mused, over the crackly line. "As an RNA virus, VSV is pretty mutable, but it's not prone to recombination. Still, as Zack likes to say, if it can be done, a virus will figure out how to do it."

"Very true. So, are you willing to take a look at our sequences so far? It's only a handful."

"Sure, email them on over and I'll give you my assessment of the likely progenitor strain, no charge. As you probably know, there isn't much VSV in this country—I'm actually funded by the USDA. Whereabouts did y'all pick up this recombinant exactly?"

"Estuary Kent—the Isle of Sheppey."

"Well, it so happens there was a small outbreak in Sittingbourne last year, from some livestock exported from Mexico, and we were the main lab that DEFRA was using to get to the bottom of it. So that would be the logical first place to start."

When Artie hung up, she experienced a small surge of hope. There was something about Lucy's can-do attitude that had cheered her up. *If it can be done, a virus will figure out how to do it.* There had actually been a VSV outbreak in Kent prior to the appearance of the Minster virus, and if Simon's model were correct, it was when the mutability of the virus was in the process of peaking. Perhaps there really had been some crossover. Maybe, despite everything, this really was something natural and—by extension, wholly new and original. Maybe her theory wasn't grounded after all.

༶

WHEN MARK AND ARTIE GOT off the Tube at Westminster, Big Ben was just striking the hour, sunlight glinting off its gilt cladding. The tide was high in the Thames, choppy and brown in the warm wind funneling down, and tail-end rush-hour traffic honked and roared across the Bridge. About a ten-minute walk later, Freddie and Mary met them in the grand foyer of the headquarters of the Royal College of Veterinary Surgeons.

"We managed to sweet-talk them into giving us a room in the Library," Freddie said, ushering them down the plush corridor past a seemingly endless row of dour-looking men in painted portrait.

Soon they were ensconced around a round table in a cramped room off the main stacks. After a moment of expectant silence, Artie said: "We've reached a pivotal moment, as I'm sure you're all aware. Freddie, has Mary briefed you on the latest results?"

He nodded, a bit grimly.

"Mark has kindly agreed to scour the literature and give us a snapshot of the molecular biology of vesicular stomatitis, but if either of you has any veterinary insights, please do butt in at any time. Mark?"

He picked up his tablet and swiped a few times. "Apologies that this is all a bit last-minute, but I've managed to get a grip on the basics." He met everyone's eye before focusing on the screen. "VSV is endemic in the Americas, and is transmitted via an insect intermediate—biting flies. It prefers to replicate in the nervous system, though."

"Well," Artie said, "that's not necessarily a problem. Biting insects will inject the virus into the blood stream, so there's definitely a chance that it could encounter T cells en route to the brain. Go on, Mark."

"It's encoded by a single-stranded RNA genome—similar to retroviruses like feline leukemia—and shares FeLV's propensity for variation. And VSV replicates in the cytoplasm—the same compartment where FeLV RT would be making its own initial DNA copies."

"You're saying," Freddie said, "that the genetic material of these two different viruses could, in theory, be freely mixing in the same place?"

"Yes," Mark said. "The FeLV copies would eventually migrate into the nucleus, away from VSV, for the amplification step, but reverse transcription and viral packaging both occur in the cytoplasm—precisely where VSV carries out its entire replication cycle."

"So," Artie said, "during a hypothetical co-infection with VSV and FeLV in the same cell, there would be ample opportunity for a strand of VSV RNA to blunder right into FeLV RT while it was doing its job, and accidentally get recombined into the FeLV DNA copy?"

"You don't even need an accidental encounter with RT for this to work," Mark said. "If there was loads of VSV RNA floating around, it wouldn't necessarily be surprising if some of it got accidentally packaged into FeLV particles, even if the VSV strands lacked the correct packaging signal—just by sheer numbers. Then in the next round of infection, recombination would be even more likely to occur."

"Have you checked for regions of homology that might facilitate this?" Artie asked.

"I have, as it happens," Mark said. "And there are indeed a few related stretches of sequence, including known FeLV recombination motifs. But as FeLV has been reported to swap on as few as a handful of similar nucleotides, that's not so surprising."

"Okay," Artie said. "Let's take this co-infection scenario as our working hypothesis for the moment. Carry on."

"The bigger impediment, of course, is the respective host ranges of FeLV and VSV," Mark said. "The former only infects cats, while the latter favors certain hoofed livestock—although it's been known to infect wild animals such as bears, rodents and lynx."

"And we also have to factor in the fact that VSV infections here are rare," Mary pointed out.

"We may have an answer to that hurdle," Artie said, briefly reviewing what Lucy Greenswold had told her about the Mexican import outbreak.

"Sittingbourne isn't far from Sheppey," Freddie said thoughtfully.

"Are there any prospective VSV host animals on the island?" Artie asked. "When we drove down there, I only remember seeing sheep."

"Oh, we have lots of horses," Freddie said. "In fact, they're really quite wild. In many cases, they're allowed to graze freely in the environmentally protected areas on both sides of the Swale—they're actually quite useful keeping the grasses under control. We have pigs and cattle as well."

"So if the VSV outbreak wasn't well contained?" Artie said.

"There is still the Swale to contend with," Mary said. "It's a massive body of water. To get from Sittingbourne to Sheppey, you'd have to invoke contaminated boots or lorries traveling from one to the other—which isn't that unlikely, to be honest. From all the foot-and-mouth epidemics, we know quite a bit about how easy that actually is."

"Okay," Artie said. "So that's a possible route of dissemination, anyway."

"I'm not sure how far individual insects actually range," Mary said, "but they could be another possible route. Maybe less likely though."

"Agreed," Freddie said. "Depending on what farm the Sittingbourne outbreak occurred, it could be as far as eight to ten miles from Minster."

"I'll get the exact location from Lucy," Artie said.

"To summarize so far," Mark said. "We've got two viruses potentially in the same greater geographic location. But how do they meet?"

"A farm," Artie said promptly. "Cats and quadrupeds mingle on farms."

"There are no known examples of any cat ever contracting VSV," Mark said. "At least not in my limited literature search."

"But maybe it's not something anyone's ever looked for," Artie said.

"It's true," Mary said, "that if you have a sick cat in your surgery, you only test for the usual suspects. If I had a VSV-infected cat on my hands, how would I ever know?"

"Much more likely," Freddie said, "is that if it failed all the known tests, a vet would just give up and record an unknown etiology."

"The VSV-G envelope can easily infect human cells," Artie said. "We know this from its usefulness in gene therapy. So it's likely to be able to hit a wide variety of species, including cats."

"In fact, that's almost certain," Mark said. "VSV-G is so promiscuous that it can even infect cells from distantly related organisms—I mentioned bears and rodents already, but there are also reports of it hitting distantly related organisms such as fruit flies and fish. I also found some mentions of humans being infected by VSV directly."

"What are the symptoms?" Mary asked.

"I'm not entirely sure," Mark said. "I couldn't find anything really specific. All I have is an article claiming it to be 'very infectious for man' and that it's 'temporarily debilitating' in those cases. And Field's *Virology* says that it can cause an acute febrile disease—flu-like symptoms. I found one mention of a child with encephalitis. I don't think it's really been that well reported."

"*Very infectious*," Freddie repeated. "I wonder if the Department of Health has seen any cases? What we need is a medic, to let us know what's come up on the surveillance bulletins over the last few months."

Artie remained silent, just watching it play out. Despite the sheer unlikelihood of their strange hybrid virus having evolved in the wild, the possibility that it was artificial had obviously not even occurred to any of the others, despite the smoking gun of a common lab vector being involved. It just goes to show, she mused, that people see what they want to see—what they *expect* to see. Trained scientists should be immune to this very human tendency, but they were obviously just as prone as anyone else. If the men in B302 hadn't clued her in, would she herself be any different?

She knew that she should pretend to think of it now, bring it up as a formal possibility, get the idea out there on the table. But something was holding her back.

"Wasn't there something in the papers a few weeks ago?" Mary said. "A few people coming down with FMD-like lesions?"

"I remember that," Freddie said. "But the story came and went—I'm not sure what the verdict was."

"Foot-and-mouth... vesicular stomatitis," Mary said, "They have similar symptoms."

"Blisters, you mean." Mark swiped his tablet, rummaging for a particular paper.

"Except that none of the afflicted cats had blisters, or skin disorders of any type," Freddie said. "I was very thorough—I'm sure I would have noticed. But we should try to follow up on those news stories, just in case. I'll take a look on the main websites tonight."

Mark said: "I guess it's time to think about reporting this to the authorities?"

"I think so," Mary said. "Very strongly. VSV is notifiable. Sure, this isn't classic VSV by any stretch, but now that the sequencing is in, Freddie and I are honor-bound to report this to the Animal and Plant Health Agency."

"And I'm all for it," Artie said. "I've been feeling guilty that we didn't do it earlier."

"We didn't know what we were truly dealing with, until today," Mark said.

"Yes," Freddie said. "Neither FeLV or FIV are notifiable, no matter how nasty the strain. I wouldn't feel bad about waiting."

"I'm just a little worried," Artie confessed, "after some results that have come in today from our mathematical collaborators."

Earlier in the afternoon, Artie had emailed Simon and asked him to provide movies of the various La Fontaine projections. She pulled her laptop out now and, after briefly explaining the key parameters, played the movie of Simon's forecast if at least one cat made it off the island.

"Holy Christ," Freddie murmured when the red lines had run their course. Nobody said anything else for a few moments—just the ticking of the clock over the door, measuring seconds in precise sonic intervals.

"We need to ask for a quarantine," Mary said. "No cats must be allowed to leave Sheppey. This could wipe out the UK's entire cat population."

"It's just an experimental model," Artie said. "Do you think the Animal and Plant Health Agency will take it seriously?"

"I'll make sure of it," Freddie said. "And I think we need to alert the Department of Health, too, about a possible emerging human virus, with the envelope this thing is carrying. If it's not infecting humans now or making them sick, it might only be a matter of time. Leave it with me."

THE FOUR PARTED WAYS, FREDDIE and Mary towards Victoria Station, and Mark and Artie along the river path leading to Embankment. The sun was setting off to their left, bathing Royal London in a coppery haze. Along the opposite side of the river, the glass rectangles of a thousand windows mirrored back shades of iceberg green. Below, boats churned though the shifting tidal waters and a cooling breeze filtered through the riffling canopy of plane trees lining the path. As they crossed Horse Guards Avenue, Artie forced herself not to look towards the grand building that housed the Ministry of Defence, taunting her peripheral vision like a bad omen.

They walked in silence for a while, and then Mark said: "You seemed unusually subdued in there."

Artie paused, turned to gaze out over the river. Mark joined her there, elbows not quite touching. A tourist's postcard: the great Ferris wheel in multicolored dazzle, with the indigo-lit stretch of the Hungerford Bridge on the left and the stately façade of County Hall on the right. In fact, several men with professional tripods seemed to be intent on capturing the view for that very intention. How many times, she wondered, had the same scene been photographed? Millions? Trillions? And how could a panorama thus cheapened by clichéd repetition remain so stubbornly beautiful?

"Something seems wrong about this whole thing," Artie said, as close as she dared skirt the truth of her true feelings. *Please, Mark: open your fucking eyes.*

"Wrong how?"

"Too many improbable events, all piled one atop the other. It's a glaring violation of Occam's Razor."

"Sure it's improbable," Mark said. "But it's happened, and now we need to figure out how and why. We've come up with a working theory that isn't *too* crazy—and now we can run with it, see where it leads. That's a key part of our job—the part that you always seem to enjoy the most, if I recall correctly."

"I know," she said. He wasn't going to see it, she realized. Not on his own. "If it was anything other than VSV-G, I'd be running along the Embankment singing to high heaven."

"Hang on," he said, looking at her face more closely. "Are you worried this might be some sort of... lab contamination?"

She shrugged, the epitome of cool, but her heart had begun thumping against her chest. "It's a formal possibility."

"Okay, " Mark said. "In that case, let's reason it through." It was a game for him, she saw, as his eyes brightened with the challenge. Just as it would be for her, if only she were in the same state of blissful oblivion. "I could buy it if Freddie had worked up those samples in a lab that processed VSV vectors at the same time—a gene therapy facility, say, or a research group working on cell entry methods. But we know he doesn't do anything of the sort in his surgery."

"I wasn't suggesting that—"

"Fiona, then? The same goes for us."

When she remained silent, punishing him for stating the obvious, he carried on: "But the evidence against is even more solid than that. I scoured the entire Department of Virology earlier today to see if anyone was using VSV-G for pseudo-typing experiments, just to see if they might have some antibodies I could borrow. And it turns out there isn't a single person in Heatherfields involved in VSV vector work—as far as I could discover, there never has been. So even if something like that *could* get tracked around—wafting through the bloody ventilation units, for Christ's sake—it can't possibly explain our recombination."

And that, Artie saw, was that. Yet again, preconceived notions had thrown up a wall between a clever intellect and an entire universe of more sinister possibilities. She opened her mouth to enlighten him further, but nothing came out.

"Art, what is it?'

She shook her head, eyes filling with tears. Spilling over. She covered her face with cupped hands and felt Mark's arm go around her shoulders, pull her towards and against him. Déjà vu, a sense of her body acting out a part that she was destined to keep botching in the real performance. She cried with the abandon of a stone kicked over the side, gathering momentum as it plunged downwards through the empty air, splashing hard against the gleaming silver surface of Thames and burrowing further in its inky, unfathomable darkness. Past indistinct, cadaverous shapes, all the horrors of what can only be imagined. She didn't think about feminism, or dignity, or the appeal of his body against hers—it was a moment of despair outside of time.

Eventually, after the sobbing had eased, she became aware of Mark's hand, stroking her hair.

"You've been under a tremendous amount of pressure," he said, voice soft in her ear. "You've got to cut yourself some slack, sweetheart."

She raised her head, all sheepish snuffles and snot, and he offered her his handkerchief. When she was done, he took it from her, found a dry corner and used it to pat carefully around her still-wet eyes. She subjected herself to his ministrations like a child, and then he tipped her chin up and was kissing her, kissing her until the two of them were a molten core in the cooling dusk. Somewhere distant, outside the blackness of her own identity, Artie heard the dizzying sound of seagulls, crying out in a fair simulacrum of her own mixed message of joy and despair.

When their lips came apart, he said: "Come home with me."

She shook her head, surfacing from that place. Wondering if this was how life came back to Henry as his rational madness gained a temporary upper hand over his more fundamental dream disease. Finding her eyes still closed, she opened them, sunset tangled in her wet lashes. Opened them, to find his smile impossibly tender.

"I can't," she said.

"Why not?"

"Oh, Mark. For all the same reasons."

He ran a finger along the side of her face—a slowly moving trace of regret. "All right. Let me cook you dinner at the very least. Pour you a glass of wine, take your mind off science for five seconds. Hell, I'd even dust off the fucking Scrabble board if you'd rather do that than sleep with me. You need a break, Artie. You're going to kill yourself."

She stepped away from him, the warm imprint of his fingertip still flushed against her cheek. As the sensation faded away in the cool brush of breeze, it was Susan's voice in her head, then: *You must be the boss of your kingdom.*

"I really appreciate the offer," she said, "but the answer is no. Is that OK?"

He turned away to look out over the water. "Of course it is," he said.

He was still smiling, at least, although with the shadows on his face it was not clear exactly what flavor of smile it might be.

෴

THE NEXT MORNING, FIRST THING, was a faculty meeting upstairs in the main assembly room. The heavy damask draperies and gilt chandeliers were altogether too grand for the petty politics and mind-numbing minutiae on the agenda—the reading of minutes; the motion on accepting said minutes as a true record; the motion seconded. A desultory show of hands—no one ever bothered to read them. Pandemic flu contingency plans; scheduled fire drills; toilet upgrades; microscope purchases; pension scheme erosions. Even a bitch session about the Edwardian lift, which had broken down the day before when Salverson was entertaining high-powered trustees. Artie purposely sat by Susan, for the first ever time, noticing how this positioning seemed to concentrate the otherwise male presence, an optical illusion making them more numerous than they actually were. Across the polished teak expanse, Hastings glowered at her like a Jurassic-era reptile that hadn't fed for some time. She ignored him and exchanged sardonic drolleries with Susan under the general cover of shuffling papers and bored sighs.

The air conditioning wasn't working, so by the time they had adjourned, irritable and sweaty, Artie's brain felt soft and stultified. Which is why she wasn't mentally prepared when, down the long basement corridor, she saw Simon leave her office and scuttle into B302 without noticing her. Increasing her pace, she went to his door, but he'd disappeared into the inner room.

Swearing softly, she turning around and approached her own office door—only to be confronted by Mark, framed in the rectangular window. He was sitting motionless at his desk, staring at her with the coldest expression she had ever yet witnessed.

Everything seemed to happen very slowly after that. Her hand reached for the knob, turned it. As the door fell inward, the heat of her body seemed to vaporize in a blast of icy trepidation—part of her must already have realized what had happened, but her brain still didn't work, an overheated engine refusing to turn over no matter how many times she pressed the pedal.

"Simon asked me to pass on a message to you," Mark said, voice as chill as his eyes.

She tried to speak, failed. Cleared her throat. "Go on."

He looked down at a scribbled note in his hand. "He needs your suggestion for some primer sequences that might prove useful in his clients' bid to PCR the Minster virus out of the dead woman's tissues." There was a long pause. "He said you'd know what that meant."

Artie slid into her chair, more because the muscles in her legs were giving out than from any desire to. She could not believe that Simon had gone to Mark with this question. What on earth was he thinking? Surely he would have assumed that she had not shared his privileged information. But then again, what did Simon know about properly functioning laboratories and the relationships between them? Obviously not much.

Or maybe *she* was the one who needed the refresher course.

"Mark, I..." The full spectrum of her betrayal, and how it would appear to him, stretched before here. "I can explain."

He leaned back in his chair, crossed his arms. "Go on, then. I'm listening."

"I was sworn to secrecy," she said, cursing the uncertain wobble evident even to her own ears.

"Really." The scorn in his voice was lacerating. "Then why did Simon assume I knew about whatever it is you two are thick into? It can't have been *that* secret."

"I—I have no idea why he came to you, Mark. I understood it was not to be discussed!"

"Are you *ever* straight, Artemis?" he said, voice rising. "Lying seems to come to you as naturally as breathing."

"That's not fair."

"Last week I asked you specifically if there was something you were holding back. You could have at least told me the truth: that yes, you were, but that there was a good reason for it. I would have accepted that—you know I would've! Instead, you don't have the common courtesy to show me even an ounce of respect, and I'm left gaping like an ignorant idiot in front of *our* supposed collaborator."

"I tried to tell you..." Her vocal cords weren't working any better than her mind. "Last night. I tried..."

"Last night," he said. "I can't believe I thought my heart was breaking when you cried all over me. That was probably just an act, too, wasn't it? This whole damsel-in-distress thing, it's just a calculated bid to get people to do what you want, isn't it?"

"How can you say that? That's got nothing to do with anything!"

"And what, exactly, were you trying to tell me?"

"The Ministry of Defence," Artie said, "thinks our virus is a bioterrorist agent."

The silence was absolute—it was almost as if neither of them were breathing. Then Mark began to laugh. But it was not a friendly, conspiratorial laugh—it was bitter and sarcastic and cut at Artie's heart like a blade.

"You have got to be fucking kidding me," he finally managed to get out, expression sliding back into the awful stoniness. "That's patently ludicrous. So ludicrous that even *you* wouldn't make it up."

She ignored the last jibe, desperately trying to inject science into the conversation—as if that could possibly set things back to rights. "We thought so too," she said. "Until the VSV-G came into the picture. But Simon and I are still not entirely convinced. We—"

"Well, it sounds as if you two have the matter well in hand."

"Don't be like that. I've regretted you not being in on this since the day we started diverging."

"You've got a strange way of showing it."

She bowed her head. "Mark, I am truly sorry. I was wrong, and I'm ready to fill you in completely. Will you accept my apology?"

She could feel him studying her. And then heard the squeak of his chair as he stood up, grabbed his backpack.

"Actually, I don't think I will," he said.

After a few moments of stunned silence, she said the first thing that popped into her head: "But—where are you going?"

"I'm due over at the Camden Institute." He couldn't even look at her as he shoved past out the door. "I don't know when I'll be back."

∽

ARTIE WENT STRAIGHT TO THE library, found her safe haven in the carrel by the purple and green diamond window. She was finally starting to think clearly again. She hadn't cried: a good sign, proof that her newfound hardness was holding. Mark would come around, she told herself. He was justifiably angry, but once he cooled off he'd understand why she felt she'd had to keep Government business to herself. In fact, she suspected that his overwhelming curiosity would be the thing that cracked him first: the desire to know the whole picture, no matter how dismissive he might be about the bioterrorism theory; the desire to demolish with reasoned arguments. And the truth was that she craved his attack on it, that she *needed* him to help her destroy Henry's fantasy. Simon was next to useless when it came to biology. Why had it taken her so long to realize just how valuable Mark's insights truly were?

A memory flashed before her eyes from the night before: Mark, breaking down the arguments about the lab contamination. His eyes flashing with energy, the setting sun glowing in his hair; the fluid way he sketched the ideas in the air with his big, capable hands. He was becoming, she realized, as indispensable to the lab's science as they had joked all those weeks ago, lying in the tall grass on Parliament Hill. It was so obvious now—far too late—that Susan's advice about post-docs needing direction could never have applied comfortably to Mark. He was not "just a post-doc." He was a special case—an ally, an equal. Co-lab head, if she really gave him his due. And she had repaid his gift of choosing her lab to bestow his considerable skills and talents with mindless rank-pulling, with exclusion. And at the same time, she had answered his staunch kindness and support with a complete lack of trust and respect.

Something more unpleasant was trying to surface amid her feelings of shame, and Artie ruthlessly called it to the witness stand. A liar, Mark had called her. A natural liar. Although she was uncomfortable with the picture of her he had painted, she could not deny that it seemed apt. Yes, she had lied—copiously, in recent weeks— and yes, she had been using her charms to manipulate the world for as long as she could remember. Artie faced the accusations squarely; she was ready, even, to try to think about how to become a different sort of person.

But the tears, the astonishing anguish of the night before, the terrors and pho- bias—these stemmed from a raw, pure source that she could not have controlled. She wanted to defend herself against this one unjust accusation at least, but in the face of the other ugly truths, she doubted she could ever be convincing.

Never mind. One thing at a time. The most important goal was not to salve her pride, but to garner forgiveness for the main sin, to patch things up, to restore the harmony of the lab and the closeness of their friendship. Artie realized, belatedly, that it was the latter that seemed to matter more. More than science, more than success and fame, more than anything else.

He'd come round. She didn't know what would happen if he didn't.

∽

ARTIE SPENT A FEW HOURS in Salverson's office, going through the costings of her grant application and negotiating over personnel. She was hoping to get him to agree to two more post-docs joining her lab if the funds came through, but this would require more space, and Salverson was cagey about whether the Institute could provide it. Nevertheless, Artie recognized his hesitations as the elaborate dance of a skilled negotiator and soon had reached a compromise that both were happy with.

When she got back to the office, she stopped dead at the open door.

Mark's desk was entirely cleared out. His laptop was gone, his stationery was gone; inspecting the shelves, she saw that even his line of textbooks, binders and journals had vanished.

"Knock, knock," Fiona said from behind her. "Can I show you some results?"

Wordlessly she let the younger woman past as she struggled to gain her composure.

"As much as he winds me up, it will be weird not having him around," Fiona remarked, sitting down at the empty desk and opening her notebook. She started rummaging around through some images of gels.

"I'm sorry, I seem to have missed something," Artie said. "Where's Mark's stuff gone?"

Fiona looked up, grey eyes concerned. "Didn't he tell you? Someone in the lab at the Camden Institute has had to have an operation, so they said he could have more hood time. Since he's spending most of his time with Minster anyway, he thought it made more sense to camp out over there for a while. There was an empty desk going spare."

When Artie didn't respond, she said, "I thought you knew."

Artie shook her head. "I've been away from the office for a while—he's probably sent me an email about it. What have you got to show me?"

Fiona pulled out a photo of a gel, tapped at the glowing bands with a lacquered fingernail. "The latest dead cat—Mackenzie. He's definitely infected with Minster. Same size amplimer as all the others."

"Good work."

"And I've got the latest sequencing results back, walking along the VSV-G insert," she said, pulling out a printout.

"Already?"

"Yeah, that swanky service is great—they make the custom oligos for you and still have the results in 24 hours. I shudder to think how much it costs, though."

"Don't worry about that," she said. "How did it go?"

"We've managed to get to the end of the insertion on this run."

"What's was the punchline?" Artie experienced a surge of sadness: Mark should be here for this.

Fiona pointed to the bottom of the sheet, where she'd marked up stretches of the sequence with highlighter pen. "The green part is the end of VSV-G—that's its natural stop codon. Then FeLV resumes for a little while—the bit in orange."

"What part of FeLV?"

"The very end of Env. It's not a section that any of our PCR primers would have recognized."

"And too short to hybridize on Southern blot."

Fiona nodded. "And then a stretch of something I can't identify—and the sequencing dribbles out there. I've set up the next 'walk' reaction, so we'll know more tomorrow."

"Thanks, Fiona."

As she was getting up to leave, she blurted out: "Artie, have you and Mark had a falling out or something?"

Artie considered concocting some cover story on the spot. Instead, she just nodded. "A disagreement about how I'm handling the collaboration with Simon Renquist. I'm hoping it will blow over."

"*Hoping*? I suspected something was up, but I didn't think it was that serious." She shook her head. "He can be such a pig-headed idiot sometimes."

"I think it's more my fault than his."

"I doubt that very much," she said. "It's not really like him to get so upset, though. Do you think he's coming down with the Minster virus?"

"That's not even funny."

"Well, whatever. I don't want to get stuck in the middle, but just so you know—you've can still count on me."

Artie stared at Mark's empty desk as Fiona left, the warmth she felt from this vote of loyalty trickling away in the face of it. She opened up her laptop and checked her mail: dozens of messages, but none of them from her missing post-doc. She hadn't really expected one. Having to learn about his rehousing from Fiona was probably his way of getting back at her for letting him blunder around in ignorance with Simon. Fair enough, and the salvo had hit its target; she didn't even try to ignore the pain of its penetration. But how long would he stay away?

Looking back at her screen, she noticed an email from Simon:

I hope you got the message from Reynolds. Have an urgent need for some sequence information—will stop by to discuss further when Henry's state allows, but in the meantime could you have a think about it and send me some possibilities?

Such a little thing to have caused such a major ripple. She wasn't really sure what he was talking about, and wasn't in the mood to work it out. Looking off to one side, her eye was caught by something odd about the wall. There was, she finally worked out, an incongruous space next to the calendar. A missing piece. Mark had taken away his framed football photo as well, erased his grin from the office entirely.

For the first time, Artie began to conceptualize that Mark might really be gone for good.

❧

ARTIE GOT THROUGH THE REST of the day on autopilot, determined to conquer the final leg of the grant proposal. She still had yet to finalize the most important section, which explained the scientific background and initial findings of the proposed project. She found it a welcome distraction, re-immersing herself into the narrative of her Minster outbreak in the carefully couched, precise and above all unemotional language that custom dictated. Although science was a very human endeavor, performed in the midst of—depending on the day and on the people involved—excitement, boredom, joy, anger, illness, exhaustion or sorrow, there was no trace of this in the sentences scrolling across Artie's screen, which she tweaked and polished with relish and gathering momentum. Each statement had to be backed up by a recognized fact: either an older paper already published in the literature, or a new finding, which she had to include in the text and figures. There was no room for ambiguity or imprecision.

Hours slid by as she bent over her computer. Grant writing was more difficult than preparing a finished project for publication: one had to give away preliminary findings, enough to tantalize the referees, but not so much that the work seemed too mature to warrant further funding. Collating the preliminary data, putting the story together was usually a challenge—but Minster was one of those rare finds that didn't need to be shoehorned into any sort of contrived story. The excitement was all built in. And of course, you didn't yet know the *answer*; you didn't know how the tale ended. So you had to couch your assumptions, hedge your bets, propose alternative outcomes. Before Minster blew into her life, her theory had been a bit thin; now, between the cell biology and the mathematical modeling, there was almost too much information to work with, and she needed to decide what to mention and what to keep back—an elaborate word game that took all of her concentration.

Today, she even found the tedious business of putting together images as formal figures satisfying, taking solace in the fussiness of labels, of font sizes, of brightness and contrast, of cropping, of perfect placement. She wasn't yet sure how to deal with the vesicular stomatitis angle, but there were plenty of experiments to describe without that uncomfortable little detail. She had half a mind to leave it out altogether. It was the kind of thing she'd have asked Mark's opinion on, if he'd been sitting there reading articles amid his usual aura of sedate intellectualism. She shoved that thought out of her mind and carried on.

When the knock roused her, neck aching and upper arms trembling from restricted circulation, the time on her computer shocked: it was nearly 9 PM. Looking up, she saw that Henry Manfield was again lurking outside her door. His wind-blown crag of a face was composed into a semi-pleasant but somehow wholly artificial expression, as if he had been studying magazine photos to see how it was done.

She stood up and was hit by a bout of dizziness. Steadying herself on the back of the chair, she remembered that she hadn't eaten anything since a few crumbly biscuits at the faculty meeting—God, nearly twelve hours ago. The last thing she wanted was to be physically vulnerable in the face of Henry.

She opened the door.

"Good evening, Professor," he intoned. "I trust you are well?"

"Splendid, never better. But I'm actually just on my way home, so can't really chat."

"That is a pity. For I have reached a pivotal juncture and wanted to show you the Meyerhof-Hernsley model in detail, and obtain your feedback about my progress in light of the biological events."

Artie paused. Henry seemed mild, lucid. There was something else different about him; after a few beats she realized that his normally wild hair had been combed, and he was wearing a different cardigan over his tweed waistcoat, still missing that top button. She had never seen him wear anything other than the brown one, so the swap seemed symbolic.

"Do come in, in that case," Artie said. She knew it was ill-advised, but the prospect of finally seeing Henry's scientific rationale for the bioterrorism theory was just too enticing to resist. And hopefully he would make it quick.

"I am terribly sorry for the inconvenience, but we must work at my terminal. The simulation is running live on the main servers, so we can't mirror them on your computer without a lot of fuss."

"What about Simon?"

"He is on the roof, child. If previous patterns can be extrapolated, we'll have at least an hour alone. He doesn't know I know he goes up there, but I've been observing his behavior for some time now, and feel that my prediction is statistically sound."

Artie felt a little flutter of anxiety, fiercely squelched it down. Now that she was standing up, she felt fine. Fear, for her, was simply no longer going to be an issue. Grabbing her handbag with the phone inside, she followed Henry into the depths of B302.

~

ARTIE WATCHED AS HENRY INPUT some parameters, his blue-lit profile stern with concentration.

"I am going to restore the values to time zero," he told her, "and play the basic model for you. Later we can tweak parameters if you'd like to see some alternative scenarios."

Artie couldn't help looking over her shoulder at the closed door separating the server room from the blind office. How could Henry be so sure that Simon would stay up there? She recalled the urgency of his email; despite this, he had gone upstairs when he finally got a free moment, not to her. She could still remember how he'd looked up on the roof those weeks ago, glowering under the starlight. He'd said then that he fled there when he was so angry that he couldn't bear it any more. So perhaps there were greater urgencies at stake. At any rate, she consoled herself that there was a precedent for Henry asking her to come to B302 and, on balance, it would probably arouse much more suspicion if Simon caught Henry visiting her office.

The clicking had stopped. Henry, she saw, was waiting for her attention.

"Before we begin," Artie said, "can I ask you how the La Fontayne and the Meyerhor-Hernsley differ, in general terms? If they are giving radically different profiles, it would help me to understand why."

"Certainly," Henry said. "It is difficult to explain the mathematics in simple terms, but perhaps a good analogy is that the La Fontayne produces an average curve from a series of data points, smoothing out their differences as mean fits tend to do. Whereas the Meyerhof-Hernsley embraces the differences, allows outliers to remain in the equation."

"Why did you feel that the Meyerhof-Hernsley is the favorable approach in this situation?"

"I have always found it to be more robust," he said. "But in particular, your dataset is not very smooth in the time dimension. You have bursts of samplings and then many months of hiatus. To average out these instances could give an unfavorable skew to the bigger picture."

It seemed sensible. "Okay, that's good enough for now."

He clicked a button and the now-familiar grid appeared. "The readout is not quite the same as the one you've been using with Simon," he said. "X and Y are still the map coordinates, and time is still represented by the forward animation. But I've chosen to disregard standard variation; instead, the Z-height represents a more sophisticated characteristic: the spreading *fitness*."

"What does that mean?"

"To put it in terms you can understand, it is a calculation that compares past and future values of a given sequence and then plots how successfully that sequence propagates in time."

"So it's like an assessment of how successful a given strain will turn out to be?"

When he nodded, she asked him a few more questions until she was sure she grasped at least the essentials. "It seems a lot more nuanced than the La Fontayne."

"That is certain," Henry said. "Now let us begin in 2010."

He clicked the start arrow, and the doughnut began to ripple. Artie waited for the goose bumps, but they never happened. This, she recalled, was the same disappointing readout that Simon had shown her when he tried the same algorithm side by side with the La Fontayne. She was just about to remark on this when suddenly, on the right-hand side, a thin pillar—almost like a tube—shot up from the seething mass of nearly flat threads, climbing all the way up the screen and then spreading out like a trumpet.

"My God," Artie said. "What is *that*?"

"I will explain the *what*. But let's first examine *where* and *when*."

Henry clicked on the base of the tube, and the map coordinates came up. "As you can see, this epidemic is centered in Minster. Not a surprise, of course. But let me take you to the crucial moment in time."

He made the movie play backwards and Artie watched the trumpet bell shrink back into the column, and then the column telescope downwards. When the cylinder was just about to disappear into the background noise, Henry froze the movie.

"March, 2017. Just a few months ago. We can be fairly precise about this figure, because you logged a lot of samples in the period from November 2016 to mid-April."

Mary, Artie thought, and that massive survey she'd done around Kent with the help of a keen vet student who wanted some research experience. Freddie's surgery would have supplied quite a few samples in that batch.

"March also happens to be when the first human cases were picked up by the MoD," Henry said.

"That could just be a coincidence. I don't understand why you think this supports a bioterrorist attack," Artie said. "Can't this shape just be a naturally occurring, hyper-fit variant?"

"Ah, I have forgot that you are not accustomed to looking at this model," he said, "My apologies. Allow me to show you two things."

He played the movie to the end, revealing the skinny trumpet, and then made the grid smaller and slid it to the right of the screen. Then he called up two more grids, which he stacked one atop the other on the left.

"On the top, I'm going to play you a classic scenario from the literature. This is a real outbreak of a particularly pathogenic strain of HIV in one discrete location—in this case, Tanzania. It's a good comparison because, as with your dataset, there is an underlying prevalence of AIDS already in this region. And of course, it is also a retrovirus."

He played the movie and Artie watched, mesmerized, as the rippling doughnut slowly produced a fat dome off to one side, which gradually inflated like a balloon. The endpoint of the movie rather resembled a bulbous cartoon car, with the epidemic providing the main body and the residual signatures a less prominent boot and bonnet.

"Of course all viruses are different," Henry said, "varying in values such as infectivity, mutation rate and incubation period, as are their hosts, which can exhibit varying behavior, immunity and levels of illness and person-to-person contact. But I can assure you that this Meyerhof-Hernsley shape is rather typical for a minimally contagious, blood-borne pathogen that takes a long time to kill its hosts."

"It's fascinating," Artie said, trying and failing to get her head around the mathematical factors that might lead to such a difference in shape. But she was very impressed, no question: Simon had never bothered to show her any examples from the literature. It was almost as if her relationship with Henry were playing backwards too: just like that, he had morphed from scary, crazy menace back to the enthralling genius she had first encountered in this very room, seemingly years ago. Except now, he was acting and speaking like a normal person, presumably riding on the unstable crest of a wave of dementia. Today, the deterioration of his frontal lobe was keeping him above water—but what would happen tomorrow?

"And now," he said, "I will present a documented example of the release of an infectious, man-made agent into a human population. I'm afraid I'm not at liberty to disclose either the geographical location or the nature of the agent, but suffice it to say that it was viral in origin—and fortunately for the residents of that area, fairly quickly contained."

Artie leaned forward, almost tingling with excitement as Henry called up the numbers and started the movie playing on the lower left grid.

"Why isn't it rippling?" she asked.

"Because there is no baseline incidence of this particular virus. The playing field is utterly empty. But now, see—"

A cylinder sprouted from the zero baseline and climbed smoothly and rapidly to the top before opening like a flower.

"Compare our model of the Minster virus with each of these two profiles," Henry said.

But of course it was entirely unnecessary: even a fool could tell a trumpet from a car. Artie sat in silence for a good minute, just staring at the colored lines.

"But Professor," she finally said. "Why didn't this shape appear when Simon ran my initial numbers through the Meyerhof-Hernsley? All we got was a rippling doughnut from start to finish."

He nodded. "I wondered that myself, and took a look at how he generated the multivariate number matrix from the raw data."

Artie remembered that evening she and Simon had spent at his computer, assigning numbers to the hundreds of entries in her Snip database. At the time, she had thought it was more like witchcraft than science, more intuitive than objective. And in that sort of process, she could well imagine that there could be differences in opinion.

"It wasn't happy with how he treated the outliers," he continued. "Simon has a strong bias against sudden shifts in variation—always has done. I was troubled that some of your data were simply... thrown out for no good reason."

"I see." Artie was a little shocked. And torn—who was right, here? Not for the first time, she felt frustrated at the whole intangibility of the mathematics and her inability to be able to judge for herself. Instead, she was at the mercy of two polarized views, each convinced that they were correct. "With respect, Professor—you must see how it's difficult for me know what to make of this. Both you and Simon are experts at what you do but, given exactly the same dataset, you have come to the opposite conclusion."

Unexpectedly, Henry gave her a tired smile. The first genuine one she had ever seen on his face, if she recalled correctly.

"You biologists are all the same," he said. "You expect such models to work like an all-knowing crystal ball. But there is no wrong or right in this sphere: there is just a continuum from probable to improbable."

She crossed her arms. "Be that as it may, I'm sure you think your view is more probable than Simon's."

Henry folded his hands neatly on his lap. "I have explained to you the strengths and weaknesses of the two algorithms and have told you my reservations about Simon's method of assigning multivariates. One could also factor in that I have twenty more years of experience—although to be fair, there are some who believe that youth is an advantage in mathematicians, not a liability. But it is not for me to make up your mind."

"What about the MoD?"

"That is another question."

But frustratingly, he did not elaborate. Artie was about to press further when Henry leaned forward.

"Do you know," he said, "that I nearly went into biology myself?"

"Ah... really?"

"I had forgotten that fact until this morning. Many memories are surfacing now, things that I had completely lost. Lately they come to me in dreams... real dreams, I mean, not the dream of my other life. Yes... my childhood. My parents. The doctors, coming and going. A trip to Spain—strange food, warm sea, beautiful colors."

His eyes had gone distant; not catatonic, just nostalgic.

"I was in a sheltered school for mentally ill pupils, but early on I was singled out as someone intelligent, someone who might make his mark despite having been written off by most of society. I am struggling to remember the name of a particular teacher, one who championed me greatly, but I simply cannot..."

"It doesn't matter," she said soothingly. Surprised by his sudden distress, Artie put a comforting hand on his forearm before she realized what she was doing. But there was no reaction, no scream, no violent episode as forecasted by Simon's rules. He just nodded as her hand slipped off again.

"Thank you, child. I wish I could tell him now how grateful I am. I'm afraid at the time, I was very cold. But that's just how I was... before. I didn't speak at all, you know. But I could have written him a note."

"I'm sure he understood your limitations," she said.

"Anyway, this kindly teacher, he encouraged me to take all the right courses, all the right exams—arranged them so that it would suit the restrictions of my illness. I enjoyed my Biology O-Levels very much, and would have..."

"What is it, Professor?"

"Well, I am sure you can imagine that the highly social and interactive existence of a life scientist in a research team would not have suited one such as I... such as I used to be. And I did so love mathematics, just as much. It was the only real choice for me. But I have found myself wondering, in recent days, if my life would have been less solitary and unremarkable if I'd taken the more difficult road."

Artie didn't know what to say, so she said nothing. And then he seemed to shake himself. "There now, I'm boring you, and I'm sure you have places you need to be."

"Not at all."

"Nevertheless." He smiled at her again. "It's late, and Simon will return soon. And we can talk more later, can't we? I would very much like that."

"Any time," Artie said. And surprisingly, she found that she meant it.

CHAPTER 14
Absences, Those Taking On A Life of Their Own

THE NEXT MORNING ARTIE WOKE up to something strange. She opened her eyes cautiously, trying to work it out.

Although the alarm had sounded, it was still dark. Or rather, her blinds weren't bleeding their usual blazing corona of sunlight. She reached up to the window over her bed and parted two segments to reveal a grey sky. Collapsing back against the duvet, she tried and failed to remember the last time the weather had not been fine. Tried, and failed, to take it as anything but an inauspicious sign.

She had slept poorly. After leaving Henry in his lair, she'd hesitated out in the corridor, trying to decide whether to go up to the roof and talk with Simon about his request for help with the dead woman. But it became clear that her hunger was reaching a critical point. What's more, the thought of encountering Simon in strung-out mode was not appealing. In the end, she just gathered her things and headed out into the dark to catch a tube home, trying not to see it as cowardice.

Although her interactions with Henry had been civilized, almost grand-daughter-ly, by the time she got home her feelings about their meeting had gathered alarming overtones. How could someone so damaged act so perfectly normal? In retrospect, it was almost grotesque. And then there was this business with the model, perfectly replicating a known bioterrorist event: all night long, the shape of that sinister trumpet kept sprouting up in her dreams. The only thing standing between normality and despair was the thought of Lucy Greenswold up in Nottingham, comparing Minster's envelope to a VSV outbreak in Sittingbourne. She hoped that her news would come today, and that it would be good.

She trudged uphill towards Hampstead Station under a smear of low clouds the color of translucent slate. It was still very warm, not a breath of wind to disperse the cloying humidity. The cobbled streets around Flask Walk were alive with their usual morning industry: queues all the way out the doors of patisseries, well-dressed mothers or au pairs herding children on the school run. Drifting pockets of scent: coffee, bacon, incense, perfume, diesel. An unshaven shopkeeper looking her body up and down with lazy eyes as he leaned against the wall smoking a cigarette. Vibrant petunias, spilling over hanging baskets along the Flask Tavern, violet, flame and crimson against lush green. A placard outside of a newsagents still proclaiming yesterday evening's shock headline, rendered impotent by the intervening hours of night. The faraway cry of swifts, surfing the thermals above. There was nothing materially different about this scene that set it apart from thousands of others like it, but for some reason the bustle seemed undercut with uneasiness.

Her mobile went off: Mary.

"Just an update," Mary said. "Freddie managed to finagle a face-to-face with a veterinary inspector from our local Animal and Plant Health Agency for this afternoon."

"Good news. How's he feeling about it?"

"A bit nervous, I think. The whole thing is just so..."

"Surreal?"

"Yeah. Anyway, I'll let you know the minute I have the full report."

Wednesday, 30 June

Henry has been acting increasingly strangely. This morning, he spoke to me on our walk to work. I cannot remember that ever happening before. He asked me precisely what I had said to Brees about the Minster epidemic. I saw no reason not to tell him the truth: that although there were certainly not enough sick people to apply any of our models yet, I did not think that the hallmarks of the human disease thus far were reminiscent of bioterrorism.

Then he asked me if I had given them any details about Artemis's cat epidemic. Again, I told him truthfully that I'd suggested looking out for sick cats in the area but hadn't gone into any details. And I told him that Artemis agreed with me that her epidemic seemed natural and possibly not linked to the Faversham cases. When I asked him why he wanted to be burdened with these petty collaborative details—details he has never troubled himself with before—he went suddenly quiet. And this is the really strange part, stranger than him talking at all at that time of day. His lapse into catatonia was somehow... not convincing. It was as if he were faking being switched off, just so he wouldn't have to answer me. But I really don't see how that could be possible.

Simon put away his notebook, as if closing the cover would make the reality of his words go away. He picked up the third phone on his desk, the drone of the dial tone as irritating as the fly that had been trapped in his airless kitchen the previous evening. He had not had the chance yesterday to talk to Artemis about possible sequences that Brees might be able to use to PCR the Minster virus from the dead woman. At first he'd been merely puzzled when she didn't get back to him by email; he reasoned perhaps that Reynolds had not explained Simon's needs adequately, nor transmitted their urgency. In fact, the man had certainly seemed perplexed and distracted by Simon's simple question. Yet as the hours passed with Henry showing no signs of lapsing incommunicado, and no electronic reply from Artemis, the fury had mounted inside him like pressurized lava.

The arch of sky on the roof, imprinted with faint stars, had exerted its usual liberating effect. Breathing deeply, getting the anger under control—not killing it outright, never that—but soothing it, smoothing it back into its flimsy cage, he'd set up the telescope. Cool metal curving under his fingers, the concentration of optics and angles, the careful twisting of knurled brass knobs. There was nothing notable in the solar system visible this evening, all the planets having set a few hours before. Simon trained the eyepiece onto the Andromeda galaxy and took pleasure in the sudden resolution of seemingly empty air into that familiar spiral, like an oblique, trembling hurricane in space. Pleasure that this cluster would always be exactly where it should be, and could not hide from his inspection—clouds and season willing—whenever he had the whim to confirm its existence.

It was only then that he had remembered that he was already in full possession of every known example of Minster virus sequence—right there on his own server. Crouched over the instrument, he actually began to laugh. He didn't need to be at the mercy of female caprice to convince Brees to abandon his flawed bioterrorism theory once and for all. True, it was risky admitting that the virus contained this VSV envelope signature. But Simon was banking on the fact that if the dead woman had been infected with Minster, it should be easy to convince Brees that its feline components were too bizarre to have been chosen as a weapon. And even if Brees didn't buy that argument, Simon could at least use his model to demonstrate beyond statistical doubt that the virus was not only natural, but far older than the illnesses in Faversham.

True, he knew nothing about PCR, but how hard could it be if even the police used it routinely? Back at his desk, he'd found the internet full of helpful web pages aimed at life science students learning how to do their first PCR experiments. The requirements for the DNA primer sequences were relatively simple and flexible; compared to mathematics, molecular biology looked about as challenging as cooking a meal. After jotting down information about ideal lengths and melting temperatures, he'd opened up the detailed sequence database he'd made from Mark's data and came up with a few candidate pairs that seemed likely to recognize the Minster virus but not normal feline leukemia.

Now, in his ear, the forgotten dial tone ceased, the silence jolting him back to the present moment. An ascending tri-tone replaced it, and a condescending female voice telling him to please hang up and try again. As he jabbed the hang-up button, the dial tone juddered back into life and he dialed the MoD hotline.

"Brees office. Tanya speaking."

"Can I speak with Mr. Brees, please? It's urgent."

"Is this Mr. Renquist?" she asked. There was something cagey about her voice.

"Yes."

"I'm afraid that Mr. Brees doesn't require your consultation on the current matter any longer."

"I beg your pardon?"

"My instructions are quite clear, Mr. Renquist. The collaboration is at a close. You are asked to destroy any data you may have copied from our server about this matter. I was just about to ring you to request this, actually."

"Now, see here. I have very important information here that he really has to know about. Put him through!"

"I'm sorry."

He stared in disbelief at the buzzing receiver in his hand. Redialed.

"I was standing right here," Brees said, "when you called before, so I know that Tanya's instructions were entirely comprehensible. But since you seem unable to grasp its essence, let me reiterate: your services are no longer required."

"But I have some crucial information about the fatality in Minster!"

"From now on, we will be dealing with the Professor. As indeed,"—his voice grew chilled—"we had always thought we were."

"Henry Manfield will not communicate directly with you. You know that!"

"Good-bye, Mr. Renquist."

Simon stormed out of his office and into the gloom of the main server space. Henry sat as usual at his terminal, coddling his bloated, useless bird flu simulation.

"What have you told Brees?" Simon said sharply, addressing the back of Henry's oversized grey head. Speaking before being spoken to: a blatant disregard of the rules. But as far as Simon was concerned, the rules were fragmenting into a million shards all around them.

Henry swiveled around in his chair, face composed and mild. "You know that the Official Secrets Act you signed specifically forbids you to share confidential MoD information with third parties."

"You *told* him I was speaking with Artemis Marshall?"

"From now on, what does or does not get told to the MoD will no longer be your concern. And I'm sure this will come as a great relief, considering how busy they have kept you. Think of it as an opportunity to catch up with the more academic backlog that's been hanging over your head."

"But this is ludicrous!" Simon said. "I've been dealing with them single-handedly for the past ten years. And you know as well as I that occasionally theorists need to chat with biological experts, off the record—you've let me do it before, and it was never an issue."

Henry waved a lazy hand before turning back to his screen. "Minster is no longer your concern, and that is final."

Simon stared at his mentor's back, the fury building up like a tight band around his chest. "Let me guess—you're going to advise them that the Minster virus is a weapon. You're going to show them the Meyerhof-Hernsley using a numerical matrix flawed with data that clearly don't fit the standard curves." With each statement, his voice grew incrementally louder. "You're going to ensure that Abdul Farah, and maybe half of his acquaintances, get locked up. Is that what you want?"

He didn't even turn around. Striding over, Simon spun the chair towards him, but Henry was staring straight ahead, slack and seemingly unseeing, body rocking slightly as the motion ceased.

"How very fucking convenient!" Simon shouted, only an inch or two from his face. A tiny droplet of spittle landed on his forehead, glistening on the coarse, mottled skin, but Henry remained unresponsive.

Simon whirled around and blasted out of B302. As he crossed the corridor, a trio of researchers clocked the look on his face and faltered in their conversation. Ignoring them, Simon saw that Artemis was alone in her office, blond head bent over her laptop. He opened up the door without knocking.

She looked up, the evolution of expressions on her face clearly spelling out that she had been hoping for someone else. *Well, fuck her.*

"I'm sorry I didn't get back to you yesterday," she said. "It was... pretty crazy here."

"It's all moot now anyway," he said shortly.

"Sit down, please—you're making me nervous. Moot how?"

Despite himself, her soft, reasonable voice was exerting its usual effect. He slumped into the chair, reminding himself that she was not the enemy. She had become, in fact, the only person he could rely on in the entire world.

"I thought," he said, "we could kick-start Brees into seeing the obvious by proving to him that the Minster virus isn't the right sort of candidate agent to fit their bioterrorism profile."

"Ah ha. So you thought we could give them a hint about how to use PCR to identify the Minster virus from June Morris. But wouldn't they have wondered how you got the information?"

He shrugged. "I made up some mathematical gobbledegook about 'retroviral signatures'—they never question when I use jargon. But unfortunately, as of today I'm no longer involved with the MoD."

Artemis listened dumbfounded as Simon described everything that had happened. Near the end of the story, she gave him a funny look.

"Let me get this straight: Henry got you kicked off the project because you told me about the human cases?"

"That's right."

She shook her head, eyes wide.

"What is it?"

"Nothing," she said quickly. "Just—I'm really sorry this has happened."

"And it's asinine, because it's certainly not the first time I've sought a second opinion on a confidential project. In fact, Henry himself has even advised me several times which scientists to consult. It makes no sense whatsoever to get all precious about protocol now."

"God, and this is really lousy timing, too. How are we going to show them your model pinpointing the variant to 2015 and predating any of the human cases if you can't talk to them any more?"

"I have no idea," he said. "I wish I knew exactly what Henry has told them."

"Do you think he'll have the same idea about the PCR?"

"I don't know that either—I'm sure if he wanted those sequences, he could easily have copied them by now. But like it or not, we're now completely in the dark."

Artie tapped a pen thoughtfully against her chin. "This reminds me. I need to chase up a friend in forensics—he might know someone who's familiar with June Morris's case from the inside."

"They're not going to be at liberty to discuss cases, surely."

"It didn't stop you," she pointed out.

"Hmmm. That's true. Well obviously, if you think you have an in there, then you should pursue it."

"I'll follow that up as soon as I can," she said.

"WONDERFUL TO HEAR FROM YOU," Johnny Ingsall said down the phone, his voice as pseudo-posh as Artie remembered. Another recollection flashed before her then: a drunken grope at the university disco, which she'd managed to repel without causing undue offense. "Sorry I didn't answer your email sooner—glad you bashed away at getting in touch nonetheless. It's been a frightfully long time."

"It sure has. Lisa says you're in the forensics business now?"

"Oh yes—vastly more enjoyable than that wretched academic grind. No offense."

"None taken," Artie said. "Listen—I was wondering if you might be able to help me. I'm studying this new cat virus, and I'm worried that it might have infected a cat owner in Kent..."

She described the situation as blandly as she could, then said, "It's probably absolutely nothing, but I was wondering if you could put me in touch with crime scene investigators who are working up this woman's bloods."

"Well, it sounds intriguing, Artemis, and there's no doubt I could find out who's on the case, but I can tell you right now that they're not going to be able to tell you anything."

"Really?" She ramped up the honey in her tone. "Are you sure you couldn't arrange for me to meet one of them, strictly off the record?"

"Completely out of the question. We've all signed the same paperwork—breaching confidentiality is grounds for dismissal."

"You're absolutely sure?"

He paused. "Well, it does sound as if your knowledge could be important for the case. Let me make a few inquiries. There's no way anyone would talk to you as is, but if they wanted to consult you about what you know regarding this virus, they could induct you into the case on a formal basis. You'd be helping them, not vice versa, but you might learn what you need to know at the same time."

"Oh, that would be great," she said. "Seriously, you don't mind?"

"It's no problem. Don't ask, don't get and all that sort of stuff. But I'm warning you, it's probably a long shot."

As she was hanging up the phone, mildly disgruntled and wishing she'd had a crack at him in person, an email from Mark popped into her Inbox.

Heart suddenly thumping, she opened it up:

There was a great deal of cell killing in my transfected cultures from yesterday, just as we saw last time, so I've harvested some supes, filtered them and will set up infections of cat and human cells. I'll keep you posted on the outcome.

That was it—no sign-off, no hint of friendliness—not even a mention of the relocation. She supposed she should be relieved that he was still working for her, but for all she knew he could be in the process of looking for a new lab and was just going through the motions.

Dear Mark,

Please come back. I miss you, and I need you. It's not the same without you. If you give me another chance, I promise I'll make it up to you.

After starting at this pathetic string of letters for a few moments, she hit delete and atomized them back into their component pixels.

∽

ARTIE STOOD UNDERNEATH THE ARTIFICIAL sky of St. Pancras International, waiting for Lucy Greenswold to appear at the designated meeting point. The metal struts of the high roof criss-crossed overhead like a million contrails, station noise sliding into a senseless jet-engine roar whenever she stopped paying attention to individual sounds. In the lunchtime crush, there were dozens of others lingering under the vast bronze statue of lovers embracing, so she was glad that Lucy had thought to describe what she'd be wearing. Her email had arrived soon after Mark's, informing Artie that she'd been dispatched to St. Mary's Hospital at short notice to pick up some patient samples and suggesting a quick rendezvous to "discuss the results." Frustratingly, Lucy had not gone into any more detail and Artie had no idea what to expect.

So Artie stood there, scanning the crowds for a black-haired, bespectacled young twenty-something with an orange T-shirt and burgundy backpack. It was difficult to concentrate, still reeling as she was from the news that Henry had blown the whistle on Simon for breaching his confidentiality agreement with the Government—even though Henry had committed precisely the same sin with her. It really could mean only one thing: that Henry had found a convenient excuse to eliminate a dissenting opinion. Ever since Simon had told her the news, she'd been turning things over and over in her mind, trying to concoct a plausible argument or strategy to keep Henry from the path he seemed determined to go down. The more she pondered Henry's fragmented character, the more she became convinced that he would not easily be swayed from his conviction that the Minster virus was unnatural.

No, her best chance at preventing a miscarriage of justice was clear: to report Henry's erratic behavior to Salverson and get him removed from his position of power, with or without Simon's cooperation. If Calvin was right, it didn't matter how cleverly Henry tried to hide his new altered state—one simple brain scan would reveal the disintegration once and for all. Not even a mathematical genius could act his way out of an MRI result.

"You must be Artemis," a voice drawled.

"How did you know?" Artie looked down to find a slim pixie of a woman smiling up at her.

"Heatherfield's website," Lucy said. "But it's a trick that only works for women—have you noticed that men always submit ten-year-old photos?"

Artie laughed. "Yes, it's amazing how low the incidence of male pattern-baldness is on institute home pages. Someone should get a grant to study it."

A few minutes later they were seated with mugs of tea at one of the terrace tables overlooking Platform Ten.

"I'm glad you were free," Lucy said, unzipping her backpack and pulling out a folder. "I could have just emailed you these line-ups—but I thought we needed to chat about the implications in person."

"I'm guessing it's not good news, then."

Lucy elevated black brows, enhancing her elfish appearance, and fanned a few pieces of paper out on the aluminum surface of the table. "Well, your recombinant is *not* derived from the outbreak in Sittingbourne, if that's what you were hoping for. Take a look."

Artie's spirits wilted as the other woman fished out a particular printout and put it on the top of the pile. "Can you walk me through it? I know nothing about VSV strains."

The paper showed a standard alignment of three different nucleotide sequence codes, zipped together like railroad tracks with vertical lines where they were perfectly matched and missing a railway tie where they did not. She didn't know which of the three sequences was which, but it was immediately clear from the number of gaps that the bottom two were highly related and the top was a lot different.

"Right—so this guy—" Lucy tapped a finger on the middle line of sequence, "is your recombinant. And the top guy is a consensus sequence of S319, the Sittingbourne outbreak strain. There are lots of mutations, as you can see."

"How variable is VSV-G?"

"Not as variable as these two, given the relatively short amount of time that has passed. It's more variation, for example, than what one might see between a strain in Texas and a strain in Buenos Aires circulating a couple of decades apart."

"But not beyond the realm of possibility of having a progenitor strain in common?"

"Well, of course not—not formally. As Zac says, if it can be done, a virus will figure out how to do it."

"But you don't think it's likely."

Lucy shook her head. "And here's why." She pointed to the bottom sequence, which was almost a perfect match with Minster. "This third guy is what pops out as most related when you search the entire database of known VSV-G sequences."

"What is it?" But in her heart, she already knew.

"It's VSV-San Juan." Lucy paused, a strange look in her eye. Artie suspected that it was pity.

"Is that a South American strain?"

"Not exactly—well, not any more. It's one of a handful of common laboratory-adopted strains used heavily worldwide as a vector for experimental manipulation—either in basic research, or for more applied applications—pseudotyping foreign genetic information for cellular delivery or gene therapy, that sort of thing."

"And you're quite sure it, or something like it, is not circulating in the wild?" Sidney Sheppard's words hit her then: *like finding a polar bear on the Costa del Sol.*

She shrugged. "Again, one can't be sure of anything when it comes to viruses. But there aren't any natural isolates in the database that look anything near like this. Plus, my feeling is that it just couldn't compete, being so heavily adapted to life in a nice cozy Petri dish."

"Well, it does seem rather impossible, doesn't it?"

"Mmm. Do any of you Heatherfields folk use VSV in the lab?"

"No. No, we don't. And the virus samples haven't been anywhere near a lab that does." She let out a sigh of frustration. "And it's been isolated from more than a dozen animals, all prepped at different times."

"Gosh. That's just totally weird," Lucy said.

The pair talked for another ten minutes, bandying about hypotheses but coming up with nothing that either of them found convincing.

"I'm sorry I couldn't have been more help," Lucy finally said, glancing at her watch. "I've got to run now."

"Thanks anyway—I really appreciate it."

"If I think of anything else, I'll get in touch right away." They both knew it was just a formality.

Long after Lucy's slim form had disappeared into the crowds, Artie sat at the table with her dregs of tea, starting at the damning printouts in front of her. She was trying to think of anything about the lab at that precise moment that made her want return to it.

∿

ARTIE EVENTUALLY PULLED HERSELF TOGETHER and caught the next train back to Mill Hill Broadway. Taking a window seat, she tried to put all thoughts from her head and simply watch the great city unravel, dirty and dispirited but eventually giving way to grudging greenness. But there was something about the reflections of daylight on the window that reminded her of Henry's model, flashes of lines and geometrical shapes that filled her with foreboding until she had to look away.

A woman getting off at Kentish Town threw her paper onto the seat, and Artie reached over to pick it up: a bit further to the right of the ideological spectrum than she was accustomed to reading, but she was hungry for any distraction. After skimming through a few flimsy items, she turned a page and was completely unprepared for what was waiting there for her, small and insidious and turning her heart into a lump of ice.

Terror suspects arrested in Faversham.

Somehow, the matter-of-fact wording of the headline was the most disturbing thing of all. It belonged to a compact piece, only two paragraphs and drily factual. With a sense of increasing unreality, she noted that the main suspect's name was Abdul Farah and that the youth had been remanded in custody along with three other men the previous evening on charges of intent to incite terror. The item didn't go into any details except to note that it had been a "multi-departmental" operation based on "special intelligence."

Deep within her handbag, Artie's phone trilled out. Like a zombie, she reached down and fished it out.

"Artemis? It's Freddie here."

"Ah—hello."

"Are you all right?"

"Yes—of course I am. How did it go with the Agency vet inspector?"

"I'm not entirely sure, to be honest. She seemed a bit... skeptical."

"I was afraid of that."

"It wasn't that she doubted our results, exactly. She seemed impressed by your Heatherfields affiliation, for example. But these sorts aren't really attuned to domestic pet issues—it's all agricultural with them. She just didn't seem convinced of the urgency, and I got the feeling she didn't know much about feline leukemia. Said she needed to talk things over with her colleagues and would get back to me."

"What about the VSV-G angle?"

"I can't say I blame her, but she didn't seem to think that a cat virus carrying around a freak fragment of a notifiable disease actually made the virus notifiable."

"Of all the short-sighted, bureaucratic idiocies! Did you explain about the human tropism risks?"

"Of course. But then she said that human diseases weren't in her jurisdiction, and I needed to contact the Department of Health!"

"Typical. Did she say when she'd get back to you?"

"No. If I don't hear anything by tomorrow I'll certainly chase her up."

"Well, you've done your best. We have to hope that the others are more convinced."

"I wish there was a way we could get that quarantine set up *today*. Every hour that goes by increases the risk of one of those animals getting off the island. Mary had an idea about that."

"Oh?"

"Something a bit more grassroots. Basically, pet owners tend to be pretty passionate about their animals. If you want to mobilize them, the best way is probably to go by a pre-existing owner-led organization. They're bound to take any threats to cats more seriously than anyone else."

"That's a brilliant idea. Did you find a good group to contact?"

"That's the problem—there isn't one overarching national group—just literally dozens of cat fancier societies, dedicated to particular breeds or geographic regions."

"What about Sheppey?"

"As it happens, there is a group in Sheerness, and Mary's volunteered to get in touch with them and see if she can't get the word out. With any luck they might have an email list or social media page—and she'll ask them specifically to spread the word to any other groups they know." He paused. "Mary's also going to contact the local newspapers, see if they'll run the story."

"It's better than nothing, I suppose."

"And I was thinking of dropping in on the local Council, see if I could persuade them to put up a big sign on the island side of the two bridges asking drivers ferrying a cat over to reconsider. Though I think it's unlikely I can persuade them without a Governmental mandate behind me."

"You done good work nonetheless." Then she remembered something. "While I've got you here, did you have a chance to check on that news story about people coming down with foot and mouth disease?"

"I did, but couldn't find anything beyond the initial ones I remembered seeing. The story just trickles out. I guess that's a good sign?"

"Probably," she said, but thought that another explanation was that further coverage might have been suppressed. "Should I try to contact the Department of Health?"

"If you wouldn't mind," he said. "A London professor is bound to have more clout than a simple country vet."

∾

WALKING BACK UP THE HILL to Heatherfields from the train station was like struggling through a Turkish steam room. There was nothing visually apparent about the humidity, but as the sweat trailed down her skin, Artie experienced the illusion of edges smudged. The overcast seemed to be settling in further, and a few times she mistook low-flying aircraft for rumbles of thunder—the mind, as usual, warping reality to suit expectation. As she passed rows of front gardens along the main road, the scent of roses and jasmine and honeysuckle was almost asphyxiating.

Artie cut around the side of the building and through the car park—and stopped short as she saw the ominous bulk of Henry Manfield. He was leaning against a door further along from the main basement entrance: the private entrance to B302. Heart skipping like a stone over water, she scanned the car park, verifying that no one else was around, then increased her pace until she was before him. His eyes were closed, a faint smile lingering on his thin lips. And he was still wearing that cardigan over his waistcoat—he had to be boiling in this heat.

"Professor Manfield?"

The eyes flickered open, their granite color softened by daylight into a pebbly blue and set off by flushed, glistening skin, by tendrils of white hair plastered against his forehead.

"Can you smell it, Professor Marshall?"

"Ah...what?" An engine blared behind them. Startled, she looked over her shoulder. Fortunately it wasn't one of her colleagues, but a motorcycle courier, who was paying them absolutely no attention as he parked and then started fussing with a package. "You're not supposed to be out here, are you?"

"The air," he said dreamily. "That odor... is it cut grass?"

She became aware of the overpowering scent around them, and of another far-away engine buzzing from the rear garden. The caretakers must be mowing the lawn.

"Yes, it is. Shall we get you back inside? Do you have your keycard?"

"It reminds me of being a boy. We lived in a modest maisonette, but the garden was much larger than what you'd expect for such a small house. I used to love lying down in the grass after my father had mown, watching the clouds and trying to predict their patterns."

"Professor, we really ought to go back inside. This heat is crippling."

"Silly youth that I was, I sometimes fancied I had their measure. The clouds, I mean. I would predict what would happen and a small fraction of the time, it would come true." Still gazing at the sky, he held up a finger, wiggled it. "A tendril would dissipate, a bank would split into two. Of course later I learned that the behavior of clouds is governed by far more chaotic laws than a mere boy could have understood— that statistically, sometimes things happen that we want to happen, just as random events. And that random, anecdotal events supporting your hypothesis do not make that hypothesis true."

Was he mocking Simon and his La Fontayne simulation? But no, his eyes were unfocused, nostalgic, very far from B302 and its pursuits.

"But now I'm not so sure," he said. "Maybe a small boy *can* will the clouds to move, just by thinking hard enough. How can we be sure about cause and effect, how the universe actually works? I mean, *truly* sure?"

"Professor, I really must insist—"

"Maybe all of our so-called scientific laws are just a framework that happens to fit with the observed facts, but are in fact entirely coincidental. That something else powers all these acts, using laws of which we are completely ignorant. And if so, how could we ever prove it?"

Just then, the door rattled behind them, causing Artie to jump. It was Simon, face lined with anxiety.

"There you are—thank God," he said, to Henry, as if he were an errant child. Catching her eye, he transmitted a question, but Artie just shrugged and shook her head.

"Professor Marshall and I were just discussing causality," Henry said, turning towards his protégé and then sliding past him and into the dark gloom of the small service corridor behind. Simon swiveled to watch him disappear around the corner, then sagged against the door frame. Artie could feel the coolness of the air conditioning leaching out into the afternoon's muzziness.

"Did anyone see him?" he asked, voice stretched tight. A hand flopped up to push the too-long, rough-cut fringe from his brow, trembling slightly.

"I don't think so. Do you know how long he's been out here?"

"Couldn't have been more than five minutes—one moment he was at his terminal and then next, he'd vanished. He has never, in all my time here, left the building on his own."

"Except after the fight with Ben," she reminded him. They were both quiet a while, neither comforted by that memory, and then she added, "I've got something you need to see."

Reaching into her handbag, she pulled out the newspaper, folded so the offending article was at the top. Watched as his eyes scanned it, as his expression slid into a mask of anxious comprehension.

"This is... I can't believe it, Artemis. I mean, I knew they probably would, but this whole time... I didn't really believe it."

"I know what you mean." Artie was silent for a moment as Simon scanned the piece a second time, desperately seeking, as she had done, all the information that remained unsaid, the pieces of the model that would make the hypothesis fly. "What are we going to do?"

"I've been thinking about that," he said, kicking the corner of the door savagely with a worn shoe. "The model I showed you before was a hasty approximation. It would only take me about a day to firm it up, do all the statistical tests that will strongly support your virus's 2015 origins." He produced a bitter smile. "Ironically, I've got free time, now that I've been booted off all the MoD projects."

"And do what with that, exactly?"

"Present it to Henry," he said, without hesitation. "Sit him down and convince him with the sheer strength of the numbers."

"Do you really think you can change his mind?" But inside, knowing what she knew, Artie was already certain his plan was bound to fail. *How can we be sure about cause and effect, how the universe actually works?* Henry, she somehow sensed, was slipping beyond the boundaries of the rational.

"I think we have to try. I mean, what other alternative do we have?"

"We can go to Salverson," Artie said, promptly. "Report Henry's odd behavior and suggest that he be examined—medically examined—with a view towards being removed from his position of authority before more damage is done." She glanced at her watch. "I could try to get an appointment this afternoon."

"No!" The word exploded out, causing Artie to take a step backwards. Simon closed his eyes briefly, and in a softer voice said: "No. Let's give him a chance to see reason. One more day won't make a difference."

When the door had clicked shut behind him, Artie stood a little bit longer, leaning against the hot brickwork and allowing her gaze to follow where Henry's had so recently lingered. Above, the sky was a featureless expanse of overcast—not a tendril, not a wisp, not a shape of any kind, or movement allowing the prediction of future position. Just a brooding backdrop of white noise, entirely static.

CHAPTER 15

Breakdowns, Those of an Ambiguous Nature

O N FRIDAY EVENING, ARTIE SAT in the stillness of the office, flickers of uneasiness already starting to lap around the edges of her frenetic industry. She would have given anything to be able to turn to Mark and suggest decamping to the Victoria Arms for a pint or two and an evening of laughter and irreverent anecdotes. But all she had was the mocking reminder of his former desk, gleaming dully under the fluorescence.

Fiona, perhaps sensing the melancholy in the air, had brought in a potted fern to make the desk look more lived-in, but it was already starting to droop for lack of fresh air and natural light. In the past few days Artie had received no more email updates from Mark, though she expected that he might already have some clues about Minster's infectivity status. But she hadn't answered his initial email, and refused on principle to pester him for more results. For the first time, she found she didn't really want to know if the Minster virus could infect human cells. Or rather, she was pretty sure that it could, but the point had become entirely moot.

Minster had not just derailed her theory; it had caused it to tumble in slow motion down the steep sides of the railway bed. The underlying science behind mini-epidemics might very well still be true; she wasn't about to scrap her latest grant proposal in the face of this set-back, for example. Yet she could no longer rely on Minster, with its intriguing FIV recombination and brilliantly unstable RT mutation, to be an exemplar or to lead her anywhere fruitful: it had been the most enticing of red herrings, but ultimately, its artificial nature could not be denied. Although she was still terrified about the outcome of the ongoing epidemic, scientifically it was now somebody else's problem. At some point, when things had settled down, she'd have to think about turning to another line of enquiry that might shed new light on her ideas. She'd have to go back to sifting through Mary's sporadic sampling and hope that lightning struck twice—but a more honest variety of it.

That is, if there were any cats left to actually study once the Minster virus had run its course.

Nothing of import had occurred since she'd agreed with Simon a few days previously to hold off going to Salverson with her damning information. The oppressive weather had carried on unchanged, neither clearing up nor culminating in badly needed rain, the low pressure bearing down on her like a faint but omnipresent headache until she thought she'd go mad. She'd been put on hold indefinitely or fobbed off outright by no fewer than four different civil servants in the Department of Health, all of whom promised to get back to her but hadn't yet. More calls and emails lower down in the governmental food chain—Public Health England, Swale Borough Council on Sheppey—were similarly fruitless.

Her attempts to chase up Johnny Ingsall had dead-ended when it turned out he was away for a fortnight of summer holiday, and two other Oxford colleagues with public health-related bents were similarly unavailable. The famous Marshall touch seemed to have fizzled out.

Back in the lab, Fiona had finished off her sequencing of the tail-end of the Minster virus and couldn't work out its origin, so Artie had forwarded the data to Lucy Greenswold just for the record, without expecting much in return. And then there had been the unpleasant run-in with Peter Hastings a few hours previously, when she was leaving the canteen:

"I hear that Mark has moved on. Such a shame he wasn't happy in your lab."

"He's merely working off-site," Artie said, clenching her voice into a simulacrum of civility, "in facilities that are actually decent enough for his requirements."

"That's not what I heard," he replied, giving her a smirk before losing himself in the post-lunch crowd. She wanted to run after him and refute his insinuations, but what evidence did she have that he was wrong? The fact that the entire building knew of Mark's defection, meanwhile, was another weight of apprehension on her shoulders.

She hadn't heard anything from Simon either, though he'd promised it would only take a day to finalize his model. She assumed, then, that he was still hunkered down at his computer, but had no real desire to seek him out and set into motion everything that she knew would come after: the futile confrontation with Henry, the painful meeting with Salverson, the dismantling of one man's waking dream and another man's entire world.

As if her thoughts had called him into being, there was a tap on the glass. Looking up, she saw Simon opening the door with a few books and a sheaf of papers wedged under one arm.

"We need to speak, but would you mind going up to the roof? I'm in need of some fresh air."

His voice, she noted, sounded different. There was a ring of hard confidence there, and his back seemed straighter. His eyes contained a glitter of animation that she had not seen for some time. Yet she could not pinpoint the precise emotion; his face was utterly unreadable.

"Good lord, you haven't just convinced Henry to change his mind, have you?"

"I'll tell you everything," he said, "when we get there."

She had no desire whatsoever to go to the roof—in fact, the idea filled her with a mounting sense of disquiet. Something about his tone, however, made her unwilling to decline. Instead, she just made sure her mobile was in her pocket and followed him out the door, but when she paused by the lift, Simon said, "You've obviously never been stuck in there. I always take the stairs."

So they trouped up the ten flights, Artie noticing curiously that Simon's breathing wasn't any heavier than hers at the top. He might be scrawny, but he was getting some decent exercise after all.

He lodged one book in the first door (Hanson's *Epidemiology*, Fourth Edition) and another in the second (Gibbon's *Rise and Fall*), and they cleared the short staircase and went out onto the roof. Without the stars for reference, the sky overhead was worryingly out of context; its faint orange haze offered no landmarks, no frame of reference. It could be ten feet overhead, or ten thousand miles. For all she knew, they could be standing in a bank of thick fog.

Simon took a few more paces, back to her, as he surveyed the faceless oblivion above them.

"I guess you won't be using the telescope tonight," Artie remarked, trying to ward off the sense of unreality that was slowly gripping her.

Simon turned and approached her; the attack, when it came, was speed-of-light fast and completely unexpected. His fist struck her jaw and she was down before her body had even the slightest chance to respond, her head striking the cement with a sickening crack. A blinding light superimposed itself over her vision, and when it cleared, she found herself lying on her back with pain and dizziness swarming in and Simon crouching beside her with the hatred on his face almost impossible to parse. She knew what she should do: strike back while he was distracted, while he thought she was defeated, strike back, get away and call Security. But something odd was happening: she wasn't really inside her body, but observing it from another angle. The unreality made every possible action an abstract concept; she felt something trickling down her jaw, but couldn't even raise a hand to feel for what it was, sweat or blood or saliva.

"Marshall and Manfield," Simon said, staring at her with furious expectancy.

Artie understood what the individual words meant, as his lips formed them, seemingly with the slight delay of a badly dubbed video, but she couldn't string together anything that made sense.

"What?" she finally managed to get out.

"Marshall and *Manfield*," he shouted in her face, so loudly that her ears rang. "Did you think I wouldn't find out?"

"Simon, please." She closed her eyes, trying to force the universe stop spinning. She thought she could hear thunder again, but it was hard to make out anything over the roar in her ears. It sounded like the creatures that came in the night, the demons who plagued her when she could no longer connive her mind into believing that she wasn't alone. She heard a flat, brassy repetition of her own words in her mind, over and over, growing increasingly more insistent. *Simon, please. Simon, please.* If she could have moved any part of her body, she would have covered her ears to try to blot it out. *Simon, please.* The voices were rising like a sea, and she knew that this time she would drown.

He shook her shoulder, sending a jolt of pain through her neck and head. He was still here, she noted, opening her eyes; this nightmare was refusing to end.

"But you must have known I would find out," he said, pulling out the papers he'd been carrying and thrusting the top page in her face. "Stupid, back-stabbing bitch."

She couldn't focus at first, in the faint orange glow. The words swam before her on the page, made more elusive by the violent trembling of Simon's grip. She thought she was going to be sick, but instead forced herself to concentrate as if her life depended on it. It was, she finally realized, the first page of a scientific manuscript, typed out in the traditional double-spaced style of a draft in preparation:

Epidemiology and origins of a novel bioterrorist agent
By A. L. Marshall and H. S. Manfield

Below it was an abstract, whose font size was beyond her fogged vision, and a further twenty-odd pages which Simon slowly fanned past for her benefit—a mess of charts, grids, reams of impenetrable mathematical equations melding into one grey, meaningless muddle.

"Well?" he said, finally.

"I have no idea what that is," Artie whispered. "I have never seen it before in my life."

"Liar!" The words seemed to echo inside her own skull, and were appropriated and taken up by the demons. "He told me all about your cozy collaboration. All the times you met behind my back to work with the Meyerhof-Hernsley—preparing this paper."

"No," she said. "It's Henry who's lying!"

"Shut up!" The slap rocked her head into a red sea of pain, crashing against her skull like a tide. "It's a little late for you to expect me to believe you now."

"We're not writing a paper together." She paused as a wave of nausea threatened to overcome her. "Or... maybe he's writing something, but I know nothing about it."

"Henry would never make something like that up—it's not in his nature to deceive."

"Simon, he's going senile—you know it. He's completely lost touch with reality."

He brushed this aside with a bony hand.

"I saw you, you know."

"Saw... what?"

He folded his arms, all jagged angles. "Coming out of B302 on Tuesday evening. I was in the stairwell, coming down from the roof. Just as I was about to push the door open, you came out of our office. I assumed Henry had summoned you, and that you'd tell me all about it the next morning—but you never mentioned it. And now I know why."

If Artie had been whole and unharmed, she might have been able to talk her way out of this. But though he was wrong about the letter of the betrayal, he was spot on about its spirit. Maybe they hadn't been writing a manuscript together, but the rest of the lie was too big for her to cover up—not sprawled out on the hard concrete mired in the complete immobility the fall seemed to have imparted. Idly, she wondered if her back was actually broken.

"Nothing to say to that, then?" He stood up, looking down at her almost dispassionately now. The anger was still there, she knew: she could almost see it like an aura trembling around his body. He'd gone beyond physical fury to a place far more frightening: a place where he might do anything.

"We did meet," she admitted. "He *did* try to convince me that the Minster virus was artificial." She had enough of her faculties about her to decide that saying she believed the evidence was not a good idea. "But..." She paused to swallow something sharp-tasting at the back of her throat. "You know what he's like—it's not as if I could easily have declined when he asked to see me."

"Yes, but you could have come straight to me, told me what he was doing."

She was silent: there was no way to defend herself further. Somewhere amid the shock and pain and vertigo, she felt a creeping weight of shame.

"He left the paper right in plain sight," Simon said, voice soft, contemplative. "Right there on the round table in our server room, face up. He wanted me to find it. To rub my face in it."

Artie wondered if she had lost consciousness for a few seconds, because the next thing she knew, he was crouched down beside her, his hands around her neck. Not applying any pressure, just loosely arranged. Even so, the slight weight set off an agonizing wave of pain.

"It's illuminating," he said, almost thoughtfully. "Illuminating that even with all your privilege and success you are, after all, completely powerless."

"Don't do this, Simon." She could barely get the words out. And then things slipped; shifted: his hands had started to squeeze; reddish light bloomed over her vision, patched with black as the panic rose in her, as even the crushing accumulation of oxygen's lack could not propel any fight into her. Red and black, and the shouting in her ears.

She was flying over the roof, shedding a tail of demons like a glistening comet.

The roar filled the infinite reaches of space.

Beyond the orange fog, she could see all of the planets, all of the stars, every last speck of dark matter and dust and singularity, spiraling into a faraway point in the distance like a celestial plughole.

And she was completely and utterly alone in the universe.

❧

AWARENESS CAME AGAIN AS A ruffle of air over skin, ferrying the fluid melody of blackbirds. A dull ache of head and neck followed, and more superficial complaints of pressure points of body against concrete. Then memory: where and why she was there, surprisingly tidy and matter-of-fact. Was it the simple relief of still being alive that made her so clear-headed?

She opened her eyes: a mushroom-colored sky, swarming with the black forms of diving swifts, so high on the thermals that she couldn't hear their incessant cries. Simon, of course, was long gone. A glance to her watch confirmed it was early morning, not quite seven: the cool calm before the searing heat of another summer day.

Managing to sit up with surprisingly little trouble, she did a quick inventory and found herself very stiff, and bruised on elbows and tailbone from the hard landing, but with nothing seemingly wrong with her back that might explain her paralysis the night before. Her karate instructor would have been bitterly disappointed.

Shock, she told herself. Shock, and a blow to the head were surely adequate excuses. Duly reminded, she reached up a hand and pushed fingertips cautiously through hair, exploring her skull until the lump revealed itself with a jolt of pain. It was massive, but she couldn't detect any crusting or broken skin. She slid a palm to her neck and throat, which felt bruised, and then up to her jaw where Simon had hit her—the flesh was tender, and a bit of dried blood rubbed off on her fingers, but working her jaw she found that the injury seemed largely superficial.

Artie got slowly to her feet, supporting herself on to a waist-high cube of fretted metal. She was dizzy, with that strange feeling of euphoria intensifying as she found she could walk without pain. The door was closed: Simon has obviously taken his books with him. Rattling the handle, she confirmed it was locked, the electronic box on the wall next to it warding her off with its red eye.

To what end? Why would he try to strangle her, then abandon the job half-way through? He must have lost his nerve; or maybe when she passed out he'd come to his senses: but if so, why lock her out here? He was obviously over the edge of some sort of rational boundary, but even if he hadn't known she had a phone on her, he must have realized that she'd be able to attract attention with some healthy screaming.

Artie pulled out her phone. A variety of options occurred to her then, the most attractive involving ringing up Mark. But Mark was gone.

Instead, she dialed the front desk.

"Professor Marshall here," she said smoothly. "I went onto the roof for a smoke and didn't realize the doors locked automatically—can someone come let me out?"

"I can open them from here," came the reply, too full of ennui to even be censorious.

Five minutes later, Artie had made her way through the deserted Saturday building to the staff shower room. Inspecting herself in a mirror, she saw that the bruising on her jaw and throat were fairly obvious, but the cut on her chin was minor and overall, she'd got off lightly. Pausing naked under the shower head, just before turning the knob, she thought fleetingly of forensics. She knew she should go straight to the police, to hospital—after all, she was the victim of aggravated assault and had been unconscious for nearly nine hours. She might feel fine at the moment, but a concussion could be serious.

Yet there was a force of something light and airy pushing through her—she wanted to be clean, to be free, to be unencumbered. Going along with the euphoria was a sense that there was something very obvious that she needed to remember—a piece of a puzzle waiting to be teased from the darkness. That nagging sense had been with her ever since she'd woken up, trying to get her attention. But every time she tried to face it squarely, it slipped from view. There wasn't time to deal with the police. She felt its urgency pushing her forward as her hand turned on the tap and the hot, soapy water rinsed the telltale traces of Simon's DNA forever from her skin and hair.

Artie went down to the basement, somehow completely confident that Simon was not there—she didn't even bother to peer into the gloom of B302 as she passed, and felt not the slightest hint of fear. The entire department was empty, of course; she knew that some of the keener post-docs and students occasionally made an appearance on weekends, but nobody would be stirring this early. Strangely, though, the situation did not endanger her mood—she felt no trace of loneliness or despair, or anything other than this deep-seated sense of wellbeing and purpose.

Going straight to Fiona's desk in the lab, she sat down and found what she was looking for in the top drawer: hairbrush, pocket mirror, make-up. She combed her wet hair and covered up the bruising fairly well with the various pots of beige liquids and powders. After pausing for a hot coffee and a chocolate bar in the common room, she collected her handbag and headed outside.

On the walk to the overland train station, everything looked crisp and sharp despite the overcast, the flowering gardens along the roadside almost radioactive with pulsating colors. Her hair dried in the heavy warm air and she seemed to float more than walk, the pain of her various injuries muted and diffuse behind a curtain of lucidity. After a quick check of the map on display at the station, she bought a ticket to Faversham. Something was pulling her down south, down toward the epicenter. She felt as if she were gliding along on the jet stream of destiny, that all the answers were there waiting for her to find them.

The trip was a strange blur, navigated as if in a dream: the crowds and announcements on the platform at St. Pancras International, the black rumbling through the long tunnel underneath the Thames then, sometime later, shooting out into the light and sliding through Kent's dreamy greenness. When the conductor passed to check tickets, she found one still clutched in her hand with no memory of having purchased it. Always the thing that she could not remember luring her onward, glimmering just out of reach. Over the River Medway and past the Rochester Docks, through Chatham and Gillingham and Rainham—gently rolling fields streaked in shades of moss-green, brown and straw. The greyness of the sky seemed to intensify with time, grow heavier and more troubled. As the train was pulling away from the platform at Sittingbourne, Artie noticed a sign advertising something called the Kent Bioscience Park, which struck her as an incongruity; how could there be any science here, mired in the middle of nowhere? And this, too, tickled her back into the tantalizing dance of not-quite-remembering.

Somewhere beneath the immediate imperative and clarity of her thoughts, she was aware that all was not well: her head had begun to ache more severely, her hands were trembling with hunger and her mouth was papery dry. Alighting at Faversham station, she walked right past a sandwich stand but could not bring herself to stop and buy anything to eat or drink. There wasn't time. She jabbed at her phone, but there wasn't enough signal for the map app to fully load her immediate vicinity—or at least, not in the time she felt she had to spare. Heading straight for the old town center, she paused at a bookshop, emerging a few minutes later with an Ordnance Survey map of the area.

The Isle of Sheppey looked obscenely large, taking up almost the top third of the map as she unfolded it against the outside wall of the shop. There was a prominent footpath wending along a tidal channel that led most of the way, and a path branching off at Nagden that would offer a shortcut through the marshes. It was only a couple of miles. She set off with a purposeful pace, down past the old warehouse district and then through a snarl of boats dry-docked for repairs. The few people about seemed to look at her oddly, and several ragged dogs snarled and barked. Eventually the way coalesced into a worn public footpath edged with elder flowers, nettle and brambles, and she left all traces of human life behind. It must be low tide, for the "creek" marked on the map was just a steep wedge of mud with a thin trickle of water threading through it.

Now that she was moving steadily towards her goal, the discomfort receded again and the world seemed to flow by, conveyor-belt smooth. After a time, gusts of cold wind began ruffling the flat expanse of grasses ahead in mesmerizing waves, full of the scent of rain, and she could see that the skies behind her were darkening further as the front moved towards the coast. It wasn't yet midday, but the air had taken on the quality of dusk.

After an hour of steady walking, the land above seemed to rise as she approached the sea wall. Here and there she had seen a few other walkers, but only as dots in the distance. Her main company had been the skylarks, hovering high overhead and singing their high-pitched, frenetic call.

Going right up to the wall's edge, she caught her breath as Sheppey came into view. The island was a dark bulk squashed on the horizon, skirted by the wide water-way of the Swale ahead, and then by a ribbon of permanent mudflats—the Oaze. For the first time that day, she felt a stab of uneasiness.

The squalls were very close now, a black mass shedding diagonal sheets of rain, and Artie began to feel cold in her impractical summer top and shorts. She was here now, and could get no closer. But *why* was she here? What had she hoped to achieve, and why would being here advance that goal? Although the niggling feeling of an unanswered memory still remained, her sense of purpose and the glow of euphoria were wearing off like a local anesthetic after the dentist's drill.

Feeling dizzy and scared, she sat down with her back to the sea wall, but the wind was coming straight at her now and the wall offered no shelter: there wasn't any in sight, just acres of flat grassland rippling and rearing like an epidemiological model gone mad. Her head pounded. There was now not a single person visible, even in the distance, who she might hail. What had she been thinking, walking this far in a desolate, depopulated place with no food or water, or even a raincoat? She hadn't even thought to take some painkillers back at the lab—she'd felt invincible. But that sensation, too, was long gone.

"Pull yourself together, Artemis Marshall," she whispered. She struggled to get the flailing map under control in the gusts, and saw that if she walked a bit more than a mile down the coast along the sea wall, she'd find the end of a small road—the map indicated there was a place to have tea, and with any luck, they could probably call her a taxi as well. When she stood up, the nausea swooped over her with full force and she bent over to retch into the dust.

"Walk," she commanded herself, after wiping her mouth. So she walked, slowly and with acute awareness of the various aches in her body, and especially of her great thirst. It didn't seem possible she'd just traveled two effortless miles—she wondered if she'd be able to manage two minutes now.

At first, she tried to force everything from her head and focus solely on what she could see—a trick she often used to distance herself from the discomforts of long karate training sessions. But she couldn't seem to let go of the thoughts whirling around inside: fear of the elements, of her concussion; fear of the nature of the mental state that had brought her here, and what it might mean. Fear of Simon, and what he might try to do to her once he regrouped.

And then, still, there was that almost panicked sense that she needed to remember something. Something important, something that would make everything else make sense. She was almost positive that it was something to do with the puzzle of the Minster virus. The secretive bulk of Sheppey on the horizon seemed to taunt her, and various memories slid through her pain-fogged mind: Sidney Sheppard's voice: *that's like finding a polar bear on the Costa del Sol.* And then Lucy Greenswold's: *my feeling is that it just couldn't compete, being so heavily adapted to life in a nice cozy Petri dish.* If Minster shouldn't be successful with the weak, lab-strain genes it had been designed with, then how on earth was it managing to thrive?

The first droplets of rain began hurl down, stinging Artie's skin. At first she tipped her head upward, trying to quench her thirst with the moisture, but soon the sheer power of it cowed her. The gusts whipped up tiny particles of dirt into her eyes, and the wind kept forcing itself into her nose and mouth, making it difficult to breathe. She turned her head seaward, squinting and trying to keep her pace. The mudflats below were born from a stripe of shingle beach and fanned outward in stripes of improbable colors, the eventual demarcation where land met sea impossible to discern with the tears flooding her eyes. Sheppey, too, had succumbed to the pelting rain, but further out to sea a shaft of sunlight lit up the water a disturbing shade of jade, as if illuminated by some drowned kingdom underneath the waves.

Just like that, she knew the answer.

～

THE LOCALS IN MOLLY'S SEASALTER Café had made a big fuss over Artie when she finally staggered through the door, half conscious, blue-skinned and dripping wet in the middle of the worst storm the area had seen for years. Later the proprietress would regale her husband with an only slightly embroidered tale of the London lady doctor who was as young as one of their daughters, as pretty as an actress and yet who despite all her learnings had been wandering around the Cleve Marshes in flimsy sandals and no provisions in the middle of a Force Eight gale. She doubted even a desperate cat would have dragged this one in. Well, these city folk didn't have an ounce of sense between them, and it seemed that even a scientist could be just as daft as the next body. The young woman had suffered some sort of head injury as well, but after demolishing a pint of water, two paracetamols, three sandwiches and four cups of tea, had politely refused repeated offers of one of the local fisherman to run her to the station or hospital. No, if she weren't overstaying her welcome, she insisted she'd rather wait for her "ride."

When Molly got a closer look at what eventually walked through the door, she reckoned she herself would have done no different.

～

MARK REYNOLDS BLEW INTO THE café along with a blast of cold air and a temporary increase in the noise of the storm, which had settled into a steady downpour that hissed against windows, roof and waterlogged earth. He raised an eyebrow when the dozen or so people inside ironically applauded his entrance, but otherwise, his expression on meeting her eye was worryingly neutral. Artie noted that although he'd only had to walk a few yards from the Fiat, he was fully decked out in waterproofs and Gore-Tex hiking boots. Somehow it didn't surprise her to find out that he wasn't an umbrella sort of man.

He didn't say much of anything, just waited patiently while she settled up at the register and hugged the older woman her thanks, as she tried to give back the borrowed old fleece jacket but was firmly refused. As he pulled out and opened up an umbrella to escort her back to the car—when would she learn to stop underestimating this man?

It was only when they were both safely inside that he reached over without warning and pulled her close.

"Thank God you're okay," he murmured, his grip intensifying. She was so confused by the abrupt shift in her expectations that she couldn't say a word, just soaking in the warmth and solidity of him, and the relief of not being shut out any longer. "Sorry I was so cool earlier," he added as they drew apart. "I didn't feel like airing my feelings in front of what looked to be the entire population of Seasalter."

"Does this mean you've forgiven me?"

"The truth is, I'd forgiven you ages ago," he said. "But once I'd cleared out my things, I felt too embarrassed to come back. I was trying to work out the right way to do it. And when you didn't answer my email..."

"I know—I'm sorry. I guess I was feeling stubborn."

"Not half as stubborn as I was. It doesn't matter. What matters is that you're really all right." His eyes on her were serious, questioning. "What on earth happened, Art? What brought you down here?"

"It's a long story," she said.

He reached out to touch the side of her face; when she winced, he flicked on the light and took a closer look.

"What's this? I thought I noticed something in the café, but it was too dim." He lifted her chin lightly, and got a good look at the bruises on her throat. Artie had forgotten that the make-up would have long since washed away. He switched off the light again, and for a moment the only sound was the pattering of rain. "You've been assaulted, haven't you? By Calvin. And this is you, trying to run away." He paused. "And I wasn't there for you, because of my stupid male pride."

"No. I mean..." She started to shiver a little, and Mark fished the blanket from the back seat and tucked it around her carefully as she tried to think how to begin. "I *was* assaulted, but not by Cal. I need to tell you everything."

"I'm listening."

"The thing is... there are still a few more things I've been keeping secret from you. I'm afraid that you'll get angry with me again."

"Artie." He covered her hand with his, where it sat there between them on the seat. "It's okay. That's one of the things I've been stewing over these past few days. We're lab mates, and close friends—" he gave her hand a squeeze—"but that doesn't mean you're obliged to tell me everything. I should have respected your privacy."

"No, I should have trusted you. I feel awful about it. When I thought I'd scared you away forever..."

He shook his head. "You must have had a good reason for your decision—I know you too well not to believe that. You don't even have to tell me now, if you feel it's better that way."

"I *have* to tell you," she said, gripping his hand. "Right now. Please. It can't wait another second."

And so she began at the very beginning. How she had first chased after Henry into the shrouded glow of B302, the evening that felt like another lifetime ago, and admired his lily projection on the screen. How she had *made* him start talking to her. How his magnetic personality had cast a spell over her, had impelled her to keep his suspicions about Minster from Simon—and by extension, from Mark himself.

"I should have told you then," Artie said. "I still don't know why I didn't."

"It's okay, honestly. Carry on."

She felt almost light-headed at the relief of letting go of these secrets, one after the other. How she had slowly gained Simon's trust, even as Henry seemed to deteriorate. How Henry had continued to confide in her: about his illness, about the situation with the MoD and his suspicions about the Minster virus; about his desire to use Artie's own dataset to prove the virus was artificial, because Simon wasn't doing it properly.

"I wasn't one hundred percent convinced then," she said. "He's such a well-respected epidemiologist, though, so I couldn't discount him outright. But Simon was on edge—I assumed Henry's counter-analysis would all come to nothing, so it didn't seem like a good idea to tell him that Henry was going behind his back on top of all the other unpleasantness he has to deal with from him. I see now that was a mistake."

"And you couldn't tell me," Mark said, nodding, "because I wouldn't have been happy keeping crucial scientific information from a collaborator—no matter how bizarre that information happened to be."

She studied his face anxiously, but there was no anger there. So she told him more—the frightening trumpet shape that the Meyerhof-Hernsley threw up, the arrest of the Faversham activists, the way she and Simon had tried to come up with a case against the bioterrorism theory, and how Henry had scuppered this by arranging for Simon to be cut off from the MoD's trust.

"I thought Henry was losing it, then. But his model looked so compelling—and Simon was terrified of Henry getting institutionalized if I went to Salverson. He asked me to wait... and then... he found out I'd been colluding with Henry. Last night. He thought that I had betrayed him."

"Jesus Christ." Mark's eyes widened. "What did he do to you? Where is he now?"

Artie explained what had happened, her voice and body starting to tremble as she relived the attack on the roof. Mark slid over and put his arm around her, but the shaking wouldn't stop.

"I... I don't understand why he ran away," she said. "Why he didn't... finish me off."

"He's a coward," Mark said, a fierce tightness to his voice. "It doesn't surprise me in the slightest. But I'm infinitely grateful for it. Then what happened?"

"Next thing I knew, it was dawn, and—"

"You didn't come round until the *next morning*?" he said. "The cops can wait—we've got to get you to hospital." He was reaching for the keys, but Artie grabbed his forearm.

"Please. I have to tell you the rest. Five more minutes won't make a difference."

He hesitated, arm as hard as steel as his body resisted her wishes. Then he slumped back in the seat. "Okay. Five minutes, and not a second more."

"When I woke up," Artie said. "Something was wrong with me."

"Well, obviously!"

"No—I mean, I wasn't right in the head. I was..."

Rain drummed the roof, measuring the seconds. "What are you trying to say?" he said. "Just spit it out."

"I've been waiting for it all my life, and I think it finally happened." When Mark just looked at her, clearly mystified, she took a deep breath and went on: "I think, today, that I had an acute manic attack. I think I've developed late-onset bipolar disorder, just like my mother, and my grandmother before her. I think what I've been terrified of all my life is finally coming true."

He stared at her wordlessly, and she cast her eyes downward, braced for his probable reaction.

"Oh Artemis, sweetheart." He gave her hand another squeeze. "Is that what the phobia is all about?"

She nodded, touched by his insight. Neither of them said anything for a long time.

"You said 'you think' you had a manic attack," he said. "You're not sure?"

"Not one hundred per cent, no."

Mark shifted in his seat, his eyes intense with the challenge of a new theory.

"Okay," he said. "Let's work this through." He put his arm back around her shoulders. "Why have you been expecting this to happen? I know next to nothing about manic depression. Is it that hereditary?"

"Well, it's got a strong genetic component, and both my maternal grandmother and my mother developed it much later than average—when they were in their mid-thirties."

"Shit. That's pretty scary, all right." He mulled this over for a moment. "So what were your symptoms?"

Artie thought she should have felt defensive, but again, there was only that great sense of relief, even peace, to be saying this out loud to someone so calm and sympathetic. Calvin had laughed her out of the room when she'd finally got up the courage to confess, and even though he did not believe she was at risk, he had ridiculed her and used her fear against her at every opportunity thereafter. Mark's scientific approach made her feel like her fears were at least justifiable.

"I felt no pain," she said. "I was euphoric. I thought that nobody could stop me. I didn't even check to see if Simon was in the building; I thought he couldn't hurt me." She didn't realize she was crying until Mark was offering her his handkerchief. "I didn't need to eat or drink. I thought I had to come here, down to Faversham, because I was part of some grand plan—that there was something hidden that needed to be revealed. That it was Fate, and I was the linchpin." She gave a shaky little laugh. "It all made sense at the time."

She wept a little bit, then blew her nose, all the time Mark holding her, every last inch of his body language respectful.

"When I snapped out of it, down at the sea wall, it was as if I'd been sleep-walking," she continued. "I didn't know why I was here. My mother used to come down exactly the same way; once moment she'd be doing something crazy, and the next, she'd be staring at me in confusion."

"Darling Artemis," he said. "I do hope you didn't bear the brunt of that."

"It was just me. Dad only lasted about a year into her illness until he ran away. I was about eight at the time."

"Brothers, sisters? Aunts, uncles?"

"No brothers or sisters. She had a brother, but he lived in Canada. The NHS used to send someone around regularly. And there was a neighbor who was very kind to me." Artie swallowed, trying to get control of herself.

"I know exactly what that's like," he said. "I know what it does to a person. If you come out of it at all, you come out very strong—but at a cost. In fact, you make a lot more sense to me now."

Artie mopped her face with the handkerchief. "So do you think I've got it? Bipolar I?"

He reached over, rearranged a strand of her hair. "I'd like to consider another hypothesis, if you don't mind. Just to be thorough. You wouldn't be offended?"

"Of course not."

"Okay." He tapped fingers against his chin, considering. "You're not really the depressive type, are you? Can one be unipolar?"

"Not really," Artie said. "You can be depressed, or both depressed and manic. I always thought the phobia attacks might be some sort of depression. And this thing with Calvin..."

"I don't buy it," Mark said. "You're basically a stable, happy person. Just because something sad is happening in your life doesn't make you depressed. I've known a few clinically depressed people in my life, and you just don't fit the profile."

"Well, maybe it's on the cards for the future, now that this has happened?"

"Maybe," Mark said. "But you had a nasty crack to the head. It's known that injuries can produce endorphins—you might have been feeling pain-free and euphoric as a side-effect of being hurt. Traveling down to Faversham was a weird thing to do, I'll grant you, but on the other hand, subconsciously you were probably trying to distance yourself from a terrifying situation, and again, the head injury itself could have caused a lot of confusion. This sense of destiny, of hidden things needing to be revealed... are there any other explanations for it?"

"Well." Artie considered things from this angle, a little surprised. "I did come up with a very good explanation for the Minster virus while I was struggling towards Seasalter. It came to me in a flash."

"I can't wait to hear about it—later. But first things first: maybe what was pushing you towards Faversham was an expression of your own subconscious, which had come up with a solution and needed some way to clue you in. It wanted you to stop worrying about the thousands of other distractions in your life, so it propelled you out to the middle of nowhere where you were a captive audience."

"Hmmm. Damn it, Reynolds. You should have been a lawyer."

"Or a shrink. It almost sounds as if you'd be disappointed to be proved wrong."

"No," Artie said. "I just want it to be over, one way or the other. I'm tired of living in fear, of not knowing what's going to happen. When I realized it might have been a manic attack, I almost felt relieved."

"Please don't take this the wrong way," he said. "But you are extremely suggestible. Isn't it possible that you've been priming yourself for years to expect your worst fears?"

"Of course. That's more or less what Calvin thought."

"Fuck Calvin." His voice was gratifyingly sharp. "That's only one theory. And your five minutes is up—let's get the hell out of here."

The engine revved, and he floored it out of the café car park and into the darkness.

CHAPTER 16
Resolutions, Some More Comfortable Than Others

ARTIE WAS SURPRISED AT HOW little she minded being fussed over by the combined and irresistible force of the Reynolds siblings in full caretaker mode. Maybe in a few days it would start to annoy, but for the moment, it was such a relief to be out of hospital that she was content to relax on the squishy brown sofa in Mark's flat and be waited on like royalty. After about the third energetic scolding from Rebecca, who had driven down the moment she heard, Artie gave up trying to do things for herself.

The scans had come back clear, but the consultant had warned her to take it easy and issued strict instructions that she not be left alone for the next 48 hours. This suited the police too, as Simon was still at large and nobody had any idea where he was. The thought of his bony hands around her throat was still enough to send a chill whispering across her skin, so she was more than happy to accept Mark's invitation to stay at his place for a few days. The storm had washed away the evidence on her clothing as thoroughly as the hot shower had from her body, but she needn't have worried about being believed; it turned out a CCTV camera on the roof had captured the entire episode unequivocally. This, and other gossip, came courtesy of Ben, who dropped by to visit on Sunday afternoon soon after Mark had collected her from St. Thomas' Hospital.

"Salverson's going to put an interim caretaker into B302," Ben told her, sitting on the edge of his chair and utterly failing to hide how worried he was about her. Rebecca and Mark were around the corner in the kitchen, in the midst of a good-natured quarrel about dinner preparations. "Just off the phone with him—sends his good wishes for a speedy recovery, by the way."

"Poor Henry," Artie said, with a twinge of uneasiness. Now that the hospital and police had been dealt with, she was anxious to get the next bit of unpleasantness out of the way. But there was something that she and Mark had to look into first.

"Not sure how he'll cope without Simon," he said. "Henry thrived on stability—bound to be confusing for him. I wonder, actually, if he will ever be able to bounce back."

Artie entertained the idea, just for the moment, that her future actions might actually be a kindness in the long run. But try as she might, she couldn't feel good about what she had to do. "Ben, while I'm thinking about it, could you give me Salverson's home number? There's something I want to speak to him about, and I'd rather not wait till next week."

"I'm sure he'd be delighted to hear from you," Ben said. "He was genuinely worried." He pulled out his phone, pressed a few buttons and scribbled a number down on a scrap piece of paper. After handing it over, he hesitated.

"What is it, Ben?"

"I do hope..." he cleared his throat. "I mean, this was a terrible business, and coming so soon on top of the yeast incident. I do hope it won't drive you away from Heatherfields."

"Not a chance," she said. "It was my own fault all this happened—you tried to warn me at the very beginning that collaborating with Simon was a bad idea. I should have listened."

"*Nobody* could have predicted that he would have done... *this*." Ben shook his head. "Blame myself—should have made more of an effort to help him integrate."

"I think you did amazingly well just being civil after the whole assault thing."

"Goes back a lot further than that," he said. "Before my time, but they say Henry forced Simon to drop his steady girlfriend when he was a student, because she was a 'distraction'—issued an ultimatum, him or her. Totally against all HR rules, but nobody intervened." He sighed. "Least I could have done was befriend him."

"Really, Ben. Don't beat yourself up about it. There was far more going on in B302, psychologically, than any of us could have guessed." Except herself, of course. And she'd just made everything much, much worse.

"Have the police made any progress in finding him?"

"Not really," she said. "The investigation is still ongoing. He bought a train ticket into Central London, apparently, but the trail runs cold after that. The only thing they're fairly certain of is that he hasn't left the country." Despite herself, she felt a little shiver pass over her skin.

Right on cue, Rebecca appeared at the doorway to the kitchen. "Visiting hours are over," she announced. "She needs to rest."

As Ben was standing up, he blurted out, "It's made such a big difference to the basement having your lab around. You've got people talking to each other instead of muddling along in their own little universes. Feels like a real department again—a *community*. Would be such a shame to go back to how it used to be."

"I'm not going anywhere," she promised. "It would take more than a knock on the head to scare me off."

After he left, Rebecca perched herself on the sofa arm, serving up yet another cup of tea.

"Whatever you two are doing in there smells amazing," Artie said, taking the mug.

"Just like old times," she said. "Fighting over the herbs and spices. Still feeling okay? Any dizziness, nausea or disorientation?"

"I'm fine, honestly."

The other woman smiled. "Sorry, am I driving you nuts yet? I'm just so relieved that you're okay—when Mark rang me up yesterday, I was really scared."

"It's sweet of you to be so concerned."

"Don't be silly. I almost feel like you're part of the family. Which reminds me—I'd like to apologize on behalf of the entire Reynolds gene pool for what an arse he was last week. I gave him a good talking-to, I can assure you."

"Oh, Becky. It was all a big mess, and I don't blame him at all for being miffed."

"Nonsense. He's always butting into other people's business."

"Runs in the family, I guess?"

"Touché." She was quiet for a moment, a smile lingering on her lips. "Listen, Artie." She looked over her shoulder, then lowered her voice: "I think you made the right decision. About Mark, I mean. Friendship is the most important thing in the world. And for someone like him... well, it's all he has, really. It works this way—I can see that now."

"T minus thirty minutes on the curry," Mark said, sauntering in. "I hope you've got an appetite, Artie, because Becky's made enough sides for a small army."

"I'm starving," she said. "And if you've got half an hour free, can we finally talk about my virus idea now?"

"Can't all that science stuff wait?" Rebecca's brow furrowed. "You're supposed to be resting your brain."

"As curious as I am," Mark said reluctantly, "she's probably right."

"It's actually really important," Artie said. "People have been arrested on what I think are false pretenses, and I suspect we might be able to gather the evidence to vindicate them."

"Okay," Rebecca said, glaring at her brother. "But don't let her get too excited."

"Yes, ma'am." Mark pulled up a chair as Rebecca drifted back into the kitchen. "So what's the score, boss?"

"It just came to me," Artie said. "Minster is undeniably artificial, but the things about it that are natural are also pieces to the puzzle."

"How can you be so sure it's manmade?"

"I checked my work email on my phone, when Becky wasn't looking."

Mark grinned. "Don't tell her, or she'll confiscate it."

"One of the messages was from Lucy. Fiona's final sequences show the presence of a lab watermark."

"What do you mean, watermark?"

"Besides VSV-G itself, Lucy found that our Minster virus contains a common vector sequence—a polylinker that VSV people use for cloning purposes. It's a thirty base-pair stretch of completely artificial code derived from bacterial constructs that could never be present in a natural virus."

"Wow." Mark shook his head. "I didn't want to believe it, but that's pretty much the nail in the coffin, isn't it?"

"Yes and no," Artie said. "Yes, the VSV-G is highly unnatural—but that doesn't mean the entire virus was manmade."

"What are you saying?"

"According to Simon's model—which I think on balance is sound—the FeLV/FIV hybrid has been brewing in the Sheppey area for some time. Even without the model, our raw sequences confirm that. So what I'm *saying* is that a manmade VSV-G portion of the virus was—"

"A recent addition!" Mark said. "Recombined into the natural, feline-derived part of the virus."

Artie nodded. "A manmade DNA, commandeered by a very promiscuous, strongly circulating and highly variable new cat virus strain. Both Henry and Simon were right, in part—but neither of them got it quite right, colored as they were by their own particular interests. Simon is keen on natural epidemics, and Henry, on bioterrorist attacks. Each interpreted the same data to draw conclusions that suited his own bias."

"But where did the VSV-G come from?"

"That is indeed the question," she said. "But I have a little hunch about that too."

"I'll bet you do." His gaze was half bewildered, half admiring.

"I remember reading, a few years back, some review articles about feline immuno-deficiency promoters being used for gene therapy."

"Really? It seems so... obscure."

"You'd be surprised," she said. "There's hardly a virus that hasn't been at least considered. People have been tinkering with HIV, herpes, cold viruses—even canarypox. FIV is in some ways ideal—it has the two desirable properties that all lentiviruses share, namely the ability to replicate even in resting cells and the facility to integrate permanently into the patient's genome. Yet it doesn't inspire the knee-jerk revulsion of HIV."

"I guess big pharma's products are as susceptible to PR issues as those of any other."

"Quite. So FIV was in fashion for a while—for all I know, it still is."

"So you think," he said, "that someone was designing a gene therapy vector with the long terminal repeats of FIV coupled to the human-tropic VSV-G, and... what? It escaped?"

"Yes. I'm assuming it was a cat-owner, or someone in close contact with one. The theory makes more sense if the VSV vector originated very close to Sheppey—I doubt virus particles could live very long on someone's hands or clothing."

"Well, that's a problem. The University of Kent does have some virology research groups, but both campuses are miles away from Sheppey."

"I'm not sure academia is where we ought to be looking," she said. "There's something else I think we should check out."

A minute later they were scrolling through an overview page on the Kent Bioscience Park website. "I saw a sign for it on the train at Sittingbourne," she said. "I think that was one of the things that triggered the idea later."

"It looks like a bunch of start-ups," Mark said, scrolling down. "You might be onto something here. A lot of them seem agricultural, though."

"What about that one?" Artie said, pointing at one of the logos. "*Genex Therapeutics*. That's suitably medical sounding, don't you think?"

He clicked into the site—and then began to shake his head in wonder as he read the general description of their research strategies—and the patented feline vectors they were using to achieve them.

❧

On Tuesday morning Artie insisted on going to work, and neither Mark nor Rebecca—via a phone call from Birmingham—could talk her out of it. Artie didn't want to admit that she was actually very tired. It had been busy Monday, even though she hadn't left the sofa. She had managed to track down contact details for the Chief Scientific Officer at Genex and, while at first he didn't believe what she was saying, all it took was a copy of the Minster virus sequence and a description of its devastating symptoms to convince him to cooperate.

Armed with this evidence, she'd rung up Salverson and had a very frank discussion with him about Henry's future. Salverson, perhaps aware that Simon's absence now made Henry's continuing residency problematic, seemed only too happy to have an excuse to order some medical tests for midweek, and also agreed to take the burden of communicating the news to the MoD from his youngest professor's shoulders. And then Mary had visited, full of the happy news that the Sheppey grassroots quarantine had exceeded her wildest expectations.

"It's amazing," she said, showing Artie a few photos on her mobile phone. "The Minster Cat Fancier's Society talked the Council into letting them set up manned volunteer roadblocks on both island exits—it probably didn't hurt that one of their most passionate members is a councillor herself. They're waving over every car, checking there aren't any cats being taken somewhere in a travel box. So far they've caught two, and the owners voluntarily agreed to turn back."

"That's wonderful!"

"Even better news is that, since Mackenzie, no vet on the island has seen any cats fitting the symptoms of the Minster virus."

"So maybe it's burnt itself out?"

"Let's hope so—but we'll keep the quarantine going till the end of the week, just to be safe."

Salverson rang back later that evening to let her know that the MoD had been unexpectedly helpful.

"Apparently," he said, "one of the technicians who transferred the virus out of the Genex facility lived in Faversham, but had a grandmother he visited every Sunday in Minster—recently deceased, apparently—not from the virus, but from entirely natural causes. From what you've told me, I guess that makes sense?"

"Definitely, " Artie said. "The technician must have passed the virus to his grandmother's cat, or to one of the other felines in the neighborhood."

"All of the people who got ill from it either worked at Genex or had immediate contact with someone who did," he said. "It doesn't look like the gene therapy virus was actually contagious from person to person—poor hygiene practices at the factory just led to a number of dead-end infections."

"Did they mention anything about the arrested activists?"

"They didn't, but it sounds as if you missed the evening news. Farah and his cohort have been released without charges." There was a pause down the phone line. "Pretty neat footwork on your part, Professor Marshall, if I may say so. The Sanctum will be very pleased to hear about this. They always like it when our members have a civic impact."

It was a bright but hazy sunny morning as Mark maneuvered the Fiat up the Ridgeway, which was unusually beset with traffic. Twice they'd had to pull over, once for a fire engine and again for two ambulances, all with full light shows and sirens blasting.

"Is that smoke on the horizon?" Artie asked, squinting at the line of trees at the crest of the hill. She thought she could smell something burning as the warm air funneled over them.

"If so, it looks pretty close to Heatherfields," Mark replied. "Come on, sweetheart,"—this to the driver of the blue Ford in front of them—"move your *arse*."

The scene that greeted them as they turned into the Institute's entry drive was pandemonium. A policeman in a fluorescent yellow vest immediately waved them over.

"You can't drive any further," the man said. "We need to keep the roads clear for emergency vehicles."

When the cop got distracted by the next car, Mark pulled over on the grass and they got out and rushed towards the building on foot. The smoke didn't look too serious now, and the fire engine was nowhere in sight. There was a crowd of people milling about by the rose gardens out front, faces in turn excited, scared and bemused. Artie saw Susan Tavistock and went up to her.

"What's happening?" she demanded.

Artie still hadn't accustomed herself to people's reactions to her bruises. Although the light summer scarf covered the lurid finger marks on her throat, she was aware that even with makeup, the purple coloring on her chin was hard to miss.

"Artemis," Susan said, gripping her hands in both of hers. "I was so sorry to hear of your ordeal—yet so happy that you're relatively unscathed. And what's happening?" She swept a hand towards the Victorian monstrosity. "We are on fire, evidently."

"It doesn't look so bad from the front," Mark said.

"It's hard to get any solid information," Susan said. "But Ben Crombie's a fire warden, and he told me that it started in the basement—and fortunately has been largely contained. There probably hasn't been any structural damage."

"Oh, my God," Artie said. "Is everyone okay down there?"

"Yes, yes—sorry, I should have said at the outset. Your technician was a marvel, apparently, helping Ben make sure everyone was out. The only casualty—and it's just minor, Ben says—was Henry Mansfield. The idiot new caretaker was out for a cigarette and did a runner when the alarms started. Ben and Fiona managed to rescue him fairly quickly—he inhaled a lot of smoke but seemed otherwise fine. The ambulances just went by on their way in."

"I've got to get over there," Artie said grimly.

"Artie, don't be stupid," Mark called out behind her, but she was already jogging around the left side of the building towards the rear car park.

"You'd better go keep her out of trouble," Artie heard Susan say to Mark, and then he was running beside her.

"You're supposed to be looking after yourself," he said. "I never should have let you come in today."

"I'll be fine," she panted, a bit surprised at how weak she actually felt. Slowing to a dizzy walk, she pushed her way through the confusion of scientists and emergency workers in the car park. The blaze looked to be out, just a solid column of smoke still rising from a hole in the ground—the damp, collapsed remains of one corner of the basement.

"Artie! Mark!" It was Fiona, appearing from behind a knot of Virtual Immunology colleagues jabbering into their mobile phones. She was grinning and sported streaks of soot on her forehead. "You lot missed all the fun!"

"Are you all right?"

"Yeah, just a bit shaken," Fiona said. "I should be asking you the same question, Artie. So glad it wasn't more serious—everyone's been dead worried about you."

"I'm fine, honestly. Is the lab okay?"

"Untouched, thank goodness," she said. "And your office too. But B302 is totaled, and there's been a bit of damage to parts of Immunology and the coffee room. But it could have been a lot worse. They're going to rehouse us upstairs while the builders set things to rights—could take weeks. So no more stairs for a while!"

"Do they know how it started?"

Fiona's face darkened. "They're saying it was probably arson. Let's just say that most of us have our suspicions about who struck the match."

"Have you seen Henry?" she asked. Fiona waved an arm towards the ambulance on the far left, and Artie approached with a heavy heart. Henry was on a stretcher, just getting loaded into the back. He turned his head and his eyes, lucid and alive, met hers directly. Removing his oxygen mask with one hand, he grabbed the arm of one of the paramedics with the other. "Can I please have a brief word with this woman before we go?"

"Make it quick," the paramedic said to Artie. "We need to get him checked over."

Artie took his hand, and he gripped it tightly.

"How are you?" she said, feeling the unexpected prick of tears behind her eyes. "I'm so glad they got you out of there."

"I received a note from Salverson today," he said. "Apparently there have been concerns raised about my mental health. I assume that Simon has lodged a complaint—and that that's why he's left, because he didn't even have the decency or courage to face me."

He didn't know, Artie realized. He didn't know about the attack.

"No, Professor," she said. "It was me. *I* went to Salverson. It broke my heart, but I had to stop you from working with the MoD on the Minster virus. You were wrong about it being a weapon—we have the proof now. I'm so very sorry."

He didn't appear to be listening.

"I am truly touched, child, that you're trying to take the blame for Simon. But I can assure you it's not necessary. I *know* it was him. And I will never forgive his betrayal."

"But Professor, it really was me who went to Salverson!"

He shook his head. "Your sense of honor is admirable, my dear."

"I've got to make you understand," Artie said. "It was *Simon* who wanted to protect you—I overruled him. He loved you like a son."

"Truly admirable," he continued, as if she hadn't spoken. His eyes, she saw, were starting to go a bit unfocused. He coughed a few times. "And I know you will help me now. Don't let them give me drugs—don't let them take away my new life. Please."

"I'll..." she swallowed hard. "I'll do what I can. I promise."

"Thank you," he said. "And if they won't let me come back, will you see to it that our paper is published? You'll find it on my computer. I believe it to be the most important work I've ever done."

"Sorry," the paramedic interjected, sparing Artie from having to make a promise she couldn't keep. "We've got to take him now."

Tears flowed down Artie's face as Henry disappeared into the back of the ambulance. After a while, she realized that Mark had come up beside her and had put his arm around me.

"I think I'd like to go back home after all," she said.

∼

CALVIN LOOKED REMARKABLY PLEASED TO see her when she popped by his office at University College Hospital the next day.

"Is this a bad time?" she asked.

"Not at all—please, come in." He cleared the chair of a stack of journals and waved her into it with a flourish. "I heard about the attack—and the fire. It's been quite a week for you, hasn't it?"

"And who says academia isn't exciting?" she said.

His gaze was roaming over her bruises, but all he said was, "So what brings you to this neck of the woods?"

"I was trying to visit one of the patients," she said. "But the strangest thing—there's a security guard on his door, and I couldn't charm my way past him for love nor money."

"I wouldn't take it personally, Artie dearest," Cal said. "These hire drones are practically robotic."

"It's that colleague I was telling you about—the Asperger's one who you thought might have frontal lobe dementia. He's in for smoke inhalation—I don't think he's considered dangerous."

"We usually have guards to protect patients, not the other way round." Calvin frowned, picked up the phone. "Let me see what I can find out. What's his full name?"

Artie watched as he navigated his way through a series of people with his usual persuasive efficiency. "Really?" he said. "And when was this?" He raised his eyebrows at her, listened a bit more, then thanked whoever it was before putting down the phone.

"It seems," he said, "that your Professor received an unorthodox visitor last night, after hours."

She felt a little twinge of apprehension. "What sort of visitor?"

"One up to no good, apparently." Cal leaned back in his chair. "A man, fiddling with his IV drip when one of the nurses came in and frightened him off. He got away—these drones are all muscle and no action. Apparently the police have linked him to the arson at your place, and think it might have been a second thwarted murder attempt."

"My God. Poor Henry." She hoped he would mistake the surge of raw fear for mere sympathy.

"Don't look so stricken—he'll be all right now. If you couldn't get in, no one could."

"Listen, Cal. Could you do me a favor?"

"That depends, obviously."

"It's about Henry. I was wondering what sort of medication they might be putting him on. Not for the smoke, obviously... but for his condition."

"I'd have to invent a reason to see his notes, and of course it depends on the diagnosis—but why do you ask?"

"He doesn't want to be drugged up into oblivion. He wants... he wants to enjoy his newfound state of mind for as long as possible. I promised him I'd fight his corner on this."

Calvin was silent for a while, fiddling with a quartz paperweight.

"That's a pretty big ask," he finally said. "If it's deemed necessary to medicate him in particular ways, then I couldn't really interfere with someone else's patient."

"But, Cal—listen." She leaned forward, suddenly seeing exactly how she could hook him. "I've been pondering your theory about the dementia somehow overriding the autism. If his condition is of scholarly interest, wouldn't it be in someone's best interests to study it? In a safe and carefully monitored way, obviously."

"Hmmm." His eyes had brightened, just as she'd hoped. "You might be right. Perhaps a collaboration..." He tapped fingers against the paperweight. "I could cover the personality issues, with a neurologist colleague studying the underlying physical deterioration in parallel... Brigsby, perhaps. No! Stein. It's right up his street. It would make a most interesting paper, if my theory is true... we might even..."

Artie sat back and listened to him elaborate, suppressing a little smile. When his pager went off mid-rhapsody, he shrugged at her apologetically and she waved goodbye, making her way out of the building. She was satisfied that Henry's wellbeing would be in good hands as long as it was attached to the coattails of Calvin's ambition. But all she could think about now was Simon, lurking in these very corridors the night before. Bent on—what? Revenge? Redemption? Forgiveness? Closure? Somehow she had convinced herself that he would have fled the area, possibly even the country. The fact that he was sticking close to Henry—to her—was frankly terrifying.

When Artie's mobile went off in the car park, she pulled it out and looked at the screen. *Unknown number*, it said. With a shiver of premonition, she put it to her ear and said "Hello?"

Silence on the other end.

"Hello?" she repeated. "Who is this?"

"I can see you," he said. "You've just been to see him, haven't you?"

"Simon?" Artie resisted the urge to cast the mobile away from her like a burning hunk of metal. She scanned ahead of her, to the sides, behind. There were literally dozens of cars, hundreds of windows, vast crowds of people moving about in the lunchtime shuffle. He could be absolutely anywhere.

"He thinks it was me," Simon said. His voice was emotionless, yet as taut as wire. "He told me last night. He thinks *I* went to Salverson. After everything I did for him; after wasting my entire life to serve his needs: he *accused* me."

Artie kept her voice soft, reasonable, even though her heart was practically galloping out of her chest. Somehow, the finger-mark bruises on her neck seemed to be throbbing in time. "I tried to tell him that I was responsible, but he wouldn't listen. Where are you, Simon? Let's talk this through like adults."

"I don't believe you," he said. "It must have been you who told him the lie, told him that I'd betrayed him, planted it in his mind."

"It wasn't, I promise. I was completely straight with him, but he didn't want to know."

There was a short, crackly pause, and then the flat voice intoned: "I will never forgive either of you. I will never forgive, and never forget."

"Simon," she said. "Be reasonable and turn yourself in. You can't run forever."

The phone went dead in her hand. Aware of his glacial blue gaze boring into the back of her head, somewhere in the crowd, she forced herself to calmly replace the phone in her bag, to walk with measured strides towards the station—forced herself not to scan the crowds for an awkward, skinny man livid with hatred.

Forced herself not to run like hell.

IT WAS A WEEK FOR hospitals. A few days later, Artie sat across from Augustus Faber in his office at Guy's, on the other side of the river. Sun filtered through oyster-colored Venetian blinds, patterning light and shadow across his earnest face.

"I'm so sorry to disappoint you, Artemis." He slowly took off his glasses. "But I'm afraid I'm simply unable to give you the certainty you crave."

She looked at the window for a moment, with its shafts of dusty light, trying to take the news in her stride.

"I guess I already knew that you couldn't offer a firm diagnosis," she said, meeting his eye. "I *was* hoping you'd be able to give me some sort of odds about whether it really was a manic attack."

He shrugged. "What can I say? It isn't an exact science. It's not as if we can take a blood sample, examine your spinal fluid, take tell-tale pictures with the MRI. Bipolar disorder can only be diagnosed after the fact, by what happens to the patient, and how often. Sure, your little jaunt down to Faversham had some of the elements, but so did it, too, of certain post-traumatic episodes."

"So what do I do?"

"The only thing you can," he said, green eyes glinting at her sympathetically. "Be patient. Wait and see. Try not to expect the worst."

"That is so not as easy as it sounds."

"I know, my dear Artemis. Especially not for someone like you: highly driven and wanting to be in control at all times. But even if you didn't have this genetic legacy hanging over your head, you still wouldn't be in control of your life. None of us can predict the future."

"I'd convinced myself that I'd have some sort of resolution here, one way or the other. But now I'm no better off than before. Worse, maybe, because I've had a taste of what it might be like."

He regarded her for a few moments.

"Forgive me for asking, but what's the worst that could happen if you really were to come down with this affliction?"

She stared at him, wondering if he were mocking her. But his expression was perfectly serious.

"My career as a scientist would be over," she said. "The same drugs that I'd have to take to control my moods would also blunt my creative spark."

"I don't think that's necessarily true," Gus said. "We've come a long way, therapeutically, since the bad old days of people being bombed out on high doses of lithium. There are a variety of additional drugs now. And there are thousands of successful writers, artists, musicians and scientists who are also bipolar."

"I'm sure there are, but what about the ones you don't hear about who aren't successful?" She could hear the sharpness in her own voice, reined it in. "Or who don't get the chance?"

"I take it your mother didn't fare so well on treatment?" His voice was impossibly gentle.

"I watched what the drugs did to her with my own eyes. Each day, a little bit more of her passion and thirst for life, sucked away. She couldn't work, she couldn't write. She could hardly talk."

Artie cleared her throat. When Gus said nothing, she went on, more quietly. "It's not just about losing my competitive edge; I could live with that. It's about losing the excitement that keeps me going back to the lab day after day. The *wanting-to-know* that makes me think about my experiments even when I'm not in the lab—the excitement that even infiltrates my dreams. It's about the sheer... joy of it all. I'm not sure there's much point in doing science without it."

"This might be your fate," he said. "Of course it might. Equally, it might not. But I can see that I will not be able to convince you; your scientist brain will only accept direct evidence. We will wait and see—and if I am proved wrong, so be it."

"I'm sorry," she said. "I didn't mean to cause offense."

"None taken." He gave his glasses a polish and slipped them back over his nose, tapping them into place with a fingertip. "Speaking of competitive edges, I do hope that this business with the escaped virus hasn't thrown a terminal spanner into your line of research."

"I was worried about that at first," she said, "but on further reflection, the entire scenario turns out to be a wonderful example of evolution in action."

"Really?"

"Yes—now that I've seen the original donor sequences, it's fascinating how the escaped vector was appropriated, which parts were used and which abandoned—it throws up all sorts of insights I would have been lacking otherwise." Despite herself, Artie could feel her spirits rising. "And it's the type of experiment that health and safety regulations would never have allowed me to do, to release something into the wild like that. I've already had a word with *Nature*, and they say they're interested."

"I have always suspected," he said, "that opportunism is a large part of successful science." He glanced at her conspiratorially. "And in that spirit, I myself am scientifically curious about one thing: can you tell me how your phobia is doing in light of the Faversham incident?"

"How it's doing?" Artie paused, thought about it. "Well, I haven't had any episodes since then, so it's hard to tell if there have been any changes."

"Is that unusual?"

"What do you mean?"

"How many days have elapsed now... a week, I guess?"

"Yes, that's right."

"And no feelings of loneliness or discomfort when alone?"

Artie ran through recent events in her mind. She'd been constantly with Mark since Tuesday, but the last few nights she'd been back by herself in Hampstead. She only realized at that moment that she'd felt normal in that state—so normal that she hadn't even noticed.

"No," she said. "Do you think it means something?"

"Again, there are no certainties. But it may be that in addressing the root cause of your fears, in living through a manic attack—or even the illusion of one—and sharing your fears with others, you might very well have gone a fair way towards dealing with them."

She shook her head. "Well, I'll be damned—what an irony. Though the cure is almost certainly worse than the disease."

"Not if you never develop bipolar I. I'd call that a definite win-win situation."

"Gus, you are an eternal optimist. Thank you for this conversation."

"My pleasure—do keep me posted."

"I will." As Artie was standing up, she thought of something. "If I might ask one more, wholly unrelated question?"

"By all means."

She stood there, hand on the chair back and trying not to feel embarrassed.

"Are there people who are unable to love... I mean, clinically?"

He shrugged. "Certainly. There are various detachment disorders, and obviously a whole spectrum of sexual ones as well."

"I mean more... someone who has no problems with platonic love or sex, but who is unable to fall *in* love. Could it be a mental illness?"

He smiled. "You don't need to invoke pathology for that. I'm quite sure that a few of my colleagues manifest that precise symptom."

"What causes it?"

"Who's to say? Childhood trauma, neglectful parents, negative experiences... even genes. They can all play their part in knocking us one way or the other in this continuum of behavior we rather arbitrarily call *normal*."

"And can people change?"

"Again, I can offer you no certainties, Artemis. Sometimes people never do." He leaned back in his chair, smiling at something invisible in the middle distance. "And sometimes, it is *you* who has to change—to meet the problem halfway."

EPILOGUE

WHEN SOMEONE LIKE ARTEMIS MARSHALL throws a party, it's a hot ticket.

And so it was that, about two months later, the entire population of Heatherfields tried to squeeze into the labs and corridors of the newly refurbished basement departments, with a considerable, good-natured overspill into the car park out back. They were there to celebrate three momentous milestones: the reopening of the basement for business, the acceptance of the lab's mini-epidemic paper by *Nature,* and her promotion to Head of Virology. Artie had refused the grand office on the fourth floor that Hastings had abandoned when he quit in protest, explaining to Salverson that she found it more stimulating to mingle with her theoretical colleagues in the basement. The stylishly done-up, brightly lit B302 now housed an energetic female epidemiologist whose work was making waves, and Artie had found joining forces with Susan to persuade the committee to get her hired almost as stimulating as bouncing ideas off the new arrival and her small team now that they had settled in.

It was a crisp autumn night, with just a touch of chill and smell of fallen leaves, as Artie stepped outside with her glass of champagne to get some fresh air. A full moon was rising over the tree line, but its bulk caused not even a twinge of unease this evening. She still had her moments of fear—both of being alone, and of the thought of Simon, still at large after so many months—but the therapy Faber had arranged was helping tremendously.

"Congratulations," Philip Cox said, materializing out of the darkness with a lit cigar in one hand and a half-full flute in the other. He was, she thought, the only man she knew who could pull off a bow tie.

"There you are!" She hugged his gaunt frame, which he suffered gallantly, patting her back somewhat awkwardly in return. "I was hoping you'd show up."

"Well, I have a special interest in Heatherfields," he said. "It's always good to visit."

"Phil..." It was the alcohol egging her on, she knew. "You're part of the Inner Sanctum, aren't you?"

"If I were, I certainly wouldn't divulge it! The cheek." He grinned down at her, then took a puff on the cigar. "But I do owe you an apology."

"What for?"

"For grossly underestimating your almost supernatural ability to propel a dead virus back into the limelight. Masterfully done."

They clinked glasses, and after a few more minutes of conversation he glanced at his watch. "I promised Salverson I'd have a word while I was in town. Come visit me soon, you hear? We can catch up properly—when both of us are more sober."

Artie watched her former mentor disappear into the crowd, then turned at the hand on her arm.

"There you are," Mark said. "Having a good time?"

"Oh, yes," she said.

"Aren't you cold? That dress doesn't offer much in the way of coverage."

She stuck her tongue out at him. "Quit fussing, Reynolds."

"I thought you'd be used to it by now."

"I'm not sure I want to be," she said. "Which reminds me. I was wondering if I could go home with you tonight?"

When he hesitated, she hastened on, "That is, if you don't already have plans." She had noticed a fair number of tipsy female post-docs giving him the eye throughout the course of the evening.

"No, I don't," he said. "But in what capacity, if you don't mind me asking?"

She slipped arms around his neck, enjoying the feel of his warmth and rough stubble against her cheek and his arms wrapping around her, and not caring who saw them. Somewhere underneath, a heart was pounding—she wasn't sure whose. "I'm not entirely sure, yet. Can you live with that?"

"I expect so," he said, moving back just far enough to get a good look at her. His habitual grin was just a shade away from coming to life. "The question is, can you?"

A dozen different responses occurred to her—answers involving probabilities, hypotheses, reasonable suppositions. In the end, she didn't opt for any of them.

"I have absolutely no idea," she said.

The End

ABOUT THE AUTHOR

Jennifer Rohn leads a cell biology research lab at University College London in the United Kingdom, studying how bacteria subvert human cells during infection. In her spare time, she moonlights as a science writer, journalist, broadcaster and pundit. She blogs about the scientific life at *Mind The Gap* and on the *Guardian,* and has written for a number of outlets including *The Times, The Guardian, Nature, The Telegraph,* and *BBC News.* She also created and continues to run the science culture online magazine LabLit.com, which has been highlighted in the *New York Times, US National Public Radio,* the *Guardian* and the *Boston Globe.* "Lab lit," a term she coined, is a tiny but growing genre of mainstream fiction about scientists and science as a profession (as opposed to science fiction). She is the author of two other lab lit novels: *Experimental Heart* and *The Honest Look,* and has also published short fiction. She is also no stranger to rebellion, having founded Science is Vital, a well-known grassroots organization campaigning for UK research funding. Born and raised in the United States, Jennifer became a naturalized British citizen and now lives in Gravesend, Kent (not far from the action in this novel) with her husband and son.

ACKNOWLEDGMENTS

Feline leukemia virus was already long out of fashion by the time I started my Ph.D. in Microbiology at the University of Washington, Seattle back in 1990. But under the expert guidance of my supervisor, Dr. Julie Overbaugh, I managed to make my modest mark with this simple but endlessly fascinating cat pathogen. I always knew that one day, I'd write a story with FeLV firmly in the starring role. Many thanks to Julie for her scientific inspiration as a research mentor those many years ago, but also for helping me to decide what sort of configuration my mutant virus might have. The recombinant described in the story is fictitious, but FeLV is a promiscuous gene-thief in real life, so the premise is plausible.

I relied on the advice of a number of experts for some of the mental health and neurological issues raised in the book. I'd like to thank Prof. Marilyn Lucas, Dr. Adil Akram and Dr. Charles Fernyhough; any errors in rendering these issues are entirely mine.

This novel was many years in the making and raked over the coals by too many people to count. I'd like to particularly thank the following people for going above and beyond the call of duty in reading and commenting on drafts at various stages: Julie Coryell, Matt Day, Richard Grant, Becky Marlowe, Seeyle Martin, Joanna Porter, Diana Rowe and David Weinkove. More general support as always was provided by the regulars of Fiction Lab, the monthly science book club I run at London's Royal Institution. Their often bracing commentary on the portrayal of science and scientists in novels—the good, bad and ugly—has become the little voice inside my head as I write and edit my own fiction. Apologies to them that, after the advice of a number of non-scientifically inclined readers, I had to allow a small but necessary bit of exposition into this current work (please be gentle with me when next we meet). Thanks also to Kris Franks for helping with elements of the cover design, and Jay Nadeau and the team at Bitingduck Press for believing in my work and making the whole process a lot of fun.

Finally, I can never thank enough my husband Richard and son Joshua, the two people in the world who make it all worthwhile.